D0675343

Among Thieves

Among Thieves

Mez Packer

**Tindal
Street
Press**

First published in March 2009
by Tindal Street Press Ltd
217 The Custard Factory, Gibb Street,
Birmingham, B9 4AA
www.tindalstreet.co.uk

A CIP catalogue reference for this book is available
from the British Library

ISBN: 978 0 955647 62 8

Typeset by Country Setting, Kingsdown, Kent
Printed and bound in Great Britain by LPPS Ltd,
Wellingborough, Northants

The paper and board used in this paperback are natural recyclable
products made from wood grown in sustainable forests

Birmingham City Council

For A & J

PART ONE

PART TWO

PART THREE

EPILOGUE

PART ONE

PART ONE

JEZ

Cov Lads

There was a drought on. Everyone was gagging for a spliff but Cov'd been dry for a fortnight. I'd been hassling me contacts for days just so's I could score an ounce to share with the boys. It was Arlo who came through first. Arlo was a Dylan lookalike who wore winklepickers and drainpipes and managed the upstairs bar at the Wolf. You could always count on Arlo to find someone with emergency supplies. I'd called him, Wednesday, for an early nod so I wasn't surprised when he called back Friday to say it was worth me going down there later on that night. The Wolf was filling up when I arrived and Arlo, whose real name was Arnold Braithwaite, was already on his jogs cos he had a pack of dope-starved lads hanging off him like oily shadows. Luckily with Arlo *I* got preferential. He was a proper Cov lad, see, part of the old crew, but we didn't hang out so much no more. Not since he'd shacked up with Claudette. Miserable. French. Ex-student. He'd got her up the duff in her final year and now they were stuffed in a one-bedroom on the third floor of Selina Dix – one of the Hillfields tower blocks; pissy stairwells, syringes, knocking shop on the top floor. Grim.

It was Arlo who introduced me to Andy that night. I'd seen him before, of course. Always in a crowd. Lads coming up to shake his hand. Confident he was. Different. He cut it. Sometimes in ancient patched jeans with a real smart jacket; sometimes British army fatigues with a hammer and sickle T-shirt. He had his own style, y'know? Andy smiled at me, wary, while Arlo did the intros.

'This is Jez,' says Arlo, holding me shoulder. 'He's all right. He's cool.'

Cool meant 'one of us', not drug squad, not likely to shaft you. But you could never really be sure. People'd get sloppy when there was a drought on. Find themselves scoring off a pig down some back alley and coming out in handcuffs.

Me and Andy shook hands, then touched knuckles like the black lads, before he nodded over to the bogs, saying, 'Shall we?' I knew them bogs. I'd written on the walls and puked me guts up in the sinks, and bought and dealt and fought and threatened in there. So when we squeezed into one of the cubicles it felt a bit like home. Still, it felt too small for strangers but then, y'know, that's what droughts can push you to, squeezing in a place, three by three, with someone you've never met before. I put the seat down so we weren't talking over a yawning shit hole and leaned against the door. Andy said I was lucky Arlo had recommended me. He could've sold the bag ten times over in the hour before I arrived, people were that desperate. It was every man for himself in a drought. As if I didn't know.

But I says, 'Yeah, thanks for savin' it for me. I appreciate it.'

And he says, 'S'all right man,' like it was nothing really.

Then he stops for a second, listening to make sure the bogs are empty 'cept for us, before fishing an ounce of Rocky from his underpants.

The bag was warm as an armpit when he pressed it in me hand.

4

The draw turned out to be better than anything I'd smoked in six months. So when I next saw Andy down the Wolf I collared him for more. It's all right to do that if you've already had an intro. He seemed more relaxed than the first time I met him, not so nervous I might be drug squad undercover. You had to be careful cos you could still get a custodial back then, even for a poxy quarter. Supply or intent to supply carried six months to three years if you was unlucky. But Andy didn't nod to the bogs this time. Instead he leaned up close and said he didn't really deal in pubs these days, too risky, it was only cos of Arlo he'd brought some stuff over the last time. I said I was sorry; I hadn't meant to put him on the spot. Then he looked right at me. Direct. So direct I had to look away, scratching me fingertips with me thumbnails, pretending to try and read the track lists on the jukebox on the far wall. In the end he said praps I should come round his house instead. He wasn't looking for new customers but I had a good vibe about me so he'd make an exception. I said, 'Cheers, man,' and fiddled with one eyebrow like a twat.

He had a way about him, no argument. It made me edgy. He was tall, see. Tall so you'd notice, and he had that film star thing going on, like Charlton Heston or Paul Newman; broad shoulders, rugged jaw. He looked like he was in charge. Some people just have it like that, I spose. Then he smiled broad and wide, a big old beamer that filled his whole face and switched lights on in his eyes.

'Yeah, I mean it. Come round,' he repeated, nodding.

And that was it. I was a customer.

We got on, me and Andy. He was into music same as me. He had all this recording equipment and we'd talk for hours about bands and gigs and shit. We only did bits of business here and there at first but after a month I was buying a coupla kilos off him each week and selling it on to the other lads in nine-bars. His deals were always spot on for weight and, without fail, whenever I scored off him, he'd give me something special for personal, a bag a Redbeard, some Pollen or some Temple Ball. He was making easy money to be fair, but still it was those little touches that made him stand out, y'know, that and whenever he spoke directly *to me* there was no disagreement between his body's language and his words. Knowing who to trust was important them days. Still is.

Now Andy's crew was a real mix so I would never've guessed in a million years he was a student, not till I met Pads. I'm round at Andy's one night, puffing away while he's sat cross-legged on the living-room floor, weighing out ounces on these huge cast-iron scales like your gran would have, when this shadow looms out the darkness in the hall, like a spirit from the other side. Andy never said there was anyone else in the house and I hadn't heard the doorbell go, so it makes me jump to clock someone lurking.

But I goes, 'All right, mate?' more to draw attention to him than anything, me heart racing, thinking about all the dope scattered round in whiffy chunks.

The lad doesn't answer. I can't make him out at first cos he's still behind the door, but then he takes a step forward and leans against the doorframe so the light catches his face. I can't help thinking how *controlled* he is, like an actor in a film or something. He's about my age but shorter'n me I reckon, thinner, with long smooth cheeks like a girl. There's not a trace of stubble, not a mark or a spot. He's like one a them old statues with his chin jutted forward and his steely eyes needling into Andy.

Andy knows he's there, but he doesn't look up.

The lad pulls a Benson from its box and bounces the tip on the lid. 'Hmm.' He frowns, not at me but at Andy. 'And who's this?' he says.

'Pads, Jez. Jez, Pads.' Andy's still not looking up; he's concentrating, making sure the weight's dead on, but still it's like there's a bit of an atmosphere between 'em.

Pads is everything a Cov lad hates. His first words've already given him away, *bosh*, like that: toff. And after all the posing in the doorway I'm expecting a pretty cool customer. But when I see the whole package he looks like his mum's dressed him: tan brogues, 501s with iron-in creases, corduroy jacket, all topped off with these neat little Bo Derek dreads. I nearly laugh. But then he says, 'Pleasure,' and gives me his hand to shake. And I take it, interested to see if it'll feel as soft as he looks. But he's got a man's grip and he searches me eyes while he squeezes, smiling and frowning at the same time so a nerve in his cheek twitches and I feel me own face jerk in sympathy. It's only then I notice he has a scar, a shiny V in his top lip, on the right side, that makes him look like he's been hooked, like a fish. Then he lets go of me hand and leaves the room without another word, just a quick glance back at Andy.

'Who the fuck was that?' I ask, sitting forward, paying attention all of a sudden.

Andy goes, 'Who? Pads? We share . . . the house, I mean.'

Andy's bagged up all his ounces now and he's adding up columns of numbers, still not looking up.

So I goes, 'He sounds like a right twat. Like one a them students.'

'Yeah, well, that's cos he is. A student, I mean.' Andy stops to think, then points over his shoulders with both thumbs. 'Correction . . . was a student . . . we're dropping out.'

I nearly choke. 'I don't believe you. You're not a student. Nah! No way.'

Andy nods. 'Politics and Sociology.'

So I goes, 'I hate students.'

And Andy goes, 'Fuckin' right, man, me too.'

*

Till I left home me and me brother shared a room, bunk beds, him on top, and all his kit laid out neat everywhere so there was barely space for any of me stuff what with his records, his clothes and his boots lined up all spit-polished. His black bomber hung on the back of the door and his smellies decked the top of the chest a drawers; always the great smell of Brut wafting out his armpits. I'd peer at him from the bottom bunk while he got ready of a Saturday night and he'd give me *the lessons*, same as Dad's, while I sat gawping or counting Dexies into coin bags for him to sell down the Commonwealth Club. Ten to a bag. He'd dive in and pop a couple while I counted. He reckoned everyone needed a bit of a whiz to get 'em going.

'Lesson one, little un,' Kev shouted over the buzz of his shaver this one time. 'You gotta let the newbies know who's boss. Every fuckin' year it's the same, corduroy baggies, all "Hwah hwah, Tarquin, Mummy's got a villa in Onteeebs" or wherever the fuck it is. Watch 'em! Lookin' down their noses when we walk past. Thinkin' they're better'n us. They're askin' to get twatted, I'm telling ya. They have to learn.'

He was talking about students. All Kev's crew hated students.

'Yes, Kev,' I says.

'At least the wogs know who runs the streets.'

He ran his hand over his scalp, feeling for any hair he might've missed. Then he caught me reflection in the mirror and fixed me with his good eye. 'Lesson two: twat 'em before they twat you. Got that?'

'Yes, Kev.'

He faced me and gave me the wink of triumph. 'Me and the lads beat two of 'em up just last night.'

8

'No!'

'Yep, you shoulda bin there. We waited for 'em after last orders at the underpass up by Spon End, then WALLOP. What a laugh.'

'What had they done?'

'Done? Jez. They exist, don't they? They deserve it.' Then he pointed at me with his shaver still buzzing away and did that pitbull snarl he was good at. 'They come along with their money and their cars and their poncy accents. Start struttin' round *our* city, nickin' *our* birds. Excuse me!'

He could've been talking about the Jamaicans, or even the Pakis, I spose. Still, it was always the same kind a speech. Thing is, I could hear meself squeezing out nervous little laughs whenever Kev got fired up. If ever I argued, or even talked back, he'd hold me in a half nelson till I cried out. 'Think you're hard?' he'd say and I'd feel his lips on the back of me ear. Sometimes he'd razor me hair off with his Remington, pin me down and *zzzp zzzp* till me bonce was smooth and shiny as a snooker ball while he pissed himself laughing. The Dexies would've kicked in by then and he nearly always got too frisky.

'There, Jez. Now you've got a proper little skincut like your big bruv.'

'Yes, Kev.'

Kev was only hardening me up like Dad had told him. Teaching me how to protect our territory. Teaching me how to protect meself an' all. We was city lads, nothing but muscle to our name; no money, no education, not a chance unless you was plucky. We knew those students'd be lawyers, judges even, in a few years. They'd be the ones sending us down.

Jeremy Stanley Cross, you have pleaded guilty to the charges brought by this court and it is now my duty to pass sentence.

Hah, you know the sketch. Or vroom, vrooom in their Porsches, zipping into the city to make another wadge while half the Styvechal crew was losing limbs in the Falklands. Or looking at you daggers through the glass as you signed on, thinking 'scrounger' while you shrunk inside with the shame of it. Three million of us. Fit for nothing, so they said. That's why the students pissed me off. When people have it dripping like treacle off their silver spoons and still they wanna lord it cos they think you stink worse'n their own shit. Later on I knew them students were taught to act biggety just like I'd been taught to act tough. I never picked fights with them or nothing though. Not like Kev. My crew liked to beat them students in other ways.

Of a weekend, dressed in our gear, y'know, we'd pile on campus cool as you like. We knew the guys on the door at the union cos they bought their draw off us so we'd just stroll in, artful dodgers, eyeing up the lasses, giving the posh lads evils. We had a whole routine for scoring birds, not that I was much of a ladies' man, but our pick-up sketch was like this, see. There was no point chatting up the girls before ten o'clock cos if they was sober they'd spot you for a local in a flash and most of 'em were too hoity toity to go for a decent Cov lad without a skinful. So you had to hang back and watch for the right girl. Plump ones was the best. Not so full of themselves to tell you to piss off and not so shy and retiring they'd run away. By eleven o'clock all the beautiful girls were in their clicks with the Hugos and Tarquins (I swear to God they really did have names like that), but the plump ones watched from the sidelines, langered, checking the popular girls as they posed about. You know how they do. We used to say it was the difference between Labradors and greyhounds, and we were grateful for them Labrador girls.

So, at about ten thirty you goes over to a Labrador girl and starts saying stuff like, 'Hello there! What's a beoooutiful girl like you doin' all by yourself?' And you'd say it in your best twang but still keep a bit of *street* in there. They liked that. If they acted suspicious, you'd say, 'Haven't I seen you in one of my sociology lectures?' That was a good ploy cos most of the poorer students did degrees like sociology or teacher training so you could get away with a slightly dodgy accent. If you was unlucky and hit on a girl who actually *did* sociology she might say she'd never seen you in a lecture, so you'd say, 'Oh, I'm a *post grad*.' That always impressed 'em. Of course, sometimes a group a posh lads would clock us and try to get us thrown out. But like I said, we knew the guys on the door and they'd tell 'em where to stuff it. It could get right edgy though. Them Tarquins couldn't believe their birds would choose one of us over one of them.

Nicking their birds; yep, I reckon it made us Cov lads feel like we was pulling the balance back. Then Andy turned all that on its head. All those years hating students, *us and them*, and a thump of pride when you crashed their parties and stole their booze or their vinyl or their wallets, then suddenly I was hanging out with 'em. Day in day out. They were me mates. Students. I mean, students!

You know you can lump people in together too much I reckon. Start seeing 'em as all the same till something comes along to make you question. Andy said, 'We represent the Zeitgeist,' and it sounded important, like the army or something. Andy believed people should 'overcome social barriers' and 'fight the enemy shoulder to shoulder'. Andy said beliefs, right or wrong, have a kind of momentum to 'em and it takes a while to slow 'em down and turn 'em round.

Course, the more time I spent round Andy's I didn't think of him as a student or ex-student. He was the leader of this new gang I was part of and he became part of the rhythm of me life. Sign on Mondays, giro and Post Office Thursdays, the Wolf on Fridays, Brum on Saturdays and in between there was hours and days working for Andy, running round, delivering dope, picking up packets. Or in Andy's room doing bucket bongs and hot knives with the other lads till none of us could move we were so stoned. Till none of us cared about *them and us* or nothing.

Pads was in and out doing his thing. Always busy busy. Organizing. Planning. Andy'd get in a huddle with him and 'talk business', or sometimes hoik off together in another room for privacy. Pads would come all Bank of England like a bleeding accountant or something. Always saying things like 'I'm not sure we can afford that venture right now, Andy' or 'Let me check the balance before we commit to this.' Bollocks like that, or so we thought. He'd smoke a spliff, y'know, but he wouldn't hang out getting shit-faced like the rest of us. It was beneath him.

He comes in this one time going, 'For fuck's sake, you degenerates,' cos someone hadn't flushed a dump or had left a chip bag under the sofa. I can't remember what it was.

Andy's lying on the bed; up on one elbow, skinning up. 'Pads, stop fussing,' he says. Andy's voice'd get all long and drawly when he was stoned.

Pads is grinding his teeth. Then he goes, 'What a waste. Look at you all.'

So Andy goes, 'Chill out, man.'

Pads sits on the bed. 'I'm chilled! Seriously, I really am. But this is insane, Andy.'

Andy reaches for the spliff box and rummages for roach. 'Nah man, this is *political*.'

'How is *this* political?' Pads is using his chin to point at all the shite everywhere.

Andy eyes Pads sullenly, but he explains all calm like. 'Because, we're saying "no" to *their* rules,' he says. 'We're saying "no" to *their* laws. We're refusing to enslave ourselves by working and paying the taxes that underwrite *their* corrupt values.'

A couple of the lads snigger. Andy could always pull his own *them and us* speech out the bag.

Pads fumbles in his pocket for his inhaler, curling his lip right where his scar is, making his nose look crooked and setting off the twitch in his cheek. He takes a tug with his eyes closed then says he knows all about what Andy's saying, but some things are beyond the pale. Then he starts going on about the fact that if Andy's gonna make a proper *statement* he should stop signing on. Stop being a hypocrite.

'Shit, you make enough money dealing so why be a burden on the public purse?' he growls.

Andy sparks his spliff, takes a long old toke and speaks between blows. 'That's a bullshit argument, Pads, and you know it. Me, you, none of us is a burden. Our twenty quid a week from the DSS doesn't even pay the J Cloth bill to polish the nose cones of those cruise missiles down at Molesworth or Greenham.'

More laughter. Andy flashes us all a wink.

Pads pretends not to notice and carries on. 'Surely it's the principle we should keep in mind.'

'Exactly. That's why I keep signing on. It's my duty to subvert. I put *their* money to good use in *my* community,' and Andy grins and points at the spliff as he offers it to Pads.

We all crack up.

'Anyway, Pads, when did you get so moral? I thought it was "free markets" and "transcending petty mores" with you.'

Pads is beaten, but he does a little laugh through his nose and takes the spliff. 'Don't listen to me,' he says, jolly all of a sudden, like it's all been an act. 'I'm only playing devil's advocate. Got to keep you on your toes.'

But his armpits are drenched and the vein in his neck pulses hard under his skin as he tries to smooth out the V in his lip with his finger.

Andy laughs and says, 'I know you are, man.'
Andy stopped signing on after that, though. I sussed that.

Andy said being a dealer's a bit like being a rock star. You get flunkies popping up everywhere. A hundred sweaty good-time buddies smarming round you just cos you've got what they want. Course, a top night's only guaranteed when the dealer turns up with the goods. You walk into parties and it's 'Jez mate, wicked to see ya,' and girls push their tits at you and everything. But soon enough it's 'So did you bring the stuff?' behind their hands.

I had me taste of it, but Andy and Pads had the real clout. They were the top team, what with the campus scene sewn up tight as an arse. When you hung out with Andy and Pads blokes acted like you were James Bond. Man of mystery. Risk taker. Prepared to get yer dick shaved by the law for their benefit. Girls pretended to fancy the cacks off you at least until there were some fat lines racked out on the cistern or a bag a weed nestled snug in their bra. I didn't mind. It was good fun.

But then it all stops. Hey presto. Big bust up. It's always the way.

Andy and Pads had razzed off somewhere, just the two of 'em, leaving us to keep the biz ticking over. But Andy comes back on his own. No sign of Pads. Andy's trying to make out he's not bothered about anything, but he can't look us in the face. And he won't talk about what's happened. He just says Pads and him are going their 'separate ways', 'the time has come', 'a mutual decision' – stuff like that. And however hard we push, the topic's off limits.

Everyone knew Pads liked coming the king on campus, swaggering around, thinking he was the boss. I reckon Andy put him straight, that's all, and they fought. I've seen it all before. There was no blood on the floor so I didn't get it when everyone started acting like a bunch of schoolgirls. But things started to change pretty sharpish after that.

When he gets back, Pads takes a flat in Southtown opposite the church, gets on his high horse, makes it clear the campus biz is his, not Andy's. Andy moves in with Spud for a coupla weeks and we all tiptoe round him. He's so touchy. Some of the lads stop showing up and we know they're clocking on with Pads. Finally Andy finds a cottage right out in the sticks at a place called Hampton Kirby. Sold his four track. Grew a beard. Said Pads could keep the campus biz, why should he care. He wasn't interested in selling to the students any more anyway. He needed a 'change of direction'. It was all final.

Hampton Kirby was a country estate, about ten acres what with all the fields and stuff, and Andy was in a shitty little cottage by the woods. But there was a big house, five or six other cottages, stables, a massive pond in the woods and loads of outhouses, perfect for hiding gear. It was all owned by this weird geezer called Al Fey who'd been left the house and land by his old man. He'd been big in sugar, or condensed milk, or something. Whatever it was, Fey was minted. He wasn't married, had no kids and lived like a tramp while the estate rotted round his ears. You'd see him in his kitchen round the back, grubbed up, spooning cream rice or cat food in his mouth. Straight out the tin.

Just him in that huge house, unless you count the lads that lurked round the place. Young street lads they was. Come to do up cars, or drive dirt bikes through Fey's private woods. Fey would get 'em doing odd jobs on the land and pay 'em in whisky, sometimes food. It was like twisted scouts down there them times, with Al Fey the freaky scoutmaster setting 'em tasks, *dib dib dibbing*, oh yes. Fey was soft in the head, I reckon. He rented out the cottages and the flats over the stables to anarchos and hippies and criminals. He was drawn to our sort, being an outcast himself. He looked like a troll, see, ugly as sin itself. Five foot nothing with his hump, warts on his knuckles and under his jawbone, and a fat, drinker's nose bulbous as a cauliflower. He snuffled when he laughed and often had his hand down his trousers and a faraway look in his piggy little eyes.

Andy rented the cottage off Fey for £80 a month. It was damp, no heating. An open fire with a blackened chimney barely took the chill off. But Andy seemed to want it basic, like he was beating himself up for something. You know how some blokes go when their wives leave 'em? They don't wash. The bills stack up. They drink too much. Sink's always full a cups and half-empty take-away trays. The toilet gets shit-streaked and there's pubes in the sink and everything smells rank. Well, Andy was like that after Pads and him split.

He rolled over too, let Pads keep the campus operation even though it meant losing income. The phone didn't ring so often now the dealing had fallen off and Andy spent days helping Fey dredge the pond and move bits of old cars off the estate to the breakers up in Keresley. He kind of closed off. He'd taken Pads's nous for granted and now he was gone Andy lost his nerve. He wasn't a natural criminal, see. What I mean is he was a glad-hander, he kept relationships sweet, kept things ticking, but he didn't have the teeth for crime, not really, and that mattered especially cos of what came next. I couldn't see it when Pads was around. It was almost as if Pads's nitpicky pansy shit made Andy seem hard and dangerous. Now he was gone, Andy was just floating about. It was obvious who'd been the rudder of it all.

Soon autumn's come and gone, whoosh, like that, and it's January. The cottage is unbearable. The pipes have burst. The water in the loo's frozen. Andy gets less visitors cos it's too cold even for the roughest lads. But Hampton Kirby's wicked. A Cov lad knows his derelict houses, his alleyways and underpasses – the dump bins round the backs a buildings, bike frames in the canal, fountains full a cans and bottles. Nature for me was the brambles on the bomb patch, bushes you got stoned in at the edge of Memorial Park, dog shit on the high slide, pigeons in Mr Spivey's shed. Don't get me wrong, I loved Cov, but spending time out there, in them fields on that estate, looking at how the wind and ice could change the world, man, it made me heart swell. I'd go out and stomp in it, poke about down by the pond, trying to see where the carps and sticklebacks were hiding now it'd all froze up. Then I'd go over to the stables so the old white nag could bury her muzzle in me hand, looking for sugar. The winter ground was hard as concrete, even in the woods, and every twig and blade of grass had its own crystal coat on. I'd hail Al as he shuffled round, always a lad in tow, dragging engines and old exhausts in and out of outhouses. Then I'd go back and make a brew for Andy and build the fire up nice and hot again. I never knew any of that stuff till then.

Then, out the blue, Andy gets his spark back. Just like that. He's got some new contacts, he says, Irish, and supplies start moving through again. Some of Pads's customers have come to him too, saying, 'We'd rather do business with you,' and Andy gets a roll back in his walk. He has a shave. There's cash in his pocket. He tells me I'm his right-hand man now Pads is off the scene. Gives me the keys to the Escort. And one night, a week or two into the new year, he sits me down, right casual, and says, 'Jez mate, I've got a proposition.'

Of course I'm all ears and I says, 'Oh yeah, what's the deal?'

'Listen, comrade. I don't have to tell you how it's been these last months. The truth is I've had it with dealing.

That's Pads's show now. I don't mind keeping a little bit of business turning over on the side, but I want to branch out.'

'Cool.'

'Actually . . . I've been invited to be part of a new operation.'

He's talking like he's been asked to go to some posey party, but it's good to see his eyes shine.

'So what is it?'

'Plastic!' He looks up with a twinkle, all cheeky, the old Andy.

I takes a lungful of me spliff then and says, 'Plastic? You mean credit cards?'

He doesn't look so cheeky now. He scrunches his eyes before he speaks, like he's thinking hard about whether he should go on. 'I don't want you coming in on this, Jez, if you're not up to it. No . . . listen.' He has one hand up now to stop me talking. 'It's not compulsory to say yes, that's all I'm saying. There's a risk and you have to be aware of it.'

'Up for it, why wouldn't I be up for it?'

'I'm serious. It's not just credit cards. It's investment. Big money.'

'With the Irish?'

'Yep. But I'm *serious*. It could be risky.'

I shoot him a grin and say, 'Shut up. I'm in, you know I'm in.'

2

MEHMET

The Gjak and the Fis

A man cannot be considered wise before he is old, until he has experience. Only then might he realize that his passion can be full of heat on one day and cold as a whore's buttocks the next. Only with hindsight can he know that the fears of one decade are embraced and applauded in another. Only then will he understand that evil can dress up in many costumes, as a general, a banker, a spiritual leader, even a cousin or a friend. Ech, yet maturity cannot shield us from the skilled conman; in fact, it can heighten vulnerability, because with age there is the pride that we have become the better judge of things. A clever upstart is often the downfall of the vain master, no?

I have a new English friend. He is a little younger than me. I met him when he came to Tallinn to perform at my club. I have many clubs now, and casinos, bars, discotheques, restaurants, in several cities. He played on tour his music with a band, electronic music. I hate this robot noise, but this man has made a special weave of sounds, new and old together, like the folk songs from my homeland with a beat that makes the young ones dance all night, on and on. So I ask him to my house. Something in his face and his demeanour is familiar to me.

Now, I am a private man. I have learned not to lay my history open to a stranger. But I trust this man instinctively. He has an easy confidence about him. So I open a bottle of cognac and this encourages us both to tell some stories from our lives. First he tells me of his decision to dedicate his life to music. Then he speaks of his wife and children, his love for them, his aspirations for their futures. It makes my heart a fist to hear stories of love come by so easily. But then he listens to some stories of mine with the attention I imagine from dearest sons or brothers, with admiration also, and I want him to think well of me. Perhaps because so many years after I lose Rafiq on that cruel mountain I still see my brother in other men's faces, his charm, his honesty.

So I open my heart to this man even more. I explain about my family in Albania, Rafiq and Razlan and Gabriel, and I explain about *gjak*, the blood, Ismail, Jules and Juan. I even tell him of my deepest love. And through the story my new friend is full of disbelief that so much can happen in one lifetime to one man.

'But all this,' he says, making an arc with his arm. 'This mansion . . . this empire, I have heard from people that you are the richest man in Estonia and here you are telling me you were once a simple farmer and then a petty thief.'

'A thief only from necessity, you understand,' I explain.

'Believe me, sir, I'm not judging you. I have a past of my own. But I want to know, how did you get from thief to business tycoon so quickly?'

'Ech, this is not a long journey. All businessmen are thieves, they exploit the law perhaps, the taxman, even their customers. I learn this when my enterprise begins to flourish: the only difference is when a man has money he is called a businessman; when he has none he is called a criminal. No, the real journey of life is towards wisdom. This has nothing to do with morality, with good and bad.'

My new friend nods and laughs, remembering something from his own life, and I think my words are poignant and it swells my pride.

'I met my good friend Juan in Barcelona many years ago. He is my friend still,' I go on. 'After teaching me to trust and then to steal, a strange combination I admit, we hatch a plan to make some money, to get rich quick as they say. But to get rich quick is harder than it sounds and we end up with nothing. We spend all the money we save and like every poor man in the world we wonder why other men are born rich with everything they need, without working or striving. What accident is this?

'You see, fortune, my friend, is an elusive thing. When you glimpse the barest thread of it you must grab it, snatch it, like this. Perhaps my actions have hurt others; one man's deeds create a new reality for the next man. There are always consequences. What I mean is . . . of course, my actions can affect others but just as I must make the most of what is in front of me so must the person who is the *victim* of my actions.'

My new friend looks confused, so to illustrate I say, 'OK, say I steal your wallet tonight.'

'Hypothetically, of course?' He laughs.

'Of course. So then tomorrow you have many more possibilities in your life than if I didn't take your wallet, yes?'

'I don't follow you.'

'If I didn't take your wallet you simply get the taxi, catch your plane and go home to your lovely wife as planned. But now I have your wallet you must choose a different path, to go to the police, to confront me, to have your revenge, to steal another wallet so you can have your money back, to forget the wallet and let it go. Do you see? By stealing your wallet I could teach you a valuable lesson . . . or ruin your day or your life. It's entirely up to you.'

'I'm glad I left my wallet in the safe.' He laughs freely once again.

'I own the hotel where you stay. I could have your wallet in a second, but do not fear, your valuables are safe with me. What I am saying is the people I stole from are only damaged by my actions if they choose to be. Ech, they might even have benefit if I steal from them.'

'I suppose I understand what you're driving at, Mr Lucca, but isn't your argument a bit like a criminal trying to justify his crime?'

'Listen. If like me you have taken a life, a very dear life, you will know that stealing a man's money is nothing. Now to rob a man of his existence is to steal from the whole world.'

My new friend looks uncomfortable and sidesteps my confession. 'So you made your fortune by stealing,' he says. 'You made mistakes, but you invested in the right things, the gods smiled and here you are.'

'Here I am.'

'I still don't understand. Wasn't Albania impossible to leave? I mean, how did you get out in the first place? I heard it was Stalinist, or Maoist, and sealed at every border. Or am I mistaken?'

'No, my friend, you are not mistaken.'

'So how did you escape?'

Since coming to Tallinn I never talk to one soul about my life, Albania, Hoxha. Now, here is a young man with a genuine eagerness to know my adventure, so that I feel overcome with a desire to speak. The cognac, the warmth from the fire, the light and shadow caressing his handsome face, so like Rafiq, so like my dearest brother. It takes me back and welcomes an exquisite nostalgia into my breast.

And I tell him everything.

*

Women tell stories of wolves; the wolf that runs with the pack, a hunter, the wolf that prowls the mountain villages at night, a silken shadow, fearing nothing. This wolf is chancy. He knows not to eschew opportunity. He creeps into the house on the heels of the men as if he was the family dog, head down like a boot-whipped mastiff, whining, but not guilty. He dissembles, slinking through legs and lamplight. He sniffs out the orphaned, mucid lamb brought in to suckle by the fireside. He smells survival so that some immanence, some imperative, keeps his heart a stone. A man must learn to check the shadows round his hearth and never leave his door unlatched. Such carelessness presages ill, for this wolf will coolly lick his chops, strike softly and snatch that lamb in silent jaws. This wolf would even slide the newborn from his crib, oh yes. Tragedy, like the wolf, is quicker than moonlight and remorseless as any man.

It is true; wise men must watch their backs in the mountains. The mountains – proud generals of thin air, handsome, mighty and cold-hearted – are the craggy conquerors of altitude without a mote of pity above their barren tree lines. If you love them you are cursed. But how can one not love when the sun reflects lavender off banks of scree and bathes a man with some refulgent purity, rare as truth? I am a mountain man, so I am doomed to honour those wolves and those proud generals. I take inspiration from them both. It is my culture. Albanians have too much pain to remember so we must empty our hearts, and harden. Pray that the bitterness from before Hoxha and Zog, from before even Skanderbeg, before the dark times drenched with blood; pray this has not festered for too long.

I say all of that, but now I weep. I am become rheumy with my middle age, visiting my past again, scratching at old sorrow. I reach out to grasp my history, because I own it, like I own this face and these hands. These hands have done unpardonable things. I am not a bad man, not in my heart. I am from a tree of honourable poor whose roots reach back into ancient times, before this desolate era, before even the Ottomans reigned. I am Mehmet Lucca, the first child in my family. My mother bore my father six healthy children, four boys, two girls. She knew this was not chance, that only meticulous observances could make strong babies bloom in her belly. And by squeezing each perfect bundle from her womb she was further enslaved to her superstitions, appeasing the *djinns*, warding off evil, protecting and encircling us with magic. So in time her rituals became more elaborate. She could never stop, lest a chink in the armour of her belief let misfortune in.

Now all my brothers are in the ground and what good did superstition do her? They were only boys when it happened, virgins every one. Young men die in Albania. Ech, old men die too. My father was carried to his bed after Rafiq and Razlan were murdered and we knew he would not get up again.

Before his light is extinguished my father calls for me.

'Mehmet,' he whispers, so soft that I must come in close, smelling the anise on his breath. 'You must do everything to make them pay.'

'Shh, Father,' I say. I do not want the burden of this last wish in my ears.

Threads of spittle make a web across his mouth and I go to drip a little water from a moist cloth onto his lips. But he is strong even when the cloak of death is fastening around him and he grasps my wrist to push my hand away.

'Did you hear me, boy? *Gjak! Gjak* is how they pay.' His voice is become forte like the tough man he had been, and I get the fear of him I felt when I was a boy, when his stick would come across my back like this . . . so hard. It was for my good, for the good of the *fis*, the family.

It does not feel strange to me that Albania was closed for the world. Shut off by Hoxha, no one in, no one out. The mountains are closed to all but the strongest anyway. Of course some came in, Serbs maybe, and spies. A few, only a few got out. In my village we think all the people in America, the West, are millionaires, so rich and clever. Rafiq would say, 'The cities in US have money everywhere, lying in the street for men to pick up.' How my brother heard these things, I do not know. These days I meet Americans often. For all their wealth their children bleat like the sick sheep I would weed out from the flock. Ech, there. See, I am too hard. I am not at home now, not in Albania. But I *am* rich. I can have anything I want for my pleasure, for my entertainment. But then life was harsher than we realized. Without comparison a people will bear intolerable things. For a while at least.

My father used to say, 'A true man who sees everyone as his equal, none below him, none above, is a rare man indeed.' This is what Communism was supposed to be in my country. But no. Our glorious Comrade Hoxha stole what men had for the sake of an *idea* and called it fair and equal. In some ways he did make us equal. Yes. Equal poor, equal fear. He stole our land and suppressed the ancient law. But he couldn't suppress our blood. There has always been blood in Albania, this we call *gjak*. The blood of honour, the blood of truth, our fathers and their fathers have fought for this blood and all blood must be paid for, to keep the balance. Everyone in the world knows this deep inside, but only the Albanian says it to your face. All of you say, 'Turn the other cheek,' like good Christian men. Such sanctimony.

My dying father asked me to extract the price for Rafiq and Razlan. I must kill other men's brothers to pay for the death of my own. This law is the *Kanuni*, the law that says how murder must be handled and how to pardon the *gjak*.

Blood feuds often do not end until all the men in one *fis* are dead. Nevertheless, in grief my father asks a high price from me and I promise him to do my duty.

It was spring and Rafiq and Razlan had taken our sheep up to high pasture for the new grazing. It was their first time away without an elder and they might be gone for two or maybe three weeks, with these things it is never sure, but when they did not return by the full moon I said we should go to find them. Father agreed, but he was not strong. He had a peculiar weakness in his gut and my mother was scared for us to travel. She said the weakness was because of *Syy Kec*, the Evil Eye, and that bad spirits were at work. She begged us to stay. For two nights we did as she bade. Eventually my father ignored her fuss and got provisions ready while she rocked back and forth beside the hearth, holding her face in her hands. All women are prone to panic.

We left for Sylvicës under a cloudless, purple sky. It seemed the very air reflected a sullen light upon our journey. But I dismissed this presentiment. My mother's nonsense had already set my teeth prickling but still we wore the blue brooches she fastened to our clothes before we left. The pack mules, borrowed from my uncle, were laden with food and bedding and our guns were slung across our backs. All the elders agreed that a man is not safe without his rifle, but even so I never knew a rifle kill a *djinn*.

Our *fis* used a *stanë*, a shepherds' hut, a few kilometres from Sylvicës, where we slept and cooked when the sheep were grazing. It had a special view down to the valley and on into the mountains. Before Rafiq and Razlan left for the *stanë* I gave them my advice. The area we pastured was dangerous in many ways.

'Keep to the northern track or the army might spot you and arrest you,' I said.

My brothers knew that our ancestral land was Hoxha's now and highlanders were not supposed to be there, but of course we were and so were the other lawless *fis*, especially in spring when the snow melt exposed the vivid new grass. But worse than the army were the bears and wolves. Since the Communists had cleared the land of all but the bravest people, the wild animals had reclaimed the mountain ridgeways and beech forests for themselves. Bears could take many bullets before their rage was finished so a well-oiled rifle was a vital tool.

'And never talk with man, or woman, from another *fis*,' I told them, repeating what they already knew to calm myself.

You see, Rafiq, my nearest, was my best friend. He made me laugh, he joked about our father so that the punishments he gave us were reframed as foolish and funny, not cruel. He was the finest brother.

We found Rafiq and Razlan's bodies by an outcrop not thirty metres from the *stanë*. I could not feel my heart for grief. They had been bludgeoned, their heads caved in, their rifles gone, their pure white *qeleshes* still crimson with their blood. They had not died where they lay for the pasture showed two broad rusting lines leading from the *stanë* to where they rested. Left for the wolves, propped against one another, legs on legs and one arm flung across the other's chest. Rafiq's face was nestling so gently in Razlan's neck that I wondered why their murderer had arranged them so; or was it an accident, had they been flung there, dumped, and some providence placed their limbs to look like they were dozing, affectionate? Cruel, deceptive tableau. I pressed my face against each of their cold cheeks in turn, shouting for them to 'Wake up, wake up.' These things are a reflex, these irrational commands to the dead. My father, fingering my shoulder, saying, 'No, son, leave them,' so softly he was like another father from a dream.

We found most of the sheep scattered on the mountainside, but the mules my brothers had ridden and the mastiffs that protected the flock were gone. My father became a lamb then, no longer brutish in the face of this carnage. He barely spoke as we gathered up their bodies and wrapped their heads in strips of cloth to hold their brains in tight. They had been dead for less than two days and, from some miracle, no wolves had found them. I was afraid but this fear was spiked with vicious anger too. I knew that if my mother and her foolish *Syy Kec* had not kept us in the village then my brothers would be alive. I begged my father that we bury them right away but he would not hear it.

'The ground is too hard,' he said. 'And they deserve the last respect of the whole *fis* when they go into the earth.'

If he knew it was right, then why ask for them to be buried straight away?

After we had searched for any sign or clue and found none, we secured my brothers' bodies to our mules and set off on foot with the sheep before us. It was too painful to spend one night where they had perished. But on the way back down we saw soldiers in the distance. It was a unit on horseback heading to the border. We had seen them in time to evade them, but we had to hide for hours as they passed an old camp we often made in the low valley. We ate a little yoghurt and maize bread and drank only water, too dangerous to make a fire. We did not speak. Our minds were afflicted, imagining the last moments of our beloved kin. Father cast his eyes over Rafiq and Razlan every minute and I know his wrath, it builds. We noticed also that there had been a recent camp close by, maybe five men had been there, perhaps Serbs come from across the border, or another *fis*, not soldiers, and we were nervous. In the mountains man is still a predator and whoever took my brothers' lives would not be scared to try for ours, so we knew we must get home.

But after some time had passed and we thought to carry

on our journey, my father began to vomit hard. Then he runs off to the wood with his rifle and he shits so strong and long I hear him cry out with the pain of it. I watch where he goes in the trees, to protect him from a bear or man, and when he doesn't come out I go to find him. He is curled up like a puppy on the moss and he is very sick. I help him up and notice his shit in a soft pile behind the tree and it is full with blood. His face is damp as a dying man so I must carry him back to the mules in my arms like a child. He has great need of the mule, I know, and I think, Should I bury one brother to save a father? But as I decide my father seems revived and says that he can ride with the body of Razlan, they are both small and the mule will bear them both. Eventually we set off, but I can see my father is close to fever and his eyes wander round inside his head.

I put the pace on for the mules and we reach the *kula* by nightfall. The *kula* is empty, eerie. With my last strength that day I make a bed from sheepskins and hay in one corner of the room and I help my father to lie down. Gently I lay my dead brothers at the other end. I can smell ammonia in their mouths and see that the blood on their faces and in their hair has become dry and brown as lichen. I want to wash them. I want to bless them. I want to hold them. But I cover their heads with their *qeleshes* and in the candlelight they look like their souls are still inside, like they have fallen into sleep on one another's shoulders.

The sheepfold beside the *kula* has walls two metres high but I know that without the mastiffs the wolves can still get in. It is the longest night. I pray the mules survive or we will be stranded. The wolves howl so close to the door I think they have their snouts against the wood; and my father, he groans and sweats and I help him to shit again and again until his bowels deliver only bile. I thought he would not live. I thought I would be bringing only dead men home to my mother.

But in the feeble dawn I find the sheep alive, and in the fold with them, cowering and cold, Rafiq's mastiff come to find the flock. The dog must have caught our scent and followed us from the high ground, but he is bony and weak with a deep wound on his hindquarters from a wolf. He must have fought hard when they first came for my brothers and the lambs, so I pet him and talk to him like he is not an animal. It was his scent that kept the wolves at bay in the night. I half expected the whole flock to be in woolly butcher's pieces in that fold. So once more I strap my brothers to the mules and set my father last upon the leader and leave the *kula* in dense fog that drenches our clothes and keeps us and the horizon lost from one another. I listen and sniff the air like I am a roe deer. If soldiers found us with dead men strapped to pack mules and grazing sheep come down from pasture, it would mean certain prosecution. But I cannot keep the animals from bleating. It is the other *fis* that scares me most. All morning I sense people around me in the fog. I think I see the flame for a cigarette and hear the low growl of a mastiff, not my own. In the end I think my mind is playing tricks because any man could have taken me that day . . . but they did not.

I knew I was near the village when I heard the sound of cowbells and sheep herds about me and at that moment the sun broke through the mist like a sign and shone a wide ellipse of pinkish light onto our path. Soon there was a group of women from our *fis* following the mules, howling as they touched my brothers' heads, ululating, and making noisy procession to our house. My mother fainted when she saw us. Dropped like a stone to make a heap of skirts and arms. The men carried my father into the back room. My mother would clean him when she regained her strength. But my father would never speak to her again.

'Who has done this?' everyone asked. 'Who has killed our sons and wounded our brother?'

I could not explain. I did not know.

'It is the *fis* Geci. Who else can it be?' the women said, so sure.

The *fis* Geci was an age-old foe. Uncles and great-uncles, cousins and second cousins had all been lost to this *fis*, as had their kin to us. Anything bad that happened was blamed on them. It was women's talk at first, as it often is, but when talk occurred blood soon followed. It was the way. I was too exhausted to argue, although I know I should have, but then I too wanted blood for my brothers' blood. Yes, who had done this? Serbs come from across the border. We all said, 'Serbs, Serbs,' but we knew the soldiers sealed that border tighter than a pickle jar. Soon the news came that Ismail, my cousin, had seen Jules Geci with my brother's rifle. How he knew this thing I do not know, but my clan decided that *fis* Geci was culpable and must pay in blood for the death of my brothers. It was whispered in every house like a forbidden prayer.

3

PADS

The Revolution Will Not Be Televised

I met Andy in 1981. I'd been at university a week, possibly two, billeted in one of the low-rise residences the university offered on campus. I was learning to ignore the banality of the syrup-faced first years in my halls and had taken to hiding in my room after lectures with a bottle of something cheap and potent. Vodka usually. I owned little (a few clothes, books, records) but I'd bought some posters in the union (Lou Reed, Blondie, the Cure) and on that particular day I'd set about Blu-tacking them to the walls, taking healthy swigs from the bottle as I worked.

I don't remember what time I passed out, three, four p.m., but when I regained consciousness my face was pressed into the floor. I could see the nylon fibres in the carpet in close-up. Beyond the empty vodka bottle and my chair lying broken on its side, slipped under the door, was the first of many 'little notes' from the girl in the next room. A fat dollop of a girl with lumpy tits and greasy hair who had told me enthusiastically in the 'meet and greet' that she was a biochemist, from Cheam (of all places). Her notes, I would discover, always began, 'Just a little note to say,' followed by some passive-aggressive bullshit, politely threatening me with wardens and disciplinary procedures. As if she had the wherewithal to implement anything more complicated than a cleaning rota. I must have been making a drunken racket. I often did. I could taste acidic cack on the back of my tongue. My head hurt. But the light outside had faded and the room was now a blur of twilit suicidal gloom, so I dragged myself off the ground and staggered to the door. 'Got to get out of this cell,' I remember shouting as I lurched about.

Outside a tangerine penumbra haloed the city to the north, leaching light into the blackness of the southern sky. The university, perched at the edges of rural England and the industrialized Midlands, was one of the *new* ones that made traditionalists pull patronizing faces when you mentioned its name. I sat on the grass beside the union for half an hour, looking at the stars, thinking, Who am I? and What the fuck am I doing here? The light from that star started its journey to me twenty million years ago, before I was thought of, before my DNA existed. This life, this slice of existence is my own private eternity. I know nothing before it and will know nothing after. Those kinds of thoughts. I was a speck. I knew it then.

I'm not painting an attractive picture, am I? I sound like the kind of miserable drunk you meet at uni and avoid. I'd thought about death often enough. I knew that my suicide, if I managed to get round to it, would not be like my father's. Not the ground-down act of a ruined man. No, my death would be an act of protest. A huge *fuck off* to the world. In my own mind I was a *rebel*, an *angry young man* who had his reasons for seeking oblivion. It's tempting to try and explain everything, to list the paltry humiliations that steer a person's life one way or another, but I've never had time for sentimental scab-scratching. All good and evil is bred in the bone anyway. I was who I was. I did what I did.

33

I also knew I needed more alcohol to oil the engine of self-pity, so I stumbled into the union looking for liquor. Inside, the heat and reek of other people was overwhelming. The taste of them prickled in my throat, but I held my nose and eased around the edges of the throng. I was never one to stand at the front at a concert rinsed with other people's sweat. I preferred to lurk at the back where I could observe the habits of my peers. But that night I stayed close to the action, watching the crowd as it rippled and pulsed in time with the music. Each individual reacted to the movements of his neighbour as if some telepathy or choreography governed them, like starlings flocking or wasps swarming. And without thinking I closed my eyes and slipped among them, wondering if I too would become part of the mass.

I was subsumed. I relaxed my shoulders and allowed myself to be massaged through the crush like an inert turd. In the centre of the crowd their bodies were packed so tight I was buoyed up by them. I could even lift my feet up off the ground. I felt the benign pressure of them all, their warmth, their beery breath, their teenage perfume. After a while I tried to sing what they were singing, lifting my voice with theirs, shouting out the hook line of their song. Me, Pads, announcing that 'the revolution' would *not* be televised or some such thing. Imagine.

I was caught up in the moment. Drunk and abandoned. But I didn't dwell on it for long because the mood at the front, near the stage, was changing. Some chaps had begun to push people around, not fighting, just elbowing, doing a jagged macho dance. I could feel the new mood as a force, or a current, vivifying everyone. I knew there would be no room for alien objects like me and on cue I was squeezed from the bowels of the crowd at the steps to the Marcus Garvey Bar.

I pushed on towards the bar then, where it was calmer, where people stood in groups of three or four chatting and smoking. There were dancers here too but they moved less energetically. Two girls made suggestive circles with their hips and smiled to themselves with their eyes closed. In the corner, propping up the bar, I noticed a tall man half in shadow. He was nodding to the rhythm and rolling a cigarette with care and concentration. He was graphic with the light bisecting him so precisely from the top of his head to his torso, revealing one wide shoulder and half a head of dark blond hair. I think he caught my attention because I recognized something of myself in him, surrounded but alone. Detached. Self-contained. Just then he lifted his head so his face was in full light and I saw faint acne scars and tiredness perhaps had combined to give his skin an antique patina. I must have been staring hard because he caught me looking. But instead of passing over me he held my gaze for five, maybe six seconds. I nearly looked away. But he grinned at me so that lines formed around his eyes and deep grooves stretched from the wings of his nostrils to the splits of his mouth. And I grinned back automatically. He widened his eyes and looked as if he was about to shout out to me when the perimeter of the crowd suddenly burst backwards. The jagged dance, as I'd predicted, had got further out of hand. I tried to step aside as people stumbled clumsily around me. But the spillage caught my right leg and propelled me sideways so that the grinning man and I were crushed together. It felt perilous, almost violent, my face squashed into his chest, my heel gouging his toe. I could smell him. We nearly fell. Some people toppled while an eager, fearless group pushed back against the rupture, roaring, youthful. And this chap . . . this man . . . put his arm around my shoulder. Sure, he was trying to steady himself. But he gathered me in. He didn't even think about it, and as he regained his balance he drew me closer and planted a firm kiss in the middle of my forehead.

'The revolution brother,' he yelled at me, eyes burning, 'will be LIVE.'

4

JEZ

Students, Scams and Stitch Maginnis

Stitch Maginnis – Irish, ex-boxer, ex-con – had the hardest crew in Cov and thumbs up guys' arses on both sides of the fence. The Jamaicans did business with him and so did the hard-nut white guys (and if the rumours were true he had an arrangement with the drug squad an' all). Stitch had been a featherweight, won some belts and silverware with that runtish cruelty little blokes often have, but he was a real heavyweight on the underground scene. Since giving up the boxing he'd filled out a bit. Gone paunchy. He was bald early and his head shook very slightly all the time, giving him an old man look that you could mistake for weakness. I knew not to mess with Stitch. I'd seen him at work. Stitch and Andy wouldn't normally blip on each other's radar but somehow he'd heard that Andy'd carved himself out a piece of action with the Irish guys in Brum. Stitch wanted some of it. How? Why? Cov's a small city and if there's something sweet going down everyone'll hear about it in the end. And if you've got the muscle you'll move in and take your due. Job done!

Andy'd hooked up with the Irish guys through Mickey the Paddy. Arlo knew Mickey from the Wolf. Warned me he was trouble and Arlo never badmouthed a lad without reason. Grey eyes; they were the first thing you noticed about Mickey, grey like old dishwater. Skin like chalk, but see-through, like a smackhead who's not seen daylight since cashing his last giro. Hair as dark and glossy as crow's feathers and a slow straight walk to match. Arlo said women found him irresistible, but I couldn't see it meself. I told Andy what Arlo had said but he told me him and Mickey had 'an understanding'. OK, I thought. Business is business and not everyone you make a deal with is gonna have a halo.

After Andy moved out to Hampton Kirby, Mickey and his lot started supplying him with a steady stream of credit cards. We'd take the cards, spend the limit and pass a portion of the proceeds back to Mickey and the Irish crew. The money soon starts turning over and we go from sad fucks sucking on nub ends in a freezing, shit-heap cottage, to wadges of cash in our back pockets and springtime in the country. It's like the sun's come out. Andy's all full of it again. Pads is history, forgotten, and Andy's winking at me and getting brash on the phone organizing this deal and that scam. The crew starts to grow. Andy recruits some drop-out student mates along with Basil Johnson. Basil's a Cov veteran. Jamaican. Built like a brick shithouse with sleepy eyes and dreads that shave his shoulder blades. Andy wants Bas on board cos he's a professional driver, done some getaways, and got good contacts on the Yardie scene. I didn't mind working with him, though he could come a bit high and mighty. But Andy needed lads to keep up with all them cards coming down the pipe. Ten a week, then twenty, then thirty.

The outhouses on the estate start filling up with goods before we can sell 'em on. Andy comes all *Father Feed 'Em*

All handing out VCRs and stereos to the anarchos in the flats over the stables, throwing parties in the woods, taking bottles of single malt round Fey's to keep him sweet. I've grown up with this kind of thing but it's new ground for Andy. I tell him to take it easy, keep it quiet. 'One cock up and we're fucked,' I say. But he gives me one a them old-fashioned looks and says, 'These Irish guys are beyond the law. The credit cards are nothing, just a cover, Jez, you wait and see. Anyway, the anarchos won't dob us. They hate the pigs as much as we do.' I don't say anything cos I'm not so sure.

Andy wasn't listening to anyone anyway. He was firing off about politics the way he used to before he fell out with Pads. Said it was greed that made the card companies fall over themselves to lend people money. Said we was at war.

He'd shout and thump the sofa and go, 'American Express, Access, Visa: see the names they choose? They promise freedom and movement but debt's a prison, debt's a millstone and a crime. They're trying to trap us all, you see. Do you see?'

And we'd all nod.

Then he'd walk round the cottage, chuntering, 'Ignorant, reactionary, bourgeois, yes crime is the only legitimate response, yes . . .' I didn't understand the politics of it. All I know is the only time I ever saw Andy angry was when he was talking about 'capitalism' and 'corporations'. He'd use all them mad dictionary words, trying to explain that by ripping off the card companies we were simply – what was it? – 'Stealing from thieves who were sanctioned by a corrupt establishment.' I didn't care *why* we were doing it. I didn't have a choice.

Anyhow, the sketch with the credit cards goes like this, and this is your basic credit card fraud; there are plenty of others. The Brum crew would find some patsy willing to get mixed up with the bad boys for a chunk a change.

This can be anyone but they've gotta be squeaky clean, no previous.

So the patsy, let's call him Charlie Chump to make it simple, gets on a train in Brum with a direct ticket to Carlisle or Glasgow. By Crewe, Charlie's fallen asleep. His story is he's been up late the night before and it was all he could do to keep his eyes open. Somewhere after Crewe (he remembers Crewe clearly cos he's heard the platform announcements) he nods off.

While Charlie Chump's asleep the robbery occurs.

Someone 'steals' his bag or briefcase but because he's asleep Charlie doesn't realize until he's almost at his destination. Then he wakes up and starts flapping round, saying, 'Hey, has anyone seen my bag?' and looking panicky and stuff. Then he goes to the guard and reports it and the guard says, 'When did you fall asleep, sir?' and when Charlie says, 'Crewe,' the guard says, 'Well, I'm sorry but the thief could have got off at any number of stops so there's no point searching the train.' Charlie reports the theft to the pigs in Carlisle and phones the credit card company from the station to get the card stopped. He's a responsible citizen after all and he's kept his side of the card contract and *informed* them of the theft at the first opportunity.

So what's the scam?

Well, there's been no theft. *We've* got Charlie's credit card the whole time. Andy's picked it up, along with a bunch of others, from the Irish guys the night before and Charlie's just playing a bit of theatre for the guard and the police at the other end. The card'll often be a new one that Charlie's never even signed, but no one knows that, so we can sign his name in our own handwriting. There's not even any fiddly forging to do. At that point we've got between two and four hours to spend the credit limit before Charlie reports it missing in Carlisle. And man, we fucking spend. We have to start spending at the right time, though. The time it takes to get off a train at, say, Lancaster and get to the city centre. But we're already in Lancaster or Liverpool looking at our watches and it's 3-2-1 *bam* . . . into the shops to gather the harvest. It's risk free. The signatures match. The card's valid. The credit limit's nice and juicy. Ta-da! Free cash, free consumer goods.

Sometimes we'd just walk right into a bank and take money out on the card, just walk in, head high, and get, say, a grand in cash. Of course we'd be in disguise. Not so it would arouse suspicion, like, but I'd wear thick-rimmed glasses, praps, and a hat. God, we had a whole dressing-up kit at the cottage. It was pure fucking Mr Benn. We only dressed up for the cameras since bank staff didn't take much notice of you them days. Not that there were many cameras around but some banks had 'em and you had to be careful.

The trick with the cards was timing. You had to check your watch to make sure you weren't spending when the card was stopped cos then the card was fucked. Afterwards we'd destroy it. Burn it. You didn't want the card and your fingerprints ending up in the wrong hands. If the fraud squad got hold of it, then Charlie'd be buggered for sure, specially as it didn't have his signature on. The downside for Charlie Chump was that whatever happened he had to take some heat cos he was the one that had to talk to the pigs. Andy said the Irish warned them patsies they'd be grilled but then people will risk most anything for money.

You see, your average bloke can't lie too well. Lying's all right if it's a quick off-the-cuff porky, but to keep a whole story spinning, to remember every thread when the pressure's on; man, that's tough. Your words might come out clean but your body'll give it away; sweaty top lip, shaky knees, a little tremble in the voice or your eyes flicking off instead of staying steady. Basic stuff. Andy said the Irish coached them patsies to say the right things but the fraud squad knew all the tricks.

They'd be like, 'So you fell asleep on the train?'

And Charlie'd be like, 'Yes, officer, and when I woke up my bag was gone.'

And they'd be like, 'And did you know, Mr Chump, that this is the twentieth offence of this nature this month, on the same train, going to the same destination?'

And Charlie'd gulp and his hands'd go all slippy.

And the officer would be like, 'Is there something you'd like to tell us, Mr Chump?'

They'd question those Charlies for hours, knowing the scam as well as we did, and every so often they'd grind one of 'em down and they'd confess and start spouting and blubbering. But we were clean. Besides, it was the Irish guys that recruited them and meetings were always in pubs with fake names and . . . well, you know the sketch. No shit stuck to Andy . . . until the dollars.

It was a band night at the Wolf when Stitch Maginnis turned up to put the screws on Andy. On a Thursday five or six bands would get up and thunder out their sets without a sound check while the crowd got tanked and rowdy. I could never hear properly till the next day cos the decibels and feedback would put a muffle in me ears. By the end of the evening the floor'd be sticky with beer and sweat, and condensation would rain from the ceiling. Stitch, who had no cronies with him that I could see, collared Andy at the bar just as the third band started playing. I watched him walk straight over and put the flat of his hand in the small of Andy's back. Andy gave him a 'what the fuck' sideways glance, but let himself be guided outside as if he was a flouncy bird off *Come Dancing*. Me and Bas followed.

'Andy. It is Andy?' Stitch smiles once they've turned the corner into the alley. 'I hope your dogs don't bite.'

Stitch means me and Bas of course, but he's not worried by us. Andy steps to one side and brushes his jacket down and I clock that he's shaking.

'Yes, my name is Andy,' he pipes, all joky. 'And who, may I ask, are you?'

Andy could come all la-di-da when he was nervous.

It's Bas who steps up and whispers in Andy's ear while Stitch cocks his head. He's the real dog. And when Andy hears his name he knows his reputation an' all. But Stitch starts chatting away and he's all sweetness and light and Andy relaxes, begins talking with the same rhythm as Stitch, small stuff, people they have in common.

Then Stitch says, 'Look, I won't fanny around. I'm here on business.'

And Andy says, 'I didn't think we were standing in the cold for fun,' but I can tell he's lost his stride a bit. Stitch knows how to steal the advantage.

Nerves and the force of Stitch's nature persuade Andy to cut him in on the Irish deals in less than five minutes. I hear snatches, even though I've got cotton-wool ears from the music. Andy tries to spell things out.

'No dead certs, Stitch . . . never any guarantees,' he says.

'I'll consider you my stockbroker . . . use yer noodle . . . invest where you see fit . . . you have a reputation,' are just some of the things Stitch says back at him.

Then, when Andy argues a bit too forcefully against teaming up, Stitch's tone changes. 'I'm a reasonable man . . . don't push me into not liking you . . . I'm here alone as a show of faith,' all with a smile that's slime and shrapnel rolled up together. Stitch had the menace of ten men and that's a fact.

I was twitchy about getting fingered by Stitch Maginnis. I knew Stitch from the bad old days when him and Kev went out Paki-bashing for fun. Stitch was from an Irish Cov family; Loyalist, tough as tanks. Him and Kev had fallen out over 'a matter of pride' years back and done bare knuckles to see who was right and who was wrong. Kev came back a pulp but wouldn't let Dad take him off down Walsgrave for three whole days. Kev lost the sight in one eye cos a that. The whole jelly-ball of it went cloudy like a bit a heated Perspex. Kev and Stitch stayed on terms, though. Kev said he had to 'take a view'.

Andy made light of Stitch crashing his scene. He said, 'Hey, he's a persuasive man. He made me an offer I couldn't refuse,' and did one a them Don Corleone voices, goofing it up. But when I filled him in about Stitch's history it shook Andy to know someone like that had the lowdown on his deals. What I didn't hear in that alley was that Andy hadn't offered Stitch a cut on the credit cards like I first thought. Instead he'd offered him in on the 'investment scheme', an even bigger deal the Irish were running.

The investment scheme had started small. The Irish got Andy to invest £500 first off and gave him £650 a couple a weeks later. Then the stakes got higher. Andy invested his first grand and got £1,300 ten days after; fairytale stuff. Then the Irish said they were working on a big one, a really big one. They would all be rich. If Andy could get a wadge together then he'd get a piece of it. He'd never have to work again. Not for a while at any rate.

That's when Andy fell in with Stitch. He saw a way to raise cash quick and he pulled Stitch in for £25K. Yeah, no shit stuck to Andy. Till then.

5

MEHMET

Ismail and Jules

To understand Albania you must understand three things: *besa*, the *fis* and *gjak*. I am not an educated man; I am a simple farmer, or at least I was. To me, to an Albanian, the *fis* is all and without *besa* he is nothing. If a man gives his word of honour and then breaks it, where would we be? *Besa* is the truth of honour, the truth of an honourable man's word. If *besa* is broken who can protect us and support us? Where can we go for our revenge? We can go to our clan, our *fis*. This is the strongest bond that holds men together. Without this we are like the wolf shunned by the pack and we will starve and die. So, if anyone attacks or dishonours any member of your family there must be *gjak*. Only blood will assuage the offended, only blood will quell the anger of the dishonoured. We know this. Why do you other people pretend you can forgive without blood? I do not know. Only in *gjak* is there equality.

But when my cousin Ismail comes to me and says, 'Jules Geci has your brother's gun,' I feel a pain inside my head. Sometimes thoughts and feelings are too big for my brain and they try to break out and it hurts. Now I know Ismail has a thirst for blood. I honour him because he is my cousin and his father is second only to my father, but his lust for violence always kept him strange from me. But I cannot betray him. I try to be the shepherd, to guide him.

I know this thing about Ismail. Two days before he left for the high pasture Rafiq confided in me a secret of our cousin. He said he saw Ismail dishonour a girl in Bajram Curri. Rafiq and Ismail had made a secret trip to Bajram to sell illegal meat. Uncle Ali knew the supervisor there and borrowed a cart to take them. There should have been permission from the commune but we had our ways to avoid the law. I am not ashamed to break the rules; it is only a way to survive . . . not dishonour. So Rafiq and Ismail went to Bajram to collect provisions and take the cart back to our village the same night. But after their work is done, when they are leaving town, Ismail says he has 'some business' and asks Rafiq to meet him on the road. They agree a place and my brother goes to smoke tobacco with our uncle Ali, and to thank him for his help.

Some time later Rafiq comes to the place to meet Ismail, but there is no one. He looks around and he finds the provisions hidden by the road, so he waits and smokes a cigarette until Ismail returns. Rafiq thinks maybe Ismail is gone for toilet or something. And then my brother sees some bright colour in the forest and thinks, 'Oh yes, Ismail has been caught out,' and he laughs to himself and calls out for our cousin.

'Ismail,' he says, looking through the trees to where he sees the movement.

And Ismail shouts, 'Hey, cousin, come over here. I have a gift for you.'

Rafiq looks up and down the road to make sure no one will come to steal the cart and the bags and he walks slowly to the forest, looking at the sky. The darkness would soon come but, ech, they have their guns so they

45

are safe from forest animals. But when Rafiq comes upon Ismail he sees he has a girl. She is lying face down in the old leaves and her dress is up above her nether parts. She is shivering and naked from her waist down and Ismail is sitting on her like it is a warm spring morning and she is a log or a chair. He is smoking and smiling as my brother comes towards him. The girl is whimpering very softly like a whipped dog and every time she moves Ismail reaches back and slaps her head with a swift hard stroke, but his face is still welcoming my brother.

'Cousin, what are you doing?' asks Rafiq, horrified.

'It's all right,' Ismail assures him. 'She is an orphan, she has no *fis*. I know her from the town.'

Rafiq does not understand at first, so he stands there for a while and looks disgusted and confused by the whole sight, the girl and her wool stockings and her shoes strewn around in the leaves kicked up from a scuffle.

'Come, Rafiq, I've saved her for you,' says our cousin as he turns and straddles the girl like she is a mule, but backwards so he is looking at her feet. And then he roughly kicks her legs open and she is crying into the earth.

'Quickly, cousin,' urges Ismail, grinning. 'If you don't get a move on I will have to go again.'

Rafiq shakes his head, understanding all. 'Ismail, I am betrothed, and this girl is a child.'

Then Ismail becomes angry. He wants Rafiq to share the crime and so share the burden of the blame. I don't know, but Rafiq's words have shown a deep ravine between them in their hearts and minds.

'What are you, Rafiq? Do you prefer the boys?' shouts Ismail.

'I am tired, cousin. Let us leave this girl in peace.' And my brother tries to beckon him away and closes his eyes as if to say he has not seen the wickedness as long as they both leave this place together.

But there is bravado in the Albanian spirit and Ismail stands tall then and drops his trousers, in full view of Rafiq, and says, 'Go away then, little *Rafiqi*, there is men's work here,' and he gives my brother such an evil look that while Ismail does his business Rafiq hides behind a tree, all the time ashamed he does not save the girl.

When it is over Ismail strides past Rafiq like a big man, doing up his belt, but saying nothing. Rafiq comes from behind the tree and sees the girl still on the ground so he goes to her and whispers, 'Shh,' and tries to stroke her hair but she pulls away from him like he is a viper. So he collects her shoes and stockings and her undergarments and when she is dressed he offers her one hundred lek from his pocket. But she shakes her head and limps away alone towards the town.

Rafiq told me he recognized her. Her name was Yana. The Communists had taken her family, like many others. They would be in Hoxha's gulags, or dead.

'That is not an honourable thing you have done, cousin,' Rafiq tells Ismail as they load their bags onto the cart. 'This could bring trouble to our family.'

'Do shut up, *Rafiqi*. You are worse than the women,' sneers Ismail. 'She has no one to avenge her so there is no reason why I should not take my pleasure.'

They travel all night to Korrës without a word running between them. When they arrive in the morning Ismail is suddenly remorseful and begs Rafiq not to tell a soul about his deed. My brother is aggrieved, but agrees and hugs our cousin like a brother. He makes him swear he will not touch the girl or any girl like that again. But the next month Rafiq hears Yana is dead, found in a hovel on the other side of town. She had been violated and beaten and some say she might have lived if somebody had found her. She was fourteen.

Rafiq told me all this before he left for the high pasture.

He had done as our cousin asked and kept his secret for him but, now the girl was dead, Rafiq needed to share the weight of his knowledge and guilt. Even so, we agreed that we would say no more about it, but would try to keep the distance between us and our cousin. We had no doubt that it was Ismail who had caused Yana's death. Some men are savage in their desires. Ismail, it seems, was such a man.

My father died the day after my brothers were buried. His last breath came in the early evening as the women herded the cows to the milking sheds on the edge of the village. I could hear the rusty clank of the bells and the high 'ayee' of the herders as they passed behind our house. My father's room was dimly lit and it made a sombre sight to see so many of my *fis* standing silently there, and my mother kneeling beside him in the candlelight. But he did not acknowledge her even at the end. He blamed her, I think, for everything. I stood in the doorway, watching, and when I looked down on his waxy skin, slackened off with age, and his big moustaches become limp and yellow, I was fearful. I knew his death would mean a new kind of life for those of us still living.

Eventually the people went to their homes and left us to sit with the body for the night. My mother and her sister went to tie blue beads around the house. Too late for warding off the spirits, I thought, but I could hear my mother weeping and my aunt comforting her as they walked outside and I understood they needed something, a ritual, to ease the pain of thinking. In the room it became so still without them and their superstitions. I did not weep. I don't know what I thought in those moments. But I know I caught myself with an accursed face staring at my father. I had imagined him dead a hundred times and there he was, small, like a doll. Just a body, the third in as many days. I'd learned that bodies are useless when the heat's gone out of them. They're only good for the dirt. Then my mother came back in the room and tried to tie a coin onto my forehead, an ancient custom to send the *djinns* away, but when she got close she sensed I would reproach her so she retreated with her eyes cast down. It would do her good to cook for me and not dwell upon my father, I thought, but she was too distracted by her grief for me to chide her.

In the morning I took my father's gun and his clothes and boots and sorted through those things that had become mine in his death. Among them a knife I had never seen before. It had a smooth, bull's horn handle with a silver hilt and on one side was a wolf's head carved in relief. The blade was about four inches long and elegantly curved with a crescent cutaway near the base. It was a beautiful weapon and I handled it carefully at first, noticing the blade had recently been made sharp, but soon I was thrusting the blade into the air, imagining my brothers' murderer, Jules Geci, before me. There were other items among my father's things, but this knife called to me like a noble friend and I put it safely in its sheath and strapped it to my belt.

Some time later I slipped out of the house and set off across the valley, making sure no one saw me leave the village. But as I moved swiftly through the woods I heard a twig snap far behind me so I found a place to hide and waited to spring out at my stalker. As he approached I felt my hand move instinctively to my new weapon. It was my quiet companion; it would not give me away, not like a rifle. When I exploded out of the undergrowth brandishing the shining blade it was my baby brother I was scaring half to death and I had to stop the knife from doing what it knew the best. The knife was like a horse that wanted to gallop, that wanted to race the wind, and my job was to hold the animal back from some ulterior destiny, lest it took me on a journey I had not planned. Yes, this knife knew its fortune. I could feel the power of it and I wondered if it was magic, a moon *kustura*, black-handled, consecrated at midnight when the moon is full. I had heard these knives had a potent magic, that only sorcerers and princes should use them. I felt proud to own it.

My little brother's fear made me realize that my own motives had forced me to forget the grief of my living siblings. So here was Gabriel, following behind me to find out who he was and what was expected of him now his brothers and his father were dead. His eyes were thick from weeping but because of his young age I knew I must forgive the weakness. Still, I took his shoulder hard in my hand.

'What's this?' I shouted. 'Following me like a sick dog, ech? And wearing tears on your cheeks like a girl.'

Gabriel could not look into my eyes and he rolled his shoulders forward and clutched his *qeleshe* to his chest.

I softened. 'Ech, Gabriel, go home,' and signalled back towards the village. I had made a decision not to become my father and so I touched the top of his head. 'I have work to do, boy, and this is no work for children.'

But he took a step back from me and fixed me with his bright blue eyes. 'I am not a child,' he screamed, summoning some courage he had stored secretly away. 'I am your *only* brother.'

His wrath touched me. I had paid no attention to this boy since he was born. He was a child to me, more often in the company of women, hiding in their skirts and only good for feeding the chickens, not killing sheep or feuding. Now he was forcing me to look at him anew. This is how men grow. He was half my age and expressed in his own anger was my own despair. I pulled him to me and I felt a pain in my chest that sent me hot, then cold and it was all I could do to keep from weeping. I was mourning Rafiq and

Razlan. I was mourning lives taken arbitrarily in a moment, lives I took for granted. I think Gabriel was surprised by my reaction, but I felt his little body relinquish itself to my embrace before I pulled myself back into one whole piece.

Afterwards we sat in the woods and shared some maize bread he had brought and I showed him my black-handled knife. He held it as though it was a sacred object and I saw the shape and weight and curve of it impressed itself on him the way it had on me.

'Please don't send me back to the women,' he said at last.

'I am walking into danger, little brother,' I explained. 'I am going to the house of Jules Geci.'

'Why are you going *there*?'

'To watch and wait for him, to spy on him and see if he has our brother's gun.'

'What will you do if he does?'

'Why, I will kill him of course.'

By now some false honour or perhaps some blunt manliness had shrouded my mind. Despite my misgivings about Ismail, I felt sure – sure in a way that defies the rule of logic – that Jules Geci would have my dear Rafiq's rifle.

'I will be your aid, your trusted helper,' begged Gabriel, wide-eyed. 'Please, brother. Do not leave me behind.'

I looked him up and down. He was blond like my beloved Rafiq and although there was no hair on his face, no irreverent smile or impish wink, he had the same strong bones that distinguished him from lesser men, the same fervid eyes. And for the first time I felt a wave of feeling for him, for his innocence and youth. I had never known this feeling. So I agreed that he could come but only if he did exactly as I said.

'You must carry out my orders, even if you hear me cry out, or see me fall. If I send you for a mission you must not waver, even if you hear gunshots and fear for my very life. And when I tell you, whenever that might be, you must run faster than a roe deer in the forest, run to your mother and your sisters, run to your *fis*. Do you understand?'

Gabriel nodded eagerly. But I took his shoulder in my hand once more and made him look in my eyes to push some reason further into his mind and I repeated, 'You must not waver from my command.'

'I will not waver,' he trembled.

We had a pact and I believed that he would keep it. He understood *besa*; that absolute fidelity to one's word, come what may, was the only way to live. So he kept my pace with smaller childlike strides through the new growth on the forest floor, the first tender flowers of spring poking through the detritus of winter and blanketing the woodland with a juicy carpet. Ech, the deer would be about if we weren't stirring up the leaf mould. But when we approached Geci territory I slowed and took an arcing detour westward across a small stream, swollen with the snowmelt from the mountains. We stopped a while and drank as deeply as we could of the gelid water. It felt like we were drinking life itself. And for one instant I thought, 'What am I doing here?' I and my brother could be heading for the new pastures. I could be showing him how to live the highland life, how to sense the wolf or kill the bear and how to protect the sheep. And we could be in our *stanë* right in this moment, laughing about the women and their superstitions, but secretly wondering how we might find a *zana*, a mountain spirit who dwells in the springs and waterfalls and offers protection and strength to warriors such as us. Or picking out a bride from the young women in our village and thinking of all the things they would do for us to make us happy men, although the truth was, until that day, I already had my hopes pinned on a girl of peerless beauty.

But I was Gabriel's father now. I was his guardian and the head of my *fis*. And here I was on Geci land to extract blood, too quickly, too foolishly. I was unwise and my love for Rafiq was leading me by the heart and not the head. And even though I knew this, something kept me moving forward. Some engine in my mind, some pattern that told me this was the only course for men like me and neither doubt nor another man's persuasion could interrupt me. This was a strange mechanism that makes men behave like the wolf. And I thought, Maybe the wolf does not want to kill but, like me, he simply cannot help himself.

The Geci farm was isolated, not part of a village, but there was a main house and stables and outhouses dotted over half an acre. The main building stood in front of a rocky cliff and, on either side, the beech wood came within fifty metres. In front of the house the stream ran freely down towards Bajram where it joined the River Drin and the Valbona, then travelled a long, long way until it disappeared into the depths of Lake Ohrid. It was a perfect place and one that I have watched over many times. 'Why?' you ask. Why has a good boy from another *fis* been spying on *fis* Geci for years, since he was young with no hair on his face like his brother Gabriel? I will tell you. I have to tell you soon, so why not now? I am in love. I *was* in love. But more of that when it comes.

So Gabriel and me, we positioned ourselves on the cliff behind the house. It was not too high, perhaps twenty metres, and there was a small ledge hidden from the ground by a glossy crop of rosemary. From there we could watch the comings and goings in the courtyard in front of the main building. At that time of day there would be only women at the farm, I knew this. The men – Jules, his younger brother and his father – would be out with the animals or in the village.

From our vantage point the Geci farm did not seem like the home of savages, of men who could climb high into the mountain passes and break my brothers' skulls open.

It was serene: the sun was shining on the shingle roofs and haughty black chickens were strutting and pecking in the yard. The crystal stream offered a picture of purity and beauty and life and I felt immediately that this was a place of goodwill. It had always felt so, whenever I sat and watched there. Years before, the army had briefly requisitioned the farm. It was not that it was strategic, only that an officer had been beguiled by its charm and thought to have it for himself while he was stationed in the highlands. The Geci family were evicted and moved down to Bajram. It was humiliating for them and my father and uncle were delighted that fate had taken everything from *fis* Geci so speedily. But father Geci had connections in high places and the family was soon returned to their rightful place while other allowances were made to compensate them for their inconvenience. It was said that the officer responsible for the requisition was disappeared soon after and everyone in our village knew that *fis* Geci should never again be underestimated. Reinstatement such as theirs could only come from Hoxha himself. And afterwards I wondered why, if they had such muscles, they had not simply crushed our clan? My father and uncle would have sent all hell upon Geci if they had the power. So why did father Geci not do the same to us? And why then would he stoop to send his sons and nephews to the mountains to batter young men's brains out?

But these questions were not with me on that day. I had left my reason by my brothers' graves.

6

PADS

The Dollars

The whole episode with the dollars began during a week of impenetrable fog. It had sat stagnant around Southtown, holding the pollution in the air, aggravating my asthma. Then, on the Friday, a menacing wind whipped down from the north before first light. I was already awake when the first gusts went whistling round the soffits, or perhaps I hadn't slept at all, but I remember standing at the window watching it chase the fog down the street in ghostly eddies, driving it down drains and around corners, as if it had been conjured to clear the brume. I was thankful. But later, when the howling would not cease, I became irritated. The wind seemed impertinent, rattling my consciousness, tugging at every loose hinge, sending empty cans skidding along the gutters. Perhaps I knew a change was coming. Perhaps I just felt skittish after so many days of muffled stillness.

It was mid-afternoon when Andy turned up unexpectedly. We regarded each other across the threshold for a few drawn-out seconds while his scarf slapped around his face. He didn't try to tame it, or his wild hair, which had grown to a mass of tangled white-man dreadlocks in the three years I'd known him. He'd made the mistake of fastening ugly metal beads at intervals along random strands. It was a messy look, but one that had a certain cachet among our group at the time.

'I suppose you'd better come in,' I said eventually.

He said nothing but cast his eyes down and thrust his hands deep in the pockets of his army coat as he slid past me in the doorway. His shoulders were hunched over in that too tall way he had that said, 'I know I'm one of the master race but I'm not going to rub your nose in it,' and I remember thinking how some people are unfairly blessed – you know, good looks, princely stature and all the rest of it. Andy must have been – what? – six three, and languidly confident in his skin. I was indifferent to his appearance by then, but he struck me that day because he seemed distracted and awkward. So different from when we first met.

I hadn't seen him for a while, not alone, not since our disagreement. I don't think either of us divulged the nature of our argument to friends, or associates. Besides, we'd stayed on speaking terms, on the scene, doing business here and there. We had mutual acquaintances, we drank in the same pubs, we were in the same line of work, so we couldn't avoid crossing paths, although when we did, those who knew us from the old gang, the uni gang, would momentarily hush, waiting to see how we'd react in one another's presence. We'd been a team, you see, a duo. Inseparable. And then . . . it was as if we were lovers who'd split up acrimoniously. People said they were worried about inviting us both to the same parties. Think of it. Two men.

I opened a couple of beers and joined him at the table. He was in the shit. I could sense it. Actually, I'll be honest, I'd heard things round town. It's crazy, but I knew he'd come to me when there was trouble and I realized, as we raised our cans of Stella in a parody of celebration, that the anticipation of this moment had kept me going. I wanted him to need me, to seek me out.

'Cheers.'

'It's good to see you, Pads, my friend,' he said sheepishly, now avoiding my gaze.

'Yeah man, you too.' I reached over to pat his shoulder, trying not to grimace at our mock *bonhomie*.

'Look, I know I haven't seen you for a few months and I know you well enough not to insult you with small talk but –' he closed his eyes '– I'm in a bit of bother.'

'A bit of bother. I'm sorry to hear it. What's the problem?' I managed to sound grave.

He touched his temples, head down. 'Well, you know that business I've been involved in?'

I thought about my response. I didn't want to sound like I knew too much but I also wanted to avoid seeming disingenuous. 'Yeeas . . . kind of.'

'I knew you would have heard. Well, it's fucking backfired . . . and I'm . . . well, I'm freaked out if you want the truth.'

At this point he looked up at me. There. Vulnerability. Beneath the deluge of ropy hair his eyes blinked a limpid mournful blue and his discomfiture, I noted, was giving me some unexpected pleasure.

With both hands cupping his cheeks, he stretched the skin on his face outwards so his lips were flattened, grotesquely, against his teeth. 'Maybe it's paranoia,' he went on. 'But I keep thinking I'm going to get a nasty surprise one of these dark nights.'

'Shit man, you sound scared. Are you scared? Andy?'

He didn't reply. His eyes were closed and he was breathing in through his nose and out through his mouth in what I realized was an attempt to calm himself. I looked idly round the kitchen while he tried to get a grip. This was the kitchen we should have shared. I'd organized the contract on the flat for both of us. *A two-bed duplex in a sought-after location with central heating and views of the church to the front.* It even had a balcony and a fire escape that descended into a brick-paved alley. On the work surface were the remnants of the lunch he'd interrupted: a bread crust, a dirty plate and a butter-smeared knife. I tried not to think about clearing them away. That would have undermined the gravity of the situation. I knew that. Instead, I found my eyes drawn to the notice board above the fireplace and, in particular, a photograph of Andy on South Anjuna Beach from two Christmases before. There was the flea market in the background, and in the middle-ground a couple of Karnatakan women, all pierced flesh and collaged clothing, selling their wares, and there, the bony backside of a cow plodding mildly in the sand. Andy's dreadlocks were just hedgehoggy nubs back then and he was looking at me sideways, not smiling, his nostrils flared, like horse's nostrils flare when you come up along their flanks unexpectedly, and he was craning his neck away from me. I knew it was me he was pulling back from because I had taken the photo. I remember gambolling along next to him, snapping away. He'd been annoyed with me. Some *thing* had happened, some silly thing, and I was clowning, foolish, trying to make him crack. Yes, *things* were beginning to deteriorate even then. Even on a clear blue Goan Christmas Day Andy had found *things* to criticize.

I had pinned the photo to my notice board exactly a year later, pissed, alone, on Christmas Day, to remind me that Andy was a fuck even before he betrayed me. Now I had a terrible urge to take it down and rip it to pieces under his nose as he sat there trying to pull himself together at my table. I had cared for Andy an enormous amount, I'm not ashamed to say it, but there are always shortcomings. People rarely come up to the mark. But then none of his faults mattered until what happened at the farm. Our *disagreement*. The offhand betrayal. Loyalty reduced to doormat status. And after the farm, after that, I knew I would have to exorcize him, no, not him, but his false friendship. You see, I'm determined to be honest. And I'm not going to carp on about betrayal and loyalty; it's not at the top of everyone's agenda. Besides, I should have seen it. People always say that, don't they, 'I should have seen it coming,' but that's precisely the nature of tragedy or betrayal; it happens when you're blissfully confident that all is well. When the fabric of happiness is sheer and limitless and it seems inconceivable that a needle of sorrow will flash through the weave and embroider some garish pattern on your complacent joy. I was broken. But Andy didn't get it. He thought I'd taken it on the chin. It was all a big joke for him; none of it meant anything at all. So we agreed not to share the flat after it happened; we would 'spend some time out of each other's pockets' as Andy put it. He offered platitudes ('no hard feelings', 'water under the bridge'), taking my silence as an acceptance of his paltry apology. He must have known there were things that were unforgivable. Pah, it's pointless going into all that again now. Pointless. Suffice to say that he did what he did and for all his bleeding heart principles he never could appreciate how he'd made me suffer.

Now Andy was in my kitchen, suffering, and I was enjoying it. His eyes had been closed for a while and I wasn't sure if he'd fallen asleep. Under the weight of the giant army coat his shoulders rose and fell as his breathing lengthened into a steady in and out. There he was, what? Twenty-one, twenty-two? 'Pirouetting on the parapet' was the phrase he'd used to describe our lifestyle at the time, blasé with the invincibility of youth. Andy was convinced crime was a political statement. We'd all listened to his speeches about subversion and 'our implicit right to undermine authority'. I can't believe we weren't more afraid of retribution, but it wasn't authority we needed to be scared of. The pigs were kittens compared to the heavy-duty professionals Andy had started messing around with. Those guys were genuine gangsters, born to it, staking out their territory and fighting to maintain it. They thought nothing of taking on the law or upstarts like Andy, pretending to be a *criminal of principle*, trying to be heroic.

Let me explain how it all happened.

Andy took drugs, we all took drugs, but our drug use inevitably led to the realization that if Mr Dope Dealer could make a few bob selling eighths and quarters on campus then so could we. It wasn't about making money really, not for Andy and me. I mean, I had the trust fund. No, for both of us it was about putting two fingers up to society and, more importantly, to our parents. And I'll admit his friendship, his certainty, cured me of my ennui.

As time went on and the quantities of hash we were procuring got larger it meant we had to rub shoulders with the 'less sophisticated' elements of the subculture, those who didn't aspire to the same principles as us. For example, some of the guys we scored off would drive stolen cars or offer us hot stereos when we turned up to buy our kilos. They were minions, most of them, working for other guys who didn't get their hands dirty, committing crimes that filled the gaps between getting off their heads. You had to keep it businesslike with those types, keep them at arm's length. But over-familiarity was one of Andy's weaknesses. He had this whole class war thing going on. I played along with that for a while.

By the second year we were making so much profit selling dope there was no point staying at uni, even as a front (Andy was doing some bullshit degree anyway). He called dropping out 'beheading the monster'. We would 'put to death the straightjacket certainty of a force-fed education followed by Sandhurst or the City before it swallows us whole,' he said. We outgrew the playground deals of handing out hash in the union and soon we were taking the business to another level. But, despite 'beheading the monster', it seemed the beast had two heads and slowly it began to eat us from the other end. Andy would never admit it, but entrepreneurialism was hardwired in our sort.

After the farm, Andy and I went our separate ways with the business. I stuck with bigger and better dope deals while he hooked up with some guys in Birmingham, tough guys, Irish. Small deals became big deals. Big deals turned into a small business and his centre shifted from drugs to fraud. Sharon Cross told me that Andy's boys (Jez, her brother, being one of them) were running a lucrative credit card scam, passing half the proceeds to the Irish. The O'Grady twins said we should jump on the bandwagon and carped on about Andy's lads 'raking it in' and that we should consider 'getting a piece of the action'. But I was more cautious. I liked to see long-term success before plundering my assets. Don't get me wrong, I don't mind a risk, but it has to be a considered risk and I was already hedging substantial sums with my Indian imports.

I'd just finished skinning up when Andy suddenly sat bolt upright and inhaled sharply as if coming up for air.

'Truth is,' he carried on, as though he hadn't had his head slumped on his chest for five minutes, 'I've borrowed a significant amount of money from a number of people for this deal. I asked you for some cash, in the pub, remember?'

I nodded, blinking smoke from my eyes. He'd mentioned me coming in on a deal for a couple of grand a few months earlier, said it was 'risk-free', that I'd get three grand back within a fortnight, a nice return for doing nothing except stumping up some capital. I'd made a play of chewing it over and then declined. I couldn't believe he'd approached me at the time. Our argument was still raw and it scalded my guts to even speak to him. But that was Andy all over.

'It was all looking so good,' he continued. 'And then . . .' His voice trailed off.

'Have you lost it *all*?' I asked, trying not to betray myself with a condescending tone.

'I've sort of lost it all. Now I owe people money. I mean . . . a *lot* of money.'

'Andy!'

'I know, I know, *you* would have been more circumspect. I can't tell you how many times your voice has been ringing in my ears.'

'Anyone can get fucked over, man.'

'Yeah, yeah. I know. Well, anyway, I went over to Birmingham to meet the Irish lads. I'd given them £30,000 three weeks earlier and I was due to collect the pay-off. Actually, I was supposed to make the pick-up on two previous occasions, but both times it'd fallen through, so you can imagine how jittery I was. Finally we arranged to meet Tuesday night just gone. The pay-off was fifty K.'

I whistled. 'Fifty K. That's what you've lost?'

'Yep.'

'Shit, Andy. What was it . . . drugs?'

'No, just cash, the deals were all at *their* end. I was just part of the money.'

'But did you know what it was *for*?'

'You don't ask questions like that, Pads. Not with guys like this.' He shook his head, incredulous at his own stupidity, I assumed, and mine for asking. 'Anyway, I knew as soon as I arrived I was out of my depth,' he continued. 'Mickey was with me. You remember cool Mickey?'

I knew Mickey the Paddy, of course. Cool, hmm, yes. Like I've said, he was possessed of the kind of sangfroid you associate with trained assassins, men without the glow of humanity to warm their eyes. I'd thrown a party at New Year and Andy had turned up late with Mickey in tow. I'd observed him at the time, watching us all disdainfully, while Andy slid around him, slimy and sycophantic. It was unusual seeing Andy like that. It made me wonder.

'I picked Mickey up from the pub and drove over there . . . the bastard.' Andy paused, remembering. 'On the way he was laughing and joking like everything was going to plan. But when we got in there –'

'Where?'

'Oh, some fucking warehouse on an industrial estate, south Brum. It was deserted, creepy, like those places are when there's no one around. Man, I thought I was in a gangster movie.' Andy looked at the ceiling and stretched his neck from side to side then took a long draw on the spliff I'd passed him. 'Then Mickey just went . . . strange.' He mouthed the last word softly, then blew a column of smoke my way. 'There were these three guys in the warehouse, well, there were the other two I'd met before, the ones I'd done a couple of deals with, you know, and then there were these other three. New guys. All wearing dark glasses . . . and suits. For fuck's sake, Pads, suits!'

People like us didn't wear suits unless we were doing a job. Suits were oppression, suits were Babylon, suits were 'pinstripe prison uniforms' that meant you had signed up and bought into the bad world, Thatcher's world. Ha, funny now I think of it. I still can't bear to feel a tie around my neck. 'If it's tied like a noose and feels like a noose, then guess what?' That's what Andy said. But those guys were the real deal. They chose to feel some tightness at their throats.

'As soon as I saw them,' he went on, 'I knew they could piss all over me. So I tried to stay calm and play at being, y'know, hard. But the Irish knew exactly how to handle themselves.'

I covered my mouth and tried not to smile. Mr Chameleon, Mr Do-Unto-Others was finally coming unstuck. For all his glottal stops and borrowed bravado he was just a sham, a middle-class boy who fought with Queensbury rules. Those chaps wouldn't know a rule if it buggered them. Not like us. I mean, Andy was one of the elite, for fuck's sake. His dad was a junior minister in health or the foreign office or something. But Andy thought he could change his whole identity. Yes, I know, we were both trying to be street and alternative, but I understood that it was short term, an act, a means to an end. Andy actually believed in it. He thought he could *be* one of them.

'So what happened?' I prompted, knowing it must have turned out all right because here he was, sitting in my kitchen, unscathed.

'They said it straight out, they said, "It's all feckin' off, the money's gone." I was livid and even though I was shitting myself I said, "You're fucking joking, aren't you?" and started getting agitated. They just watched me with these poker faces saying nothing. Then I felt weird all of a sudden because it came home to me that I was on my own. I mean, entirely alone. I thought Mickey was with me, that we were mates, comrades even, but he was saying, "Keep cool now, my man, keep it cool," and holding me back and I knew right then that he was *all theirs*.'

'You're kidding me.' It was a throwaway comment, but I wanted Andy to believe that I thought Mickey was a mistake anyone could make.

'Would I kid you? He even had a gun.'

'No way.'

'I saw it with these eyes,' Andy insisted, poking the flesh that padded his cheekbone. 'It was down his trousers. I'm telling you, man, he flicked his jacket back like an American gangster and I saw the butt end of a weapon. If it was a joke, or a replica, I swear it was *not* funny. My bowels turned to liquid. I thought I would shit my pants.' Andy looked down at the floor.

'Weeeell,' I encouraged. 'You're safe, man, yeah? You're here.'

He nodded. 'They told me straight, though. They said they liked me. *Liked me* – hah – that if Mickey hadn't petitioned for me they wouldn't have even been there, they would have just "blown me off".'

'They would have killed you?'

Andy rolled his eyes. 'No, not blown me away man, blown me off, dropped me like a hot rock so I'd never hear from them again. It was hard to understand everything they said. They were all Irish and their accents were thick as potato soup.'

I laughed. 'Yeah, but they didn't threaten you or anything?'

'Well, I got a bit shirty.'

'Understandably.'

'And one of them . . . scary fuck said' – Andy attempted an impression – '"Yow've got tree choices here, my man. You can walk away quiet like. You can have yr kneecaps blown ohf or yu can take a consolation prize. What's it t'be?"' He looked at me and held his palms up with a 'what was I supposed to do' expression on his face.

'Knees blown off. Shit, Andy, you must have been cacking it.'

'I knew they were bluffing.' He looked unconvinced as he gave the ashtray a long stare, shaking his head. Then he reached inside his shirt. '*This* was the consolation, which, of course, I had to take.'

Andy pulled an envelope from inside his shirt and placed it on the table. It looked innocuous enough. It was A4, manila, not full, not empty.

'Go ahead.' He signalled with a slight incline of his head. 'Take a look.'

I admit to feeling rather uncomfortable at this stage. Those chaps sounded heavy in spite of Andy's propensity to bluster. From his description of them and what I knew of Mickey and the steel in his eyes I wondered if I might be faced with some appalling photo of a mutilated body, the consolation being that this hadn't happened to Andy. You have to imagine how calculating men can be when pushed. Tentatively, I picked up the envelope and slipped two fingers inside to catch the contents in a pincer movement.

I pulled out three twenty-dollar bills.

I looked quizzically at Andy. 'What, sixty dollars for your trouble or . . . what?'

'Take a closer look. There's plenty more where they came from.'

'Uh.' I examined them. They looked ordinary enough. Fresh, new, crisp bills. I turned one over. It looked normal.

'That one's mine,' said Andy, rubbing between his eyes with his index finger, the way he did when he was stressed. 'Look at the other two.'

'Jesus fucking Christ – they're having a laugh.'

The dollars were counterfeit. The fronts were defined, clean, authentic, but the backs were pretty bad. The reproduction was so-so, but not good enough for anyone to pass off safely. Andy was impassive.

'As I said, the bottom one's mine. I only got it from Thomas Cook to prove to myself how bad the backs were,' he explained. 'I didn't really need confirmation. I know what dollars look like, but I tried to kid myself for a day or so.'

It didn't make sense. The backs were like photocopies but the fronts were scarily good. So good you knew that some big people had to be involved in a racket like that.

'Seems like whoever produced these only had plates for the fronts, eh? So how many have you got?'

He looked at me directly then, obviously interested to observe my reaction. 'Fifty thousand dollars,' he said.

I stared back in disbelief. 'You what?'

'You heard me.'

'Yeah, but what the fuck . . . I mean . . . Are they all like this?'

'Yup.'

'Fuck!'

We opened another couple of beers and Andy started heating up some dope. He preferred his hash clean, no tobacco. Pipes and chillums wiped me out in the day, but I needed more than a spliff right then so we both took little sucks on Andy's pipe, passing it back and forth until it was spent and Andy tipped the charred remains into the ashtray.

'It doesn't make sense,' I said. 'Why give you fake dollars? And why so many? Why not . . . I don't know . . .'

I didn't finish the sentence. Andy was squeezing the bridge of his nose between his thumb and fingers, his eyes shut. I wasn't sure he was listening to me and I didn't want him slipping off into another trance so I raised my voice.

'You're going to burn that pile of crap though, yeah?'

'What . . . these?' He blinked and stretched his face, bleary but still blasé.

'Yeah, it's best. Take them into the woods and set fire to the whole lot. It'll be a laugh. A lesson.'

'Well, I can't spend it, that's for sure. Not here anyway, I wouldn't last a minute – and before you ask, yes, I've checked what I could get if I was caught with this much counterfeit fucking bollocks.'

'How long?'

'Twenty years.'

'Twenty years!'

'Yeah, man.'

Confessing his situation was obviously helping Andy regain some of his composure. It was rare for anyone to see him fazed. We sat and smoked another pipe in silence. Every now and then one of us would take a bill and look at it, then shake our head and place it back on the small pile as though looking and re-looking could make the backs become crisp and bright like the fronts. I got to know my twenty-dollar bills that day, staring into Andrew Jackson's face and crossing my eyes, trying to make the blurry White House come into focus.

By late afternoon we were completely stoned. Andy's pipe was packing Double Zero that some friends of his had brought back inside their stomachs. There were always small cargoes of rectum-shaped hashish to be found in England in those days. There still are if you move in the right circles, although for a few years all you could get was slabs of industrially produced soapbar masquerading as black Moroccan. Andy had some reliable contacts in Marrakech and we'd been close to investing in a 'route' the year before, when we were still partners. Back then there were no databases of suspects, no X-raying every bag, no government strategy, no War on Drugs. As long as you were cool, had taken some Valium for the nerves and a couple of Imodium to stop you shitting, then you could make a nice living swallowing dope. I had an associate at the time who worked for customs and she gave me a wealth of inside knowledge about procedure, when and how they searched, who they pulled and why. It came in handy later on that year I can tell you. But that's another story.

'Listen, man,' I said, still experiencing a rush of secret delight at the thought of Andy's deal going up in smoke. 'Why not put this down to experience? A few key moves in what you're good at, a few kilos here and there and you'll have paid back most of what you owe. Seriously, Andy, burn the fuckers.'

'Sod that,' he said, almost disgusted. 'It would take too long to pay off the debt. Twenty-five K I owe – twenty-five K!' He slowed down as he repeated the figure to emphasize the size of the task ahead. 'No, Pads, I've got another plan.'

'What?' I was suspicious, conscious that knee-jerk reactions to crises like these almost never provide the best solutions, but interested to hear what he'd come up with.

'Trust me.' He smiled. 'This one's a beauty.'

I'd fallen foul of Andy's madcap schemes before. He tended towards a kind of bi-polar over-exuberance. It was part of his charm. I'd spent a lot of time reining him in early on, but I'll admit his enthusiasm was a breath of fresh air at first. I went along with various scams. Benefit fraud, insurance schemes. Everyone was doing it. Holiday scams were useful if you wanted a free break in the sun. They involved a trip to, say, the south of France after taking out a fat policy with Endsleigh or the Pru. First you'd spend a week soaking up *le soleil* but soon you had to set to work. Then it was '*Oh mon dieu, mon sac est perdu,*' followed by a quick trip to the local *gendarmerie* where you did the whole victim of theft routine. A week later, return to Blighty, fill in the claim form, *et voilà*: a few hundred quid to pay for your much-needed vacation. The insurance companies got wise after a while so the scams had to become ever more elaborate to circumvent the clauses and the caveats in the policies. In the end, the legwork needed to persuade them your claim was authentic (hijacked hire cars, dodgy hotel rooms, interminable form filling) meant you got no holiday at all. So the holiday insurance fraud was good, but the house insurance fraud was better as it yielded the healthiest return for the least effort and capital outlay.

Andy and I did our first house insurance scam together. We took out a policy with Legal & General covering the contents for as much as we could (or as much as was feasible for a couple of students) and eight months later we put our plan into action. It took some setting up. It had to look authentic.

It was the year I shared with Andy. We were renting a

Victorian end terrace in Southtown, a dilapidated slum, flanked by a dismal recreation ground on one side (cider-swilling adolescents, dog shit, discarded glue bags), our neighbours on the other (four generations of Indians who had concreted their back yard so thoroughly and so inexpertly that it lapped against the garden walls in stiff grey waves) and a damp brick alley at the back. The alley connected all the back yards in the row, their dank out-buildings, coal sheds and privies reeking of poverty past and present. It suited our *Citizen Smith* image at the time, but rather than make the best of it Andy proved a total slob. His room was a suppurating hole where slick green mould grew in forgotten coffee cups and congealed fried egg art graced greasy plates with occasional dog ends planted in the glair. There were filthy rags, overflowing ashtrays, cartons of curdled milk. I won't mention the smell but for weeks a gradually dwindling pool of vomit (in a paralytic stupor Andy had abandoned any attempt at the downstairs loo) remained on the flat roof directly below his window (what was eating it? Birds, cats? I shudder to think), its biley tang wafting up under the sash on the lightest breeze.

I wanted to clean up for the burglary, of course.

'Why clean when we're just going to trash it again?' Andy argued.

'Because it has to look as though we are civilized enough to have owned things of value *before* we were robbed.'

'It doesn't follow, Pads. These burglar types come in the house and fucking vandalize everything, you know, spray-paint the walls, shit on the sofa . . . Cleaning up will only give us more to do when we break in.'

'Help me out, Andy; just the really disgusting stuff, that's all I'm asking.'

'OK, but I'm telling you, we don't want it to look like we got turned over by a bunch of fruits.'

The queer references upset me. My tidiness and need for basic hygiene were scorned as both inherently feminine *and* homosexual. But then Andy took the piss out of camp guys *and* homophobes. It was all skew-whiff. It was the times. Once I overheard Biff talking about me at a party as a group of them leaned over the hob doing hot knives.

'There's feminine and there's effeminate,' he said in one of those put-on falsettos. As if they didn't know the difference. The knife dangled loosely as Biff let his wrist go limp and blims of hot dope melted pinholes in the lino. Everyone laughed. Andy choked on his draw so hard Biff had to beat him between the shoulder blades. Still, he overcame his paroxysms enough to say, 'Leave him alone, man. Pads is just very particular about things.'

So there, I knew the jibes had become a kind of habit, a genial, blokey piss-take. Interestingly, Andy always chose the androgynous girls. The ones with small tits and shaved heads who drank pints and rolled their own. There was a steady flow of women in Doc Martens prepared to risk bacterial poisoning in Andy's room. I rarely had female guests. Don't misunderstand; it's not that I felt inferior listening to him night after night. I could have brought girls back if I'd wanted, but it's the principle. It's about not shitting where you eat.

For the insurance scam we broke into our own house on a moonless night. We even wore balaclavas and dark clothing. Andy smashed a small rectangular window at the back, using a towel to deaden the noise. Then with a wire coathanger I hooked the main window handle, opened it up and climbed through. Very quietly (just in case some busybody saw or heard our secret drama and called the pigs) we set about messing the place up. It was all going to plan. I even remember feeling a kind of sphincter-loosening excitement as I pulled things from drawers and emptied cupboards. I was role playing, fantasizing the life of a burglar, or a spy, you know, going through the files and papers looking for the secret documents. But then Andy announced quite seriously that he was going to shit on the table. I mean, the table! The spell was broken.

'I told you, man, it's what burglars do,' he said. 'It'll make it look real.'

'No, I don't want your steaming turd in the middle of the dinner table. I'll never be able to eat off it again. No turd. Full stop.' I thought that was the end of it so I went upstairs to carry on making it look like Johnny Burglar had had his fingers in every cranny.

But when I came back down again Andy had defecated where we ate. He'd climbed up there in spite of what I'd said, pulled his trousers down and squeezed one out. It was the size and shape of a Cumberland ring. It made me gag. But Andy was in stitches. He thought it was hilarious, utterly hilarious.

'You are filthy,' I told him. 'When the time comes it's you who's wearing the Marigolds and scrubbing that spotless.'

'Chill out, man,' he countered, like I was over-reacting. 'This shit will clinch it for us, believe me.'

We called the pigs at two in the morning after making a pantomime of rolling home merry and stumbling through the front door. I have to say that although we'd trashed the place ourselves the chaos was a shock when we switched the main lights on. You hear conservative types on the television saying how a break-in has made them feel *invaded* and dirty, as if someone fiddling in their drawers has defiled them, robbed them of their very dignity. I would always scoff before that day, shouting at the TV, 'It's only stuff,' and despising their suburban sensitivity.

Our messed up house definitely had an impact and I had to concede that Andy was right. His shit was the clincher. The pigs were sympathetic and not suspicious of us in the least when they saw it, wrinkling their noses and edging back into the hall. To them we were well-brought-up students who'd been abused by the rougher elements of *their* town. We didn't need to ham up our middle-classness, we simply used our home voices, enunciating our 'pleases' and 'thank yous' and 'yes, officers' with every consonant clear as cut crystal, every vowel sound round and BBC.

'I'm afraid to tell you boys that we're unlikely to recover what's been stolen,' said the taller officer apologetically, and we feigned sadness and disappointment in response.

'But my grandfather's watch,' started Andy. 'It's an irre-placeable heirloom.'

'I'm very sorry, sir,' was all the officer could say to soothe him, then ventured, 'Are you insured?'

'Why . . . yes, I think we are,' I answered, one finger on my temple trying to remember. I stared at Andy with a 'was it you or was it me who kept up the premiums I bloody hope we have' look on my face – it was classic stuff.

Then the officer was all, 'There you go, this cloud has a silver lining,' and we grinned bravely, turned our lips inwards and nodded.

The insurance assessor was not such a pushover. We put in a claim for £8,000. Naturally the company was suspicious that a couple of students were wealthy enough to own personal effects worth anywhere near that value. The company was right. The house, as I've mentioned, was a complete pit, half-furnished with thrift-shop tat, mass-produced in the 1950s, deeply worn carpets from two decades before and white goods that had gone past grey and turned to rust. Our own possessions were meagre despite our well-to-do families and our Oxfam/Army Surplus dress code said, 'Eight grand? Who are you trying to fool?' It was a dead give-away to anyone paying attention to detail and the assessor's job was to do just that.

Mr Snell, the assessor, introduced himself with a wet

handshake when he arrived two weeks later. He was like liquid, moving through the house so fluidly we could barely keep up with him as he ticked boxes, made notes and smirked at us with his fishy lips and bulbous eyes. But we had upper-middle-classness on our side, or so we thought, not realizing that this eel in a tight suit had seen it all before and that our type was the worst type.

'I see you have no receipt for the Pentax SLR,' he said, looking slyly at his notes, but mysteriously managing to keep one eye on us. 'Or the gold watch – maker unknown, or the Les Paul guitar, or . . . well, the list goes on and on.'

Mr Snell spoke in slow deliberate tones and put unusual emphasis on random syllables, which made us cup one ear like pensioners to try and catch his meaning. We'd put on our smartest clothes for the encounter; I think Andy wore a shirt with a cravat. Looking back, it was a bit overdone and we were defenceless against his acuity. I saw him glance at Andy's dirty fingernails and spot the cannabis leaf postcard on the fridge. He'd found our level. We really hadn't been thorough enough. That's youth and inexperience for you.

The company didn't turn down our claim entirely but in a polite letter drew our attention to section c, article 2b in their code of practice, which stated that, on the company's discretion, payment may, or may not, be made in circumstances where receipts were not forthcoming. I remember the precise amount to this day. We got a cheque for £760.23, yes, and a right to appeal for twenty-eight days. We took the cash, they knew we would, and we became another statistic that meant our premiums and yours were higher for no reason. It was a paltry success and worth it for the experience, but then Andy said, 'Let's do it again!'

I said, 'No way.'

I was categorical. Less than four hundred each didn't seem enough for all the anxiety and form filling and pigs poking around the house. But Andy had an axe to grind with the Legal & General and that was all that mattered, not the hours and weeks of work just to squeeze a few hundred quid from a reluctant bureaucracy.

And so it was that a couple of months later I came home to find the house a shambles and a knobbly man-shit in the middle of my bed. The back door had been jimmied this time. But Andy was 'away' in London visiting some girl he was shafting. Away, my fucking arse. This had Andy written all over it. I recognized the smell of his excrement, goddamnit. I didn't call the pigs. I just turned round and walked out again. I was so angry. It was already late and the pubs were closing so I had no choice but to slope round to Zoë's.

I slept with Zoë once in a while but she wasn't a girl-friend. I could only handle her in small doses. She was intense and diligent when she wasn't taking psychedelics, willing and undemanding when she was. She took LSD most days, so it was difficult to know her true nature. There were times when she didn't even notice I was there and she'd just moon around in a colourful world born of misfiring neurons. I can't imagine where she ended up. I heard rumours she'd become a sanyassin, but that was years ago. Back then Zoë lived in a block of municipal university halls at the top of town with buzzer entry and carpet tiles and cold strip lighting that crackled off and on as you walked along the corridors. It took a minute for Zoë to let me in.

'Hey, man,' she said when she saw me, smiling and touching the buttons on my 501s.

'Hey, Zee.'

Zoë's room was warm as a womb. Some sickly joss stick was burning on the windowsill while Zappa oozed urbanely from the stereo. There were a couple of long-haired chaps I didn't know sitting on the floor. One of them managed a nod of acknowledgement as I squeezed into a corner. By the look of them they'd had several bongs already and had only paused in their serious discussion (about Nietzsche) to make sure I was 'cool' (not the hall's caretaker come to hassle them for smoking pot).

I wanted them to leave. I wanted somewhere to expend my anger. I wanted the mechanical release of Zoë's easy sexuality. But she was entertaining her clever friends. Of course, I knew that the whole 'Yeah, man, Hitler failed to understand the fundamental humanity of Nietzsche's thinking . . .' bullshit was pretentious space-cadet philosophy. So I gritted my teeth and willed myself to fall asleep.

When I woke Zoë had despatched her visitors. A single candle flickered by the stereo and Zoë, who was now completely naked except for a chiffon scarf tied around her waist, was dancing to some dull hippy tune, apparently unaware of me. I shifted and took a couple of deep sucks on my inhaler. She must have heard my movements because she turned round then and danced for me, all opiated smiles and fecund demonstration. I think she was pretending to be an eastern goddess, grinding into an invisible priapus. Girls' fantasies are so obscure. I stood up, stripped, then stretched out on the bed. Zoë straddled me, managing to keep the rhythm going. Andy would have said it was all that talk about Nietzsche that got her horny. He said girls got turned on by intellectual debate, but I know Zoë was just, you know, a bit of a whore.

Andy loved women, thought they were – what did he call them? 'Mother Gaia, life givers.' What the fuck? Women are not interested in intellectual debate, they want power. Your power. Still, I miss those days if only for their unrepentant baseness. When you're young you don't realize, you think it's the beginning of a lifetime of sexual freedom. Then you get older and discover that the tiny slice of time between eighteen and twenty-five was *it*. That was the harvest and after that it's barren and dried up. 'Halcyon days' my dad called them, but I wasn't listening. He was at Oxford, of course, but he never told me much about his youth before he topped himself. He could barely get a word in with my mother. He spent his life slaving to keep her happy. He became a shell. If I'd tapped his skin at the end it would have sounded like a blown egg. So there it is.

I woke at lunchtime and left Zoë sleeping. When I got home there was a squad car parked outside the house so I knew Andy must be home. Sure enough, he was standing in the hallway looking traumatized and talking to the police, acting his head off. I couldn't blow it for him. Instead I came in saying, 'What in God's name is going on?'

'Thank Christ you're here. You'll never believe it.' Andy let his arms flop resignedly at his sides. 'We've been burgled . . . *again*!'

'Never.'

'Yep, Tris, I'm afraid so. Didn't you come back last night?'

'No, my friend. I was at Zoë's.'

The officer stayed silent throughout our exchange, but looked from Andy to me as we spoke. He may have got a sense of the impending rancour. But all he said was, 'You'll have to make a list of what's been stolen.'

'There was nothing left to steal, eh Andy?' It was barbed, I know, but I couldn't help myself. 'The bastards got all the good stuff the last time.' Then I laughed cynically to add weight to the irony.

'Speak for yourself, Tris,' Andy objected. 'I've replaced all *my* stuff, hadn't you noticed? I even borrowed money from my parents so I could get everything back.'

You had to hand it to him, he was on the ball, and I know his little speech was for the pig's benefit as well as mine, but it was a surprise and it hurt. He'd schemed without telling me, left me out of the deal, and there he was shaking his head and tutting, making me look ridiculous.

'Well,' I said, losing my cool a little. 'I hope you've kept all your receipts *this time*.'

The policeman cleared his throat and made the same apologetic speech about not recovering our property, then left us standing stiffly in the hallway exchanging caustic glances.

'You twat,' Andy hissed as soon as Plod's footsteps had receded far enough for comfort. 'You were trying to make me look stupid in front of that fucking copper.'

'Making you look stupid does not appear to be my job, man. It's been your sole occupation for a while now.'

I walked past him towards the kitchen and cuffed him with my shoulder as I went.

'Hey,' he shouted.

'What?'

'You got a problem?'

'Yeah, of course I've got a problem.' I lowered my voice and got this deep rumbling anger thing going. It wasn't an act, it was genuine, although I wasn't stupid enough to shout so prying ears could hear. I told him all about himself through my teeth. 'You fucking do this job without my say so, you shit on my bed like an animal and engineer it so I'm the one who finds it all. Did you really think I was going to call the pigs like a good little boy when you knew I didn't want all this to happen in the first place?'

It didn't take long for him to become conciliatory. I had never stood up to him before. He had betrayed me, you see. Granted, it was a small betrayal, compared with what came later, but by going against my specific wishes he was saying, 'Your opinion doesn't matter.' Oh, I know it was trifling, but he was beginning to feel he'd outgrown me. So I had to flex my muscles. Power play is important in every relationship.

'C'mon, man,' he said. 'I had to do it this way. You were dead against it. But I promise you it will come off perfect.'

'Yeah,' I drawled sarcastically.

'You'll see.'

I sighed. 'I'm going back round Zoë's and I'd be obliged if you could change my sheets before I get back.'

I didn't go to Zoë's. I went down the pub. Our local was a converted terrace just off the towpath where antique sewing-machine treadles served as tables and a succession of life-worn barmaids served behind the bar. It was here that all the freaks and lowlifes congregated, sipping their halves in the flock and fug. The landlord, a huge West Indian called Horace, with a face as round as a chocolate moon and a belly to match, always had a welcoming smile, but you had to check your change even if you were a regular. He was a cheeky sod, but he did weekend lock-ins and we were grateful for it.

'Ah right,' came Horace's broad salutation as I approached the bar. 'You look like someone put chilli pepper up yer rass.'

'Just give us a pint of Director's,' I said, eyeing the pump.

The place was empty apart from a couple of old boys playing slap domino by the bar. I nodded to them and they each raised a hand of greeting before continuing their play. I sat in the corner by the window and made up my mind to get drunk. An hour later Andy arrived and put a fresh pint in front of me.

'I called at Zoë's,' he said eventually. 'But you weren't there.'

'Evidently.'

'Listen. I'm sorry. I've cleaned up the shit and I promise you won't hear another word about any of it. Honest.'

'Pah, I'm cool,' I lied.

It was after midnight when we fell out of the pub. We

were intoxicated, stumbling, and Andy grabbed me and embraced me as he flopped about. He told me I was the best friend he'd ever had. He said he 'admired me', that we'd 'be mates for ever', until we were 'old men', and even then we'd still get together on a Friday night for a beer and a spliff and to set the world to rights. I said, 'Course we will, old chap, course we will,' knowing it was beer talking, but still I melted to hear him say it. We made our way with our arms across one another's shoulders, laughing so hard our knees buckled. I was full with fickle happiness.

Two months later Andy came into my bedroom and threw an envelope onto the bed.

'What's this?'

'Open it and see.'

He had a sparkle in his eye as I ripped it open. Inside was £500 in grubby tens and fives.

'For you,' he said. 'For being a good mate, for being . . . *understanding*.'

'What?'

'I got the insurance money through.'

'You what?'

'Stop saying "what", you fuckwit. I'm telling you I got the money for the insurance. I sorted it all out.'

'I thought you promised you'd drop that shit?'

'I never said that. I said you'd never hear another word about it and I kept my word.'

I was chagrined, but I decided to be good-natured. 'Andy,' I said. 'You're a genius and although I'm tempted to take your money I want you to keep it,' and I handed the envelope back to him.

I wanted to hurt him, to show him I was bigger than him. It was spiteful, but then again maybe I knew, deep down, that one day I'd be glad I owed him nothing. Maybe I just wanted to punish him for leaving me out of the deal. For using me. I could tell he was wounded, but he tried to brush it off.

'It's nothing personal,' I explained. 'Truly, I appreciate the generosity . . . but that insurance scene, well, it wasn't for me and I'd feel better without profit from it. You understand that, yeah?'

Although he was frowning, he said, 'Yeah man, I'm cool,' and pocketed the notes.

I found out later that Andy had been as shrewd as an actuary and got hold of thousands of pounds' worth of receipts for goods; a camera, a video recorder, TV, synthesizer and a four-track studio, you name it he had proof of purchase for it, from this dodgy chap or that – God, who knows where from? – all acquired in those intervening months to 'replace' the goods we hadn't had nicked in the first place.

He made a claim for £6,000 and saw the same fishy assessor, without me of course. Andy told him that he would go 'directly to the ombudsman' if he pulled any crap or offered less than he'd rightly claimed for. The company had been happy to take the premiums and now they'd pay the price. Unbelievably, the company didn't quibble and paid up in full. But a week later Andy received a polite but assertive letter returning the last two premiums on a computer printout cheque with a note that said, 'With regret, Mr —, we cannot continue to insure you, blah, blah, as you represent too high a risk et cetera, et cetera.' Something like that. They could have said they'd carry on insuring us if we installed a state-of-the-art burglar alarm or window locks but they didn't and, well, we all knew where we stood.

Andy didn't care. He'd got what he wanted out of those bastards. He was going to cancel the policy anyway after screwing them for six grand. He'd proved that he could beat them at their own game. That was Andy all over. He was a risk taker, and a terrier. I loved him if only for that.

*

This time audacious, brazen Andy wore a terrier's grin that was about as genuine as the dollars on the table in front of us. In fact, I knew he was flummoxed, impotent. He had been monumentally conned and it was eating him up. I knew his body language well enough to ascertain that. But he kept that helpless smile stretched across his teeth for just a fraction too long and I remember that on the wall behind him was the giant Che Guevara poster he'd given me. The juxtaposition was delightful: Andy, a little boy lost, but bluffing it, with that scowling revolutionary looming large at his shoulder.

There were many reasons why Andy came to me that day. Obviously he underestimated my capacity for resentment and therefore mistook reticence for a kind of cooling off after what had happened at the farm. Also he had clearly missed my insight and my moderation in the time since our paths had diverged. No doubt he respected my business mind and the razor sharpness of my financial judgements. But most of all (my nose told me) he needed money. He'd take his time to come around to it but he'd slip the request in somewhere. I didn't mind that the motive for his visit was entirely financial. In fact, it occurred to me, with him in this weak state, that it was an ideal opportunity to even out the scores between us.

Impatient to hear how he intended to shine up his disaster, I gave him my sincerest stare and said, 'So come on, man. Tell me your plan.'

'Well, I've been thinking. How can I offload these dollars, I mean realistically, without being busted? Not here, it has to be abroad, somewhere where they're not going to be so on the ball or check each note.'

'Where would that be? These aren't drachma or krona or something obscure like that. Everyone in the world knows a greenback, it's international currency, you know that.'

'Thanks, Pads, I knew I could count on you for encouragement. C'mon, go with me here,' and he did a drum roll on the table with his fists. I gave an exaggerated shrug, pretending to concede.

'I wouldn't change them all at once, of course,' he went on. 'I'd do, say, two to three hundred at a time, in little places, Bureaux de Change, you know, in a tourist spot where you won't be noticed in a crowd and where the workers on the counters won't be suspicious.'

He paused and looked to see if I was on board.

'What do you want me to say? It's a risky piece of shit whatever way you do it, and you know me, I'm up for a lot of things . . . but this?'

'Oh, man,' he moaned. 'I can't close on this. I have to turn this round. I just have to.'

'Your mind's obviously made up, so what do you want from me, Andy? My blessing?'

'Nah.' He laughed, although he looked away and couldn't meet my eye.

I was waiting for a moment, a chink where I could deliver a blow to whatever scheme he'd put together. I make no apologies for it. He was buggered anyway. Besides, his pain was salving a hitherto deep and unreachable ache of my own and as he described the details of his plan I wondered if I could perhaps eliminate my discomfort for ever. His demise could be my salvation.

A couple of guys, he explained, would take the dollars down to southern Spain, the Costa del Sol, there they would take their time and change all the notes into currency: sterling, pesetas, marks, it didn't matter as long as it was 'real'. They'd mail the new currency back to Andy so they wouldn't end up with a rucksack full of genuine notes and another full of fakes. Andy would stay in England to direct the whole operation (although I sensed unease, rather than a hands-off managerial approach, was the prime motive for this particular decision).

83

I said I thought the plan might work but that the lads should change no more than one hundred dollars at a time. They mustn't arouse suspicion. And they must watch they weren't followed. If those notes turned up in the wrong hands or if some observant bank clerk noticed a shaking hand, or a tremor in the voice or such like, then the law would track them down. This wasn't small fry. Interpol would be very interested in fifty thousand counterfeit dollars.

Andy was lapping up everything I said.

'Which guys were you thinking of sending?' I asked.

'Jez . . . and Bas. What do you think?'

'Perfect.'

'Yeah, you think?'

'Yes, absolutely.'

He pushed back in his chair, expelling a long breath as he rolled his eyes and shook his head. 'Mental,' he mouthed, meaning all of it, the situation.

I couldn't believe he would dig his own grave like that. Jez (minuscule IQ, borderline psychopath) and Bas (Jamaican, ex-con, loser) were precisely the wrong people for the job. He had sunk further than I'd first realized.

'You'll be all right,' I assured him.

Then he said, 'Mate, there is one thing you could do for me.'

'Name it.'

He paused. 'Lend me five hundred quid. Just to finance getting the lads over there. Once the money starts changing I can get it back to you, you know I can.'

There it was, the request. I held my chin in one hand and shook my head, considering. I milked that excruciating moment for twenty, maybe thirty seconds until at last I said, 'I really need what I've got for a deal I'm arranging in Manchester tomorrow. But . . . if it's that bad?'

'There's no one else to ask,' he admitted, on tenter-hooks.

'You mean there's no one else you don't already owe.'

'I've even had two grand off my parents.'

'Shit!'

I could taste revenge. I put both hands flat on the table. 'I know I might not get my five hundred back,' I said. 'But what the fuck, a friend's a friend.'

'You'll get it back, I promise, with interest. I'll double it.'

He was letting out a little held-in tension, relieved, but he was still cool, still not desperate.

In the bathroom I locked the door and pulled up a floorboard behind the toilet, feeling for the box I kept hidden in the cobwebby space beneath. I took out a wedge of notes from one of the plastic wraps inside and counted off twenty-five twenties onto the toilet seat. For the first time I appreciated the authenticity of valid currency. I'd never thought about it before, the fact that something I'd taken for granted all my life could be fake, worthless. Maybe it was because I was stoned, but I held the twenties up to the light and thought about burning them right in front of Andy's face, to demonstrate my power, to show him that destroying his lifeline was no different from putting rubbish on a fire. But I slotted the floorboard back in place and carried the bundle to the kitchen, where I slid it casually under Andy's nose, as though I threw hundreds around for fun. It made me feel potent and I know I swaggered and thumbed my nose as the money swooshed in front of him. He was grateful, thanking me over and over. I felt important and magnanimous. Can you blame me?

We shook hands on the doorstep. Andy said something about it being 'big of me' to let 'bygones be bygones'. He meant the farm, of course. I held his shoulder and said,

'All forgotten.' The fog had cleared entirely, but the wind was stronger, dragging all kinds of rubbish around with it, and I had to hold the door firmly to stop it leaping away from me. I watched Andy walk to the end of the road, his collar high, and at the moment he rounded the corner he raised one hand in a valedictory gesture, without looking back at me. I closed the door and made a fist, triumphant.

Curiously, when he was gone I felt dissatisfied. I would almost say annoyed. No, not annoyed . . . empty. I knew it was the hash so I got some munchie food and watched TV in a daze, eating mechanically and chasing round the channels for something to distract me. The shiny, normal people on the TV were scrubbed and urgent, their faces making expressions of continual surprise, the world they inhabited simply fantasy, or a drama, or a news report unfolding. Yet the girls with workmen's shoulders and voluminous hair and men in *Miami Vice* jackets and un-flattering trousers talked to the camera, to *me*, with something like conviction. I got on all fours and crawled over to the screen, getting as close as I could before their faces became dots of electronic dirt. Yes, they actually seemed to believe in it all. They weren't pretending, not exactly, but the newsreaders, the actors, the pop stars, even the public being vox-popped in the street, all of them, they all held themselves a certain way when the camera was on them. And I thought, Some people consciously act out their lives. Others change automatically depending on the stimulus. There, right there, it occurred to me: you can spot a bad fake a mile off but a good fake, a really good fake, well, you just can't tell.

7

JEZ

Reactions

I loved Cov. Cov was wicked, no word of a lie. Coventry. The bomb patch down the road, swimming in the canal in summer, chaos on the Foleshill Road, the colours of the saris, Mandy Jessop stripteasing in Johnny Ray's shed, Mum at the caff and free bacon sarnies after the match. Cov City FC – *wey o wey o wey o wey* – go Sky Blues. Excellent! I understood it when Kev said he wanted to protect all that. Cov always gets a slagging for being dirty and ugly and everyone craps on about the ring road and Hillfields and the crime, but more good stuff's come out of Cov than any other place on earth. The music – Ska, 2 Tone, the Selector and the Specials, man! I'd go down Tiffany's with Errol Sweeny and blag into all the gigs. We reckoned we had mates in all them great bands. This was the new vibe, see. All of a sudden the whole world knew what a great city Cov was. Instead of it being 'that place that got flattened in the war' it became the centre of the world. Jerry Dammers and the crew, local boys we actually knew, or felt we knew. London had punk and puke but we had real music; we had 2 Tone.

Kev didn't wanna protect 2 Tone. There was no multiculturalism, community relations, black and white goodwill bullshit in our house. Kev felt the same as Dad. We was gonna 'swim in rivers of blood' and we had to be ready. Dad crapped on about those rivers so often when I was a nipper I had this nightmare, night after night, where a wave of bitter old blood would come whooshing down our street, drenching the Tarmac, lapping up over all the doorsteps and rising higher and higher till we were up to our chests in it. Then, mad as it is in dreams, we'd all be wearing rubber rings and armbands, floating about on this crimson foam, with Dad in his armchair bobbing along Leicester Causeway, puffing on his pipe, saying, 'I told yer, ya bastards, but would you listen?'

No one ever told me whose blood it was and where it came from and I didn't think to ask. All I knew was Dad hated how Cov was going. He cut a picture of Enoch Powell out the paper and Sellotaped it over the shot of Aunt Flo with Uncle Wally at Weston-super-Mare, the one that was taken before they were married. Mum was upset when he did that since Flo was hardly cold in her grave. Aunt Flo was Mum's only sister. She hung herself from the meat hook in the pantry while Uncle Wally was out at work. He came home and waited in the lounge wondering where she'd got to. She was never out at teatime. He didn't find her till he got so hungry he went looking for grub and when he opened the cupboard door there she was, bug-eyes and black tongue and packet food all messed up on the floor. Mum said Aunt Flo wanted kids so bad it sent her loopy, but Dad reckoned Uncle Wally could make any-one want to slit their wrists. Course, Uncle Wally still visited from time to time and always said how 'nice' it was that Mum kept Flo's memory alive with her picture on the mantelpiece and everything. Then he'd launch into 'My! The time we had at Weston-super-Mare that day,' and go on about the pleasure gardens and how Flo'd been flashed by a carnie after she'd relieved herself behind the hedge at the fair. You know how people hoot at the same old stories.

Dad told Mum straight when it came to politics, though. He said, 'Mr Powell's the only man talkin' sense in this whole fuckin' country,' and he flicked Enoch's face with the back of his hand like it was still a piece in the paper he was banging on about.

Mum knew not to square up to Dad when he was firing off like that.

That was the same year Dad got all the union flags out the loft, 'bunting from the Coronation', and hung 'em in the winders. They stayed there too, advertising Dad's 'position on things' along with his Enoch moustache, slicked down with a flat comb each morning. He could steam on and on about 'another bleedin' Paki family' moving in on the street. Course you could get away with it then, you know, calling black guys wogs or nignogs or fuzzy wuzzies. That's what they was called on the telly. Me old man called all the Sikh lads 'ragheads' and any other Paki without a turban was just, well, a 'Paki'. Them Chinese were chinkies and Dad always made us kids laugh down the take-away when he asked for 'fly lice', pulling the corners of his eyes back and waggling his head, you know, the way you do. I don't know how Mr Woo kept that sweet-n-sour smile on his little old face.

'These Japs don't feel things the way we do,' Dad said behind his hand.

So I goes, 'He's Chinese, Dad.'

And Dad goes, 'Same thing.'

I'm sure Dad didn't really *hate* 'em. He just didn't understand 'em. Mum said you couldn't expect everybody to understand everybody else just like that, now could you?

When 2 Tone came along, it was cool to have black mates. But in our house it was as bad as treason to mix so I kept me mouth shut about Errol and our nights down

Tiffany's. Once I said, 'Some a them black guys are quite English, you know, 'cept for their skin.'

'English! English! English is bred in here, boy, and here.' Dad pointed to his heart and his head with a look on his face as if I'd wounded him physical. Kev, who was sat in the armchair reading the *Sun*, shook his head and gave me one a them 'easy now' looks from under his eyebrows while he whistled inward and rolled his eyes.

Kev knew as well as me that they'd been born here same as us, and at school you had to mix unless you was real NF. Then you wore the bovver boots and braces and got a skin-cut to show which way you went. Kev reckoned you couldn't let your guard down else the black guys'd start getting ideas above their station. 'Those blackies are defiant. You can see it in their eyes, Jez. You start tellin' 'em they're English and they'll want what's ours like it's their right.'

Kev had his point. There were some scary black guys round an' all. Real Yardie stuff. They hung out down the snooker hall on the frontline and rumours grew it was right lawless, a no-go for the white lads. We imagined it was like the blaxploitation movies, pimps and guns and brown-skinned girls with big arses and hotpants rolling round the place. Errol said it was just a load a guys playing snooker or slap domino and Lynval's brother, Levi, weighing out weed on a table out the back. I spose it didn't look much from the outside, but still, there was always a group a black guys hanging out the front. They'd be keeping watch for the enemy; pigs, or NF or rival gangs, and some a them were so huge you knew they could ball you up and bounce you down the street easier than the Harlem Globetrotters. Whatever Errol said, there's mystery in what you don't know, or can't know. Kev and his lot didn't dare go near the snooker hall. They'd have needed a proper army to get in there. But Stitch could. He had the ins with the West Indians. He had real clout.

*

Before I met Andy I was used to people saying I was off me head. 'You're fuckin' mental, Jez,' 'You're nuts,' 'You're a mad bastard.' Yeah, just something people said, part of the lingo. They'd say it to me and I'd say it back to them. It was a badge of honour being fearless, taking on the dares. I knew how to put a swagger in me walk and talk the talk, acting tough. If you can pretend to hold yer nerve you rarely have to fight. It's a bluff. You have to get the body language just right and keep yer voice smooth like the cream off yer milk. So part of the mental shit was blag, but part of it was cos we *were* nutters; hard-drinking, speed-snorting, bong-for-breakfast boys the lot of us. Me, Kev, the likes a Stitch and all a them lot. It didn't feel criminal, it didn't feel anti-social; it was a way of life. Everybody did it. Sure it was rough, but you know what you know, right?

I knew Cov but Andy didn't, and the night the Irish fucked him over he realized he was in over his head for the first time. He pleaded with the Irish; he said, 'I'm dead meat if you don't pay up. Man, you don't know Stitch Maginnis. It's him I owe. I'm dead. Dead.'

He aimed his pleading at Mickey the Paddy.

Mickey set the record straight. 'Oh, we know Stitch Maginnis –' he laughed '– don't we, boys?' Looking over his shoulder to where his hard men were stood, flicking their jackets back to show off the metalwork shoved in their waistbands.

Mickey's men thought it was a laugh that it was Stitch Maginnis who stood to lose.

'Stitch hates the Provos and we hate him,' Mickey explained. 'Look, this is a high-risk game you're playing, Andy my man. You rolled the dice. This time you lose.'

Mickey was a fuck, but he was right. Andy had made the gambler's mistake: put all his chips on one colour to win. He'd gone in with Stitch, then pooled everything of his and Stitch's, and handed the Irish thirty big ones.

Lost it all in one fell swoop.

You didn't have to be a genius to see Andy'd been crying when he got back from Brum that night. Me and Bas heard the key in the door and sat to attention, ready to jump when Andy gave the orders. But his shoulders were rolled forward, eyes puffed and his skin fleshy as raw chicken. He didn't say a word. He didn't have to, we knew it'd gone bad. He sat in the armchair and started cutting up speed on his Hawkwind album, snorted a line, rolled a spliff, then sat drumming the chair arm for two hours, more, staring at the phone until he picked up the receiver, dialled, and spoke to Stitch.

Turns out those Republican guys were raising cash from every sucker who'd hand it over to finance a campaign later that year. They'd have these rackets: drugs, credit cards, fencing hot goods. They'd turn cash over nice and gentle for a few months and then they'd do a blitz with their contacts and have 'em for everything they could get. Andy couldn't believe it. It was a professional con though, no doubt about it.

Bas was like, 'Didn't you aks how your money mek the money?'

I said, 'Money makes money, Bas, everyone knows that.'

'Well now, Jez, that depend on a whole heap a tings, y'nah.'

Andy shook his head. Said he couldn't believe how 'naïve' he'd been. Said he'd always reckoned the sketch was simple. He explained it for us like this:

Andy puts £30K towards the deal with the Paddies, but he's only part of it. The Irish've raised £30K each from, let's say, nine other people like Andy, all of them out to turn a dollar and a blind eye. All the contributions combined give the Irish a nice quarter mill or more to invest. The money pays for a few guys to go to Morocco, say, where they buy a coupla three tons of sweet Moroccan black. They stash the hash, beautifully, professionally, in a truck, a car and a boat giving a cool three-pronged attempt at importation. First off, the drugs arrive in Spain. Then they're driven on to northern Europe, probably Amsterdam. Here the big boys of the distribution network are waiting in their dark glasses to whiz the gear off to London, Copenhagen, Paris, Brussels, where they pass it on to their guys who buy, say, twenty kilos each. They take this to other guys who buy a coupla kilos each who sell it to their guys who buy a nine-bar each who sell it on in eighths and quarters to the happy tokers of the northern hemisphere. Hey presto, a home-grown deal, everyone's happy, everyone's like you and me, it's not even really a crime, just dope heads ensuring the free and easy flow of Mother Earth's own wonderful weed through the lungs of a grateful population. And Andy's helped underwrite it and profit from it. Bonus.

Bas goes, 'And you didn't think that duns this easy mus' have a nasty smell on 'em?'

And Andy goes, 'I didn't think.'

Then Bas goes, 'Only the baddest crimes mek that much cash. There's always a man ready to tek risk for greed, or for a *cause*. They don't cyare if it dope or heroin, they don't cyare if it a nuclear bomb, nah rakstone.'

The Irish were happy to let people like Andy, like us, believe it was some heroic dope run through the Atlas Mountains.

Andy said, 'Fuck, man, just the fact they were Irish should've given me a clue. I'm a fucking fool. Terrorism costs money. Blowing up pubs and hotels costs money.'

If I was Andy in that sketch I'd've done a runner. You see, Andy's background was soaked in privilege like bread in yer gravy; I mean the whole nine yards. He'd been to one of them posh schools like Eton but up north – you know, a proper toff place where you sleep in dormitories and they bugger the little uns for fun. His dad was a diplomat or a politician or something. What I mean is Andy had a get-out. He didn't have to do all that shit like we did. So when he comes the fall guy in an IRA–Loyalist turf war it would've made sense to disappear, yeah? Specially since he'd lost twenty-five grand belonging to the meanest bastard in Cov. He could've fucked off to London, left us high and dry. But he stayed. Then I spose it wasn't in *any* of us to bail out that way, to be fair.

It wasn't till the next day Andy showed us the dollars the Irish had fobbed him off with. Fake! Fake, fake, fake . . . Faker than Mickey's 'hey, comrade' bullshit, faker than the handbags on Cov market, faker than the videos in Parminder's on the Foleshill Road, faker than me auntie Gloria's tan or Mum's diamond solitaire. Andy was gutted. Like his heart had been ripped out by it all. He'd sucked up to that paddy like a mollusc and for what? He took a few notes off the pile and laid them out neatly, face up, face down, on the table, then he told me to bury the rest 'somewhere safe'. I wrapped the bundle in supermarket carriers and cling film, took it in the woods and buried it at the foot of the oak tree down by the pond while Bas kept watch for Al or any of the street lads. Back in the cottage Andy stared at the greenbacks on the table for two days, getting stoned, shaking his head. But he soon got his mind in gear.

What was weird was Stitch's reaction. I went along with Andy as muscle, but knowing I'd be as useful as a chocolate teapot if anything kicked off. It was strange, you know, and not like Stitch at all, but he gave Andy a month to get his money back – a whole month. Said he'd be satisfied with two grand interest instead of the seven grand profit he was expecting. Andy didn't tell him about the counterfeit dollars. Instead he tried to barter with him over the payback.

Said if he'd known Mickey's crew were IRA he wouldn't have hooked up with them. He pretty much accused Stitch of setting him up. Said he should've warned him about Mickey, et cetera, et cetera.

Stitch pushed him up against a wall while one of his henchmen barred my way. 'Listen, you little shit,' he spat, so close he was looking right up Andy's nose. 'Don't push your fuckin' luck, poncy boy. I'm bein' kind cos you keep good company, all right. One month or you're dead. You understand?'

Andy shook and nodded like he was clucking.

It was fucked up. I had to root around in the glove box for a Valium when we got back in the car. Andy necked two and laid on the back seat going, 'What did he mean "cos I keep good company"?' while I drove the Escort like a maniac back to the cottage, checking him out in the rearview all the way in case he had a fit or something.

Basil reckoned we should launder the dollars at the tourist change places in London, West End, where it was so thick with people you could get lost in the crowd if there was a whiff a trouble. But Andy was like, 'No way.' We had to go abroad. Spain.

'It's close to home but backward,' he says. 'That's what we want. Somewhere they're not going to look too hard.'

'Why not use the Morocco connection?' asks Basil.

'We've got to think about worst-case scenarios, boys. If we get caught in Spain then the likelihood is we'll get sent back here but I, for one, do not want to risk a Moroccan prison. No, Spain's the place.'

Andy chose me and Basil to go to Spain. It could've been Spud or Biff or any of the boys, but suddenly it seemed like the crew had shrunk again. Andy was closing ranks. He wanted a tight little unit, people he trusted. But he was desperate for cash. Money was the only reason he ever went near Pads again.

8

MEHMET

A Knife's Work

There are many things I remember from the day I went to murder Jules Geci. Some are everyday things that can be detached from the story, but that even now transport me back to that time and place. This is the way it works for me with the look of a frightened mule or a man casually walking with his gun or . . . the smell of rosemary. Such a humble herb, so full of oil; my mother would collect it from the roadside and burn it on the fire to cleanse the house and every room would fill up with its fragrance. I cannot bear to smell it now.

As I hid with Gabriel on the ledge, it was wild rosemary that obscured us from the ground. It heated in the sun so the smell became sharper and mixed with the smell of Gabriel's fear as he waited there beside me. His was a feral odour that animals sense sooner than a man, but I could smell him. And the knowledge of his fear made me question my judgement. Why had I agreed that he could come? He was of no real use to me, apart from as a messenger to say that I was dead on Geci land. That's if Jules killed me and not the other way around. And even if he did kill me then Jules would have the law beside him as it would be me that had come aggressive and brandishing my gun on *his* property. And if I killed Jules, then still I was the culprit and I would be a fugitive from the Geci *fis* and from Hoxha's thugs.

I was on a precipice with an iron hand pushing me over and with nowhere to run. I did not care for myself, but I did now care for Gabriel.

'Brother, you must leave,' I said suddenly.

He did not answer straight away. We had been sitting there for four hours by then and there was relief as well as disappointment showing in his countenance.

He looked at me from underneath his brow. 'You're sending me away. I knew you would.'

'There's nothing happening here, Gabriel. We could wait like this until the morning. Go home now and rest, and if I am not with you by first light then return along the same route and find me.'

I watched his small fists tighten and flex, but I knew he had already had enough; he just could not admit it.

And once again I put a firm hand on his shoulder. 'I know I can trust you to do as I ask, brother. And I know you will not be seen.'

'Yes, you can trust me.' He smiled and held my wrist tight to his shoulder. It was the gesture of a comrade.

He nods then, and takes up his gun and scrabbles down the cliff towards the stream. Then he turns at the last point before he is gone from view and holds his hand up to me, and he looks bigger, almost a grown man, like Rafiq there in the lowering sun, but I am glad I am sending him home to safety. As soon as he is out of sight, as if his leaving is the trigger, I see three riders coming from the south along the stream, one horse and two mules moving slowly with long shadows beside them and the water sparkling so that rings of light look like they are dancing on the purling water. As they get nearer I see the horseman is Jules Geci, riding tall and proud. He is my age, a handsome man by anyone's account. His mother's family could trace their tree back to the sultans and sultanas, or so the village people said. And on a mule beside him is Aisha, the light in my dark dreams, the sensation in my numb fantasies, forbidden and unreachable Aisha. Yes, Jules Geci's sister is the reason I know this place so well and only in this moment do I realize that I can never have her, that the story in my mind where her family and mine are reconciled and she and I are married to cement the truce – or where we meet accidentally by the sparkling stream and she swoons with the power of my presence and we embark on a secret love affair – all these stories, they are nothing more than a child's imagination. For I am here to kill her brother and there is no future now to recommend me to her in any way.

I feel something tighten up inside me and I have to clench my fists until the pain of it has passed. The riders soon enter the courtyard and are met by eager dogs that seem to come from nowhere; they must have been sleeping under the old cart or behind the grain store. Jules and Aisha's mother comes from the house then, her face contorted beneath her headscarf, her skirts billowing. She is squawking louder than the chickens and her bluster is sending them flapping to the edges of the yard. Then the old woman points her finger directly at me in my hiding place and her other arm indicates where Gabriel has headed back upstream and I understand the crafty witch has realized she is besieged and has been spying on our mission from her window.

Like the wolf I have to snatch this opportunity or I will lose my quarry. So I lift my rifle and take the best aim. The courtyard is in turmoil. Aisha and Jules are dismounted and she is running with her mother to the house while Jules is trying to calm the horses skittering on the cobbles. But the third rider is stuck upon his mount and the mule is dancing and turning on its hind legs. Jules has the mule's reins in one hand and his horse's in the other and he is shouting something. Shouting at *me*, but I cannot hear him, I only hear the noise of my own blood in my ears and the screeching of the mules. My finger is on the trigger and the trigger feels soft, like rising dough, like my hand could pass right through the metal, like my finger is not me and I am not here and the rifle is not real. But I look at Jules far off and fancy I see panic in his eyes . . . so I squeeze so gently that it feels like nothing. The gun recoils against my shoulder and makes a hard edge come back on *everything*.

And in the courtyard the third rider falls.

Jules has let go of the mules and before I get another aim he has dragged the third rider behind the grain store. The animals are prancing madly now and I throw my rifle to the ground and hold my head in both hands, miserable with anger that I miss my target. But soon I grab my gun again and make my way down the cliff on my backside determined to get in that courtyard and seal Jules Geci's fate in close-up. But as I descend I see that Jules is no fool, that he is moving to intercept *me*. He is running with his knees bent turning this way and that, holding his rifle horizontal at his side, not at the ready, and taking refuge behind each thing to protect himself from my fire. I lose sight of him as I make my final descent but in my heart I know, I just know, that I will get him. I am filled with strength and knowledge like a god and no fear is getting in and I am laughing in my head and grinding on my teeth like this is the merriest game because honour *will* be mine in that man's blood.

At the bottom of the rock face everything is different. The wood is silent and the sun has dropped behind the cliff so the forest is in ghostly twilight, not lit by a peachy sun like it was high up. Only the stream is speaking now. I can hear its whooshing babble. But Allah knows I can read a forest such as this; my life is in this landscape. I take off my *qeleshe* and rub dirt onto my face. My hair is dark, not like my brothers', but all the same I have to camouflage. I move swiftly now, my rifle slung across my back, only stepping on the old, soft leaves that do not give my position away with a *tch* and a snap. After a few minutes I stop. I cannot see him or sense him. Perhaps he waits where the trees are thin. Perhaps he has run back to take shots at me from a window. I listen and peer into the gloom.

Then I see him.

He makes a dash from one tree to another in that same way, his knees bent, his rifle in one hand. Then he shouts out.

'Mehmet, Mehmet, if it is you then show yourself. I will not harm you. You have my word. I offer you *besa*.'

Ech, ech, he knows it is me come to avenge my family. See, he knows. And I stay silent like a snake. He will not trick me to give myself away. But again he shouts out and it seems his voice is come from far, far away in the stillness of the wood.

'Mehmet, you must listen to me,' he says, and there is terror in his distant voice. 'This is a mistake, I tell you. We must be friends, you and me. We must make *besa* between us. I fear we have both been betrayed.'

My teeth nearly crumble as I grind them stronger than the millstones and it takes all my strength not to shout back to him. But for all his offers of *besa* he does not come into the open, he sneaks from tree to tree trying to close the gap between me and him, and I am glad I will kill him, glad his life will end up in my hands.

I sniff the air and I smell the fear there – not mine, no. Jules Geci's fear – and it is making the whole forest acrid. He still has not seen me, but I see the flash of his waistcoat not fifty metres yonder. So I watch and wait. I have him. I have the upper hand. I wait for five, maybe ten minutes, but he doesn't change his position. And the forest is so cool and calm it soothes me to know that I am king here, not him. I sense that the fear has paralysed Jules Geci, yes, this must be it, and yet my resolve is still strong and each breath I take is powerful and clean.

I start to move in for the kill. The light is nearly gone but my eyes have become accustomed and I feel like a wolf in the night, so much I want to howl like I have gone mad with my dark quest. I move quietly from solid trunk to trunk, even across open ground, until I am one move from his position. Then I lay my rifle down and unsheath my father's knife. The blade seems to shine, reflecting some light that is not there and it makes me look up to see the moon – but there is no moon. I am a hunter now, a predator; nothing in the world can stop me. I am behind the very tree where I will fulfil my destiny, to make it right, to make it balance, to make the Gecis pay for Rafiq, for Razlan and even for my father.

So I lunge round the trunk with the blade of that fearful knife before me, no thought of fighting hand to hand or struggling awkwardly in the dirt. I know this blade will do its work and sure enough it strikes home with the first and my heart leaps with an extraordinary joy. I can feel I have thrust straight through, right to the handle with one assault so I almost feel my hand will follow in the cavity. Only then do I feel Jules's hands come up to grab my arm – but he is already weaker than a child – a child, I tell you, yes, a puny grip and fleeting because I twist that blade in the darkness and know I have a lethal strike. I know, I just know.

There is a moment, a thin slice of time when all your knowledge can be proved in a dreadful right and you understand that you knew the tragedy of your life before it happened. That if you trace back the minutes and the hours and the days or even the weeks before some catastrophe, you discover that you knew that it would happen long before it did. And you say, 'The night before that fateful day I had a dream and woke with a strange premonition,' or, 'I laughed at the old man in the market who grabbed my arm and pierced me with his wild eyes and told me I had to take a journey,' or, 'For a whole week the goats' milk curdled as soon as it hit the pail, imagine, I did not see the signs of it.' Yes, the spirits provide us with the signs and the old women prognosticate. But did I listen? It had been a week of signs and what other tragedy could I have imagined after the bloody discovery at the *stanë* or my father's bland dismissal from this world? What sign, I ask you, what sign?

But I knew, even in the darkness, that it was not Jules Geci twitching on the end of my knife. Oh God I knew, so clearly that I could not bring myself to look. I could not force myself to discover so I pulled the knife out and slumped onto my knees and put my face on my bloody hand and I wept and rent my clothes.

I did not notice the lights coming through the trees, the Geci men and women with their lamps like sprites and fairies come to illuminate my tragedy. I did not hear the twigs and leaves kicked up by footsteps. I did not care if my life was over or if the *djinns* had come to take my soul away.

But it was Aisha who shone her lamp on Gabriel's still face. It was Aisha's light that fell upon my misery.

PART TWO

PART TWO

9

PADS

The Manchester Connection

The day after Andy came to show me the dollars I left for Manchester. The wind had dropped and rain set in. On the train I watched as vast bands of weather lashed the landscape, turning pastureland to slurry, stippling the surface of the rivers and canals. Sheep, cows, horses all stood in their fields, dejected as the squalls beat down on them. I whooshed by, cocooned against the elements, but the mayhem in my carriage made it difficult to think; the clatter of rails, the trolleys, the passengers. There was a woman travelling alone with her young son, about ten yards down the aisle from me. She was letting him run amok. She had her forehead pressed against the window as the boy darted up and down between the seats making jet engine noises, occasionally spitting machine-gun fire at face level while infuriated passengers tutted and blinkered their eyes with their hands. A man in a suit, shiny at the knees, and wearing tatty shoes continually coughed, wheezed, brought up and swallowed back his phlegm. Opposite me, an elderly woman slept with her head back and mouth open, only slightly, but enough for me to see the flesh-shine plate of her false teeth plasticizing the roof of her mouth. Lobes of loose, powdered skin quivered at her neck with each stertorous breath she took. A book was open in her lap. A romance. I read the title: *Love Lies North*. Perhaps she was heading up country for a geriatric tryst. It made me shudder to think an old turkey like her could still be stirred.

I looked out of the window and I tried to imagine the heft of those dollars. Fifty thousand of them, two and a half thousand twenty-dollar notes. Altogether I estimated the package Jez and Bas were carrying to Spain would be about the size and shape of a kilo of grass. I wagered that in the interim Andy would hide the money in one of the outbuildings at Hampton Kirby, either that or he'd bury it. We'd dealt together long enough for me to know his foibles in that regard. He was a burier. I used to call him the Pirate when he went off with his trowel and his Tupperware. He'd laugh and say, 'Ooooarrrgh' and 'Pieces of eight' as he pulled his collar up around his ears and headed into the night to shift soil. But it wasn't a joke. If you dealt drugs then the gear had to be hidden. The safest bet was to keep your main stash off your property; otherwise, if the drug squad got the dogs in, you were done for. They'd pull up carpets, fish around in your water tank or toilet cistern, empty the freezer, go through the flower beds looking for freshly turned earth, and all the time their eager bitches would prance around your legs, their snouts delving in deep where their masters directed. Bright-eyed. Loving it.

Andy used to bury a large portion of our dope in a small copse at the edge of the recreation ground behind our terrace. Obviously you had to be careful you weren't seen, but as long as there were no fingerprints on the packaging who was to say who the dope belonged to if it was found? Andy lost half a kilo of Gold Seal in that copse. That's what you get for stashing gear when you're off your head. Me, Spud, Jez and Andy spent one spring night with spades and garden forks digging the ground looking for it.

We wore head torches, but switched them off and stopped our work when anyone came past; dog walkers, piss heads.

I remonstrated with Andy, *sotto voce*, as we worked. 'Five hundred fucking quid's worth,' I whispered. 'Lost. This is insane. You must have some memory, you must have put a stick in the ground . . . or something, so you could find it again.'

Andy and the lads kept their heads down and dug on in silence.

One dog walker, who must have heard us, wandered right up to the edge of the trees no more than fifteen yards from us. No doubt he had seen our lights wink on and off and come to investigate. I froze and waited for him to move away, but he just stood there, squinting through the tree trunks. Then he cleared his throat and stepped tentatively to the middle of the copse, craning his neck forward while his dog turned her pointed snout this way and that. It was quite surreal. Five men and a dog standing silently in the darkness. Then I edged behind a tree and the man took my movement as his cue.

'Helloo, lads,' he cooed. 'Can anyone join the party?'

I saw the glint of his belt buckle.

'You've got it all wrong, mate,' gruffed Andy in a voice designed to give the impression of bulk.

'What? Well, what are you lads doing then?'

His dog, a greyhound, with impossibly attenuated legs and delicate paws, turned her head away, aloof. The orange streetlamp that illuminated the playground through the sycamores highlighted the sheen on her brindle coat.

'Territorials. Night manoeuvres.'

'What here? Here in the park?'

'Yeah, we're practising.'

Impatient for the man to leave, Jez switched his head torch back on and shone the beam directly in the man's face while emitting a throaty growl. The man held his right hand up to shield his eyes. It was a chubby hand and behind it was a plump middle-aged face with puffy jowls straining away from the light.

'Hey!'

'Just fuck off, yer poofter, before I twat yer,' snarled Jez.

The man fingered the bulge below his chin, mumbled an expletive and exited the copse, the greyhound trotting beside him with her head high as if such low behaviour was beneath her. We all laughed, relieved, but Jez kept saying, 'Fucking faggots,' as his spade cut into the ground.

Andy said he'd been approached once before when he'd been burying his dope. 'It's amazing the people you find wandering around at three a.m.,' he remarked.

That half-kilo is still buried somewhere in that copse.

I preferred it when contraband was elegantly and cleverly concealed. I would find, or design, several exquisite places round the house and distribute my hash and cash in them accordingly. You could never hide gear and cash together as this was evidence of 'supply' and thus carried a longer prison sentence. I also spent a number of months working on dog-repellent scents and sprays, as well as dog-attracting scents. 'Olfactory decoys,' I called them. I used the sprays to disguise the smell of any dope I had to stash in the flat or take on trains with me. I got the idea from the saboteurs. They used hormones and fox scent to lead the hounds away from their quarry, thus disrupting the virile fun of the horsy set during hunting season. If hounds were susceptible then so were Her Majesty's sniffer dogs.

Birmingham, Stoke-on-Trent, Macclesfield, Stockport; at each station the train disgorged its passengers then swallowed new ones destined for the heathen north. I disembarked at Manchester Piccadilly heavy-limbed, freighted by the journey. Midday was like a wet dusk, grime-opaqued. Here progress itself seemed eroded to a pagan core. The aggravating boy and his wrung-out mum were met on the platform by a man, too old to be her husband, not intimate enough to be her friend. The boy was subdued now, dragging his toes along with every step, scuffing the leather on his shoes. I lit a fag and turned away.

My 'man in the north' had a flat in the city centre. Carl Simpson, Simmo, was an old customer from uni, a quiet man who'd graduated with a first in Social Administration and moved back to his native city to set the world to rights, or at least ameliorate the suffering of the urban poor of Manchester. He was a well-meaning toker with a political vision that didn't quite fit the times. Disillusioned, signing on, he agreed to help me find the right people to carry hash over borders from India to England. He got a small fee for every lead he generated and an ounce of top-grade Charras for each successful run that resulted. He sometimes worked in tandem with Sharon, Jez's older sister oddly enough, who'd moved to Manchester to escape a bothersome boyfriend and had become an interesting addition to my network. The object of my visit was to interview the potential couriers they'd found, recruit them and prepare them for upcoming 'missions'.

Importing a top-quality product meant tighter margins but still, I was cutting out the middlemen, going direct to the producers. It made good business sense and the profits were handsome. Even allowing for a fifty per cent failure rate I made a healthy return. As long as there were four or five couriers working off the same trip I could break even if just one courier in four got through. But the risks were high. Customs officers knew how to interrogate a runner. However, my recruits never knew my name or where to find me. I bought their tickets, cash, from the bucket shops in Earl's Court. I never carried the dope myself. I was never on the same flight as them. I made sure there was nothing material that could connect me with any of them, except

Simmo, who hated Thatcherism in all its manifestations enough to be as tight-lipped as *la Résistance* and take a martyr's fall in the event of a bust. Anyway, even *his* connection to the couriers was too tenuous for the police to get a handle on. If they had trawled his accounts and his movements, or his flat, there would be nothing untoward for them to find, except perhaps a tolah of Charras or a few anti-government pamphlets in a drawer. But who didn't have these things around the place in 1984?

Simmo had set up meetings in Manchester with three potential runners. Usually we held interviews in a pub off Whalley Road, but as the hauls got bigger we got more nervous and needed more privacy. So Simmo procured the keys to an empty house in Chorlton. It had been a student house but now it was derelict, with bindweed strangling the borders at the front and boards masking the windows, save for one rectangle gone astray from the downstairs bay. Simmo checked up and down the road before he let us in.

'We'll do the interviews in there.' He nodded, indicating a door to my right. 'Kitchen's through here; they forgot to cut off the gas,' he added as he went off down the corridor.

I opened the door to the 'interview room'. It was empty apart from a stack of old newspapers in one corner. The air was stagnant. Where the board was missing, one grainy slab of light penetrated and stretched trapezoid across the floor. There was a damp patch on the ceiling above the bay. Classic 1970s paper covered three walls but most strips had peeled away two or three feet from the top, as if the room was shedding its skin, revealing chintzy patterns from an earlier dynasty. There were dusty rectangles where pictures had hung and I wondered what images could have worked against the geometric brownness of the paper. The fourth wall was taken up entirely by a monstrous inglenook with a gas fire insert and plastic-veneered shelves fitted into the recesses. The contents they supported were long gone but I noticed an empty box of Marlboro and a two-pence piece.

Simmo came in with two red milk crates. 'To sit on,' he explained, placing the crates in the light. It looked stagy.

'It's grim,' I said.

'Let's wait out back.' He nodded. 'The first one won't be along for a bit.'

The first interviewee didn't turn up at all. Simmo said he'd expected as much. 'Space cadet,' he offered by way of explanation, and went off to the corner shop for teabags and more fags.

The second interviewee was a young lad, with hair shaved short at the sides and straggly dreadlocks. He wore cotton leggings that showed off the fleshy dangle of his tackle at the fork of his legs. His nose was pierced. His ears were pierced in several places. He had an obvious tribal-style tattoo on his neck, and body odour.

Later, when we'd despatched him, I chided Simmo.

'What the fuck was that?' I said.

'Sorry, man. I thought he might scrub up. I told him to look smart.'

I sighed and shook my head.

The third interviewee was early. Me and Simmo were in the kitchen drinking tea when we heard the door click open.

'I think I left it on the latch,' grimaced Simmo apologetically.

I poked my head round the door and checked down the hallway. A girl, nineteen, twenty-ish, stood chewing one fingernail, eyeing the surroundings, sexy not nervous. She wore pink baseball boots, skin-tight jeans with a loose cotton tunic top. Her hair was long, unstyled and hennaed a deep red, but fading to orang-utan at the roots. I experienced a seldom-felt click of desire in my loins.

I cleared my throat to get her attention. It made her jump, her mouth making a pretty O, before she quickly recomposed herself to say 'Hiya' in that nasal way northern girls have.

'Hi, yeah, you're early.' I tapped my watch.

'Am I? Sorry.'

'Just go in that room there.'

'This one?'

'Yeah.'

She did as I bade.

'This one looks better, Sim. Where did you find her?'

'Mate of Sharon's, actually. I've never met her.'

'Bit hippy, but it's workable.'

The girl laughed out loud when Simmo and I walked in the room, then covered her mouth, stifling giggles and looking at the floor. 'Sorry,' she said, but gave no explanation for her outburst.

I felt my collar and secretly checked my fly. Some people titter like children when they're anxious but she seemed genuinely undaunted by the situation, even though she was sitting awkwardly, all limbs, on one of the crates while Simmo and I paced round her, her knees together, heels apart, toes touching, girlish.

'OK, Rebecca. It is Rebecca, isn't it?' I began.

'Becca, yes.'

'How old are you?'

'Eighteen.'

'Eighteen! And why are you here?'

She looked from me to Simmo and back again.

'I'm not right sure,' she answered tentatively. 'Will you explain it to me?'

'Do you mean to tell me we've come *all* this way and you don't even know what you're here for?'

'I only meant that it'd be foolish for me to say before I'm, well . . . sure about the both of yous.' She finished with a simpering smile, but there was a hardness in her voice and her eyes. It was compelling. There was something animal and potent about her behind the studied coquetry, the big-eyed, nail-biting charm.

I walked round the room, then offered her a cigarette. 'OK, Rebecca – Becca,' I corrected, lighting her cigarette, then mine. 'We have to make sure you're good for this. Not because we don't trust you, but for your sake you understand?'

She nodded assent, blowing out smoke. 'Of course.'

I sat down on the crate opposite her while Simmo leaned back against the inglenook, looking up the road through the gap in the window boards. She said she understood what she was about to do, that she knew the risks she was taking but was happy to see it through. The atmosphere became more relaxed as I explained the details of the trip and the set-up.

I explained as much as was necessary. 'Now, on the way back we'll get you a low-risk flight, through Amsterdam or Belgium. Then you'll have to make your own way overland and across the channel. Do you feel OK with that?'

'Yeah.'

'You must have nothing, I repeat *nothing* in the bags that can connect them with you or anyone else you meet while you're in India. No letters, pictures, phone numbers or personal items. You want to be able to dump those bags and walk away if you have to, but only if you have to. Even if the airline labels say they're yours there's no way they can prove that the bags haven't been switched. OK?'

'OK.'

'As soon as the bags are in your possession, wherever you land, rip all the airline labels off. A phone number will be given to you in India that you must memorize. When you get to London, call the number. You'll be told what to do next. Any questions?'

'No.' She was confident, almost cocky.

I took a last drag on my cigarette and ground it into the

floorboards with the ball of my foot, then turned to Simmo, who shook his head as if to say he had nothing to add.

'One last question,' I said, leaning back on the milk crate. 'Call it more of a role-playing game. You're in . . . Paris, say. You're walking through customs and you're feeling pretty terrified. You can feel your knees wobbling. A customs officer calls you over and says, "Are those your bags, mademoiselle?" Well, you're pushing them so you have to say, "Yes." He asks you to put them on the counter. You're trying to stay cool but you're feeling pretty ropy. He starts to rummage through the first case and . . . well, he finds the stuff. What would you say, Becca? What do you tell them when they've got you, all alone, in a room, pumping you for information?'

She stroked a strand of claret-coloured hair from her forehead then touched her jawbone with her fingertips, thinking, looking at me, then off to one side, a sliver of a smile suppressed about her lips.

'I'd say . . .' she began, biting a fingernail thoughtfully and looking at the ceiling. 'I'd say I met this lad and we had a scene.'

'A scene?'

'You know – a fling!'

'Oh.'

'I'd say, "This lad helped me pack me bags but I didn't think anything of it." I'd say, "Now I come to think of it, he was in the hotel for several hours the day before with all me kit while I went shopping." I'd say, "His name was . . . John Wilkins," that I knew it was his real name cos I saw it in his passport. I'd say, "He was gorgeous . . . from London." I'd say I was "*in love*". I'd say, "He made me give him back the photo I had of him even though I begged to keep it but he wanted to send me another. A better one. But I do have his address, in St John's Wood." Then I'd look for the address and not be able to find it. Then I'd cry . . . like this.'

She cried. On the spot. It was uncomfortable. It was convincing.

Simmo and I looked at each other and raised our eyebrows.

Eventually I said, 'Good, good, that's very good.'

'Thanks,' she said, immediately composed again.

'You'll get two hundred pounds now, to help you get what you need for the trip, and a thousand pounds when you deliver the stuff in London.'

'A thousand pounds?' she shrieked, losing her cool for the first time.

I held up my hand to silence her. 'OK, twelve hundred – but that's all we can stretch to.'

'Twelve hundred!'

'OK, thirteen but that's it, absolutely no more.'

'Fuckinell.' She grinned. 'I hadn't even thought about bein' paid till you mentioned it.'

Rebecca Jarvis had been brought up by her dad. Her mum, twelve years his junior, died of breast cancer when Becca was eleven. The father, a retired miner, was a man's man despite his passion for dahlias. He kept a basic house with beer in the fridge and traditional food on the table. To get what she needed Becca, an only child, had learned to play the little girl, realizing early that most men including her father responded to coy persuasion better than they did to confrontation. Rebecca's dad, on the other hand, realized too late that he possessed few strategies to cope with his bright and wayward daughter. He withdrew, burdened by a burgeoning rather than diminishing grief for the loss of his wife. Becca grew to hate him for the pall of sorrow that continued to permeate their lives. She believed he nurtured rather than tried to overcome his despair.

Her one A-level got her a job doing admin at the local technical college. She'd never even thought about university.

No one she knew had ever been so the idea was simply out of the question. Instead, Becca ran the family home, such as it was, while her father spent ever more time on his allotment or watching sitcoms on the TV. Becca was bored. Becca was desperate for excitement. The decision to run drugs was the corollary of all this, an escape, the route from prosaic to extraordinary. She was prepared to accept the consequences that went along with such a choice whatever they might be.

She told me all this as we sat in a café off Cotton Street two days after the interview. I had decided I would try to tempt her into a more permanent association with me, rather than a disposable one-off like the other couriers. In truth, I hadn't been able to get her out of my mind since the day of the interview in Chorlton. Past the pouting, off-beat *femme fatale* image there was focused tenacity. It existed as a discrete thing inside her, an indivisible core. Granted, her body was female, complex, but her mind, her soul, was male and fearless and sharp. I saw it straight away. In the normal course of events I would only have met Becca again in India. Runners only ever met me twice. Once at the interview and once in India where I would meet up with the trip organizer to pack the bags and make sure the couriers got safely onto their return flights. That was it. Relationships had to be clean and businesslike. Getting to know or like a runner was like befriending a lamb before sending it to slaughter. There was no point. But I was rarely attracted to a woman in this way. It made me falter.

On the phone she sounded surprised to hear from me but agreed to meet me again without question. It was in one of those greasy spoon, coffee shop hybrids with pretensions of sophistication you got in the 1980s. They did frothy coffees but there was squeezy TK on the tables and hollow-cheeked men in flat caps reading the *Racing Post* up at the counters.

I got there early and ordered a cappuccino. Then I leaned

back in the corner of one of the sticky booths, lit a cigarette and thought about how I would 'present'.

When Becca walked in her beauty asserted itself with the same physical pang I had felt the first time I saw her. She had dyed her hair deep mahogany and it hung in heavy tresses over her shoulders. Her long printed top worn over tight leggings was cut to plunge at her breasts but underneath she wore a tight T that still revealed the firmness of her cleavage and advertised the fact she wore no bra.

I patted the seat next to me as she walked over but she slid onto the bench opposite and lit a cigarette of her own. I liked that.

'Good to see you again.' I smiled.

'Yeah.'

'You alone?'

'Like you said on the phone.'

'Good, good. You OK? Not scared or anything?'

'No, course not.' Then, 'You look different without the suit, though.'

'Hah, yeah. The suit's a disguise, a precaution. It lets recruits know this is a serious business.'

'You do this often, then?'

'Now and then.'

'You and yer mate looked like the Blues Brothers the other day. You ought to watch that. People'll think you're on a mission from God.'

I laughed and pulled at my earlobe. 'I like to think what I do is . . . inspired.'

'Whatever you say, chuck.'

'That was meant to be tongue in cheek.'

'I know.'

I checked about the café warily. 'Look, I'll come straight to the point. I've got a little extra job for you before India if you're interested.'

'Oh yeah.' It was a world-weary reply.

'Yes, a trip to Spain.'

She looked at me blankly. Different from the day of the interview. Like the girls at uni she had the air of someone used to being chatted up – arrogant, scornful. 'What kind of a job?'

I leaned across the table. 'Well, there are a couple of guys down on the Costa del Sol . . . and they have this thing of mine. I want it back.'

'What thing?'

'It doesn't matter what it is . . . not yet anyway, but I want *you* to come to Spain and help me get it.'

'It'll be just *me* and *you* then.'

'Well, yes.'

'And when you say get it back, like, how d'you mean?'

I felt my hand bunch into a fist, but as I answered I unfurled my fingers to show Becca an open palm. 'We'll have to, sort of . . . steal it.'

She made a small but audible gasp and put her fingertips on her chest. 'Why, I've never stolen anything in my life' – an obvious lie in a southern belle accent.

I laughed. 'It's not really stealing, Becca, it's more retrieval.'

'So these guys that have this *thing*, do you know them or what?'

'No. Well yes, kind of. Look, it's complicated. But trust me, it'll be like stealing rings off a corpse.'

She curled her lip at my macabre imagery.

We stopped talking while a matronly waitress with a nylon zip-up over-apron, grease-stained, ambled up with Becca's coffee.

'There y'are, luv. Sugar's there.' She pointed at a mug of single-serving sachets then moved off again with a peculiar fat-thighed gait.

Becca stirred three sugars into her cup. 'So, why are you asking *me* to do this? It's not like you know me.'

I considered how to play her. 'I have my reasons.' I said 'reasons' with a rolled 'r', trying to sound light-hearted and theatrical. 'Besides, you're exactly the right person for the job. You'll be my honey trap.'

'You what?'

'Bait. You'll be the bait to catch these lads out, down in Spain. A pretty girl like you.' I winced at my own clumsiness.

She wound a strand of hair round her finger, mulling it over. 'I'm not right sure.'

'You'll get another five hundred, and all expenses paid.'

'When will I get the money?'

'When you get back from India.'

She thought for a few seconds, pushing her fingertips through the dense hair on the back of her head. 'No,' she stated, definitely. 'I want the money now, in advance, and I wanna take a friend wi' me.'

'What? To Spain?'

'Yeah.'

'This isn't a bloody package holiday, you know, this is a job.' I lowered my voice and stretched towards her, speaking through gritted teeth, but strangely desperate to know what she smelled like. 'This is *serious stuff*.'

Becca reached out and closed a hot dry hand over my fist, her lips thrust forward in an unsubtle, kittenish moue. 'It's just, I need some cash. And I can't keep *two* gangsters busy by meself, can I?'

'They're not gangsters.' I sighed. 'OK, I can stretch to an extra ticket, but all my cash is tied up right now. You can have the five hundred quid once we get to Spain, but there's nothing extra for your friend, you'll have to finance her yourself. And if she's not cool . . .'

Her eyes lit up. 'She's cool, I promise. The best sort.'

'Hmm.'

She pushed her chest forward so her breasts rested on the Formica, then exerted extra pressure on my hand.

Wrinkling her splendid nose, she smiled. 'Thanks . . . whatever yer name is.'

'It's Pads.'

'Pads. Funny name. So when do we leave?'

'Day after tomorrow.'

'Fuck me. So soon.'

We spent another half an hour chatting about details and times and so on, during which time I had this vision. In my mind's eye I could see us together in Spain, playing at Bonnie and Clyde, dashing around, getting in scrapes, pulling off capers. She'd be drawn to my intellect; I to her feral wit. We'd have fun and steal those dollars from Bas and Jez. And I'd exact revenge. But then Becca said she had to go, so we both stood up. It felt like we should shake hands to clinch our deal, but she was right-handed and I'm left-handed so I ended up gripping her all awry and she did one of those imperious one-note laughs my mother was prone to, which rattled me, I'll admit. My hand was as cold as an undertaker's compared to her untamed heat.

'Good, good,' I said about nothing in particular. 'We're all set then?'

'Yeah, all set . . .' She paused. 'I was thinking though, you know, how strange all this is: Spain, India. Last week I didn't even know yer and here we are off round the world together.'

'Yes, wild.' I straightened the front panels of my jacket. 'One thing, Becca.'

'Yeah?'

'Not a word of this to anyone.'

'Course!'

'The Spain thing I mean, not to anyone, not even Sharon, not under any circumstances.'

'Oh-kay,' she said slowly, with a sardonic smile as if to say 'chill out'.

It was an effort but my face was granite. 'Everything could fuck up if you do.'

'All right, all right, you can trust me.'

I'd crossed a line. I didn't trust her as far as I could spit, and she certainly didn't trust me. For some reason I liked it like that.

10

JEZ

Hola Amigo

I'd never been abroad. I'd been on a school trip to Wales once. That felt foreign. Air like menthol it was so fresh and all them sheep and mountains and shit. It was like a film where the scenery goes on and on. No end to it. Another summer I went on the coach to Weston-super-Mare with me mum. It was 1976. That hot year. Mum said she wanted to 'walk on the beach where Flo'd walked'. Said she missed her sister *so* much. Said she couldn't do without her 'little prince' either, that's why she was taking me for company. Dad went down the pub while we packed and never came to Poole Meadow to see us off even though Mum'd asked him to.

At Weston Mum let me have ice-creams whenever I wanted, but the sun was so strong in the day we spent our time indoors fanning ourselves with anything that came to hand. We stayed in a B&B right by the miniature golf, with a lounge that had a drinks cabinet in one corner; Cinzano, gin, whisky, sherry. You could help yourself if you put 50p in the honesty box. On the third night Mum cried like a baby. Kept saying, 'It's all too much,' and I had to sit and stroke her hair. I could feel her body sobbing and juddering through me hand as I looked out the winder. A boy about my age was hacking at a golf ball with his club, then stamping the ground and laughing. I wished I was him out there having fun. Eventually, Mum sent me out for fags and gave me a pound note to get fish and chips. When I came back the man who ran the B&B asked if Mum was 'quite well'. Mum had told me not to let anyone see me carrying food in, so I held the fish and chips behind me back. I could feel the grease seeping through the newspaper onto me fingers as I stood with one foot on the bottom stair. I told the man that Mum 'could be better' and hoiked off up to the room before he had time to say anything else. After ten minutes he turns up at the door with a glass of sherry. Stood in the hall all polite and said he 'recognized a damsel in distress' when he saw one. So Mum had to dry her eyes and say, 'It's nothin',' and 'I'm so sorry for the chip smell, you know kids.' She was always right polite. Later, she went down to the lounge to 'chat with the nice man', a widower it turned out, and left me in the room on me own.

Looking for me toothbrush, I goes through her case. It had everything important in it near enough. She'd even brought a picture of Sharon and the one of Flo and Wally from off the mantelpiece, still with the Sellotape marks where Dad had stuck Enoch Powell. She'd brought her NHS card too, and mine. Mum stayed downstairs talking with the B&B man till I was soundo. Early next morning she packed us up to catch the coach back to Cov. It was so early that half the sky was still dark as sin and the sun had only just cracked over the bus station. 'You make yer bed sometimes, little prince,' she said. She made all the beds at home. I remember that.

If you're talking serious travel, though, I was green as schoolboy snot. Basil had travelled a bit. He'd spent a week in Spain, in the seventies, with some rich white bird twice his age who'd wanted a 'young stud'. I thought that sounded well cool, but Basil said, 'It reek to blousebait,' whatever he meant by that. Man, it blew my mind that some poor ex-con black boy from Cov had managed a bit of jet-setting in his youth. I mean, he grew up in Hillfields just like me, and he was on the make just like me. If you were struggling for a crust, you could rest easy the black guys were striving more'n you. It's the only thing that made the world seem fair. Their dads were on the buses or the railways and their mums were cleaners, or praps nurses if they was lucky, and they always had a whole clutch a kids an' all; pop, pop, pop, one a year till there was raggety urchins all over Hillfields, dirt-streaked on the doorsteps. That's just the way it was. Basil shook me up with his foreign travel lark.

Andy took us to Gatwick in the Escort. Gatwick–Malaga. It was exotic. After check-in we stood by the entrance to the departure place. Andy's brain was racing. He'd had a line of speed in the car to keep him going for the drive back up so he was yab yab yab, a hundred miles an hour, and chewing the side of his mouth like a good un.

'Let Basil do the driving when you're over there.'

'K.'

'You do the money changing.'

'K.'

'Keep your wits about you.'

'K.'

'Basil.'

'Yeah mon.'

'You've got everything?'

'Safe and sound.'

'Call me every day.'

'Yes.'

'Both set?'

'Set.'

'Yes ayah.'

'Shit there's something else . . . damn, damn – what was it? I was going to say something else.'

'It doesn't matter.'

'No, it does, it's important.'

'You'll remember. We'll call tonight.'

'Fuck . . . it's gone. Shit.'

'It doesn't matter.'

'Gone. Shit. OK, OK. Good luck.'

'Cheers.'

'Solid.'

'Lickle more.'

Andy touched knuckles with both of us; nodding, worried, wired.

Then we was queuing at departures and Andy was still standing by the wall opposite, scratching his head, trying to remember. The light in the airport was harsh. I wondered if they did it on purpose. Then we was in the passport place and I couldn't see Andy no more.

Basil says, 'Him cyaan protect you now, bwoy.'

And I goes, 'What d'you mean?'

'Mi jos mean we on our own so you can stop stretchin' yer neck to catch a glimpse a him.'

'I wasn't "stretchin' me neck".'

Basil wouldn't talk on the plane. After take off he pushed his seat back and closed his eyes as if flying round up there in the clouds was what he did every day. I looked down on the land far away. All the real things that mattered getting smaller and smaller through me double-glazed porthole. It was just like pictures out of aeroplane winders you see on the telly, but with that wobbly feeling in yer belly when you drive over a bridge too fast. I thought of all the spirits that filled the space between the plane and the earth. This was where they lived, up here in the thin air. I could feel them. Hundreds and thousands, even millions of dead uns, airborne, just like me. It got me thinking about all that again.

When I was a nipper Auntie Gloria'd come round once a week to do tea leaves and tarot with me mum. They'd squash up over the kitchen table, all bosoms, trying to work out the future. I had a thing about them cards. I loved the pictures and the stories that went along with them and at night I'd dream hefty old dreams about towers and fools and emperors. Course Mum didn't have the gifts that Gloria had, so to make up for it she had all these little rules and regs that we daren't forget: no shoes on the table; no open brollies in the house; we never wore green; if salt was spilled she always threw some at the devil; she'd never cross knives or put a hat on the bed and on and on.

Auntie Gloria – she wasn't me real auntie – was a brassy old bird with crimson nails and rings on every finger, even her thumbs. She wore low-cut tops that showed the deep wrinkles in her cleavage and even in the thick a winter her skin was like a jacket potato. Mum said she did the sun beds, but in my kid brain I thought she was made from old leather sofas like the ones at the dentist on Gosford Street. Auntie Gloria always had a fag on the go. She lived in a cloud of smoke that wound up through her hair and spilled out of her mouth when she talked. At the end of a visit, when nub ends overflowed the ashtray, I'd try and read the patterns they made by copying the looks she gave the leaves in Mum's teacup. Fact was, Auntie Gloria had visions. She could see people trapped on the *other side*.

'You know it's only a membrane,' she'd whisper. 'Thin as net curtains, holding all of them dead uns back from our world.' She'd be so close I could hear the phlegm move in her throat.

Even at five years old I reckoned I could see the wispy bodies of them that'd passed over wafting round me bedroom, all milky and see-through. Auntie Gloria said I had a gift; I was sensitive to things that other people would never notice. So even though I was a 'little man', Mum and Gloria said I could stay up for their women's sessions.

Holding hands round the table of a night would be me mum, me sister Sharon, Auntie Gloria, Mrs Millington from the Co-op, Miss Miles, who Mum said had been a 'lady of the night' but now she called the numbers at the bingo, and Geraldine Loy. There'd be candles and sherry and pots of peppermint tea and fag smoke thick as the mist in a graveyard. There'd be talk of loved ones taken early. Often there'd be tears. But it was always Auntie Gloria who called the dead. She'd twitch and roll her eyes and do this death rattle breathing with her shoulders poking forward like an old witch. Then she'd 'channel'. Dead husbands, lovers, brothers, sisters, sons and daughters. Strange thing was I *could* feel them coming. It was like ice in yer veins or someone blowing them shivery hairs on the back of yer neck. 'One of them's here,' I'd whisper. Shitting me schoolboy pants I was. Aunt Gloria said I was her 'early warning system'. That's why I was Mum's prince. She knew I had 'the gift'. Sharon just called me 'freaky-boy' and poked her tongue at me when no one else was looking.

When Dad found out about the séances he went ballistic. Said they was ruining me with women's nonsense, like embroidery or knitting, and Mum and Auntie Gloria were stitching chat and mischief into fairy stories, filling me head with gobbledy gook. So he rescued me. Took me off down the Red Lion whenever Gloria came round and scolded Mum for feeding me with mumbo-jumbo. In the pub he'd sneak beer in me lemonade and once he was pissed he'd let me smoke his Navy Cut. He'd make a man of me, he reckoned. Kev took over where Dad left off. But however hard they tried, and even with the booze, and pills and spliff, I could always sense things other people couldn't. Whatever Auntie Gloria said, it never felt like a gift to me.

An air hostess poured me neat whisky from a tiny bottle into a plastic cup.

'Ice?' she said.

I shook me head. Whenever she looked in my direction the hostess did an ugly pretend smile that made me want to retch. She did it to everyone down the aisle. I watched her as she worked her way along. I thought of all the people she'd smiled at. I wondered if all of 'em smiled back at her in that slit-eye way. Just polite, wasn't it? Nah. It felt like a slap, that smile. I imagined all the people in the aisle holding the sides of their faces cos they'd been slapped by her vicious little grin. It brought me back to earth.

The airport at Malaga was small and weird. Basil took charge. He could do that, he could get all bolshy and treat me like a twat. He sorted out the hire car. Said 'gratsi' all the time to the locals. Said, 'Mi know this place,' and 'Mi know that place,' as we drove along the coast, like he was a regular Spain freak or something. It pissed me right off.

At last we get to Nerja, our base, and we check into this hotel with a reception desk about the size of a ticket booth. I used to do portering on Saturdays at the Leofric so I know a posh hotel when I see one – this is more like a guesthouse. It has tiles on the floor in the bedroom, like a kitchen, and a funny smell everywhere. The woman who runs it reminds me of Auntie Gloria. Painted nails. Fag out the corner of her mouth and a wicked laugh we get a taste of whenever Basil says 'gratsi' cos it makes her cough and cackle.

'Is grassias,' she explains to him, then winks at me and wobbles her boobs, giggling again so I can see a film of fag smoke coming out of her mouth like she's running on hellfire.

During the next week we make trips up and down the coast to change the dollars, though it takes me a coupla days to get the guts up. Now I can't remember the name of the first town where we change dollars, but I remember Basil walks into this bank, cool as a bottle of Pils, and changes $200, easy. Then he strolls back out to meet me, in the café, and we're like 'Yes!' and it feels great.

'Bank man didn't even check dem,' he says.

'What, he never looked?'

'Jos graze 'im eyes cross de pile, that's all.'

'Wicked.'

I think, If Basil can do it I can do it. But I have a bit of the *fear*. Still, I do a money-change in another bank across town and Basil's right, the bank clerk hardly looks. We're both high from our first success so we kiss our pesetas when we're sure no one can see us and grin at each other like a coupla monkeys. But driving back I notice a car tailing us. I can see it in the wing mirror, turning when we turn, stopping when we stop. Just as me heart starts a brisk beat the car turns off and I have to rub me chest and puff a bit to settle meself down. Best not to worry Bas with it though, I think.

Next day we do $600 between us and we say stuff like, 'This is it, we're in our stride now,' feeling light with the thrill of it. But then I see the car again. A Beemer. This time I clock the plates just to be certain and sure enough the next day it's on our arse *again*, four cars back, as we leave Nerja. I adjust the wing mirror to see it better.

'Hey,' shouts Bas, miffed I'm messing with his all-round vision.

I can feel a bit a sick rising in me throat but I says, 'I don't wanna freak you, Bas, but you need to know.'

'Wha?'

'We're being followed.' I say it like it's everyday. Like it could be nothing.

He's looking in the rearview now. 'Nah! True?' says Bas.

'Yeah, a black BMW. Behind us. It's been there both times we've changed dollars too.'

'Mi nah see it.'

I adjust me mirror again. 'I'm telling yer, it's there. Shit, they've slipped off.'

'Same car both times, you say?'

'Yep, I checked the plates.'

'Mi watch fa it.'

And I think, There, I've said it, and swallow the sick back down.

Two days later and it's fucking hot. Hotter than I've ever been before. Hotter than '76 at Weston-super-Mare. It's dry heat, but sort of chewy. It gets in yer mouth and throat, like you're eating hot-air pie. I'm dripping. I'm stripped down to me jeans and trainers waiting for Bas to come out the bank down this side a the road. As he comes towards me he has a wide old grin. Success again. We go to a café, out the way, and Basil whips his shirt off too. He's panting, going, 'Wooah, it's a rush when you walk out with the duns.' It makes me wish I'd gone first this time.

Then Basil says that *I* have to put me shirt back on to do me bank bit, just like he did. I notice how smooth and shiny Basil's chest is. It's the colour of me dad's old Bakelite radio and here I am all pasty and white like one a them spirits in Mum's kitchen, only difference is you can see the purple veins pulsing up me arms. What a pair we are. Fucking ebony and deathmask white. Fucking United Nations of crim. Dad and Kev would cough up six-inch nails to see me taking orders from a blackie like this.

'I'm keepin' me shirt off,' I say.

'You don't want to do that, Jez.'

'Look man, no disrespect, but I'll do what I want, OK?'

Bas sucks his teeth. 'You want to think bout the impression you is givin'.'

130

'I'm a tourist. I'm givin' a *hot* tourist impression.'

'Mi thinkin' more bout that *tattoo*, right there.'

He points at me tattoo. Sign of allegiance to *Das Bombers*. Me old gang. Kids all of us back then, of course, hanging out on the bomb patch, making dens, digging up shrapnel left over from the war. Boys love all that. Me and Terry Royston, Peter Daventry and Johnny Ray, even Tim Jessop, in short trousers. We had a proper code of conduct and initiation ceremonies and everything. Yeah, boys are like that. We weren't Nazi. It was just a sign scratched in skin. But we knew it had power. We'd seen it in the movies. Black and red. Flags the *SS* hung on their walls. We'd seen it on all the wall hangings in the Indian shops on Foleshill Road. 'An ancient symbol of peace and well-being,' that's what Devandra said. Dad said it was sick. Said people had died with that sign burning its shape on their brains. Course Kev loved it. Reckoned it was the only thing that gave him faith I'd chosen the right way. Later when I saw it on the badges him and his mates wore on their bomber jackets I knew some people, aside from Dad, could get fucked off with my tattoo. Kev wore his swastika badges for gigs and marches and Paki-bashing. I wondered if Dev had ever been Paki-bashed. I wondered what he'd make of the swastika badges his attackers wore.

All this thinking makes me hate Basil right then like a swift fist in me gut. Knowing what was right and wrong, so sure of himself. Coming all big and righteous with me like he knows everything about me and me life. I grind me teeth so hard a chip of molar turns to powder on me tongue. But I keep schtum and put me shirt back on. I am hot. Burning hot. Fear and anger. Fear and anger. Striding off across the cobbled square to this Bureau de Change chuntering to meself, saying, 'Ancient symbol of peace and well-being. He doesn't know shit,' and feeling well fucked off with Basil.

Inside the Bureau de Change the air's damp and close, but I feel a cold sweat creep onto me lip as I pass the security guard. He's squat and swarthy, bending over to peer into the aircon vent on the wall. He has a gun. It's a neat little handgun, holstered in black leather. He's wearing a thin white sash that goes across his chest and round his waist that I can see the outline of after I've looked away, like sunshadow. I blink to make it disappear but it won't budge. The woman behind the counter is scribbling on a piece of paper. It's a form she's filling in. I can see her big, looping, joined up writing coming out of the nib of her pen, filling the boxes on the form like magic. She clocks me but carries on. She's fat. Her wrist flab bulges onto the tops of her hands. I can see greasy sweat where her skin folds over on itself round her neck. I think of those toads whose necks bulge right out when they croak like they have giant goitres, inflating and deflating. Big puffers. Big bellows.

The woman stops writing and clears her throat before looking up at me. She narrows her eyes. Her neck flab wobbles. Her neck flab could set up home somewhere on its own.

'See,' she says. Then 'See, see.' She's impatient. Pissed off that I'm interrupting her form filling.

'Oh. *Si*,' I say and hand over the $200 I'm gripping. She snatches the notes from me, just whips them out me hand. I'm sweating so much it's running down me face. Heavy drips of it keep plopping off the end of my nose. It must be a hundred degrees or something and me guts are churning like a bloody washing machine. I try and stop glancing over me shoulder at the guard. It'll look suspicious. But I can't help meself cos the bad feelings I'm having about Señora Neck-Blubber are gripping me belly something chronic, forcing me to wriggle and squirm.

Fear and anger. Fear and anger. Basil's a shit for coming all mighty with me.

'Him cyaan protect you no more, bwoy.' He'd said that

like he was threatening me. He said it at Gatwick, just out of reach. Just as we stepped over the edge of the known world. Yep, no doubt that had a threat in it. Then telling me to wear a shirt. As if he was the boss.

She's signalling to the security guard by the door now, sneaking out slimy looks like wet farts and taking for ever to count out me pesetas. I'm drumming the counter, thrummity thrummity. I try to stop it. I use me willpower on me fingers, mind-bending, going, 'Stop it, stop it now,' in me head, but on the fingers go, thrummity thrummity. I can see she's mucking about with this little machine under the counter. There's a button under there. I'm sure of it. There's an alarm. I'm gonna throw up.

Fear and anger. Fear and anger. Fear tears through me like floodwater, like KABOOOSSHHH and me insides are drenched with it. Yeah, when the dam breaks yer thoughts get swept off. Reason's jerry built, like wooden houses, it breaks up like matchwood with the force of it. I have to run. From guards with guns and heifers with flab enough to suffocate the average man. Thrummity thrummity thrummity stops all of a sudden without willpower. So sudden I'm surprised and stare at me fingers. I have the exit in me sights. But then she says, 'Grassias, señor,' and some other gibberish that comes out her mouth like shit off a shovel and she pushes a bunch of pesetas at me over the counter, just like that. Did she even look at the dollars? I don't remember. I should remember. I should have a mental picture of her turning them over, holding them up to the light . . . or something . . . but no, all I can see is her mumpy, greasy neck bellows. I take the pesetas.

As sure as there's an underworld the notes are marked. They're on to me, these two. They're gonna follow me. They're gonna have me for sure. I turn to leave. The guard is looking at the fat señora and adjusting his balls. Men do that before they strike, I've seen it time and again, they touch their dicks to remind themselves they're men, just a little touch then WALLOP.

Outside, the light almost blinds me, and it's oven hot, blistering, but I stride back across the square, blinking, man on a mission, and walk past Bas like I don't know him. But when I'm close enough I say, 'Quick, man, quick,' out the corner of me mouth so he knows to follow me. I don't look back till I'm in a side alley. It's shady and cool down here and I rub round me eyes to try and clear me vision. There's a woman hanging washing from a pull-along line, high up. I can hear a telly from a window further down and Spanish voices speaking faster'n Peter O'Sullevan commentating the Derby. Too fast. The fastest language in the world. Faster than Paki. Spanish is a wall of babble. I try and blank out the voices.

Basil's caught up now. He squeezes me shoulder in his big black hand. 'Chill, mon, chill,' he says.

'She was onto me, man, that fat cow in there was onto me.'

'Who, Jez, where?'

'Her in there, in the change place.'

I'm wringing me hands and looking around at the floor. There are rats in alleys like these. Vermin breed in dank places. Basil walks down to the corner and looks back into the square.

'What are you doing? Get back you fucking –' and I grab him and try to pull him back. He's sticking his neck out, taking a risk of being seen, for fuck's sake. He can take risks if he wants, but not with me.

'Chill out, mon,' he says and I can feel the muscles in his arm tighten up. Then he looks at me with his big cow eyes and talks softly so I have to concentrate on his voice above the sound of the telly down the alley. 'I'm going to look round the corner,' he says. 'And I'm gonna check if that car there or anyone followin' us, see.'

He's nodding, trying to make me agree. 'You can go back a hotel if you want and mi meet you there.'

'I'm not a fuckin' kid, Basil. I'm not a coward, right.'

'What you sayin'? Of course not, mon.'

'I'm not scared at all.' I stand tall and pull me shoulders back and push me chest out and grit me teeth. I know how to look hard. 'I'm bein' fuckin' cautious is all.'

'Well, mi glad to hear it, Jez, but you know what? I is scared, so mi need to find out if mi have somethin' to be scared of.'

'You think I'm fuckin' paranoid, don't you?'

'JEZ –' he raises his voice a way now '– ress yourself. Mi hope you *is* paranoid cos that would mean we not bein' followed, see.'

Fear and anger. Fear and anger. I'm glad it's more anger now than fear. Anger has a nice hard nudge behind it that puts a twinkle in yer eye. Basil's back at the corner now, twisting his head round the wall to look out on the square.

'What can you see?' I whisper.

'Nhuttin. What did *you* see, exactly?'

I think for a second. 'Well, I handed the woman behind the counter two hundred dollars, yeah . . .'

'Yeah.'

'. . . and she stared at me, I mean like this . . . fat greasy cow. Then she looked over to this security guard while she was fiddling with this machine under the counter, yeah . . .'

'Yeah.'

'. . . and she nodded.'

'Nodded?'

'Yeah, y'know, like raised her eyebrows, like this, and made a kind of signal with her eyes to him, to the security guard.' I show Basil the face.

'What did security man do?'

'Well, he must have had a device, like a wire or somethin' in his trousers.'

'Why must he?'

I show me teeth. 'Isn't – it – obvious – you – stupid – cunt?'

Fear and anger. Me words come out slow, slow like sharp sand through a funnel. I know how to look hard. But then Bas steps away from me and pushes his own chest out. Basil's a big man. Basil knows how to look hard too. Shit, Basil *is* hard.

'There's no point to mek trouble with me, y'understan', Jez.'

Then he checks the square one more time and walks past me down the alley without speaking to me. Past the winder where the telly's on, under the washing the woman's hung out. He doesn't even care about vermin or nothing.

'Where are you going?' I shout, chasing after him up the alley.

'Back a hotel.'

Fear and anger. Fear again. Basil's a shit, but I'd rather have Basil than no one. At least I can trust Basil.

I catch up with him. 'Look . . . I'm sorry, mate. I'm stressing, man,' I say.

He keeps walking. 'You need to get a grip.'

'I saw what I saw, man. And you . . . You're not the boss here, you understand, Basil, *you're not the boss*.'

He stops firm in his tracks and turns on me. He has a long jawbone. As long as the span of my hand, and it is pointing up and out as he speaks so I can see the shine of sweat on his neck. 'Who de boss then, Jez?' he asks. He's smiling too. It's a real smile, not pretend, not like that air hostess. It's a real big beamer. A dazzler.

I say nothing. I just shrug.

'Cos mi wonderin' what it take to be a boss man here.'

He's still smiling. His eyes are warm.

He starts to count off on his fingers. 'Mi older than you, mi cleverer than you, mi *stronger* than you, mi have more experience than you . . . an' mi cooler than you by one hundred degrees, mon. So mi aks you again, who de boss, Jez?'

I look over me shoulder and shift on me feet like a schoolboy. I'm thinking, Yeah, who is the boss? Then I scratch me cheek. I am hot hot hot. 'Neither of us is the boss.'

'What you say?'

'I said, neither of us is the boss.'

Basil laughs. 'OK, Jez, none of us is the boss. That suit me down to the ground.'

On the way back to the car Basil does that black man swagger. He knows he's harder'n me. He's showing me that he knows I know. But mostly I'm still checking to see if the security guard is following and keeping me eyes peeled for the BMW. Once we're in the car I feel better. We have wheels. We can escape. I know Bas is a wicked driver. I feel safe knowing he's in the driving seat.

I say, 'I don't want any bad feelin' between us, man. You know that.'

'Ahright.'

'And you have to understand that I'm not a racialist . . . if that's what you were thinking.'

'Mi nah think pon it.'

'Some of me best mates are black, you *know* that.'

'Jez.'

'Yeah.'

'You nah think to get that swastika on your arm turn into a flower or a heart or something pretty like dat? Dem tattoo artist can do that now, y'know.'

I pull at the skin beside me tattoo so I can see it better. I was twelve years old. Science lab, Sydney Stringer Community College. Johnny Ray pricked me upper arm with that compass two hundred, three hundred times till it felt like the devil's torture itself while Pete glooped the ink out the end of the plastic inner and rubbed it into the pinholes with one dirty finger. Blood and ink. Red and black. Pete saying, 'You're bleedin' like a good un.' Me saying, 'Get on with it, for fuck's sake. It's tutor groups in two minutes.' Then doing the *Das Bombers* handshake when we went our separate ways. It was a thing of beauty that tattoo once the scabs fell off.

Basil's waiting for an answer.

'Flowers and hearts, fuck. Why would I want that?' I say.

'Well, that sign there, that *swastika*, give man a man a message bout your true self, you nah think?'

'This symbol –' I tap the tattoo three times with me finger '– is like, part of *my* culture.'

I'm about to explain but Bas butts in. He's not smiling no more. 'Swastika not your culture, mon. It a symbol of your old enemy, Germans, Nazis . . . remember? World War Two and all a that jivation.'

I push the heel of me hand against one eye.

Bas carries on. 'That symbol tell a black man that you cyaan be trusted, that you sympathize with Babylon.'

I shake me head and screw up me eyes. 'What? Look –'

'It mean you is a racist, ignorant raasclot and mi rather eat mi own shit than look at you flash your skinny white arm at me with that sign on it, y' understan'? And you know what? Of course mi is the boss of you. Look at you blousebait. You is scrawny and weak and pathetic and wet and wrung out in the midday heat. When you get tattoo up with that swastika you think you is a big, big man an' you cyaan bear that a black man over reach you in every lickle ting, eh?'

Fear and anger. I know how to look hard. I can fake it. Bin doing it all me fucking life. At home. At school. Down the pub. Out on the town. With the lads. You gotta stand yer ground. You can't let anyone push you around. Fatal that. You become the whipping boy. I've seen it. Oh yes, I know how to look hard. I take me knife, four inches of steel, flick knife. It's done damage this blade. That's a lie. That's bluff, but I push it gently into Bas's ribs while he's driving and put enough pressure against it for him to feel the sharpness of it on his bare skin. The car wobbles around on the road when he realizes I'm sticking him, but Bas gets his fear and the car under control. He's quicker'n most men.

'Woah, ress yourself,' he says. Then, 'Put it away, Jez. That not sharp enough to break mi skin.'

I push the blade a little harder. Feel it slice. A trickle of blood runs over the bowl of Basil's dark belly. Red and black.

'Woah. Ress up, mi tellin' ya, Jez. Mi only aks you to cover up a swastika, mon. It only a lickle ting mi aks.'

That's better. That's polite. You can't let anyone push you around. Fatal that. I flick the knife back into its housing and wipe the sweat from my forehead with me T-shirt. You have to know when to look hard, but it makes me heart beat against me stomach so fast I want to chuck up right there in the footwell.

Instead, I say, 'If I cover up me swastika you have to stop baffling me with your fucking bad English.'

I'm making out this is cool. That this is just a little spat. I'm negotiating. I'm swallowing back vom.

'It not English me speakin', mon, it *patois*. It a different language altogether.'

'It's English, pigeon English, and I know you can talk the *Queen's* English cos I've heard ya . . . in the hotel, in the airport. You just speak to me so dense cos you think you can scare me.'

It was true. Basil could talk proper English without all the pattywah. I mean, he still had an accent, but without the tooth kissing: 'Hey bwoy, y'nah, rrrackstone an' tunderation.' The patois was an act.

Bas sucks his teeth. 'Where you comin' from, rasta? Mi not tryin' to scare you. Mi talk in patois cos mi expect bredrin to tek mi fa what mi is.'

Bredrin, Black Power, Black Panther, Mohammed Ali and *Shaft*, y'know, all that 'shut yo mouth' stuff. The *blacker* they acted the more clout they had. It was 'Roots' and 'Dread' and 'Star' and 'Blood'. I'm not saying it wasn't Bas's culture. I'm just saying *The Two Ronnies* and chicken vindaloo and Cov City FC and a lager down the Dog and Trumpet was his culture too.

But I say, 'It's tough to understand you sometimes is all.'

And he says, 'I will try to mek meself clear den, Jez.'

I watch him wipe the trickle of blood off his belly like it's coffee he's spilt or something.

When we get in the room I pull the bottle a vodka from me bag. I need to calm me nerves so I'm swigging from it hard. I strip down to me pants and build a loaded spliff, knocking back the voddy while I roll. Sometimes getting fuckfaced is like hunger pangs, like a nag in yer brain going, 'Drink, spliff, drink, spliff.' Basil paces round the room. He's shaken, trying not to show it.

Then he says, 'We both need some space, alright?'

I nod and he leaves.

I'm not happy when he leaves. I'm not happy at all. I start getting twitchy and have to check out the winder. I can see Bas off by the prom, or whatever you call it in Spanish, staring out to sea. He stands out from all them pasty arses milling round him. He's a six-footer. Built. I decide he has a welcome face. It has high cheekbones, a straight thin nose with wide nostrils. I'd be scared being black. I'd know there were people like Kev on the streets who hated me for nothing. Basil isn't scared. Basil is proud. He holds his shoulders back and his head high like an African prince. Like that bloke off *Rising Damp*.

*

Fear and anger. When we got back from Weston-super-Mare Mum made her 'little prince's favourite dinner', neck of lamb stew with dumplings. (Dumplings, dimpled dumplings.) 'You are my saving grace,' she said. 'You keep me on the straight and narrer, yes?'

'I'll help you make yer beds,' I said and Mum did one of her sad smiles.

When Dad got in from work he was all 'Dorothy, my love' and trying to grab her round her haunches. They stood in the kitchen till after nine just talking. Kev said Dad was pathetic. Said he hadn't eaten all the time Mum and me was away. Said if *he* was Dad he'd never have her back.

Mum's been having it off with Uncle Wally, Kev whispered. He never said it right out loud.

'Liar.' I screamed so hard I was sick on the carpet, even though I didn't have a clue what he meant.

White on white. These are better colours. The tiles in the shower are white. The shower tray is white. The curtain, the soap, me body, me arm – all white. The swastika is black. It's got all blurred round the edges as the years have marched by. Now the edges are grey. Degraded? Basil's right. It's in need of a spruce up, don't yer fucking know. It's in need of a total fucking redesign. No less than a total fucking redesign. I shouldn't do it pissed. But it's best to be a little razzed to dull the pain. The razor blade is silverrrr, or is it white, if I turn it this way so it reflects the light then it's white, that way and it's silverrrr. Red and white. That's better.

'Baaaasssiiiillll,' I shout when he comes in. I throw me arms in the air cos he's a hero, yes he is. If I was black . . . fuck. 'Me old mate, come 'ere.'

He steps closer but stops. I, Jez, need to be treated with caution. Ha ha. I'm well spruced up. Shitted showered shaved and redesigned and I'm so happy to see Basil. Basil!

'You seem happy now, mon,' says Bas, big cagey lump.

'I am happy, happy, happy, I tell yah, I've never been so happy.'

It calls for a dance so I do a little jig on one leg then the other. Still got me voddy. I look closely into the bottle as I dance, give it a shake, give it a shake, but there's only an inch left. Me axle goes and I bowl into the wall. It makes me laugh to hit the wall so solid. Thwump.

'You eaten?' says Basil from a long way off.

'I don't need *food*. I don't need that shit they serve here, bloody octopus shhhiit. I need more *booze*, man.'

'Come now. Mi see a nice place that do sausage and mash and Guinness, mon.'

'Yahey, Guinness.'

I stumble over to him. It's a journey. I put me arm across his shoulder, but I know he deserves better'n me.

'You deserve better'n me,' I say, then I gently kiss his face. 'You're the fucking Zeitgeist, Basil my man, the fucking Zeitgeist, I swear.'

Basil doesn't know what a Zeitgeist is. I don't really know neither. Praps he thinks it's some kinda swastika. Still, he says, 'Come,' and leads me by the hand out the room.

We walk down to the beach and out along a huge paved land jetty that juts out of the rock and over the sea. It has seats running up either side and palm trees down the middle. At the end it's so high up the views go right across the land and down the coast, but it's not like Weston-super-Mare. Here, instead of one great slab of sand to put yer deckchair out on, there are coves with new moons of golden sand and cliffs rough as pumice stone. Bas buys me Coca-Cola and we sit for a while breathing charred air and watching the people parading up and down. They're all dressed up pretty for holiday party time, families and couples and groups a lads and lasses. Basil points to a row of fishing boats setting off from beaches somewhere round the coast. Each one has a man in and a yellow lamp burning at the front. Basil says they'll be out there on the water the whole night. Says they call to each other when they're lonely and sing sea shanties when the clouds rub out the moon. I wonder what the night would be like on the big, big ocean in a tinsy winsy boat.

'Looook,' I say then, rolling up me sleeve.

'W'happen, mon? Did you fall?'

'*Naaoo*, don't be daft.' I laugh and throw me head back. 'I ffffucking got rid of it man, fffucking . . . fucking got rid of it.'

'You're dread, mon,' says Basil. 'You try and tek off that swastika?'

'Ffffucking right, man. Fffuckin' redesign.'

'But look there, you is bleeding bad.'

'Nothin', nothin', it's nothin'. I tell you, nothin'.' I decide I like saying nothing. 'Ffffucking nothin'.'

'Let me see,' says Bas, all worried.

'Nah man, it's nothin'.'

But even as I'm arguing I'm pulling the bandage up a little way. I have to show him. I want him to see me new red flower.

'Fuck, Jez, you nah jest. Bwoy you is dread, uh huh, you is dread.'

'Of course there weren't enough duns fa all of us to mek the journey to England so Mom and Pop leave me and Delroy behind a JA till they have some big money comin' in. That's the way wid our family . . . wid Jamaicans on a general, y'nah. Family is family and every pickney have tree mudda, the mudda mudda the father mudda and the baby mudda, aint no arguin' on it no way. Whoever closest rock the cradle, it make no matter.'

Basil's talking about his childhood. He's smoking a spliff, leaned back on one a the white plastic chairs on our balcony.

He's speaking all soft and looking off into nowhere. He's never spoke to me like this before. We've talked about jobs and scams and whether this typa grass is better'n that typa grass, or who's gonna win the Cup. But already this evening he's gone on about Jamaica and school in Cov, the trouble he's been in, doing time in Winson Green, the beatings, the friends he's made. Now he's saying he would never have gone to prison if he'd stayed in Jamaica. Except, he says, that's probably not true now he comes to think of it, cos Jamaica's where he got his taste for 'the mighty 'erb' and his need of it has led him astray ever since. I say it stands to reason.

Jamaica's where he learned to fend for himself. Grew up with his grandma while his mum and dad made the beginnings of a life over here. He spent 'dazzlin' days out in a bush'.

'What *is* a bush?' I say.

'Bush jos mean nature. It where you can plant tings wild, like banana or yam or 'erb. Instead of a field mi have plant in a wild in JA, y'understan'?'

I say, 'Like the woods?'

'Kinda like the woods 'cept green and lush and full a tropical plant and ting. Woods in England fusty and musty and dirty. It all about mud and decomposin' in England. In JA it bright and light and full a colour. In Revival, the town where mi born, mi have a big light room where mi can step out in a yard in mi bare feet and roll up the track to the beach or stamp through the bush looking for lizard, playing target with mi catapult. In England mi share a double bed wid tree a mi bredrin in a dark lickle yard that Mom and Pop have, with no heatin' an' a ice cold journey to the share toilet out the back.'

Bas stretches across and passes me the spliff. 'Yes mon, it was rough dem first years in Cov.'

'Was there anythin' you liked about England?'

Basil's looking up at the stars and scratching his chin.

'Television,' he says at last and laughs. Then, more serious, he says, 'Y'nah, mi like that feelin' a bein' different from the rest, y'understan'? When mi come to England mi realize mi not like him or him or him. You can pick me out in a school photo, you can spot me in a crowd. Even though mi tek some grief from ignorant raasclot white bwoy sometime, mi have a identity that mark me out. An identity that tell the world I and I is a rare ting.'

Basil's stoned now and coming all Black Power the way he does. Then he says, 'But the ting I love the best bout England, mon, best of all, mi love de gals dem, mm mm.'

'White girls?'

'White gals, black gals, big, small, short, tall, thin, thick, mi nah cyare. Mi a grindsman fa true. Mi have no preference fa colour. When man a man accuse me a wanting jos white gal, mon, it vex me. Dem gal at the West Indian Club see me and come up a hand on hip and waggin' finger and sucking them teeth saying, "Hey, Mr Mention, why you go out with them maga, flat batty, white bitch when you can have a strong black sister like one a us?"'

Basil's stood up now, doing an impression of the Jamaican girls you see up at the Community Centre, pouting his lips out and wiggling his arse.

I can't help laughing. 'What do you tell 'em?'

'Mi say mi waitin' for the right sister to come along. But mi have to admit some dem West Indian gal too facety for me, bwoy, yes ayah, too facety. But mi walk out with most gal, whatever they colour or they creed. Mi eat where the table is fullest, y'undastan?'

I shake me head. 'Let me show you a reasoning,' he says. 'First up mi know many more white gal than black.'

'Well, you live in England, don't ya?'

'*Hexactly!* Second, the white gals them *intrigued* by a black man. Them want stretch out mi kinky hair and say, "Wah, look how long 'tis," when it seem so short curl up

145

on mi head. And them want check if mi blackness run all over mi body, you know what I'm sayin'? And dem white gal dem believe mi well-endowed before mi even start to conjure with mi *mojo*.'

We're both laughing now.

'Yes ay, it help a black man to have a reputation. Some a dem gal ignorant though, y'nah, mi have a gal one time who pinch me so hard on a backside when we making love it mek mi stop mi work and yell out, *aaiiiieeee*, like a kick dog.'

'What did she pinch you for?'

'She say she "just checkin".'

'Checkin' for what?'

'She say she checkin' to see if I and I bruise!'

'What?'

'Yes, mon, she act like it the most natural ting in the world to pinch a man while him busy in a bed. If I bruise! I aks you. So mi say, "Of course I bruise, you jos cyaan see it so well on mi dark skin." Whah! She think she sleeping with a alien fa true with green blood and . . . two stomach and eyes on stalk and ting. It did not last with that gal, uh uh, no way.'

From the balcony we watch the late-night partygoers going up and down the street below. We're looking down on the tops of people's heads. I can see their hair, their shoulders, the bulge of girls' boobs peeping out their strappy tops. There's a couple kissing against a wall, half in, half out the arc of a streetlight. The girl has her hands in her boyfriend's hair. It seems wrong for me to watch.

Earlier, Basil took me to the pharmacy. Got me these funny little clip plasters that hold cut skin together, got me iodine and Savlon, got me a crisp white bandage, got me some cotton wool, got me a pizza. A pizza. Sobered me up enough to feel pain. When we got back to the room he took off the toilet roll and the strip a towel I'd tied me

146

tattoo up with and cleaned the wound out with cotton wool and warm water. Kept saying, 'Bwoy, you is dread.' It made me feel good when he said that. It made me feel hard, like he respected me. He tipped iodine over the wound and I grit me teeth and turned away from the sharpness of it. He put the clip plasters on one edge of skin and stretched them over to catch the other edge, pulling both edges together. Blood was still seeping out, but with his soft black fingers he gently rubbed Savlon over the wound and the clips and the iodine. Black and red and white. After the bandage was secure, he said, 'Trust me, Jez, mi going to keep you safe, y'understan'.'

He held me shoulders while I cried.

Said he was gonna take me under his wing.

Said he was gonna look after me.

Then I slept.

Bas points. 'Look down there, bwoy, she's fine, eh? We should find ourselves some action one night, y'nah.'

He's singled out a pretty girl who's standing on the corner with her friend. She's wearing a boob tube and a short skirt.

'She look ready for a wild time y'nah think?'

He doesn't give me a chance to answer.

'Man a man haffa be careful, though. Y'nah this one gal mi step out with like to have sex like it going out a fashion. Wi tan pon it lang every day, mon, yeeaas I'm tellin' ya. But while wi busy she always staring where har skin meet mine, and when we done she lay har lily pink arm cross me and sigh like romantic. She a *hart* student and she talk bout the "*haesthetic* of black and white". She say tings like she love – what was it? – "the depth and shine" of mi skin against the "alabaster" of hars! Then she lay limb cross me, this way and that, like she choosing wallpaper or paint or someting. Mi say, "Jah knows, it look fine," mi jos happy she happy to be naked with me all the while. But soon mi feel like she designing us together . . . you know what I'm sayin'?'

I nod, then shake me head.

'And then, rakstone and tunderation, she start talk bout pickney and that she want *brown baby*. It then mi know we not a couple . . . we a paint palette!'

Basil slaps his thigh. His laugh is deep and clear like it has a meaning more than laughing. Like laughing for him is as important as living and dying, like water in cells, like organs in bodies, like hearts and lungs and livers and blood . . .

'This other gal there seem normal to begin. We go to flim or to a blues on a Satnight or off to see Specials at Tiffany club. Mi nah realize but she young this one . . . praps seventeen, maybe younger . . . sixteen? One day she aks me to come see har parents, and mi say nah, uh uh, parents not fa me. Mi nah like the whole *Guess Who's Coming to Dinner* vibe, y'nah. And mi no Sidney Poitier, high and mighty neither, mi nah have a smart suit, mi nah silver tongue, white wannabe – although I and I is a handsome man fa true.'

He grabs onto pretend lapels and does a dapper face.

'But she nag and nag and tell me har parents *desperate* to meet me. So mi aks if har parents know that I and I is black and she say, "Of course they do," like it a stupid question.

'So the next Sunday mi put on mi smart clothes and mek a way to Kenilwurt where she live. But walking down har road mi know this not *my* place, the houses and street and car and milky pickney in the yard all oozing whiteness. You know Kenil*worth*, eh Jez?'

'Course.'

'It a wash down clean *heducated* place with the castle and everyting. Har street have the office-man home, you know the style, suit and tie and briefcase man home. There is no man a man like that in my street or your street, eh

Jez? There is the railwayman and bus driver man and the factory man and shopkeeper man and man a man who mek a lickle stretch a long way on the wrong side of the law. So mi feel this Kenilwurt is not *my* place, it feel like Kenilwurt want repulse me like I is a ting caught in its gullet. It wan vomit me back out a that town, back to the frontline where mi belong . . . no, back to Jamaica . . . no, back to Africa . . . no mon, back to the jungle. The jungle, like it a real place that mi from . . . *the* jungle, hah.'

'Is the jungle not real then, Bas?'

'Of course the jungle is real, Jez. But I and I is not from it.'

'Ah.'

Basil shakes his head. 'Mi cyaan remember that gal name now – oh, hol' on. Emily, har name Emily. Bwoy, she wild and pretty. It Emily mudda who open the door when mi knock. Mi say, "Good afternoon," in a proper way. "Good afternoon," har mudda say back, with har rosy cheek head a one side, a half a smile at the edge a har lips. Mi say, "My name is Basil."'

Basil touches his chest with his fingertips. '"I have come fa dinner."'

'What did she say?'

'Bwoy, the mudda nah speak nah move har head. She nah move har body nor har half a smile neither and she start look dread, cos har mouth all stretch in a smiling shape but har eyes afraid and glassy to blousebait.'

'Fuck.'

'I'm tellin' ya. Then Emily come bouncing in the doorway and she say, "Basil, Basil, come in. Mum this is Basil." She's pullin' on me hand, pullin' me into har house. Har mudda still standin' there frozen. True. So y'nah, mi nah gwin.'

'No.'

'Yes, mon. It obvious that she nah tell them that I and I is black.'

'She hadn't told them?'

Basil sucks his teeth. 'Mon, not a word.'

'What did you do?'

'Mi say, "I'm very sorry, but I have just remembered a promise I must keep." And mi bow a lickle way down with one hand on mi stomach like this, then turn and walk way slowly, slowly.'

'Shit I'd've given 'er a piece a my mind.'

'Wha? And mek them think they is right to hate? Nah. Uh uh. Mi nah give har the pleasure of feelin' righteous.'

'What about Emily?'

'Emily soon come all facety at mi shoulder and mi say, "You told dem I is a black man?" She nah answer me. She look at har fingers, zif she threading needle. Then she say, "I thought this was the best way for them to find out." I aks har who it is best for. Not for me, and not for dem, uh uh no way. That mudda scare. She want mek for dead on a doorstep before mi even haul mi black backside cross threshold. And if har mudda like that, what har father like, eh? Then Emily say they need waking up. What did she say now? She say, "They need to be force to change their uptight, middle-class racism."'

Basil stopped and shook his head.

'Me mum and dad would be the same.'

'Bwoy, mi know that, Jez. Mi know your bredda and your kin from time.'

I start to scratch at the edge of me bandage. Kev, Dad, Mum, Sharon, Auntie Gloria. I'm a brother and a punch-bag and a 'little prince', a scrap, a twat, a seer. I have a gift. This hotel, even our room has signatures in it, marks made by the people who lived and died here and they could be any size or shape or colour. Their ghosts are in there now. Dancing behind the flimsy curtains. Black ghosts and white ghosts and yellow ghosts and . . .

'Jez. Jez. JEZ!'

'Yeah.'

'Stop scratchin' bandage, mon.'

'Yeah.'

Basil looks worried. His welcome face and his brown cow eyes have more sympathy than any eyes I've ever seen. He's trying to distract me with all his stories. He's shit scared I'm gonna go loop-de-loop.

'Did you chuck her then?' I say.

'Who?'

'Emily.'

'Of course. Emily want use me to punish har parents, showing off a black man so har mudda and father twist up in a rage. Bwoy, them punishing gal the worst kind.'

'Seems like the white ones are more trouble than they're worth.'

'You're not wrong, bwoy, you're not wrong. It a hard life for a black man. Mi cyaan please no body.'

'You're happy here now though, I mean in England?'

'Man a man mek a life, y'nah. All the trouble I bin in, bwoy, mi mek mi bed, mi haffa lie in it.'

11

PADS

The Pain in Spain

When I shared a house with Andy it was 'Maggie out!' and protest songs and trying to grow our hair in dreads. It was *Winter in America* and anti-apartheid, boycotts and free Mandela, but most of all it was dope, acid, shrooms and headfucks. We hadn't quite dropped out of uni at that stage, although I didn't go to a single lecture past Christmas 1982. We continued with the façade of being students for our parents' sake, pretending we were aiming to take our place in their world.

I remember walking into the living room when Andy was on the phone to his mother. He was leaning back into the cushions with his legs apart, saying, 'All the guys at uni have their hair like this, all of them.' Then a pause for her to speak and him to sigh, exasperated. 'Listen, Mum, chill, it's only fashion, it's only hair, it's not like I'm taking drugs or anything,' and rolling his eyes and making a face at me that said *if only she knew* . . . both of us smirking, adolescent, believing we were fooling them, those ignorant behemoths of the old order, whose tweed-wearing, *Telegraph*-reading rigidity was no match for our lissom intellectual newness. We should have listened to ourselves, behaving like schoolboys, trying to deceive them. I ask you.

Thankfully, Andy's parents never had time to visit. He'd go off to meet them in London or Oxford a couple of times a term and come back pensive and brow-beaten. My mother, on the other hand, made a habit of dropping in unannounced on her way to one of her horsy 'meets'. She'd pull up in the Range Rover like some hybrid farm-wife meets Cruella De Vil; Argyle jumpers and pearls, welly boots and stockings.

Once she arrived unexpectedly after we'd had a particularly heavy session the night before and the house was still full of wasted freaks, some spaced out, some sleeping. We were all there: Biff, Spud, Raff, Daz, Merlin and Dom the Hat . . . and Gollum and Frip and Rizzo and the other Andy, Andy B . . . and – oh God, so many, a house full. My mother sat amid it all as the guys woke up around her scratching their dreads and their balls, peering at her through swollen, slitted eyes, saying, 'Morning, Mrs Pads,' after I'd introduced them. Me dishevelled, mortified, my guts wrung out, going, 'Yeah, er . . . some of the chaps stayed over . . . er.' She, the picture of supercilious tolerance, knees together, straight-backed, taking tiny puffs on her menthol Mores, laughing genteelly when someone made a joke, but observing me and all of us minutely. And when the guys had staggered off to their respective homes, her saying in that haughty way she had of commenting on anything I did, 'This is all very *basic*, Tristan. And the names – Biff, Boff, Jazz, Razz – my goodness, do these *boys* have parallel lives on children's television?' I hated it when she turned up. I hated everyone seeing the pile of bourgeois faeces I'd crawled out from. She refused to accept I'd thrown off Tristan Padstock-Burroughs and become Pads, the man, my own man, so determinedly did she shine her spotlight on the embarrassing accident of my birth.

Of course, she adored Andy, who always managed to tiptoe along the charming side of obsequious. For example, on that particular occasion he sauntered into the living room where Mother was sitting (ashtrays at her feet, cans and empty bottles littering the carpet, me with a bin liner trying to clear the debris from around her), and feigned total surprise and delight.

'Mrs P,' he exclaimed in his plummy, thrilled voice. He went straight over to plant kisses on her right cheek, then left, then right again. 'To what do we owe this uncommon pleasure?' he asked, squeezing her hand, looking into her eyes.

Mother melting now, batting her lids. 'Andrew, please, call me Jennifer. I shan't tell you again.'

'Jennifer. Of course. But look at this mess. This place is all "aftermath", I'm afraid.'

'I know, boys will be boys . . . and I suppose I should have rung.'

'Don't be silly. All the best people act on impulse, there's firm evidence for it, isn't there, Tris?'

He'd had a hasty shave. I could see where he'd nicked himself with the razor below his jawline. He'd splashed on expensive Eau de Cologne that a girl he'd been fucking had brought him back from France. He was flirting shamelessly with Mother to mollify her and take the heat off me. He was brilliant.

It's all distant now. I don't see Mother any more. That's something I could thank Andy for, I suppose, but there were things about Becca that reminded me of her. For instance, Mother could be arch and machinating while appearing child-like and foolish at the same time; a caricature of villainy in one moment, fawning and sickly the next. Then, unlike Becca, Mother was vain to the point of narcissism (I saw her at her dressing table pulling the skin back on her face, daubing herself with unguents, sucking her cheeks in), yet she adopted a style that was almost careless; caramel hair piled high with random wisps curling at her neck, each item of clothing chosen to produce a wanton, upper-class country girl effect. Perhaps it was only me who saw all this. I shan't deny Mother's classic, long-necked beauty. 'Good breeding stock,' my father always said, and would have said it of Becca simply for the width of her hips and the proportions of her face. 'Horses and women, Tristan, it's all in the measurements.' Good old Dad.

But whereas Mother *was* well-bred, Becca came from common stock. Her accent sounded safe and homely all right, and when she laughed she seemed rum, almost hearty. But those cheery 'Ey up, chucks' belied an innate ferocity. I suspected Becca had an elemental heart. I suspected she could be as fierce and conniving as a starved animal.

'Just a hop. Did ya hear that, Becks? Pads says it's just a hop over to Spain.'

Valerie, Becca's plump, meretricious friend from home, was buckled into the seat beside me. Since I'd met Valerie ('Just call me Val') at the airport I'd regretted giving in to Becca's demands to bring a friend. It was clear Becca was having second thoughts as well.

'Hop my arse,' Val continued. 'Not even a hop, skip and a jump, no! This is Val and Becks swoopin' across the friggin' world. Val and Becks's big adventure.'

'Shurrup, Val.'

'But this is it, Becca. What we've always dreamed of. Shit, you wait till we tell those spastics down Bo Jangles. Fuckin' Spain. They won't fuckin' believe it.'

'Val! Shurrup.'

Val had been prepared for foreign travel. She'd had her passport ready. Her future, built on Becca's disposable drunken plans – grape picking in France, au pairing in Italy – was taking shape. Every *ping* of the 'No Smoking' signs, every cabin crew announcement, every unexpected loss of altitude, every air vent, button and overhead light elicited squeals of over-excitement. So by the time we landed in Malaga Becca had the wild look of a woman barely restraining herself from violence. It didn't help when I took Becca to one side and hissed, 'Your friend's too loud, Rebecca. Sort it out.'

Later that night, I heard the whining cadences of female recrimination and counter-attack coming from the room next door. Their argument was followed by a spongy silence during which I went to the lobby to make a couple of calls. On the way back to my room I hesitated outside the girls' door. I couldn't hear anything so I knocked lightly until Becca called, 'It's open,' in a soft sing-song voice.

I put my head and one arm round the door and saw she was reading, sprawled on her belly across her bed while Val slept lumpen on the other twin. I beckoned Becca out and she got up obediently and followed me to my room.

'At bloody last, I know where our target is,' I announced, emptying my pockets onto my bed as I spoke. Coins, a soft pack of cigarettes, passport, penknife, a roll of pesetas, a single Durex, all made their small impression on the cotton sheet. 'I've just been on the phone to England.'

'Great,' she replied, her eyes glimpsing the Durex then fixing back on me. 'It's always good to know where your target is.'

I raised my eyebrows. 'The guys, I mean, I know where to find them. We'll head off there tomorrow. I know the town they're staying in. It's only a small place so they shouldn't be too hard to find. We could be back in England by Wednesday.'

'Wow . . . brilliant.'

I pretended not to notice her mock enthusiasm. 'You and Val have got things sorted between yourselves, I presume.'

'Yep.'

'I heard you arguing.'

'Who didn't?'

'She's a loose cannon, Becca. I hope you haven't told her anything about India.'

'Nope.'

'Good.'

Becca was wearing a dark purple vest top with narrow straps and no bra. I noticed the material stretched taut across her breasts and the vague outdent her nipples made. She stood by the window, barefoot in denim shorts, hands in pockets, her weight on one leg, the other foot drawing an invisible line on the ground in front of her. Her stance was churlish, recalcitrant, but in her shorts and her vest she looked punishingly nubile – and winnable. I felt my sphincter clench automatically.

'God, it's so fucking hot,' I declared, offhand. 'These clothes are sticking to me. Hope you don't mind.' I started to undress.

Becca looked up. Her eyes widened for a second before her expression recovered its usual studied insouciance. 'No, yeah, it's boiling,' she agreed.

I continued to remove my trousers and shirt. I took off my boxers, my watch, until I was totally naked. 'Wait till India, Becca.' I laughed, turning towards her. 'The heat there will blow your mind.'

'I've heard it's *almost* unbearable.'

I took a step towards her. 'It's utter torment.'

Her gaze was on my face and she was shaking very slightly so that the fine hairs on her cheeks appeared to shiver. I could feel each expiration from her nostrils. I could see a chickenpox scar embedded in her right eyebrow, a red thread capillary snaking across the white of her eye. Her pupils covering the crystal ridges of her irises, sucking in the light. We were both wide awake. These moments are what it means to be alive, I thought.

'I'm gonna take a shower,' I said.

She swallowed. 'OK.'

I stood under the water letting the jets rinse away the sweat of the day, laughing inwardly at the discomfort my unexpected nakedness had caused her. I wondered if it had troubled her enough to send her packing to her room. If she stayed, I thought, it meant I could have her if I wanted. If she left it meant she intended to wield her power – such as it was. I couldn't resist observing her next move so I left the shower running and tiptoed to the door to spy on her. She was sitting on the bed holding the roll of pesetas I'd thrown there, flicking through them, making a rough count. Then she placed the roll carefully back where it had been, picked up the Durex, turned it over in her fingers and put it down again. Then she had my passport. Shit. She studied the first page carefully, occasionally glancing over to where I watched, hidden behind the bathroom door. I tiptoed back to the shower and turned it off before walking back into the room towelling my dreads.

Becca was already pouring wine into glasses. The thrill of subterfuge seemed to have stimulated her and I, in turn, was excited by her courage just as I had been when I first met her in Manchester. We sat together on the bed quaffing the wine in easy gulps and talking. I told her that my plan was for her and Val to follow Jez and Bas into a restaurant or bar where they would flirt, get the boys drunk and inveigle their way into their room. I made it clear that an invitation would almost definitely be on the pretext of having sex.

Becca said, 'Yeah, like they'd ask us back for any other reason.' Then she patted my knee and said she could 'handle' herself, which I took to mean that she was prepared for whatever the situation called for.

I opened my wallet and took out a wrap of ketamine.

'Half of this wrap in a drink will render a man useless. It'll take fifteen minutes to work but don't spike them in the bar otherwise they'll start falling about before you get to their room. If you can't slip the K safely in their drinks tell them you've got some coke. If they snort it, it'll have the same effect except it'll only take five minutes to work – but you'll need to get them to have a good healthy line. Just don't snort any yourselves.'

'Obviously.'

'You know how to snort coke?'

'Same as speed?'

'Same as speed. You'll have twenty minutes to search the room before they know what's going on. You're looking for a package this big.' I made the shape with my hands. 'Check it, then grab it and run. Don't wait for them to recover.'

'They will wake up, won't they?'

'They won't be unconscious, just out of it. It's ketamine, not poison. It's safe. It's pharmaceutical.'

'Where the fuck do you get this stuff?' she asked, inspecting the wrap, then lifting it to her nose and sniffing.

'India. You can buy it over the counter there.'

'No way.'

'Seriously.'

'So . . . how do I know if I've got the right package? I mean, what the fuck's in it to warrant all this *sneaky* stuff?'

'Becca.'

'Yeah.'

'I *can* trust you, can't I?'

'Of course you can.'

'I don't want to say this . . .' I paused for effect '. . . but your life won't be worth living if you betray me.' I put my hand on her thigh, my thumb just brushing the hot flesh leading between her legs.

She didn't flinch.

'You understand I have to say this,' I continued. 'It's not personal.'

'Yeah, I understand,' she said, shifting so I was forced to take my hand away. 'So what's in the package?'

I held my hands in prayer in front of my lips so that my index fingers nipped the base of my septum. 'You're persistent, I like that.' I smiled. 'You could be a secret agent, or a spy.'

'When I was little I used to pretend I was a Bond girl. I'd be one of them that works for the KGB, you know, a baddie. I'd kill James Bond with me karate chop and run away to Russia.'

She lay back on her elbows, licking her front teeth and eyeing me playfully. 'Look,' she said, serious again. 'I still have to know what's in the package else I can't be sure I've stolen the right thing, now can I?'

The sheer speed of her emotional reactions impressed me. 'You *should* know, I suppose.' I sighed, giving in. 'It's money . . . dollars to be precise. But not real dollars.'

She shook her head. 'You what?'

'They're fake dollars.'

'We're stealing *fake* money?'

'It's difficult to explain,' I said.

'How many dollars are there then?'

'Now that's *not* your business, Becca.'

She paused thoughtfully, twisting a strand of hair around her finger. 'Fine,' she said at last, sitting up. 'Well, I should get some sleep, unless there's owt else.'

'Hold on.' I stretched down and conjured a bottle of brandy from my bag. 'Night cap?'

She pretended to consider my offer, stroking her lips provocatively with her fingertips. 'Hmm,' she pouted, then capitulated. 'Oh well . . . go on then.'

How does sex happen? It begins with an imperceptible sign perhaps, or a small encroachment into another's space that they don't eschew. Maybe they cast their eyes down in response to a sensual look rather than rolling back confident and careless. You notice their breath quicken, perhaps there are small waves of attack and retreat that build . . . and build then surge until . . . an awkward stand-off . . . or a kiss. It can go any way you like after the kiss. The list is as long as human experience.

Sex with Becca was like a game of chess, politic, analytic at first, then robust and a little bit ruthless. She had to be dominated or she'd have got the better of me, so I found myself interrogating her. I couldn't help it. 'Do you like that? Eh? Is that what you want? Yeah? Deep in there, yeah?' She didn't answer. They weren't real questions.

Afterwards, lying under the fan smoking a spliff, I told her all about Andy. I didn't mention his name, but I told her that he'd betrayed me. 'Loyalty reduced to doormat status,' I said. I liked that line. 'He has to be taught a lesson and stealing the dollars will even out the scores.'

I let my guard down with that girl.

I was worried that the boys might be lying low, but the waiter in the Europa café nodded and pointed out their guesthouse as soon as I gave him their description: big black English guy, little neo-Nazi sidekick. What was Andy thinking? I kept watch on them round the clock after that and followed them whenever I could. Jez was problematic. Despite a snail's IQ, his antennae were up and he knew someone was on to them. He kept checking in the wing mirrors when they were driving and studying the street from his balcony. More than once I had to pull Becca into a clinch, pretending we were a couple as Jez's eyes swept over us from above. Finally, three nights later, I orchestrated the scenario I'd been hoping for.

It was an oppressive summer's day, and only the tourists had braved the sun's ferocity, wandering blindly round the stalls down by the waterfront or cowering under their sun umbrellas. Now it was late evening and the streets were full of tourists and locals taking advantage of an insistent breeze coming off the tepid sea. It wafted through the narrow streets where men and women turned their faces into it to better feel its touch. They closed their eyes and smelled the scent it carried; scorched sand and salt and Africa.

At around eleven p.m. Jez and Bas left their guesthouse and headed into the centre of town. They stood awkwardly on the street corner for a while until Bas put his hands on Jez's shoulders. Jez bowed his head so his chin was on his chest. Bas was talking to him, coaxing him. The tableau was comradely and I was desperate to hear what Bas was saying. Then Bas gave Jez's shoulder a friendly shake and they walked a little further down the road and went into a small bar. The place had a couple of chairs on the cobbles out the front and a neon sign in the window that flashed pink, *Tupelo Honey*, then blue, *Cocktails*. Becca and Val, looking sleazy in their short skirts and plunging tops, followed them in a few minutes later. Val was one of those lardy, undignified girls who, after a couple of drinks, becomes bawdy and shrill. The lads would compete for Becca – there was no question. To the loser a beery night of vast flesh and dangling breasts. To the winner – Becca. The thought gave me a slight pain in my chest as I recalled a snapshot of her, lithe and naked, from the night before.

They left the bar in a foursome an hour later and I followed them to the seafront at a distance. Val was already pissed, her skirt riding up on her hips, singing 'Moondance', burping and laughing. Jez looked nervous. Becca was leading Basil by the nose as I had hoped and they sat on the sand with Basil pointing at the moon and whispering things in Becca's ear while she giggled and accommodated his advances. After a while they left the beach. Jez first, Val following, Becca and Bas bringing up the rear. The streets were still full so it was easy to follow without being noticed. They paused outside the entrance to the guesthouse while Basil and Jez fell into deep discussion. For several minutes the foursome stood in an ellipse of cold white light cast by the lamp above the door. It silvered their hair and made them all appear old and heavy browed. Jez looked especially burdened, shaking his head wearily as Basil quietly cajoled. Then Becca sidled up to Basil and ran her hand from his buttock down his thigh. No one else saw her do this, but it prompted Basil to say something definitive to Jez and suddenly they were all spilling into the foyer leaving the oval of light like actors exiting a spot-lit stage.

I waited outside for three hours until the sun rose to make a vivid orange and pewter sky. The town's early risers had started to filter onto the streets with the dawn, but Becca and Val finally emerged into more muted apricot tones that made peaches of their cheeks even though they looked rough and ruffled.

Becca groaned and slumped her shoulders when she saw me. 'We're right tired, Pads, just let us go and get some sleep.'

'The package?'

'Didn't get it, all right.'

'But it's up there. Is it there?'

Becca shook her head. She was defeated. In my room she threw the untouched ketamine wrap onto the coverlet, then lay on her back smoking a cigarette in deep drags. Eventually I said, 'Well?'

'The whole thing fucked up, OK.'

'I need more than that.'

She rolled her eyes. 'All right, all right. First, that Jez, that little one, well, he's soft in the head, right, take it from me. He's off his fuckin' nut. I swear he was hallucinatin', doing this –' She sat up and did an impression of Jez with wide, shifty eyes, then slumped back down again. 'Y'know, like he could see stuff runnin' round the room. Anyway, he

163

wasn't capable of a wank let alone getting frisky with Val. He got me up against the wall in the toilet, mind. He told me I was a friggin' greyhound or sommat. I don't know. I had to fight him off. Then Basil comes in and goes, "Sorry bout 'im. He's not been well." So I says to meself, right, get this ketamine stuff down 'em, get that package and gerrout of here.'

Becca waited several moments before continuing. 'Anyway, that Jez one isn't drinkin' by the time we get in the room, not even water. Bang goes spiking the drinks. So it's time for Plan B. I says, "Anyone up for a line of coke?" like you said and Bas goes, "Mi don't touch nah chemical," and gives me this pathetic look like I'm an addict or summat. So I shrug and say, "Each to their own." Then he tells me he won't let Jez have none neither, him not bein' well and all. Course then Val wants some and I haven't told her it's a fuckin' Mickey Finn, her bein' so crap and everythin', so she starts hassling me like mad for some till I goes, "Leave off, Val." She's pissed as arseholes. Then she passes out.'

'What?'

Becca gets up on her elbows again. 'Passes out in the bog. Well, she throws up about three times first, but yeah, totally poleaxed, skirt up round 'er waist showing off her fanny and everything.'

'Shit!'

'So then Bas makes a bed for her on't floor and I'm sayin', "No, I'm just gonna take 'er home, like, cos she's not right well," and he says, "Mi carry her back a your hotel," and I think, Fuckinell, this is a bit too close for comfort. So I says, "No no no, you can't move her now," and all a that, besides, "Let her sleep it off." And he goes, "All right then, we can have a *lickle chat*." Well, I know what he means by *that* cos it's not as if I've been Miss Prim'n'Proper all evenin', have I? I've fair led him on like you told me.

'So he goes off to the bog and I manage to get a good look round the room for bags and hiding places and stuff. I've already checked the loo, I've checked under the beds and I've checked the wardrobe, don't even ask me how I did it cos that nutter Jez was just starin' at me loads. Anyway I found nothin'. Not a sausage. It's all too fucked up, Pads.'

'It *has* to be in there.'

'Well, if it is I couldn't find it.'

'You were in there for three hours.'

'Tell me about it.'

'So, did you . . . ?'

'What?'

'You know . . .'

'What?'

'Have sex with Basil.'

Becca's shoulders drooped, exasperated. 'I don't think that's any a *your* business, Pads. But I'll tell you what, he's all right that Basil. I mean, he's a good guy.'

'So?'

'So if he's a good guy what does that make us?'

I had to laugh. 'As if you care, Rebecca my dear.' I did my Clark Gable voice, but I don't think she got it.

Becca and Val's lopsided friendship started in primary school. Lesser girls were drawn to Becca in the hope that her lustre would reflect onto them and Val was no exception; she was simply happy that she had been chosen over all the others to play the passenger to Becca's fearless driver, so she could sit back and vicariously experience the rush. Boys, parties, drugs, clubs and kudos – all these would have been hopelessly out of reach for Val, but because of Becca they fell into her lap and for that she was grateful and loyal. But after their fruitless night at Jez and Bas's guesthouse, Val refused to go along with any more plans to entice the lads despite Becca's threats and entreaties.

'I'm not gonna shag that mental case for anyone,' she told Becca. 'Certainly not for Pads. Not even for you.'

Becca was ambivalent. When I asked her what drew her to Val, who was obviously her inferior, Becca said, 'Everyone knows why lookers hang round wit' skanky ones, don't they?' When I nodded, she said, 'JOKE!' and rolled her eyes. Then she went on, more gravely, that Val was a good sort and they'd ended up sharing their deepest secrets for a while, but that no one could expect loyalty to last a lifetime. Then she whispered, conspiratorially, that I should know that better than anybody. Worms turn, et cetera, et cetera. That's precisely what she said.

In the subsequent days Val took to sulking for hours in the hotel room before heading for the beach to roast with the hordes. Becca drove around with me as I tried to keep up with Jez and Bas's movements. I was looking for the right opportunity to search their car as I was now convinced that the dollars were hidden there. I remembered Andy telling me it was one of Basil's specialities. He'd worked for the Brown brothers in the 1970s driving kilos of hash around the country stashed in the engines of family saloons. I had underestimated Basil and from what I now observed he was managing to change those greenbacks into hard cash single-handedly. He couldn't get away with it for long. It would only be another week before the banks compared notes and realized a laundering scam was going down on the Costa. Then all the banks and bureaux would be on red alert and bang, he'd be nabbed. I surmised he'd risk a couple of big-money changes before bailing out and going back to England. In the meantime, I'd watch and wait and when they left the car unattended I would break in, take the dollars and leave them and Andy high and dry.

Eventually, on another blistering day, the opportunity presented itself. Becca and I had followed them from Nerja, driving behind them on the main road into Malaga, hanging two or three cars back so that Basil and the beady-eyed Jez wouldn't spot us in the rearview. They soon turned off down a narrow lane that led to a quiet coastal village. I looked at the map. There was only one road that led in and out. On either side of the lane, low, dry-stone walls corralled desolate fields of flat, parched grassland, accented here and there by cypresses and ancient olives. It was a sparse landscape that allowed us to see Jez and Bas's progress from where we waited up on the main road, wet with sweat since the BMW's air-conditioning had finally given out. After ten minutes we followed, deducing, since there was no sign of their car's return journey, that they had parked up in the village. We found the Peugeot on the shady side of the church. Jez and Bas were nowhere to be seen, but I recognized Jez's daypack on the back seat and a lighter I'd seen Basil use in the coinwell by the gear stick. It only took a minute to break in but my heart was pounding and my body dripping as I scoured the car, while Becca kept watch at the corner of the road that led to the heart of the village. Becca, I noticed, had a quickness about her, in the way she moved her head, looking agitatedly from me to where the guys might appear from any minute. I searched the glove box, under the seats, in the boot. Nothing.

There's a spark that ignites dry tinder or a switch that's flicked, or a final straw that snaps and pushes people to hysteria . . . sometimes. Not like madness or anything, but a thing that makes their sense unhinge momentarily. For some the trigger is an insult, about their mother's honour perhaps, or their sexual prowess. Words have never done it to me, but frustration with something that's out of my control – now that's my Achilles heel, all right. I know I became hysterical with anger searching that car. It was beyond rationality. If I'd had a knife I'd have sliced the seats and ripped the stuffing from them. Andy, the dollars, the whole revenge thing, it was urging me to do things I wasn't comfortable with. Revealing my identity to a runner, for God's sake, risking exposure to Jez and Bas. And yet I felt compelled, forced. Those miserable dollars had to be somewhere. They had to be under the hood and I knew that was the next place I must search but suddenly, incomprehensibly, I became exhausted. I could have lain on the back seat and fallen asleep. The whole situation had leached every vestige of energy from me. Cowardice, that's what it was. It happened to men in the war, my father said. The spineless ones curled up in ditches and whimpered, made impotent by fear. It took every ounce of strength to roll out of the back seat, pin the note to the windscreen with the wiper blade and limp back to the BMW, calling to Becca that we had to go . . . NOW.

The note I had prepared in my hotel room the night before was written out in a tall, printed hand. My intention was to thumb my nose if I found the dollars, or induce paranoia and trepidation if I did not. We had only just got back in the BMW when we spotted the lads further down the road. Basil was supporting Jez, whose arm was slung across Basil's shoulder. Jez's other hand grasped his chest as if he'd been shot or had a cardiac arrest. It was a pathetic sight and I felt confident my note would nail down the coffin of their failure. Nevertheless, as we drove away, it felt as if death's scythe was grazing my arse while Becca curled in the footwell on the passenger side going, 'Fuck fuck fuck fuck.'

Back in Manchester the rain came down in diagonal stripes, stencilling a harsh greyness onto everything. The same afternoon I packed a dejected Becca and Val off to Burnley on the train. I recognized my behaviour had begun to manifest the mania of obsession and the girls had become suspicious of me because of it. I'd overheard them in their room on the penultimate night in Spain.

'I can't handle him, Becks, he's a freak a nature. Let's just fuck off and leave the mad bastard.'

'Sshhh, shurrup, Val, just shurrup,' Becca had hissed before they fell silent.

12

MEHMET

Besa

Jules had been to visit the mediator on the day my life changed its course for ever. He had heard that his *fis* was accused of the murder of my brothers, so he went to our commune's intermediary with his father, his brother and Aisha. The mediator was a pernicious man who had his vulpine jaws clamped round every part of village life. But Jules had a way with officials, it turned out. He offered representatives of my family the freedom to search the Geci farm for evidence of the allegations. This was an unusual offer, but Jules insisted. He and his father had returned from Gjirokastër only the week before. They had been there on 'official business', he could prove this, and so he had no fear of what my family would find, for many reasons . . . I will explain.

The intermediary came to my house, with an entourage of visitors, to describe this evidence to me. But I was not there. I was waiting on the ledge above the Geci farm with Gabriel. After a private conversation with the mediator it was my uncle who accepted the 'proof' on my behalf and made Ismail retract his allegations.

'It was all a mistake,' said Ismail. He was sure he had

seen Jules with Rafiq's rifle, but he knew now that it could not be true.

So Jules and Aisha were cautious, but happy they had averted more bloodletting. Their father went back to Gjirokastër with their brother, and they rode to the farm discussing the events of the day. They met another of their *fis* along the road and invited him to take their hospitality. He told them the army had caught and executed a group of Serbs up in the mountains. He said the soldiers found all manner of booty at their encampment.

'Aye, it was the Serbs that killed those boys,' he had stated like a fact.

'We can't be sure,' Jules had replied.

So when the riders came into the courtyard it was fortunate my aim was lacking. The flood of energy a man feels before a fight will often convince him he is more skilful than he is and although I grazed their relative's ear and brought him from his mule he was otherwise unharmed. Anyway, he was not my target. And Gabriel? Gabriel must have hidden in the woods, or heard the shot and doubled back, petrified that he would lose another brother.

I see Gabriel in my mind, looking through the forest, watching Jules and me zigzagging in the half-light. He cannot cry out lest we fire on him by mistake. So he waits quietly, hiding, to see what will unfold. He is *so* afraid. He is no hunter.

Ech, you know, I cannot vouch for his thoughts. I knew my brothers at the cloudy edge of their childhood and of mine. Without adult reason, without chronology, without a sense of who we were apart from in relation to each other. And Gabriel, sweet Gabriel, I knew him for one day . . . and then I killed him.

The Gecis took me to their home the night it happened and sent for my family to collect me. I was feverish, insane, like the idiots you see chained up in the town when their minds have left them. They rant and gibber and spit and plead and cry. I remember little except that I was torn apart with shame. My uncle collected me and I regained my reason some days later, in *his* house. Ismail came to taunt me every day.

'Your mother cannot bear to look on you for disgust,' were the first words I remember. 'She blames you for all of them, you know.'

I decided Ismail was too bony to be my real family, with his hollow eyes and thin, ridged nose that rose sharp from tawny skin like a Turk or a Persian. He hunched his shoulders forward as he crept around the room. I hated him.

'She says you make Rafiq and Razlan go to the mountain. That you are too lazy to pasture the sheep yourself,' he goaded.

'It's not true.'

'She says you forced your father to make a journey he was too sick to take.'

'No.'

'And Gabriel . . . Ah Mehmet, surely you will not defend yourself about your brother?'

I tried to answer but could not.

All this Ismail said in a whisper, like a demon on my shoulder, so no one else could hear him, and he laughed as I tried to call upon some buried strength to fight him. My weakness was intolerable. But when the other members of my *fis* were in the room I could see in their eyes that they despised me also and so I believed Ismail when he said my mother blamed me and only me. I believed him to be harsh but true.

When I recovered enough to walk, I secretly left my uncle's house and went home, but there was no one there. I took some things, some food, some clothes, and I left what little money I had saved on the table for my mother. I have no *fis* now, I thought. No one to turn to. So I did something a man should never do. I asked my rival, Jules Geci, to help me. Why did I do this? Why did I go against the *Kanuni*? Why did I risk everything? Because I lost my faith and in so doing knew that everything was possible. That there was no use in rules and *fis* and *Kanuni* and *besa* – what do the Americans say? 'All is fair in love and war,' or is it that nothing is fair? I would have to make my own justice, punish myself and prove myself. This is *not* the Albanian way.

I went to the Geci farm. I took the same route through the forest that I took with Gabriel and I lived the day again, you understand?

The conversation with my brother seemed to echo there beside me and I fancied I saw another Mehmet and another Gabriel a way off through the tree trunks. I stopped and squinted my eyes, moving from this side to that, to piece together the picture cut into stripes by the beech wood.

Sometimes I think the forest holds the memory of every-thing that happens in it and plays it back, like in a movie theatre. This movie hurt my head so I moved forward. And this time I did not skirt around to the cliff and up onto the ledge. I walked straight into the Geci courtyard with mastiffs snapping and drooling round my legs and I stood there in the heat of the day and shouted, 'Hello, please, I ask for your *besa*.'

I was pathetic.

Jules comes out from the house in boots and breeches, in the old style, and with a white shirt open to his waist.

'Mehmet.' He nods, framed in the doorway. 'I will offer you my *besa*.'

I knew he would.

I walk towards him and I know he waits for me to speak, but I cannot.

'You are well again?' he says at last.

'No.'

'But you are recovered?'

I smile sadly and dismiss the question with my hand. 'I am here to ask something of you.'

'Then you must come in,' and he stands to one side and extends his arm for me to come across his threshold. Inside there is a fire in the hearth with Jules's mother bent across it attending several pans. When she sees me she makes a sound like an angry cockerel and touches her head with both hands several times as if checking that her skull remains intact. Then she spins around the room and leaves. My presence has undermined the rules that hold her world together, I think.

'She's a loyal person,' says Jules by way of explanation.

It is unusual to hear a man speak out in praise of a woman and I think of my mother and our contempt for her desperation to protect us with her beads and amulets.

Jules puts his head on one side. 'What is it that you need to ask me, Mehmet?'

Still I cannot speak. I do not know how to begin and feel I am a simpleton tugging on my *xhup* in my enemy's kitchen, moving my weight from one foot to another.

'My, my, my shame . . . it is complete,' I stutter.

'I understand. But I think you acted faithfully.'

I touch my temple, for an ache has returned there. 'Faith is nothing if it is based on falsehood.'

'I agree, but mistakes are made by all men.'

I close my eyes tight against a shooting pain. '"Mistakes", you say. This monstrosity cannot be described with so trifling a word.'

Jules nods slowly and goes to tend the hearth, where a pot is beginning to splutter onto the fire making the embers spit and sizzle.

'This is hard for me to say,' he begins, poking in the new flames caressing the bottom of the pots. 'But I believe we were betrayed.'

'What? What do you mean? Who by?'

He is about to answer when Aisha skips into the room, innocent of my presence. She has been out with the goats and chickens, for she has the smell of animals about her, but she has removed her headscarf and there is a breeze of wild flowers in her hair. In one hand she holds a basket, full with speckled eggs, while in the other milk slops across the top of a brightly coloured bucket. When she sees me the smile she is wearing falls onto the floor and she casts her head down and turns to leave. But Jules asks softly, 'Stay with us, sister?' and Aisha rewards him with an obedient gaze. Then she nods, demure, and takes his place tending the fire.

Jules sighs deeply. 'I will tell you the truth now, Mehmet . . . I believe I *do* have your brother's gun.'

I am dumbfounded, but no anger grips my stomach for I am sure of his innocence and I indicate for him to explain this further.

'The day before . . . *the day* . . .' he pauses and all three of us exchange a look that says he will not say my brother's name or what happened in the forest. 'The day before you *came* I was chopping wood, over by the stable, when I saw a figure at the edge of the wood. I am wary of strangers like all men are, and I went inside casually, so it was not obvious I had seen him, to spy on him from the window and watch what he would do. I told the women to stay inside and for a long time there was nothing, no movement, so I thought maybe I am wrong and it is not a man but only children from the village playing tricks. But then I saw him once again, moving like a cat at the perimeter, over there. The man was furtive and I knew he had come to do no good for he was carrying a gun, but then every man and boy carries a gun.

'So I said to myself he is a thief perhaps, a gypsy. But then he slipped into the courtyard and turned inside the grain store. Even a thief knows there is nothing to steal inside the grain store, well, apart from grain,' and Jules shrugs and holds his hands out. 'So I decided he must be hungry, or stupid . . . or come to ruin our food.'

'So you went to confront him?'

'No. But I did go to watch what he would do. I ran across the yard and climbed up on the wall behind the store to watch him through the air vent on the back wall.'

'What did you see?'

'Nothing, there was much to obscure my view. But I could hear him pushing around in the corn so I climbed down and went to the corner and waited for him to come out, hoping he didn't have a lookout ready to make a signal. I was listening for noises from the wood, but there were none. Then he left and slithered round the outbuildings, like he was a *djinn,* before disappearing into the forest.'

Jules stops and breathes deeply. He is telling the story without much pause and staring at me with a look that says I should understand everything. But I do not.

'It makes no sense,' I say.

Jules leans across the table. 'When he was gone two things impressed themselves upon my mind. One, he no longer carried his gun . . . and two, I thought I might know this man.'

At once I understand. Jules has been set up: Rafiq's gun planted on his property so I would have my proof to kill him. I didn't even need the proof; I was too stupid to check what was true or what was right.

'Who was it?' I say with fire in my heart. 'Who put Rafiq's gun in your grain store?'

'I will not tell you because I do not know it for certain. And of course I am not sure it is Rafiq's gun. I only suppose this to be true.'

I am angry and brutal and I stand like a fighter with my legs apart and my hands on my hips, threatening. 'Tell me,

Jules, or by Allah I will wring it from you.' And I feel my chin jutting forward and the heat in my body.

'Mehmet Lucca, remember you have my *besa*. And surely you have had enough of blood and retribution? For I can tell you this – I am sick of all of it. Sick of the commune, sick of Hoxha, sick of the cold hearts of our fathers, sick of innocent people violated in their homes . . .'

Aisha stands and goes to soothe her brother, whose chest has expanded, whose fist has come down hard upon the table so the eggs rattle in their basket. His anger is as hungry as my own.

'My brother is not a violent man,' Aisha offers.

'Some call me a coward,' adds Jules with moisture in his eyes.

'He expects change,' she explains gently.

'I demand change.'

I laugh. 'Change? I don't understand you.'

'I think you do.'

'We are farmers, Geci, not revolutionaries.'

'Perhaps we are both.' He sighs. 'Ah, perhaps it does not even matter. But I promise I will discover the roots of this mystery where your brothers are concerned. If I was meant to take the blame for their deaths then I need to know why. Will you help me, Mehmet?'

'It is I who came to you for help.'

'Then the answer is yes.'

'The answer is *no*. I did not come to ask you to find my brothers' killer. I need another kind of help.'

'Just ask.'

I hesitate and look at brother and sister in turn before I speak. 'I *must* leave Albania,' I whisper.

Jules sits down, defeated, and pulls his palm across his face with one slow downward movement until his hand holds his chin. 'And they call me a coward,' he says, resigned; not malicious, but it cuts me.

'Yes, I am a coward. Too scared to climb into the mountains and wait for the wolves to make a meal of me,' I cry.

'How can you think to sacrifice your life when you are your family's only protector?' Aisha gasps.

'I told you, I am a coward.'

'You don't make sense,' she says. 'Are you a coward for living or for dying?'

I look at Jules. 'Help me leave Albania,' I plead.

'What good will come of it?'

'I can send money to my mother. I can try to understand my brothers' deaths.'

'I have heard your uncle means to be the leader of your *fis*.'

'Ech, let him lead.'

'He will take your house.'

'I care not.'

'But if you go, what will become of your mother and your sisters?'

'I told you, I will provide for them.'

'And if your uncle throws them on the street?'

'He would never.'

'But if he does, who will stop him?'

'You.'

'No, not I, I told you. I have had enough of feuding.'

'Then you will not help me at all?'

It is Jules's turn to hesitate. He lowers his eyes. 'Yes, yes, I will help you, Mehmet . . .'

'Jules!' Aisha cries and throws her brother a look with acid in it.

My father would have struck my mother for less. But Jules puts his hand on his sister's arm. 'But you must understand the consequences if you leave, my friend,' he warns.

'I will make a new life . . . in England or America. I will be a rich man, you wait. I will make my family proud of me again. But I cannot do that here with sheep and chickens and Hoxha's hand around my throat. I have heard there is money on the streets in London, lying there for anyone to pick up.'

'I am not sure of these stories,' Jules says.

'It is the only way.'

'What if you fail?'

'I will *not* fail.'

Jules taps the table lightly with his middle finger, thinking. 'It will not be easy,' he says at last. 'It is harder to get out than to come in, I think.'

'But you have contacts in the party.'

'My father has one or two.' He shakes his head. 'But this does not guarantee your exit.'

'But you will try.'

'Yes, Mehmet.' He sighs. 'I will try.'

13

JEZ

A Fistful of Dollars

OK, don't laugh, but everything turns into a spaghetti western. You'll have to go with me here cos that's how I remember it. Me and Bas are starring in *A Fistful of Dollars*, only we're driving a car not riding horses, and then later we're actually on horses. It's all mixed up. I wanna be Joe but I'm not sure if I am and the heat is fierce, shit, it's one hundred and ten degrees, and even the locals are feeling the stress, pulling their sombreros low so we can't see their faces. We pull up hard on our reins and turn the horses round so they make that whinnying sound and we can see foamy sweat bubbling on their necks. We're gonna head for Marbella, or is it Almeria? We ride for hours and hours till the morning's gone, till we realize that here the earth is cracked and the whole world's empty as a desert. We're trying to find a place to have a beer and shake off the bad vibe we're feeling, but the journey never seems to end. I spot some riders way behind us. They're only bitty little dots on the horizon but they mean trouble. I know a posse when I see one, so we dig our heels in and ride like fucking luna-tics, till our throats are full of sand and the grit stings our eyes. It's like a fucking miracle when we find this village.

Man, I'm trembling; look at me.

The village is deserted. The feel of the heat and the scorched smell of the streets and the sound of crickets, *pirrip, pirrip*, are filling me head to bursting. There's no frigging people in this village, not one. Something's going down, I can feel it in me water. I say to Bas that the decent people are too scared to come out of their houses. They must have seen the dust our horses were hoofing up, they must've snatched their kiddies from beside the kerb where they'd been playing games in the dirt, then they must've locked down their shutters, CLACK CLACK KERCHUNK. Now whole families are hiding under their kitchen tables, squeezing each other's hands, waiting for the danger to pass. Waiting for the showdown. I look around, expecting Clint Eastwood to come sauntering down the road with the stump of a cheroot wedged in the corner of his mouth and squinting at us, cracks for eyes, hand hovering beside his holster. Clint's not arrived yet. Clint's not in the scene.

We park the horses by a church that has parched weeds growing from the mortar and old paint mottling the walls. We start walking further into the village, but Basil's agitated cos there's no saloon or nothing. He keeps saying, 'Jos a beer, mon, it's all I aks,' and I do a little *yeehaw* noise to show I agree. The streets are just rows and rows of piddly white houses that all look the same and the heat makes it all look ugly and fat. We can't even sweat cos the moisture just sizzles on our skin. We're desperate to cool off.

Then, like someone announcing that a ghost's arrived, the church bell tolls three times, slowly, slowly, slowly, BONG, BONG, BONG, and just as the echo of the last strike fades (I can see the sound like a wide shimmer in the crushing heat) I catch something out the corner of me eye. Don't ask me to swear who, or what I see because it flies out of view before I make out its true shape, yeah, but there's menace to it. So I point and I say, 'Hey, what's that?' I can feel the words in me throat right now.

Basil's doubtful and he goes, 'What?' like I've got heat stroke or something.

So I says, 'I saw something.'

'Where?'

'There, man, he just dodged behind that building.'

I say 'he' cos Basil's looking at me funny. I'm thinking, I don't want to rot in this desert.

'Mi cyaan see nothin',' says Bas.

So I run on ahead and make him follow me, calling, 'Come on, man, quick, this way.'

I can hear music. Whistles and whip cracks and a lone trumpet wailing out, mournful as fuck.

'What's that?' I say. 'Can you hear that?'

Basil shakes his head. He's worried that I'm off me trolley, I can tell. I run towards the corner where I saw the 'man' and look back over me shoulder: Basil's looking testy but breaking into a jog. I go round the bend and I'm on a wide main street and up ahead I see him. He's real. The man I've been chasing. He's got his back to me.

'Hey you, fuckin' hold up there,' I shout. Then, 'Quick, man, I have him,' back at Bas.

Basil's stopped running. He's standing in the middle of the road, legs apart, arms by his sides like a gunslinger. He's staring right at me and I turn to face him. The man I was chasing fades to nothing, just like that, like he's been beamed up. Now I understand. It's Basil I must fight. But he's miles away like he's been sucked back down this long old road that stretches on for a hundred miles and for a moment he's the teensiest speck in the distance. Lost in time. It's OK, though. My eyes are like telescopes and suddenly I focus and I can see the tiniest movements of Basil's body as if I'm close enough to kiss him.

There's a shine on his face. I can see touches of yellow

colouring the whites of his eyes, the oil in his thick black eyebrows. He's primed all right. He's ready to go. His finger twitches above the trigger of his gun. I knew it. That fucking nigger'll have me if he can. Man! I'm swallowing my beating heart back down. Burn, you fucking heart, burn in bile and stomach acid, you fucker. I draw my gun without thinking. I'm crazy. Bang bang bang bang . . . bang bang. All six unleashed in a frenzy of sweat and gunpowder. I'm crying as I shoot and I can feel the bile scald my throat. 'I'm no killer,' I scream, falling on me knees. But Basil is still standing. He's far far away, all in black; hat, shirt, skinny-leg trousers. He's Lee van Cleef in ol' Mehico, cooler than a dead man's dick. He snatches his .45 from its holster in one smooth movement and lets one off. Pop. Like a finger pop in your mouth, a comedy sound. The bullet is beautiful and sleek and shined up brighter than a brand new pin. Yes, I can see that bullet coming. I can see it getting bigger, dividing the air in front of it, cutting, slicing, getting bigger, filling me whole vision. It makes a noise like the north wind is sucking inwards, sucking in in in. Me ears pop. It's coming. I can't avoid it. THWUMP. My body accepts metal. It pierces me chest with the sonic punch of a deep bass line and all me vital organs quiver. This is it. This is it.

Then Bas says, 'Rakstone, get up. Get up, dread. Get a grip, for God's sake.'

I'm shaking. Basil has me by the collar of me shirt. I look down to see how deep the wound is, but I can't see nothing. No blood. I tear me shirt open and run me hands all over me chest. No gory hole to stick me finger in. There's metal in me, though. I can feel it. I can feel that bullet. It's on the move. It's heading for me brain. Yes, of course, of course, where else. Basil is dragging me along, saying, 'Come now, mon,' and at last I'm up, taking jelly steps. I don't know how me legs are working. God knows how I survived that bullet. God knows how long we've been lost in this ghost town. I'm thinking, Praps I'm mad. It feels like my very last thought.

Basil finds the horses, but it's a car and he piles me in. I am foldable, collapsible like an empty cardboard box. I sit flatly in the passenger seat. I can't speak but I can see everything. There is a piece of paper resting under the driver's-side wiper catching the only breeze in the whole fucking village. It looks so lonely flapping there. Basil snatches it in his enormous fingers. It seems too delicate a thing to touch with hands as big and black as his.

Basil takes hours and hours to read the note. The sun rises and sets and still he's standing by the car holding that lonely piece of paper. At last he says, 'Mon, I tek it all back,' and he shakes his huge sad head. He's a big old bear. He's lovable and strong. He doesn't want to show me the note but he shows me anyway. The note says, 'We know where to find you. We are watching you.'

It won't be long before the bullet reaches me brain.

14

MEHMET

Prison of the Mind

Razlan and Rafiq are in the mountains, bathed in a shining light. The vision is golden like the painted ikons my mother used to hide under the floorboards or deep within her skirts. My brothers' hands are outstretched. They are naked, they are pleading, with sunken eyes. Blood seeps from the bandages around their broken skulls. They rebuke me. 'How could you abandon us, Mehmet,' they wail, 'you, our honoured brother and protector?' The lustrous spectres dissolve and Gabriel appears, delicate, fresh as an Illyrian wildflower in the lichen meadows beyond the tree line; his eager face and acolyte's smile pull grief from my core, gasping like a birth.

'Wake up, ya foul gypsy.'

It is Titus's voice that rends me from my dream. Titus is a salty wall-eyed Greek, with hispid skin and yellow moustaches, who runs contraband between the islands and the heel of Italy's tall boot. My moaning has moved him only to frustration. He is hardened to human emotion and I wonder how much depravity he's seen to turn his heart to agate in one lifetime. I ease onto my elbows and scan the faces of my fellow travellers cramped in the bowels of his boat. We are all dishevelled, beyond dirty, beyond afraid. One boy, with soft down on his lip instead of whiskers, is puking like a cat, his body heaving soundlessly in the lamplight. The smell comes sharp and I turn away to try and catch a zest of sea air in my nose. But we are stowed away in foetid wood.

Anything is better than the weeks spent in Saranda, hiding, wishing I could swim, then thanking Allah I could not. At night I watched the searchlights and listened to the sirens as men, like me, took their chances in the water. Sometimes two or three a night would be machine-gunned as they tried to swim across the strait of Corfu. Here the channel narrows to little more than two kilometres. Corfu was freedom and its proximity tempted us, beckoned us, so that, as night fell, the swimmers could not help but strike out, hopeful and desperate. God bless them all. A few made it, but most were drowned in blood and brine.

Eventually Jules fulfilled his promise and I, along with a young artist from Tirana, were ferried across the strait one night by two men in a gunboat. Off-duty soldiers? I did not ask. Two months in Corfu were like a dream but I could not stay. Ech, I cannot think now of the debt I must repay.

Secretly, I reach inside my underpants to feel the outline of my Greek passport and the money Jules has given me. Both are safe, hidden there beside my manhood and my father's knife. I harden my jaw. We have been on the water twenty hours, sometimes moving, with the motor grinding and the waves slapping the hull, and I think the sea is a bully to be cuffing a thing as small as us again and again. For a while we are still while Titus lets us roil in the swell. But then we're on the move again and soon we are docking and the boat disgorges its staggering Jonahs onto a foreign quay. My companions melt into the night; they know where they are going these Kosovans, these Serbs, wary of me and one another. So I am alone. I stand in the shadows for a while, watching Titus unload boxes for a man in uniform. They exchange small packages retrieved from breast pockets and pat one another's shoulders without looking in each other's faces. When the official is gone, Titus stands with one foot firm upon the prow, gathering the ropes back in. He sees me then and shoos me off.

'Which way?' I shout in desperation.

'Do what you know, gypsy . . . wander.' His Albanian is passable, I suppose. But then so is my Greek after two months in their islands.

Leaving Albania – hah, I say it so quickly when it is the hardest thing a man can do – leaving Albania, Albania the fortress, my gulag, a nation-sized labour camp bound on one side by the sea and all others by the armies and the hatred of our neighbours. This is what we learned. Hoxha had us all held fast in his paternal arms and his ideology. Perhaps our comrade father was half right.

In Corfu, Jules and Aisha's friends hid me, clothed me, furnished me with knowledge, taught me to look unmoved instead of gaping and gawking at every car or shop or ostentatious thing. They showed me how to drive. They showed me how to trust, enough, but not too much. I still have much to learn.

In Italy it is different. For three weeks now I forage in this town, sleep on her beaches and in her doorways, using up my meagre finances for food. I am used to hardship, but I can not live this way for long. At least I am warm. With the shopkeepers I pretend I am deaf, or Greek. I do not risk speaking Albanian and soon the *polizia* will stop me and study my face from under their eyebrows and ask for my papers. They will see I am in exile and try to send me home. I do not realize I can have asylum. So with the last of my money I buy food and a map and wear an honest smile so people can see some goodness in my heart and I begin to hitch-hike.

It is an old man who stops for me first and although we have no language together I point to places on my map and he points to others to indicate how far he can convey me. He sets me down an hour later and I begin the process once again. Standing in the russet sun with nothing, waiting, but smelling olives and a tantalizing trace of freedom. And so I weave across the land. Everything I eat is scavenged or begged from the drivers or in the towns. Some take pity but others are contemptuous. So many cars fly by without slowing, pretending I do not exist. Others stop a hundred metres hence and sound their horn, but as I run to accept their generosity they speed away, leaving me in the dust their wheels have made. It is a cruel sport and at times I finger my knife through my trousers and imagine its blade flashing through the rubber of tyres, a fantasy of retaliation that keeps my jaw hard, that keeps me moving. When I see the *polizia* I crash into the undergrowth, or push my hands deep in my pockets, strolling along as if I am a farmboy out for a walk, but saying, 'Drive on by, drive on by,' beneath my breath. I think that if they catch me I will be beaten and deported. I have decided I would rather die.

'*Liria i ka rrënjët në gjak.*' Liberty has its roots in blood, that's what my father told me and I believed him. Now I know that every man is confined by a minuscule reality, a manufactured ethos that pervades everything he does. And how can it be another way? Our beliefs, taboos, ideas of what is possible or acceptable and what is not, all these things we are breastfed from the moment we escape the womb. Yes, we grow in one dark prison and suckle at another, trapped in the bosom of our families. *Gjak* was my prison, but *gjak* could be my liberty too, yes?

Of course, when we are young we do not realize we are incarcerated. Some of us even believe ourselves to be free. We stride around, confident, making choices and decisions that we believe will alter destiny. But most men can no more choose to alter what will *be* than my ragged ewes could choose to avoid slaughter. I hear some people talk of *good* men and *bad* men as if these men decide the stance they take. Our goodness or our evil is handed down state to citizen, leader to led, guru to disciple, father to son, brother to brother. The conceit of some overarching morality or universal right is a myth and it is we who peddle it, because we are all, even our oppressors, the victims of the time, the culture and the circumstances in which we find ourselves.

Now it is late afternoon and I find myself in France. A van has stopped ahead of me, layers of dirt caught in each grey corrugation on its sides. A man opens the door and looks back at me, calling. I think I have seen this van only ten minutes before driving the other way, but then there are so many like this, I cannot tell. I run to the window. It is an older man at the wheel, with drooping eyes and hair that looks too black. He chews a stick that you pick olives with, and he beckons me in the passenger seat with his head.

'Cannes?' I say.

'*Oui, oui,*' he assures me, impatient. Ech, he is in such a hurry.

The van is a Citroën, rickety, with a gear stick he holds like a gun. The back is full of boxes, plain cardboard squares sealed closed with shiny tape.

'*Italiano?*' he asks.

'*Non, Greco,*' I reply. '*May je parle le français tray mal.*'

He spits his stick out of the window and pulls onto the slip road.

The man is not as stocky as me. He has narrow shoulders and a spinster's chest, but the swell of his stomach falls over his belt like he is carrying dead rabbits in his lap. He smiles at me often and I return it, to be polite, but his drooping eyes they seem to close and open too slowly and his mouth is too much like a girl, the bow of his lip pronounced like he has drawn around it. I notice that his nails are perfect and, on one hand only, they are painted a deep blue, so I think he is a man who likes the men more than the women. My Greek friends told me of men like this, but I have never met one. It occurs to me that he might ask for more than I can give for a few kilometres in his car. I am strong man. I have dealt with wolves in my time and I wonder how I can explain him this using only actions. So I roll up one sleeve and flex my bicep as we speed through changing scenery.

Later, I wake up groggy. I am not sure how long I have been sleeping. My driver has his eyes fixed on the road, but senses I am stirring.

He utters something quickly.

'*Arrêt?*' I ask. I hear the shape of this one word, but all the others are like smears on a window.

'*Oui, dans le village là-bas.*' He reaches into the back for a package and mimes a silly scene, passing me the package then patting his chest with the flat of his hand. With some concentration I comprehend his meaning. He must make a posting or delivery. I shrug. He drives. Then he takes the next turn where spindly trees mark the edges of the road. After twenty minutes he turns off again, but down a smaller lane, then finally into a long drive that leads to a house that looks as crisp as a new frost. I am beginning to feel restless, like the young hogs when they're taken from their pens. The man senses my fear and smiles reassuringly and acts his package posting once again to the accompaniment of rapid French. His mouth pouts his words out like my sister kisses the cat.

I am assuaged and settle further in my seat as he pulls up on the asphalt. He walks the distance to the house, some thirty metres, and I tense my thigh against my knife as I watch him press a button on the lintel. I brought this knife so it would forever bring me pain, but it is becoming an unexpected comfort.

A man comes to the door and the two talk for a minute. The man shares the same flaccid corpulence at his belly as my driver, his stomach expanding the front of a sleeveless cotton shirt. He goes back inside and re-emerges with a large dog on a lead. It is a German Shepherd. The men consult again briefly and begin to walk towards me. For three seconds – but an eternity in one tiny slice of time – I consider my situation. Am I misreading this scene? I ask myself. Adrenalin is telling me it is the time to fight or run. I decide I will . . . RUN.

I flip the handle and get out of the vehicle. The men are no more than twenty metres away, but the dog is already yanking on its lead and making laboured rasping sounds in its attempt for freedom. The men seem to be grinning. It is bizarre and still I have a seed of thought that maybe this is not as threatening as I feel it to be. But caution is my friend and I make a dash along the drive, cutting across the dusty ground off to the left to skip over a low wall that marks the boundary of the property from the scrubby land in front. There are no other houses here and the tiny road we came along has no traffic on it. I glance behind me briefly to see if the dog has been set loose. Yes. Now both men are standing with arms folded, their heads on one side, inquisitive, interested to see how this race will go. The animal is gaining on me.

I am unhappy to see the dog is in good shape. His head is low and his steady limbs are pounding out his pace with beauty and precision. I know I must get further from the men so I concentrate my effort on lengthening my stride, realizing there is no time to reach inside my undergarments for my knife. The dog should be no trouble but he may take time to subdue, although one spring I killed a rabid mastiff with my bare hands in less than a minute. I get another twenty metres and the animal is almost on me. Now I must turn, so he cannot get a grip on a leg or an arm. If he does I am in trouble. But I manage to rotate enough to face him and he stops, his paws splayed, his head so close to the ground that the fur of his chin grazes the parched earth. He is intent. But I hope he's not too clever, or too well trained. I want him to pounce without thinking. I need him to pounce.

Soon, he starts to circle slowly but then looks as if he is backing off. If he corners me and does not attack it will give the men a chance to reach me before I have dispatched him. So I half turn as if to run again, baiting him, and he falls for my trick. The dog follows a deeper instinct after all and launches for the kill. So I turn again, face on as he, in mid-air, propels himself, jaws first, towards my face. I must reach past the savage teeth and grasp both his front legs with my hands. I must find my target or I will bleed. Miraculously my hands close round both his legs.

Ech, poor creature, he should have stayed low. Well-trained dogs go for trailing limbs rather than mounting from behind or jumping for the throat. And in the pack they can nip away at a cow's nose and genitals until she collapses, exhausted and resigned, to let the pack put her from her misery. Surviving cattle often looked like the victims of some perverted sport when we found them in the morning.

This canine's legs are so powerful it takes all my strength to pull them wide apart. I imagine rending burlap with my bare hands. This forces the jaws closer to my face and I can smell the offal of its last meal and something like predestination as I plead with a higher power that the animal's rib cage will give way to my exertion. And in that creature's eye, its tooth slicing my cheek, I see surprise, then sadness. I have him, a lung is punctured, and he falls.

He is not completely dead; although, judging by the supine glass-eyed panting, he will be soon and on cue he whimpers, very soft, in the brown grass. I feel a splinter of pity but already I am on guard and reaching in my trousers for my knife and without hesitation I run towards the men, whose arms are no longer folded but out at their sides as if they are balancing on very fine wire. They look like clowns with gaudy surprise painted crudely on their faces. They are disgusting.

I reach the driver first. He has managed a lame canter as I knock him unconscious with one decisive blow. I stop briefly to kick him in the ribs but his body does not flinch, it only gives way like a sack of millet as my boot invades bone and tissue. Then I make chase after the dog's master as he heads for the safety of his home. I reach the door as he is closing it and for a minute we struggle on either side. I realize my failing strength may not match his terrified energy. I am hungry and feeble from weeks of travelling without a proper meal, from snatching sleep on roadsides and in cars. But as I am relenting Gabriel appears in my imagination and I find the vehemence to give the door one final push. The man is thrown back into the hallway; he looks dismal now sitting on the floor, fear wobbling his bottom lip. It gives me pleasure knowing that he, once smug, and using the strength of an animal to masquerade as his own power, is brought onto his rear. I leap on him, unrestrained, and pummel his face with my fists until I feel the flesh has lost the fibre that holds it all together and he is minced and moaning.

I look around for something to tie him with, cut the flex from the television set and try to tie his hands behind his back, but the wire is springy and my hands are trembling so I cannot make a knot. I hit him on the temple. He is silent at last.

I am thinking about good fortune; the bag of silver you

find beside the stream, the healthy children your wife bears one after another, the horse that works tirelessly for years when three of your neighbour's have gone lame. For this you thank the *djinns*, your god or fate. But when bad fortune comes – disease or poverty, war or humiliation – you cry out and tear your clothes, or lose your reason and cut yourself and put ashes on your face. Yet it is the same capricious anarchy that torments you this year but made your life complete before.

This knowledge is as the spring that breaks the leaden clouds of winter. I can confront the future. As long as I eschew guilt I can be free. I can embrace happiness and tragedy, because beyond the sting is the salve – beyond the climax the descent. There is no good or bad, simply necessity.

Like the men, my mind becomes quite still but my actions do not have the corresponding hiatus. I do not give myself a minute. I am out on the drive and dragging my driver into the house to be with his friend. He is a dead weight and I can see that urine has soaked the crotch of his trousers. In the lean-to at the back of the house, beyond an immaculate kitchen, I find thick tape and rope among the tools and household goods. I decide not to gag them, but I tie them firmly to each other, back to back. It is not easy to find something enduring to tie bodies to inside a home. I pull the telephone from out of the wall, crush it with my foot and fling it from the front door. I gather all the knives from the drawers in the kitchen and hide them in the yard. Now, I cannot think. So I make myself some coffee and devour things from the fridge; some cheese, a cold stew, milk from a paper carton, until I have a pain in my chest from eating too much too fast.

Ech, you see, turning my back on guilt does not make me a monster. In Albania I would have killed these men but now I am free I do not have to. A good man does not always do good things. And a bad man does not always do bad things. And a free man does good and bad and sleeps at night and does not have infernal dreams of retribution. He only knows that he is dust and all his actions will eventually be like powder, forgotten.

As the men begin to gain their consciousness I sit before them eating and drinking and wiping my mouth with the back of my hand. The driver begins to whine as certainty descends upon him, but the other man is pulverized and can barely move his head, let alone allow the slightest tremor to further unhinge his lip.

'I didn't want to hurt you. That's not what I am, that's not what I want,' I explain in Albanian, my mouth full of food. 'I am a man of peace, you understand. I no longer have a place in my heart for violence,' and with a closed fist I thump my chest where my heart resides. It is almost a gesture of comradeship, I think. 'But you attack me, you set your dog on me, and so I have no choice.'

The dog man is crying but the driver slurs back at me, incomprehensible, and I know this is useless. If I were arrested now I could prove no crime against me. I cannot swear there was one. Yes, I would be the criminal. I have killed their dog and beaten them. But as I drive away in the corrugated van with the francs I found in the bedroom drawer I fill my chest with air. I am the victor and I am free.

I have been in Barcelona for five months. I kept the droopy-eyed man's van longer than I intended. Ech, it was stupid but it was my first vehicle and I am a desperado now, yes? Anyway, no one stopped me at the border. I abandoned the Citroën in the mountains; my new friend Juan showed me the place, a car graveyard, where the carcasses of vehicles lay burned and stripped among the trees. I am building some good savings now to add to the francs I stole from the dog man. Juan's brother, Ratto, bought the videos and magazines from the boxes in the back for ten thousand pesetas, so I am become a real businessman.

'Very good gay porn . . . from Germany.' Ratto nods as he slits the boxes open and thumbs the shiny books.

Juan's brother is a boy-girl, a transvestite, but Juan does not seem to mind. I thought I would be sick when I first saw him, six foot four and walking like a pop star in purple heels. Juan says, 'Friends come in many disguises,' with a look of disdain for my disgust, not for his brother. So I think about my revelation in the dog man's house and I think, OK, Ratto is happy, he hurts no one. When we go out to the bars his crotch is smooth like a girl because he straps his manhood down between his legs and wears dresses of sheer fabric that barely cover his buttocks. There are many men in Barcelona who do the same. But still I will look at the ground and concentrate on my cigarette when they are posturing and flirting with one another. They know not to tease me.

Juan is teaching me Catalan and French and how to break into cars to steal the radios and coats and briefcases. This was how I met him. I was sleeping in the back of the van one night when I heard the doors pop open, *brrup*, like that, so easy. It was Juan coming in to steal but he did not bank on me, huddled in a corner. He did not spot me right away, not until he was on his hands and knees pulling at the boxes. I had my knife at his throat before he had time to shout.

'Tell me if you are alone or I will slice your gullet,' I whispered, not expecting an answer.

But in the faint light I saw him smile. 'Macedonian?' he asked, then after a pause, 'No, Kosovan?'

'Albanian,' I replied suspiciously, my knife still shaving the flesh beneath his chin.

He touched my forearm with the tips of his fingers and

gently pushed my arm, and knife, away. 'An Albanian . . . so far from home,' he said in Greek.

Juan is a slice of bounty, my godsend and my teacher but most of all, my friend. We steal at night and sleep until midday then eat *tapas* in the cafés off the Ramblas in the afternoon, smoking Fortunas and slinging back espressos until our breath is sour and our hands shake like old women's. I am so happy. Juan can be a little crazy sometimes because he has no fear. He is Spanish and so he cannot be deported if he is caught with his hand in some tourist handbag. He says he will organize a Spanish passport for me. This will help me get to England. My Greek papers don't travel across borders too well, he says, and he reminds me that I'm lucky to have crossed through France and into Spain without a grain of trouble. No one even looked at me or my passport, in my Citroën, smoking the dog man's Gauloise out the window. Ech, you see, it is only things that make us stand out from one another. A naked Albanian is the same as any other European with no clothes on. Yes, Juan says, I am become truly European now.

PART THREE

15

PADS

India

If Spain was throbbing then Coventry barely had a pulse. I arrived back at nightfall as a clammy drizzle soaked the city, reflecting pools of light from the streetlamps on the Stoney Stanton Road, illuminating the gutter rubbish and the emptiness. It made me feel despondent, almost ill.

It was after midnight before I called Andy. We hadn't spoken for two weeks and he ranted over me with the roughshod manner of a speed freak until I cut his monologue short and asked him to call round the following day. The Andy who knocked on my door was less energetic than I expected. I led him through to the kitchen, asking after his health over my shoulder. I poured him a beer but didn't have one myself. I wanted a razor edge. Andy took slow mouthfuls from his glass, listening in silence as I told stories about my movements during the previous fortnight. I described my recruiting trip to Manchester, my preparations for India, et cetera, and filled in the gaps when I was in Spain trying to steal *his* dollars with lies about 'business', 'parties up north', tales of conquests and the like.

'So what's the news on Jez and Bas?' I asked suddenly, not missing a beat. No point in being too sensitive.

Andy rubbed his chin, considering what to say, and I got the feeling he was taking a moment to make sense of everything. 'I'll come clean . . .' He hesitated. 'There's been a bit of a hitch.'

'Oh yeah?' I was acting offhand as I poured milk into my tea.

'Yeah man! I mean those guys, they're good guys, you know, and I reckon they did their best but there was some heat over there in Spain and, well . . . they've bottled it.'

From the corner of my eye I could see he wore a guilty look. 'What do you mean "heat"? What do you mean "bottled it"?' My back was still half-turned as I stirred the sugar in.

'Well . . . it's mad, I know, but they're convinced they were being followed. Someone over there was onto them or something.'

'What? Law, customs, what?'

'They don't know, Pads. A gang maybe.'

'How can they bottle it and not know?' I was inventing irritation now, putting Andy on the back foot, but still not facing him.

'Look, I wasn't there but both of them say they were followed by some car . . . and there was, like, a chase or something, and a note. Shit, I mean, I've seen the note. Weird! And their car *was* wrecked. They had an awful time, I honestly feel for them.'

'Fuck, Andy.' I turned to face him fully then, my voice rising. 'This is ridiculous. Typical, unprofessional incompetence.'

'Now hold on –'

'No, you hold on, Andy. You owe me money. Damn it, man, you owe *everybody* money.'

'Steady, Pads. I don't deserve a roasting just yet.'

'No? Well, I think you do. I think it's time this situation was taken in hand.'

'Look, if it's the bloody money . . . shit . . . I'll get your five hundred quid, OK.'

I pointed the teaspoon at him. 'It's gone past that, you bloody . . . fool. This is about your reputation . . . and your safety. You've come to me for advice as well as money, yeah? So take this like a man.'

Andy tried to counter my criticism. 'You didn't have to lend me a penny. No one forced you,' he said. 'You're being unfair, unreasonable.'

But I was flying. Everything I said felt commanding, erudite, and Andy, although he tried to object, well, he was a lamb, a pathetic lamb.

'So what do you suggest I do?' he bleated. It was a wounded cry.

'For once, just once, let me take control of this.' I thumped the table with my fist for emphasis, and a little too much vigour.

Andy sniffed and pushed backwards so that his chair was balancing on two legs.

'OK,' he whispered.

Was that it? Was it that simple?

'OK,' he'd said.

Two letters and he'd relinquished all his power to me. Astringent glee washed through me and I felt the urge to whoop. Instead I pulled myself up to my full height, rolled my shoulders back and cleared my throat.

'You'll have to do everything I say, no question.'

'Fine.'

'And I'll need all the details: times, places, costs, all your plans.'

'Fine, Pads, I *said* fine.'

'Good. Good. I'll sort this out then, you'll see.'

He eyed me coolly and repeated his 'OK'.

I hopped up on the counter and sat looking down on him. 'So where are Jez and Bas now?'

'They're back. They got back yesterday, but Jez isn't in good shape.'

'How do you mean?'

Andy made circles with one index finger at his temple. 'Lost it, you know.'

'Had to happen one day.'

'Did it?'

I didn't answer.

'His dad came and got him from the cottage. It was awful. Like Psycho Tom all over again.'

Psycho Tom was a first-year psychology student with a penchant for LSD. He scored his drugs off us. It was the week before his exams when he began pushing a shopping trolley round campus wearing his dressing gown. Some of the other students followed for a while, laughing and clapping, thinking it was a performance piece. Psycho Tom was renowned for his theatrics.

On the third day a doctor and three security guards cornered him in the philosophy quad. It took several injections to subdue him. In his trolley they found used condoms, bicycle lights, various bones (chicken, squirrel, cat), a mangled doll, a stuffed perch and three carrier bags containing (in relatively small quantities) blood, saliva and semen. He was sectioned for three months at an institution near his parents' home in Hampshire.

'Try not to think about Tom and Jez for a second,' I said.

'Jez's fucked, Pads. It's all my fault.'

'It's not your fault, man. Jez was predisposed. Don't pretend you didn't know that.'

'Exactly! I did know it . . . so . . . then I shouldn't have sent him to Spain, right?'

'Like I said, it was going to happen, Spain, Cov, this year, next. Anyway, sorting out the dollars will take the pressure off him. It'll get Jez out of the firing line on that score at least. Is he at home?'

Andy rubbed between his eyes. 'No. Hospital. Psychiatric unit . . . you know.'

'Best place for him.'

Andy's jaw was slack and he pulled the skin on his cheeks downwards with both hands, so I could see the pink at the rims of his eyes. He looked old, grotesque.

'So . . . where are the dollars?' I tried to sound nonchalant.

'What? Oh, they're hidden.'

I nodded slowly. 'Hmm. Where?'

'In the guesthouse where the guys were staying in Spain.'

'Fuck!'

'I know. But Bas reckons they're well stashed. Plastic and tape, he's good at that sort of thing.'

'Damn, damn, damn.'

'What's wrong?'

'It's OK, they'll just have to stay in Spain for the minute that's all.'

'Why?'

'Because we need money, guaranteed money, and the only way to get it is for you to come to India with me and pay off what you owe.'

'Me come to India?'

'Yeah! I thought we could take the dollars to Delhi and change them there but there's no time.'

'I'm not doing a run, Pads. I'm just not. Been there. Done that.'

'I'm not asking you to do a run, for God's sake. I just want to get you out of Cov and out of debt; that's the bottom line. All you have to do is move the gear from Manali to Delhi and pack the bags. That's it.'

'The riskiest bit. The bit that has a ten-year prison sentence dangling over it.'

'Can you think of another way to raise the capital you need? India is the only choice.'

He closed his eyes and nodded. 'K,' he said.

My mouth was dry but my body was tingling and moist. In my dream I was in India with Becca. We had gone out for the day sightseeing. We covered some ground. I showed her the temples and the mosques of old Delhi. We wandered through the mountain forests of Himachal Pradesh. I coaxed her away from a group of street children who surrounded her at the Taj Mahal. She waved goodbye and they gave her a carved soapstone ornament of a goddess and blew her cheeky kisses. I knew the goddess's tragic tale and Becca listened as I told it. There was a deeper meaning to the story and everything I said had import. Becca understood that I was teaching her. I was explaining a complicated mystery and she was appreciative and earnest. Then it was the afternoon. The heat was oppressive so we repaired to our hotel room. In the room the light was subdued and the air fragranced with jasmine and Nag Champa. We lay naked on a bed covered with sumptuous brocade and strewn with silk cushions. Each cushion bore an inscription from the past. Becca stretched across the bed like a cat and as she stretched she kicked the cushions onto the floor one by one. She meowed, licked her lips and closed her eyes seductively when I stared her down. Then, on all fours, she prowled around me then straddled me until she was leaning over me and I could feel her hair on my face while her nipples grazed my chest. I was overcome with desire and I held her waist firmly while I penetrated her and we both gasped as if this was a wonderful surprise. Then her hips were deep in my groin matching the deliberate rotations of the ceiling fan above. We were stripping away layers, revealing the naked, implacable kernel at the core of her and me, at the core of everything. I turned my head in ecstasy and in the doorway stood Andy, watching, his mouth a pathetic gaping hole. I ejaculated, a protracted exquisite spiritual orgasm that shook me into wakefulness.

A dream is a deceit that tricks the dreamer into thinking his dreary life has some significance or meaning. He might even go so far as to believe that the characters in his dreams can impart messages from his subconscious to his conscious self. It's preposterous, of course. Pure vanity. Our lives have no importance beyond our own narrow self-love or loathing. Despite knowing this, I found this dream of mine persuasive. I caught myself imagining Becca in India with me even though I intended to drop her from my plans after her failures in Spain. Yes, I can own it now, the desire to retaliate gripped my imagination and Becca became part of the plan. Andy would want her for himself when he met her, but I would flaunt her in front of him. Still, I made a mental note to take care she should not cloud my judgement.

I'd never thought of myself as a vengeful person. There were hard substrata to my personality, of course, but premeditated reprisal? No. Think about it: I'd spent a year licking my wounds and trying to make a new life without a thought of paying Andy back for his betrayal. But now the opportunity presented itself I was seized by ideas of revenge. And since I'd tried and failed to steal the dollars in Spain, my determination strengthened further. I found myself thinking about Andy every moment of every day. It was a far cry from the dope-addled 'peace and love' persona I'd pretended at university. It never *really* was my bag. It was veneer. Society demands we pay lip service to altruism or compassion, but everyone I ever met was selfish through and through. Show me a hippy whose 'feed the world with love' bollocks isn't a cover for inadequacy or an excuse for having no material or moral ambition. Andy and his cohorts wanted society to underwrite their pothead lifestyles while they reframed their criminal activity as Robin Hood heroic, or political or creative or whatever other epithet they could think of to disguise their indolence. It was risible. The way they talked of generosity and the social good, dressing conceit in some political outfit or other, expressing their ideologies with dewy-eyed sincerity. When push came to shove they'd sell your carcass to the butchers of doom and think nothing of it as long as they could satisfy their own cravings. It's ridiculous any of us fell for it.

Becca and I left for India before the others. It was a perfect evening. As the plane surged upward I looked out on long elegant clouds, dark as slate, painted on the sky in parallel lines above the horizon. There, a blinding molten sun bronzed the stratus from below so it looked as though there was another land way off on the shores of a distant river, its broad course reflecting the sun's light. Afterwards, whenever I closed my eyes, an echo of the spectacle glowed on my retinas. I'd stared for too long. During the flight Becca didn't talk about Spain or Val. Instead, she watched the in-flight movies and took advantage of the complimentary drinks. When alcohol loosened her tongue she told me more about herself. That her worst nightmare was to stay 'up north'. That if she hadn't discovered cannabis and its attendant subculture (my words not hers) she'd have been some heels and nylon go-getter, working in customer services, redoing her lipstick during the tea breaks and sucking up to the office manager.

'Yeah, I'd of ended up a supervisor at Asda or summat.' She winced. '*And* I'd of counted meself lucky.'

The best Becca's sort could hope for was a factory job to pay for the white dress and a cheap reception in the back room of a pub, with guests staggering paralytic to the DJ dross. The groom destined to become a flop-bellied fuckwit, the bride to bear a lifetime of tedious, football-chant misogyny. I felt magnanimous knowing I was playing a part in liberating her.

In Delhi I splashed out on an upmarket hotel off Connaught Circus and set about impressing her with my local knowledge and authority. It was easy to look lordly since the natural inclination of the Indians is to bow and scrape. We had four days in Delhi before Andy was due to arrive. With him would be Jez's sister Sharon, who Becca knew from Manchester, and two more recruits from the interviews Simmo and I had undertaken several weeks before. In those four days I would ensnare Becca then parade her in front of Andy, like Caesar with a leopard on a leash. I know I'd had her already, but I was under no illusions on that score. I was back to square one. However, a combination of her isolation and my experience made Becca more amenable to me than I expected. She was attentive, flirtatious even, forever finding excuses to touch me, a finger lightly brushing the back of my hand or simply picking some tobacco or a thread from my shirt. She told me she was 'totally made up' about being in India and apologized more than once for her failure in Spain.

On the second night, standing on the rooftop overlooking the city, I tried to kiss her and she relented, then bit my top lip. I felt a stab of shame. How could she bite me there? Then she said she was 'right sorry' but she was 'on', otherwise we might have had some fun, to which I coloured crimson but she didn't appear to notice in the darkness and the heat. She admitted that India scared her: the smells, the poverty and disease. She said she was glad I was there or she'd be back to Burnley 'quick as a ferret'. On the third day I took her to Agra to see the Taj Mahal. She thanked me diffidently for taking the trouble to show her round and we gazed at the shining mausoleum for some time before she skipped off to buy a string of jasmine flowers from the hawkers near the entrance. She garlanded me, and smiled at me with such affection that I felt an insistent pain below my ribs that spoiled an otherwise successful day.

It was when Andy arrived that things started to misfire. I left Becca sleeping in her room and got up before dawn to take a rickshaw to the airport. Along the roadsides people slept, wrapped in white *dhotis*, while the dawn caressed the streets through a thin mist so that everything was blanketed with a rosy miasma. By the time I reached the outskirts of the city the sun had burnt the mist to nothing and street life was in full swing. Naked children scrubbed each other down, soaped up, rinsing off with water from old buckets. Men and women defecated openly by roads and railway lines and whole families rattled through their routines in full view of me and God and everyone. At the airport I found two taxi drivers and paid them to wade into the scrum and extract my team as soon as the terminal began discharging passengers from the international flights. I pointed out Andy first in the middle of it all, standing head and shoulders above the rest. I caught a glimpse of Sharon too, screaming at a rickshaw wallah to let go of her rucksack. And then my heart stuttered. For there, behind Andy, eyes aflame, reprimanding the baggage handlers, was Basil.

I was winded. But I greeted them all enthusiastically as they slumped into the waiting taxis, travel-weary and relieved. I bundled the recruit, a soft-faced lad from Bury called Nigel, into one of the taxis with Sharon and Basil. Andy and I took the other.

'What the fuck's *he* doing here?' I asked before Andy could deliver his first sentence.

'Who? Bas?'

'Who else?'

'Pure necessity, Pads. I couldn't warn you. One of your Manchester lot dropped out so I knew we had to get a quick replacement. Basil was on hand.'

'Fucking hell. You should have let me know.'

'How could I? Anyway, he's game. He'll do the run, and do it well.'

At Connaught Circus I paid the drivers. Andy handed out airline chocolate and fresh wipe sachets to the pavement children while I helped the others with their luggage, praying that Becca was still asleep. I needed time to warn her about Basil. I needed time to think. A visceral fear enveloped me and in the darkened lobby I sensed Basil and Becca's meeting was imminent. A minute later Becca appeared at the foot of the stairs. She had seen the taxis pull up and had come down to greet everyone. I held my breath.

Sharon had her arms round Basil's waist as they checked in at the reception desk.

'Rakstone, it hot, Sharon, it hot as hell,' he was saying.

Time slowed. Basil's words seemed to thud like rocks on dense sand. He hadn't seen Becca, but she had seen him and I watched her nostrils flare and her eyes dart with that furtive, animal keenness she tended to.

'You'll get used to it, ya whinger.' Sharon laughed, sliding her hand from his waist to his buttock to grab a mischievous handful.

Then Basil glimpsed Becca, a quick flick from the corner of his eye that made him double-take then turn and face her. I watched a filament of recognition begin to glow, then burn brighter until his whole body stiffened.

Sharon felt it. 'You all right, babe?' she asked, stepping back, looking at him, then from him to Becca.

All my function and potency was suspended and I stood helpless, neutered, waiting for my fate. I even hung my head.

But then Sharon shrieked, 'Becca! Excellent!' and ran to embrace her friend. In my trepidation I'd forgotten it was Sharon who'd recruited Becca in the first place.

Becca managed a show of excitement and an uneasy smile.

Basil scratched his head. The situation was defused.

'Fucking hell, Basil, it's mad you're here,' I declared, slapping his shoulder to distract him. There was a croaky fault line in my voice and I had to cough to clear my throat, but I went on, 'It's good to see you.'

Basil relaxed slightly as he focused on me. 'Mi nah choose to come,' he growled. 'It was I and I or no one, mon. You haffa speak to Andy bout the whys and the wherefores.'

The thickness of his voice gave away his size, but the whites of Basil's eyes were milky, tinged with yellow, and his face was wan with the shock of seeing Becca. In all, he seemed discordant, almost blurred, and so his impact was diminished. As Andy came towards us I sensed I could hijack some authority from Basil's weakness, so I leaned forward, looking quizzically from Becca to Basil with a wry but worried expression creasing my brow.

'Do you two . . . know each other or something?' I asked.

'Yeah? I thought that too,' Sharon said.

'No,' replied Becca quickly. 'We've never met.' She held out her hand for Basil to shake. 'What's yer name then?'

He hesitated, unresolved for a second, and then another, until – vanquished – he said, 'Basil.'

They shook hands. That was it. Their concealment was contractual.

Later, Basil, Andy and I sat on my balcony, wearily discussing the plan of action for the week ahead. The midday heat was a chronic ache that affected everything and that nothing could allay. The sun itself seemed weighed down with it and sagged heavily in the sky so that Delhi lay before us, ponderous, decaying, bloated, its definition all but choked in the dust haze and the smog. The monsoon was late.

'This heat gets to work in my mind like a fucking parasite,' Andy said sullenly, pinching the top of his nose. 'I'll get some sleep, I think. Manali tomorrow.'

'Sure,' I said and showed him to the door.

'Where you find that gal there?' Basil demanded when I came back.

'Becca?'

'Yeah.'

'She's a friend of Sharon's from Manchester,' I offered casually. 'Why, do you fancy her?'

'Nah man, uh uh, no way.'

I winked. 'I could put a word in for you.'

Basil kissed his teeth. 'Nah mon, 'im jos remind me a someone, that is all.'

'Sharon's the one to ask.'

Basil shifted his large frame from the chair. 'Well . . . mi get some sleep miself now.'

I stared at the chair Basil had sat in for a long while after he'd gone. There are some people whose very essence seems freighted. Perhaps their atoms weigh more and so the elements they displace and the fabric of time and being they disrupt is more than the average person. Or maybe there's no heft to them at all, they are ciphers defined only by the fact that their nothingness becomes a receptacle into which all our fears are poured. Whichever it was, after Basil was gone either the space he'd inhabited struggled to fill up again or was so full of my reservations that I could still see his outline in the air and hear his resonant, thick-vowelled argot full of suspicion, full of accusation, for what felt like eternity.

Later, when Becca came to my room, she was angry. Gone was the lip-biting coquette of the day before. Gone was my malleable disciple.

'What the fuck's going on? What's *he* doing here?' she began, too loudly. 'You're rippin' off your mates, that's what you're doin', isn't it? And I'm the stupid cow who'll take the blame. Is that it?'

I strode towards her so determinedly she looked behind her for somewhere to run. But I was on her in a second, covering her mouth with my hand as she struggled.

'Shut the fuck up,' I whispered slowly, my lips against her cheek so I could smell the rancid whiff of fear on her. Eventually, I released my grip and Becca shivered as she pulled away.

'You done?' I said.

She didn't acknowledge the question.

'Do you really think I'd have brought you if I knew that *bastard* would be here? Do you?'

She looked at the floor.

'He has no idea that you know me, or I know you, in any other context than this, here, India,' I continued. 'He doesn't know I was in Spain. As far as he's concerned, you being here is just the freakiest coincidence of his life, yeah? As long as you keep your mouth shut everything will be OK. OK?'

Becca bit her thumbnail while I paced the room.

'You'll have to talk to him, of course,' I said at last. 'Say, "How weird this all is," and "Fancy seeing you here, of all places." Reinforce the whole "me and my mate Val on a package holiday" routine.' I stopped pacing and put my head on one side, my voice softening, modulating. 'Maybe even suggest that you two might . . . re-establish a bit of a physical thing.' I raised an eyebrow.

'Oh my God,' she sighed heavily, exasperated.

'What? You've done it before.'

'Fuck you!'

'Careful, Becca!'

She slapped the palm of her hand to her forehead and laughed. 'You're unbelievable.'

I shrugged. 'I'm trying to salvage a fucked up situation.'

'D'you know what, Pads? What's worrying me most about *all this* is that we spent a week sneaking about in Spain trying to steal that money off of yer mates. I mean, it *seems* that Jez is Sharon's sister. And now he's – what? In an asylum or summat? And Basil seems to know Sharon extremely well and all.'

'Jez has mental health issues, always has had, always will.'

'And who knows where that poor Andy fits into everything –'

I interrupted her. 'There's no "poor Andy". Don't confuse things, Becca. Don't . . .'

I stopped. I'd raised my voice and now I was having to take cleansing breaths to calm myself. 'I mean, you mustn't get confused or sentimental here,' I said, more softly now, taking a cigarette from its packet and bouncing the tip on the box. 'They're no *friends* of mine I assure you, none of them.'

She appeared to understand and looked away, contemplating a corner of the room, clicking her teeth together so it sounded like someone banging nails in a wall in a room far away. At last she looked at me and said, 'And me, Pads, am I your friend?'

How to convey reassurance, sexual availability and authority? I approached Becca resolutely, and with a smile. When I was close enough to touch her I brought my hand under her chin then ran my thumb firmly round her lips. I caught a strand of her hair that had broken free from its ponytail and tried to push it back behind her ear. She didn't blink. Suddenly she didn't seem human at all.

'Obviously I'm *paying* you, Becca,' I said. 'But of course I *am* your friend.'

'Thanks, Pads, I appreciate that.' She exhaled quickly, pulling away.

I lit my cigarette. 'You're welcome.'

The shops in Paharganj were like busted cushions with all their extravagant stuffing spilling onto the street. The Indians knew how to *pile it high* – the slung together, the mass-produced, the shoddy – and the shopkeepers would call from their doorways, tempting browsers into oppressive interiors with promises of 'beautiful treasures inside' and 'I give you best price'. On the street the shoppers vied with the traffic beneath the hoardings and signage. It was an everyday jubilee of colour and chaos. You could hide away in chaos like that if you weren't faint-hearted, and plenty of the cafés in Paharganj served up a discreet, drug smuggler's breakfast.

Andy was late. The café was a regular haunt of mine and I waited with the rest of the crew, brushing flies off my face. Basil looked tired. The opacity in his eyes from the day before seemed to have colonized his whole body and now threatened his very aura. I was pleased his power was clouding in the heat. The café, an open wooden structure, extended a few feet into the road, which meant the beggars could lean through the windows on three sides. It was the only drawback to the place. They appeared as spectres, empty eyes, nurturing some unique deformity or other, the fingertips of the one hand making a bird's beak that pecked into their open mouths while they beseeched us silently. Becca gave. The beggars left. She gave again. They left. I wondered if she'd give everything she had. It was not what I expected of her. It irritated me and so I bawled, 'Chale jao, go away!' at the next importunate wretch who dared lean in. It was an emaciated woman in a filthy sari with skin the colour of bitumen. She recoiled like a snake when I shouted, but life-long desperation had made her courageous and she stepped up again and thrust a bundle at us through the window with a quiet whimper. It was a baby, naked apart from a length of rag that wound around its belly and on through spindle legs splayed open, frog-like, at the knees. In place of the baby's mouth was a misshapen hole where a cluster of flies buzzed and supped. We were looking right at the gory workings inside the creature's head. Becca turned away, gagging, but I gazed in awe, unable to move except to run my finger gently over my top lip, faintly appalled by my own disgust. Basil, half-standing, ready to give chase, looked sick to his stomach, but then the café owner, aware that generosity is worn down quickest by revulsion, shooed the woman off, catching her arse with the end of his dishrag as she retreated. It was all for show.

'Cleft palate,' said Sharon flatly as we watched the woman drift off down the road. 'They don't get fixed up here like they do back home.'

Diamonds of sweat prickled on Basil's brow. 'It rank to rakstone, mon.'

'Yeah, don't those pesky poor people just make you sick?' sniped Becca.

Basil kissed his teeth and looked down Paharganj trying to spot the woman again in the crowds. 'Righteous bitch,' he murmured, but there was no force in his words; they weren't directed at anyone although Becca poked her tongue out at him. He didn't see. The sweat was running freely now, polishing Basil's whole face.

My asthma was playing up in the heat and I sucked deeply on my inhaler before turning my attention to the recruit, Nigel, who was rocking back and forth in his chair. I held his wrist while I explained about 'culture shock' and 'heat stroke' and the need for constant 'rehydration', and he seemed comforted that there were labels for his distress. Soon our food arrived and we began to eat in silence. All of them, I suspect, trying not to think of the open chasm in the baby's face. Then Sharon, who was sitting diagonally opposite me, began nudging Becca to her left and tipping her head towards Basil and one by one we turned to look at him. His eyes had rolled back in his head so that only the whites were showing and he was scowling and baring his teeth. I snorted cynically, thinking he was pulling a face, a piss-take reaction to the baby, perhaps. But then I saw the tendons in his neck stretched tight as cables and heard the chalky grind of tooth on tooth before it started. The fit.

At first Basil went over like a felled tree but once he hit the floor he began jerking violently, his limbs in spasm, sending chairs and tables spinning across the room while his body made awkward, jagged shapes. We stared, powerless. Becca was screaming, 'Do something,' and appealing to me with the wild look of a routed officer cut off from the chain of command. And once again time slowed to a series of yawning moments with a soundscape of muffled voices and the tiniest details of irrelevant things presenting like a slideshow: a loose button on Basil's shirt, the DayGlo yellow of spilled egg yolk on his dark brown chin, a coweyed child staring through the window not at Basil, but at me. Then Andy appeared from nowhere, and he was on the floor with Basil, holding him from behind, manoeuvring him onto his side. And he was forcing Basil's mouth open with one hand by pressing where his jaws hinged with his thumb and shoving his fingers past gnashing teeth, fetching his tongue out like it was old cloth that had got caught in a machine. Basil was choking. Andy was saving his life.

It was ungainly heroic, made more so by a sudden sploosh as water drenched them where they rolled and heaved. The café owner had doused them as if they were dogs fucking on the street. This shocked us all into a momentary hiatus while Andy brushed at Basil's cheek, wiping moist hair from his face saying, 'Easy now, bro, easy.' And soon he had Basil on his feet, shell shocked but taking shallow breaths, and guided him into a taxi. It was all quick-as-a-flash.

'You go back to the hotel,' commanded Andy through the car window. 'I'll meet you there.'

We nodded, stupid. Then Andy was gone.

When we got back to the hotel we sat on the roof terrace. Sharon was ashen. Becca was saying, 'Fuck, that was mad, totally mad. Did you see his face? His eyes? And that Andy, like fucking Superman. I mean, where the fuck did he come from? Did you see? Did you? Look at my hands. I'm shaking.'

Nigel had his hands at either side of his face, like blinkers, trying to stop the stimuli. But it was no defence; the fear came from inside. He was taking quick gulps of air. Then he began to howl. It was more of a moan at first but soon his voice tightened and pitched upward. A voice on the rack. A voice popping its joints, extending into an impossible painful stretch.

He managed a couple of pointless sentences. 'I don't know . . . I . . . I . . . don't . . . he's black . . . I . . . I . . . he should . . . be able . . . to handle the heat . . . We're gonna fuckin' die . . . fuckin' . . . die.'

'Shut up, you twat,' snapped Becca.

She wasn't serene but she was in control. Nigel was losing control and rising further up the scale.

'I want to go . . . home. I want to . . . go home.' The words came out of him in taut gobfuls.

Becca tried again. 'For fuck's sake, calm down.'

I began to laugh. I think it was the northern accents. My laughter must have added to the hysterical atmosphere because Nigel began to hyperventilate and Becca shot me an incredulous, gape-mouthed look as I tried to quell my laughter.

Nigel started to wail and just as his cries reached an ear-splitting climax Becca walked over to him calmly and slapped him. It was fantastic. It was a full-force *bam* with an open palm right across his cheek as if he was a hysterical woman. It was cinematic. It was a real 'pull yourself together' slap.

'Get your shit together, man,' Becca said through gritted teeth. 'Look at me. This is NOT the time to flip out. I said look at me. This is NOT the time to be uncool. This is the time we get a grip and CHILL OUT. Do you understand me?'

She was holding his shoulders now, brilliant in her authority. Perhaps it was a northerner thing, perhaps Nigel recognized the sound of home and it quietened him. He managed a childlike nod and touched his ringing cheek where a raised imprint of Becca's hand was forming.

Becca slumped into a chair, exhausted by her fury, while Nigel snivelled softly. The sounds of Connaught Circus drifted up to the roof terrace, the car horns and tuk tuks and shouts from the vendors elbowing through the sick sweet squalor of the street.

'Becca's right,' I said smoothly. 'I know we're all a bit jittery after what's just happened, but everything will be just fine.'

Becca rolled her eyes at me and shook her head.

The next day we left for the mountains. Andy said Basil had heat stroke and had to get out of Delhi. I was reluctant but agreed we should all go up to Manali. At the bus station Becca, Sharon and Nigel gave Andy obedient nods as he pressed a Valium in each of their hands. It would 'make the journey bearable' he said. His heroics had impressed them. On the bus Basil sat by the window next to Andy, wrapped in a cotton shawl, hiding his face. He didn't speak but Andy assured us he was fine and from time to time I saw Andy talk to Basil through the flimsy material. An hour later the dizzy anarchy of the city thinned until we were driving through pastureland that had become dust and extended on either side of the road to a flat horizon. The late monsoon made everything look exhausted and drained of colour. Unowned white cows trudged the highway, their hides glued to weary bones, and at the roadside women balancing brass *mutkas* on their heads held down flyaway saris as our bus boiled up a cumulus of grime. On the road an arcade game was playing. The game was chicken and the driver was a dab hand. Bicycles beat pedestrians, motorbikes beat bikes, tuk tuks beat motorbikes, then cars, then vans, then buses . . . then lorries. Lorries were fairground attractions done up more gaudy than a gypsy caravan but deadlier than any tank. Anxiety, deleted by Valium, was replaced with our dreamy, near-death 'oohs' and 'aahs' as the driver threw the bus along its route, swerving and honking and squaring up to every obstacle. We clung on and rolled into one another on our wooden seats. As day turned to night the derelict roads kept us reeling. We made several stops until, at last, the air was cooler. Beyond the weak lights that illuminated the *chai* stalls with their garish snacks there was impenetrable darkness. We were in a new landscape far away from a civilization that leaked ambient light.

Back on the bus we crawled up, up, up. As the first light broke I could see we were inching through thick forest. I knew the stretch of road, but the old bus wasn't making more than ten m.p.h., the incline was so steep. Round the next bend a vista opened out to reveal a sheer drop, beyond which valley upon valley fell away abruptly one after another to form an incomprehensible panorama. Here the mind plunged breathlessly into every chasm. The clouds were beneath us, not yet climbing in the new morning but bathing the rice terraces. I turned to see if Becca was awake, wanting to share this view, this moment, wanting to present this to her as a gift: the experience of high wiring along the serrated ridge of the world. She was awake. But so was Andy. Basil was asleep on his shoulder as Sharon was on mine. Andy looked regal, almost beatific, and his eyes reflected the sky as he inhaled deeply through his nose, his chest expanding, and he was smiling at Becca and she was smiling back.

'You all right?' I saw him mouth to her, full lipped.

'It's so beautiful,' she mouthed back.

Then they laughed with their eyes at each other, basking in their moment of shared, aesthetic understanding. I turned away before either of them caught me spying.

Two hours later we arrived in Manali. In years to come

it would become a drug-smuggler Disneyland, but now it was nothing, just a couple of precipitous streets lined with raggle-taggle Nepalese-style buildings. There were no beggars, no foetid smells of disease or decay, only clean, cool air and views across the Kullu Valley that made me remember the flying dreams of childhood, when I would swoop above some far-off lush terrain and make impossible rolling passes over outcrops and treetops; when I would dive down to cut a line along the glassy surface of a lake with outstretched fingertips. I missed those dreams. But now that I'd seen Andy smile at Becca, the ground hurtled away from me and I was not flying. I was falling. I felt a creeping ancient panic.

We booked into a guesthouse on the main street, a wattle and daub construction with wooden roof shingles and unimpeded views from the front. I took a back room overlooking a courtyard where women squatted in their shawls to cook and wash the pots. As I unpacked I heard them gently reprimanding children who crawled too close to the fire. I ate, then read for a while, but couldn't relax, so I went to see if the others were awake. Sharon was sleeping and Nigel was in a downstairs room showing a group of men his Walkman. Mountain people are different from the plains, their eyes set wider, the bridges of their noses flatter, more Chinese. The men were charming Nigel with their easy gap-tooth smiles. They bowed their heads and touched their Kullu caps in deference whenever he spoke. I was relieved that Nigel felt safer now, comforted by their bygone hospitality.

Andy and Becca, however, were nowhere to be found.

I'm not going to lie. I couldn't bear the thought of him and her alone together. She wouldn't be attracted to him, I was sure, but he had a roguish charm that girls were drawn to and he was handsome, of course, and profligate. He'd try and snare my doe if I wasn't careful. So I set off through the village to look for them. A troupe of urchins followed me as far as the river path but they waved goodbye as I left the road. Further up, I clambered across huge, ancient boulders that flanked the River Beas and followed the cut on its northern side into the forest. Here, unfamiliar plants and flowers grew along the banks and the acrid smell of wild cannabis mingled with the tang of foxes and water rats. The forest was made up almost entirely of soaring deodars, tall as buildings, that clothed the mountainsides and added their pine-fresh scent to the aromatic mix. After half a mile or so, the forest opened into a clearing and near the far perimeter, up several steep steps hewn from slabs of rock, was a large pagoda structure that looked like a traditional house but was in fact a temple. As I approached I could see votives and offerings around the entrance. Apart from a mangy dog that limped towards me when he caught my scent, no one seemed to be around, although I noticed the temple door stood slightly ajar. I circled cautiously to my right and approached the temple from the side so I could observe whoever was inside through the slatted windows set all around the ground floor.

'Yes, this is the temple of the Goddess Hadimba.'

I could hear Andy's voice before I pressed my face against the antique wood. He was there with Becca. When Andy and I had first visited this temple it was I who told him the story of Hadimba and the legend of the carvings. After the exquisite reliefs that decorated the walls were finished, the king had had the wood carver's right hand chopped off lest he repeat such beauty elsewhere.

Now, here was Andy telling the story to Becca as if it was his own.

'She's a very approachable deity by all accounts,' he went on expansively.

He knew nothing.

The air was heavy with forgotten entreaties and the

smell of age-old incense and as I peered inside I could see little except a narrow triangle of daylight hung with motes of lazy dust. But soon I could make out offerings set out all around, bowls of seeds and dhal and withered garlands, and Becca standing next to Andy in the gloom.

'Where is everyone?' she whispered.

'I don't know. There are normally people here, or at least a holy man.'

'I can't see a thing.'

'Here, take my hand.'

In silence she reached out. What was she playing at? What act was this? A ruthless Becca ploy, playing one of us against the other, for her own ends no doubt. I was fascinated.

'I want to tell you,' she started, confessional. I pressed my ear against the wood.

'Yeah?' said Andy.

'Well . . . to say thanks, really. I mean, until you arrived this was a bit of a nightmare.'

'No. You mustn't thank me.'

I couldn't make it out precisely but I was sure that as he spoke, he lifted her hand to his lips. I wished I could see her wicked smile.

'Do you know Pads well?' she asked, a hint of deviousness now seasoning her voice.

'Yes. Very well. He's a good friend. We don't hang out as much as we used to though.'

'Why's that?'

'We had . . . differences. I was a bit of a shit actually.' Andy sighed. 'It's a long story.'

'What? Did you sleep with someone he fancied or something?'

'Something like that. Anyway, what's all this about?'

'It's just . . .' she hesitated. 'I can't tell which one of you's in charge, that's all.'

So that was Becca's game. She was trying to suck up to the source of power.

'Pads is in charge all right,' Andy confirmed.

'Oh.'

'What?'

'Nothing.'

'No, go on. What?'

'It's just you and Pads, you're both so . . . different.'

'Different how?'

'Pads seems so cold,' she went on. 'Like he could hurt people. I mean I don't want to speak badly about your friend or owt but he just doesn't seem to like anyone.'

'It's simple with Pads. He wants to be loved, but he's just difficult to love I suppose.'

'No. He's cold,' she repeated distantly.

'You've got him all wrong.' Andy mirrored the faraway tone in Becca's voice. Then he brightened and said, 'So go on, how are me and Pads different?'

'You fishin' for compliments?'

'Maybe.'

I tried to imagine their flirtatious smiles, the mischievous angle of her head, and I leaned further against the window to make sure I didn't miss a word. In doing so I dislodged one of the slats, only slightly, but enough to disturb their game.

'What was that?' Becca whispered.

I ducked down quickly and made my way to the back of the temple where I arranged myself in a nonchalant pose: cross-legged, nodding to the music on my Walkman. If they found me I would smile, remove my headphones and say 'Hey' as if it was marvellous luck we had all decided to visit the temple at the same time. But when neither of them appeared I tiptoed back to the window. There was no one inside that I could see or hear. At the front of the temple a young acolyte was sweeping the entrance with a grass broom. A hundred yards away Andy and Becca were climbing the steep path that led up the mountain.

The path continued through the forest to a huge buttress of rock, a natural viewing point from where the whole valley could be surveyed in one dramatic sweep. I should have been Becca's guide. I'd planned it all: the route along the river; the stories in the temple; the forest walk to the lookout, high above the valley. I watched them disappear into the trees and followed on behind as best I could, not on the path, but struggling through the undergrowth. For a while they seemed to walk without speaking, only stopping now and then when a gap in the deodars forced them to readjust their perspective as each new view across the valley demanded their attention.

It was hard to keep up but easy to remain undetected. Even if they saw me I didn't care. I'd simply pretend I was out for a walk. Andy knew this was *my* place. Nevertheless, the trees were thick and the white noise of the river cloaked the sound of any twigs or roots I snagged. Presently they reached the promontory and, from a distance, I watched them as they stood tall, like kings or gods, surveying their dominion. I was at a disadvantage now. The trees were sparser here, so I circled up, then down, along an old goat path, until I reached the cluster of huge boulders that supported the base of the promontory. It took ten minutes or so but I ended up beneath the overhang where they were sitting. I could see their feet dangling and hear snatches of their conversation.

'How long have you known Basil then?' Becca asked.

'A couple of years now,' Andy replied. 'No, not even that.'

Becca was being politic. Getting the low-down on the situation.

'Look,' Andy said, suddenly alert. 'Look there.'

I flattened my back to the rock. But he was pointing out

an eagle, soaring effortlessly in the distance. 'They use the thermals to stay up there for hours,' he said. 'Beautiful. But they'll take a lamb you know.'

'Predators and prey.'

'It's the way of things.'

'Which are you then Andy: the hunter or the hunted?'

He offered no rejoinder. They didn't speak for several minutes, and I sensed the mood had changed. Becca's last question had been pointed, almost accusatory, and there was something palpable in their silence.

'I'm interested to know how someone like you ended up doing something like this,' Andy asked at last.

'Like what?'

'You know, drug running.'

'I was gonna ask you the same thing.'

'I mean,' he went on. 'You seem really bright and alive and . . . intelligent. It's dangerous, what you're about to do. You know that don't you?'

'What are you saying? I should only do a drug run if I'm stupid?'

'Er . . . no,' he objected.

'That only thick people should be donkeys for people like you and Pads?'

'No!'

'What then?'

I was desperate to see Becca's face and I risked taking a peek, inching up the smooth rock behind them so that I could see their backs from an angle. Andy was sitting square-shouldered, looking to where the honeyed sun had started its descent behind the distant peaks.

'What I mean is . . . I like you Becca. That's all.' I think that's what he said. He spoke so softly that his voice seemed to coil off like smoke across the valley. Then he went on decisively. 'I want to make sure you get through customs safely,' he said, 'without getting caught, and if you do get caught I want you to know exactly what to do and what to say so you don't go to prison.'

He turned to face her. I could see their profiles. They looked briefly but directly into each other's eyes until Becca looked away. Andy hooked his finger under her chin and gently turned her face to his. He was going to kiss her.

At that moment I felt my muscles fill with blood as something murderous suffused me. I'm not sure if I would have sprung out on them but every sinew felt prepared for it, although I had no idea what I would say or do. But Becca resisted him and unhooked her chin from his finger with regal disdain. Once free, the malign captive, that creature I recognised the first time I met her, was released and reached the surface wild and angry. Andy pulled away from her abruptly, a star of surprise glinting in his eye. I was transfixed.

'Do you really want to know why a girl like me is doing a fuckin' stupid thing like this?' she sneered. 'I'll tell ya! I'm changing me life, that's what! I'm havin' an experince. I'm . . . I'm choosing not to stay in some poxy northern town where all I can live is some poxy northern life. And even if you *do* think I'm stupid . . . well . . . well it's your skanky mates what put me up to it.'

'Whoa.' Andy held his hand up.

'Whoa, my arse,' she shouted, mimicking Andy's actions. 'People like me have to take risks just to get a tiny piece of what the likes of YOU take for fuckin' granted.'

She was standing now, hinging from the hips and jabbing the air in front of his face with her finger. 'So I don't need your snotty, poor-provincial-lass bollocks, right. And if that's all you've got to offer then you can just fuck off.'

I couldn't believe what I was hearing. It was wonderful. I raised my head above the overhang, as far as I dared, to witness the vignette in all its glory, Andy getting torn apart by my girl. He was still sitting, his head bowed and his shoulders rolled forward, and he was shaking. At first I thought he might be crying but when Becca said, 'What? What?' about five times I realised he was laughing. He couldn't seem to stop and went on so long that Becca ended up saying, 'Stop it will yer? Why the fuck are you laughing at me?' Eventually his laughter subsided into long, drawn-out sighs as he wiped tears from his eyes.

'I'm not laughing *at* you Becca, I . . .'

'You're patronising me.'

Andy stood. 'No, really . . . it's a reflex, you're so fantastically feisty.'

'Oh yeah?'

'Yeah, actually! God, chill out. You think the whole world's got it in for you.'

'I know when I'm being ridiculed.'

'Listen, I just told you, I like you, I've just tried to fff – SHIT. Don't get offended so easily. We're the same . . . I mean I understand about the escape stuff . . . Becca. BECCA!'

Becca had turned and raced off with a snarl. Good girl. She had goaded him into an argument. She had led him on, made him feel uncomfortable then guilty, and then she'd stormed off and he'd followed like a clumsy bull with a ring in its nose. She was peerless. I decided not to follow them. Instead, I waited a minute or so until the coast was clear then climbed to where they had been sitting and stretched out on the rock, contemplating the vista, smoking a spliff. I tried to spot them on their downward journey but all I could see, far below, was a line of people with huge wicker baskets on their backs making methodical progress along a distant ridge and then snaking out of sight. I shivered. The breeze had changed direction and brought the night's cool bite with it. In the valley the terraces of paddy fields extended on and down until they met a sheer drop that plummeted into an unseen gorge. I knew it was there, that chasm.

It was evening when I arrived back in the village. There must have been a power cut because the streets were dark. Only timid halos encircled the lamplights in the shopfronts and the windows. On the way to the guesthouse I was passing the Himalaya Restaurant with tea lights illuminating its sign promising 'English menu' when someone called my name from the balcony.

It was Sharon. She was there with Nigel. Even in the candlelight I could see they were red-eyed. They were toking and not in the least bit worried about smoking dope in public.

'Seen Basil?' I asked.

'Still sleeping.'

'Ah. What about Andy?'

Sharon pursed her lips, then said, 'With Becca.'

'Oh!'

'Yeah, I reckon we've got a coupla love birds there.'

Sharon had a tendency to take things too much at face value.

16

JEZ

Inside (Das Bombers)

Lights go on and lights go off and on and off and on and off, over and over for ever and ever. Sometimes things have a hard edge, you know, like glass, and sometimes it's fuzzy like there's shit in yer eyes, grit, or a liquid floater. Dr Dawes says it's the electricity, yeah, the volts from the ECT, but I can't tell if it's that or another world trying to break through the membrane.

When I imagine me brain I think of a dead dog. Not any old dead dog, mind, but this dead dog I saw when I was a kid. I've been thinking about when I was a kid a lot recently. I was strolling down George Elliot Road when I saw a heap of old fur and gristle in the gutter. It was Mr Banks's flea-bitten mutt; it was always getting out and worrying the hens down Mrs Fawcett's garden or sniffing the girls' fannies as they played French skipping round the lampposts on Leicester Causeway. Banksy would stand on the doorstep for hours, morning and night, shouting, 'Cobblers, Cobblers, come 'ere,' cos that was the dog's name, Cobblers. He loved that animal but now there it was, in the gutter, just another dead dog. Some car had driven past and smashed his brains out and the juicy folds of it were still seeping out by the kerb and the dust in the gutter was sticking onto it and I remember thinking that brains really shouldn't get all covered in dust and crap like that or they wouldn't work properly, like when you get grit in a camera. Shit, maybe that's all that's ever been wrong with me – I've just had a bit of grit in me brain, hah. Anyway when I walked past Banksy's I knocked the door but he didn't answer. So I shouted through the letter-box, 'Mr Banks! I'm sorry but Cobblers is dead. Mr Banks! He's all smashed up on George Elliot Road.' I don't know if he heard me but it was the least I could do. I don't remember hearing Banksy call for that mutt again, I don't remember seeing him ever again for that matter, but that could just be me memory playing tricks.

Me ma used to step out with Banksy, years back, when she was a slip. Funny that. It always pissed Dad off when she took him a bacon sarnie from the caff. 'I'd do the same for you if you was on hard times,' she'd say to Dad. You know the first clear thing I remember after Spain is being in hospital and me ma sitting on the visitor's chair next to me bed. She wasn't paying me too much attention, just yabbering away like she did, and wearing that floral over-pinny thing she always wore. I reckon she must've come straight from clearing tables.

'Oh, I forgot, I've brought you some fags,' she says, rummaging in her handbag, 'and the *Sun*. I don't know why I'm bothering cos I reckon that old git over there's smoking all the fags I bring anyway, and look, you haven't even opened yesterday's paper. Auntie Gloria says she'll pop in to see ya tomorrow . . .' Blah blah blah blah blah blah. 'Oh and that friend of yours, Andy, that's him, he's been calling and calling. I told him you wouldn't know him if he came but he won't give over. Anyway, I told him not to come again till you were a bit more like yourself . . .'

Fuck me! Ma could talk. She'd go on till the cows came

home without taking a break, filling hours and days with meaningless yap yap yap.

'There's no substance to your prattle, woman,' Dad would say. 'Your drownin' out the telly.'

Since Weston-super-Mare Mum'd built up a fair old wall of sound round herself, she had. She and Dad just stepped around each other at home, her with her séances and blether, him with his politics and his pipe. Uncle Wally never came round no more. Went to live in Bournemouth with a divorcée from Hockley Heath and only sent a card at Christmas.

Yes, Ma in her floral pinny is definitely me first proper memory after the 'psychotic event'. There she was, acting like it was as normal as Rich Tea biscuits for me to be banged up in the loony bin. Except I couldn't speak properly, I couldn't even answer her back. It was like I'd bust me jaw or something or me mouth was full of, like, twenty chewing gums, and when I did try and speak I sounded like Raymond Jiggins's brother, the spastic one in the wheelchair who couldn't hold his head up straight and drooled down his chin.

'Nnnggrahh, myyahh, mrnnnnngyaahh.' Shit, that's all I could manage I was so crammed full a Largactyl. Fucking mental drug.

But Ma was made up that I was even *trying* to speak and she jumped up, shouting, 'Jerry, me love, Jerry, what you sayin'? Hey doctor, doctor, nurse, he's talkin'.' Course she didn't know all I was saying was, 'Shut the fuck up and light me a fag, will yer?' She's a good girl really.

I could talk better by the time Andy turned up a couple a weeks later. It was only when he began to tell me where he'd been and what he'd been doing that I got a grip on how long I'd been in that place. It was like I'd been in a time warp or something. Other worlds, you see? It had been four whole weeks since leaving Spain, four weeks in cuckoo zombie land lunched out on tranks and antipsychotics. Andy was all smiles when he clocked me and sauntered over to the bed without a hint of the nervous, freak-show stuff that Kev and me dad'd had. He could handle all sorts, Andy. Nothing fazed him.

'Jez, my main man.' He grinned. He'd brought me some grapes, a couple a copies of the *Face*, I remember, and a book, *Zen and the Art of Motorcycle Maintenance*. He even smuggled me in a tenth of Charras, which I was grateful for. Fuck, the drugs they were pumping me with in hospital were well fierce compared to a little toke of the organic stuff, although if you listened to the doctors you'd think dope was responsible for the mental fuck-ups of the whole frigging nation. Bloody ridiculous.

'God, you scared us for a while there, man,' Andy said, laughing, after we'd done the awkward 'All right, mates', with him checking if I was sane enough to hold a proper conversation. I could tell he wanted to make a big old joke of me being in the nuthouse, but hesitating cos I looked well sad with me mouth flopping open like a stroke victim or something, but I made light of it.

'Aah, don't be soft, man, it's me, Jez.' I didn't want him to feel sorry for me.

'Yeah but, you know, all that stuff you did. I had to call your parents, I just had to, you understand?'

I frowned. I didn't really know what he was talking about so I goes, 'S'all right. I don't even remember.'

'Don't remember?'

I shook me head.

'You lost it completely, man. It was pretty funny in a weird kind of way, but we didn't know what to do.' He shifted from side to side on his arse cheeks like he was gonna fart or something, but I think he might've just been nervous about freaking me out. Then he said, 'Look, man. Maybe now's not the right time to be going into all this. You're still not completely well and –'

'No, tell me, I wanna know what I was doin'. I wanna know everythin'.'

Andy looked up and down the room. I followed where his eyes went. There were four of us on me ward. There was this old bloke who lived rough mainly, but spent a month or two in hospital every year. I recognized him from when we was young. We used to call him the Marcher cos when you saw him in town he'd be marching up and down all day, left right, left right, left right, round and round the precinct. 'Here comes the Marcher,' we'd shout, as he quickstepped towards us, arms going like pistons. Sometimes we'd see him on the ring road where there was no pavement and the traffic would be indicating round him at seventy miles an hour. It's a wonder he wasn't killed. He'd always have a hard-set face and narrowed eyes, like he had a fixed purpose with somewhere to go and something to do. Then, every once in a while, he'd stop marching and start hanging around the city centre making a nuisance of himself, swearing at the housewives as they went to fetch their groceries, or surprising the old dears sat by the fountain feeding pigeons. He'd sneak up quietly behind 'em and when he was close he'd shout out and make 'em jump out their skins. It was always something filthy like 'Fucking whore bitch,' or 'Suck my fat cock.' Then he'd turn heel and march off a few yards and rock from one foot to the other, mumbling, just like that. Well, the old dears would squeal like weaners and run off quick like, cos they was real frightened. But it was sport to watch him, and as teenagers we'd hang out in a gang, lads and girls together, and some of the girls would try and goad him and walk over to where he was fidgeting and say, 'Hey, Marcher, ain't you gonna talk dirty to us today?' while we all sniggered in a group a way off. Fuck, man, that Marcher would get so flustered and start spouting the craziest shit you ever heard and we'd be laughing and laughing. Aah, those were great times. But I'll say one thing, the Marcher never hurt no one. He'd swear and cuss and stuff but I never saw him lay a finger. Then he'd just disappear. We wouldn't see him on the ring road or in the precinct and we'd think he must've been arrested for making a public nuisance of himself, or sometimes we'd make up stories for each other that he'd marched off on a long old journey to some exotic place, like France or China.

'He's making the little Chinky women howl in some precinct in Shanghai,' we'd say. 'Fluckin' whore britch, rick my cock.' What a laugh. We never imagined him banged up in the loony bin. Yeah, that Marcher was all right really. Even in hospital, though, you couldn't get much out of him before he told you to 'fuck off'.

So there was the Marcher, and then there was this young lad who'd wank for hours if he was late with his tablets. And there was this middle-aged guy, Dennis, who'd tried to top himself a few times and now he just turned up at the hospital if he felt the urge coming on. He told me about it, all factual like a teacher, cos he was that type, you know, a posh un. But he had a gentle voice a bit like a woman.

'Yes,' he said, 'this is my twelfth time. I keep trying but I'm obviously not very good at it. I suppose I'll get the hang of it in the end.'

He had such an old-fashioned look about him and you could tell he felt like he was a failure at everything, even suicide. I reckon he was a fruit meself but still, we got on.

As Andy checked out me new buddies I wondered if that was it for me, fucked in the head for ever, in and out a hospital like Dennis and the Marcher.

Then Andy says, 'Do you remember getting back from Spain?'

I searched me mind. 'No, not really.'

'Do you remember anything about Spain?'

'Oh yeah, loads of it.'

'Do you know . . . for example . . . where the dollars are

stashed?' As he spoke I spotted a flash of hope in Andy's face.

'I . . . I didn't stash 'em. It was Basil.'

'I know, Basil told me. I just haven't seen him for a bit so I was wondering if *you* could remember exactly where.'

'Can't you ask *him*?'

Andy drummed his knees with his fingers. 'Look, Jez, we've been in India, me and Bas; we went just after you came in here, and well, Bas isn't back yet.'

'No! India! No way!'

'Yeah man, it's true. Unbelievable really. Your sister was there too.'

'You're kidding me. Sharon?'

'Straight.'

'What, on a job?'

Andy nodded and gave me a knowing look. 'So you see I haven't got all the details about where the dollars are stashed.'

Every time he said dollars he'd look down the ward to make sure no one was listening. I should've told him that a mad story like his wouldn't get any attention in the loony bin.

'I'll be honest, mate, those last days in Spain are a bit of a blur.' I rubbed me temple cos I felt a small pain where the memory should've been. 'I remember Basil going off to stash the dollars,' I went on. 'It was mental. He bought all this plastic packaging and tape and stuff and he wrapped 'em up in it, layer after layer. At first I thought he was gonna bury 'em but when he came back he said . . . he said . . . he'd stashed 'em on the roof.'

I'd remembered. I was well chuffed.

'Yeah, he said the roof . . . the roof of the hotel, but what hotel, Jez, and where on the roof? Try and remember.'

'The town's called . . . aargh . . . Nerja, a place near the beach, the rooms had . . . balconies.'

I don't know why but after I got that sentence out I started to cry. I can't explain it, I mean I *don't* cry, or maybe I do, but a hot wave of prickly stuff washed through me and I was curling me mouth and snot was dribbling onto me top lip. It was such an effort to dredge up one simple fact, it hurt, like weightlifting with no muscles or like when you're a little kid and struggling to fight off a stronger lad or something. Fuck, I was feeble in there. I couldn't see inside me own mind.

'Hey, hey, it's OK, man,' says Andy. 'No pressure.'

'God knows where they are, Andy. God knows,' I cried.

Andy had his arm across me shoulder. 'Shh, shh. No worries, Jez, I can get a message to Bas. He'll tell me. It's not a big deal.'

Andy's eyes were flicking down to the nurses' station while he was trying to comfort me and I knew I had to pull meself together. 'Sorry, Andy, sorry, mate, I'm OK, I'm safe.'

'Yeah?'

'Yeah.'

We sat quietly for a while with Andy patting me back and playing with his dreads. Until I goes, 'I remember Basil on the plane, though. He was apologizin' to me . . . or was it for me? And making me take them pills.'

'Valium.'

'OK, Valium, if you say so.'

'Basil said you thought he was forcing you to take a truth drug.'

'Hmmm.'

'You did, man, it was mad, I mean it was funny.' Andy was laughing now, trying to make me forget the weeping fit, and clacking his fingers like Basil used to.

I laughed along, but ugly memories were running round behind me eyes and making me screw me face up. I could feel meself gurning. Fucking Largactyl.

Andy ignored it, or didn't notice. 'Hah, and on the way back up the motorway we stopped at some services and you walked round the shop as if you owned it. You were nicking loads of food off the shelves and stuffing it in your shirt. The manager chased you out and you were screaming, "I have to have supplies cos that darkie's gonna lock me up for ever," but then you stopped outside by the window and let the food fall on the floor while you . . .' Andy could barely speak for laughing. 'While you picked the heads off every single flower out the front. All you left was a row of stalks.'

'No!' I was chuckling along now.

'Yeah, man. We tried to explain to the manager but he thought we were all mad. I paid for the damage of course. Me and Bas had to wrestle you back into the car with you fighting us as though we were the enemy. I mean, properly fighting.'

'You're joking.'

'Straight, and back at Hampton Kirby it was totally weird cos you were speaking in all these different accents, Irish, Patois, northern, and picking at your tattoo scab till it bled.'

'Really?'

'Really.'

Andy put his hand over his mouth and looked at me, raising his eyebrows; some thought had stopped his flow. I was fingering the bandage on me tattoo, remembering things in shards like broken glass. Then he said, 'But you're getting better now.' He still had his hand over his mouth so I couldn't hear it clearly, but I know that's what he said.

'So what else did I do, Andy?' I asked, wanting to get the blokey vibe going again, you know, me and him creasing up at me being a nutter and feeling like it was all just another crazy story of us, the lads and our exploits. But he looked tired all of a sudden and started rubbing his eyes and shit.

'Aw, you know, stuff, a bit mad. Your mum and dad came to the house, and we called the doc and then you were in here and that was it really.' He paused. 'I came to visit.'

'When? I don't remember.'

'No? Well, it was the first week but you were out of it.'

'It's the drugs, man, they're all fucking downers.'

'I know.'

'Andy?'

'Yes, mate.'

'I'm still your best boy, aren't I?'

'Too fucking right.'

There was so much Andy could've told me that first visit but I suppose he wanted to measure it out and make sure I could handle the information in dribs and drabs. Like I said, he didn't want to worry me or freak me out. So he didn't tell me that he couldn't ask Bas about the dollars cos Bas had been busted on the way back from India with twelve kilos of hash in the false bottoms of his suitcases. He was in prison, in Rome of all places, and his lawyers were saying it would be a three-year custodial unless they had some money to put a case together. Another recruit of Pads's had been pulled in Copenhagen and been so freaked he'd spilled the beans, so Pads's contact in Manchester, Simmo, had been pulled but then released. Everyone had their fingers crossed that Simmo's case'd be chucked out – lack of evidence. Simmo was a good lad.

Andy *didn't* tell me that Sharon was back on the scag, that even though she'd got through customs with her cases she'd nearly killed herself with some manky ten-quid bag she bought off the Gulson Road crew a week later. Apparently it was cut to shit with strychnine or something and even me ma didn't know she had a daughter in the detox clinic half a mile away while she was visiting another one of her fucked up kids in the nuthouse down the road. Sharon never saw Mum and Dad anyway, not since her and her mates broke in and stole the video recorder and Ma's collection money for the catalogue.

Another thing Andy didn't tell me was that Arlo had phoned and warned him that Stitch was gonna kill him. So Andy'd moved out of Hampton Kirby and into a flat in Leamington Spa, with Spud. They both sat there each night, bricking it, expecting the door to get kicked in and a sawn-off pushed in their snouts.

Still, Andy came every week, sometimes twice a week. He got to know the other blokes on the ward and brought the nurses chocolate and phoned me ma if he couldn't make it in. Ha, one of the nurses fancied him and she'd always stop and join in our conversation so that Andy would have to ask her to leave, saying we needed 'one-to-one time' and promising he'd come and find her later. He had that effect on women. Little by little he told me all the bad news. Now I can't be sure if half the things he told me were real. I'm not saying Andy was lying – I'm just saying it was a strange time for me and I've had to take a view, if you know what I mean. Up *until* Spain me memories are pretty sharp, as memories go, but Spain memories have got a kind of squishiness to 'em, like liquid in a clear plastic bag: you can press the surface and it gives a bit, like you could almost pierce the membrane and step right through your thoughts and into another world. I'm not sure if 'madness' or mad people aren't just people who can see where the barriers between worlds have got thin so whatever's happening in a parallel place seeps into the way we see things here. People call 'em spooky feelings or premonitions, but I think it's space or time bulging and swelling up like a big old bubble and people like me can peer through the window like it was a magnifying glass. Yeah. That's what it is.

*

I remember I was a nipper, about eight or nine years old, when we started *Das Bombers*. The gang was made up of some of the kids in our street and we'd made this massive den on the bomb patch at the end of our road where a whole row – no, rows on rows, actually – of terraced houses had been flattened in the war and no one had built anything there again cos, like, the council was shit and everyone was poor and stuff. Thirty people had died in one night where that bomb patch was. Now it was a dumping ground full of old prams and bits of bikes and milk crates and car batteries. The brambles had taken over, mostly, and made huge thorn domes over everything, covering the remains of the buildings. Course, us kids had claimed the area like our dads before us and there was never anyone them times telling you to 'stay off' or 'be careful'. If anything the grown-ups would shout, 'Why don't you pests just fuck off down the bomb patch?' if they saw us hanging about on the street or kicking our heels outside the sweet shop, and they'd shake their fists at us like in the *Beano*.

We had a whole imaginary life on the bomb patch. Our den was wicked. You had to crawl down under a bramble curtain and into this old, blasted up parlour. The roof was gone but there was a mass a thorns and rubbish for a ceiling instead, draped over walls about four foot high, at the highest. You could still see the old tiles on the floor and the sooted fireplace set back in the bricks. That room was where we sat and smoked fags and swapped the stuff we'd found, you know, like copper piping and bits of lead, conkers and football stickers. But in the second room, the most secret 'cut yer wrist and never tell' room, was our pride and joy. The entrance to the room was hidden behind a sheet of mouldy chipboard. We had to shift it back before we could crouch down and crawl into the tunnel. The tunnel was, say, six foot long and we'd go through it on our bellies like soldiers, with the brambles scratching our backs through our clothes. Eventually the tunnel opened onto another room. We'd decked it out with candles and page three pin-ups and the foam innards from dumped settees. This was where we kept booze, stolen tapes, the cassette player and some old porn mags. But most important, this was where we kept the *sacred artefact*. It was Patrick O'Connor's idea to call it the 'sacred artefact' cos we couldn't call it by its real name, it was too big a secret, but between us we ended up calling it by its real name. *Das Bomb*.

Das Bomb was an unexploded World War Two German bomb about three foot long and as thick as a man's thigh with a snub old snout at one end and three chunky fins at the other; a proper bomb-shaped bomb. We knew it was dangerous. We'd heard the stories off our dads and grandads of poor sods who'd accidentally hit one with the garden spade, sending themselves to bleedin' heaven in a spray of earth and metal. We knew this was the real thing all right, and that's what made it so special. It had taken three of us the best part of a day to drag it into the den and set it on a bit of foam to cushion it. Then Patrick, Peter Daventry, Terry Royston and me painted swastikas all over it with our Airfix paints.

Das Bomb was power, raw power, and we used it for our initiation ceremonies. Every new gang member had to crawl through to the room and hit the bomb in three places with the wooden hammer that Johnny Ray's brother had stolen from the Magistrates' Court when he'd been up for reckless driving. The bomb had to be hit once on the fins, once on the body and once on the snout while the new member said the Promise of Allegiance. Fuck knows what the actual words were, they changed each time cos they weren't written down or anything. But the bomb banging was the same each time. The main rule was that you had to keep the secret room and its treasure a total secret for ever and ever.

Timmy Jessop was a weedy rascal who promised to get his sister to do a strip for us if we let him join the gang. So we decided that if he had the nous to pimp his own sister he deserved to join – besides, everybody fancied Mandy. I was the initiation witness that day so me and Timmy crawled through the tunnel while the other boys went outside to take cover behind the wall that marked the boundary between the bomb patch and the school. I mean, that shows we knew *Das Bomb* was not just a mascot but an actual house-shattering, flesh-ripping weapon of destruction. I'd brought me torch and some matches to light the candles and a whistle for signalling.

Inside, I told Timmy to kneel in front of *Das Bomb*. It was always cold in that room even in summer. Timmy Jessop was small for his age. He had short trousers on that day and a grubby shirt under his tank top. You'd've laughed to see him. He kept pushing his specs up with one finger, then wiping his nose with the back of his hand. Once we were settled I gave him the hammer. Two orange flames were reflected in his glasses so it looked like he had fiery cat's eyes but his hand was shaking and I remember saying, 'Easy, Timmy, you don't wanna blow us up.'

Timmy tried to nod but I noticed the glint of a single tear making a track from beneath his glasses and on down his cheek. So I says, 'It's OK, nothin' bad's ever happened. Anyway, if we're gonna die it'll be quick as lightning, so there's nothing to worry about.'

But I had a little shiver when I saw that tear, like someone was on me grave, tho I'd've rather chopped me finger off than show I was scared them times.

'Look, just a little tap with that –' I pointed at the hammer '– that's all you have to do. Tap *Das Bomb* here, here and here,' and I showed him all the places where the hammer had to fall.

Now Timmy's got a right good shake on, stronger than

me grandad's Parkinson's I'm telling you, and I can tell he can't get a grip on the fear, but he's clutching that hammer like a weapon now and I'm starting to wonder where this is all going cos I can hear him wheezing, short and shallow, and there's a faint grunting sound in there an' all. So he's kneeling in front of *Das Bomb* and I'm almost pissin' with the tenseness of it and him all teary and shaky in the candlelight and that big old rusty bomb sitting there all solid and menacing in front of him and he lifts that hammer up, way above his head so it almost gets caught in the bramble shoots, and before I can say, 'Hold on a minute there, Timmy,' he smashes it down as hard as he can on the fins of that there bomb. BADOOSH.

Now, call us all wimps, but I ain't never seen any of them *Das Bombers*, meself included, hit the *sacred artefact* like Timmy did that day. No way. The most we'd ever managed was three hard taps like, RINK DINK DINK, so the metal rang out a little while our hearts speeded up a ways. But Timmy smashes that thing as if he means to break the bomb in two and you know one a them fins comes flying off and zips right past me ear like the shrapnel's already out to get me.

'Whoa, Timmy, not so hard, you don't –' But before I can finish he's lifted the hammer up high again so the handle's touching the ceiling.

I saw another world open up to me that day. There was another universe inside *Das Bomb*, or maybe it was just the future. But the world I saw was one where Timmy was a half-skeleton, with all the flesh burnt away so that he was grinning on one side of his face and sort of blubbing on the other. It was a world where the sky was crystal blue with white clouds racing above a rainbow of debris, expanding outwards from one hard point. A whole structure lived inside *Das Bomb*, you know. It was only the metal casing that held it in. One more hammer blow would release it and let it take its shape. I knew it. But Timmy brought the hammer down again and bashed that bomb right in the guts, GADDONK. In a half second I had him on the ground, grappling with him in the dirt, and I could hear him whimpering right next to me ear.

'Tim, stop it now, you're gonna make it blow,' I shouted.

Then I felt him go limp and everything was quiet for a moment except for a tiny metallic 'click'. It was the quietest click, as quiet as when you pull one fingernail against another, but we both heard it.

Then a real live voice spoke in the stillness, a man's voice, no kidding, not in my head, and it said, 'Listen to that, Jerry, that's the sound of death.' I swear to you, stab me in the eye, it was real, cos then my vision went all weird like a heat haze rippling above the Tarmac on a summer day and I couldn't move. Then Timmy panted, 'We gotta get outta here.' Perhaps he'd heard the voice too; perhaps fear opens up other worlds for everyone. Then, in a flash, we were crawling back down the tunnel, through the room we smoked in and out into the light and we ran across the bomb patch with me blowing me whistle as hard as I could and Timmy shouting, 'Cover, take cover.' All the while that picture of metal and dirt and brambles and torn limbs and flesh was burning in me head.

We all stayed behind the wall for ages until eventually Johnny Ray got up, frustrated, chucking his weight around like he did.

'I'm bored with this,' he moaned. 'Nothing's gonna blow.'

'It is, I tell ya. I heard *Das Bomb* make a noise from inside like it was changing its mind about something.'

'Bollocks, you're just a wimp, you're both wimps.'

Johnny Ray's dad was a boxer who liked to come all feisty and hard with his kids; we all knew Johnny could be a twat because of it. So I jumped on him, fists flying, shouting, 'Bundle!' to make the other lads join in.

It was Timmy who ran off and got his dad. Then everything happened at once: the cops came, all the dads were out in the street and mums were stood in doorways wiping their hands on tea towels and soon half the road had been evacuated while the bomb squad turned *Das Bomb* from *sacred artefact* to lump of old metal in a matter of hours. The man from the MoD said there was no doubt *Das Bomb* was 'primed and ready to go' and they cordoned off the whole area for three days while they checked it over. They found two more little uns under the soil and all. The Germans dropped some lethal shit on Coventry.

We forgave Timmy in the end, especially since Mandy Jessop did a strip for us in Johnny's shed and it was the best strip of any of the girls in the street, ever. We never forgot *Das Bomb* though. Some of the lads got a picture of it tattooed on the top of their arms when they were older while others, like me, just got a swastika. It was a sign of allegiance.

'Did I tell you I was in love?' Andy came out with it like he was surprised.

'Someone caught your eye again, mate?'

'No, I mean it. I'm in love.'

Andy had come on one of his visits. He'd brought me a bag of lemon bonbons and an *NME* and he was sitting on me bed with his feet on the visitor's chair, reading the paper.

'So, who is she? The lovely Nurse Joanna?'

We both looked briefly towards the nurses' station as Andy put a bonbon in his mouth, puckering up with the tartness of it. 'No, not her, I met this girl in India. She was one of Pads's recruits.'

'You never mentioned her.'

'No. Well. I haven't seen her since.'

'Shit. Didn't she get through?'

'Yep. Got through customs in Brussels safe and sound.'

'Pads must've made a packet what with Sharon and your girl. Two outta four. I can't believe he hasn't paid you for the job.'

'C'mon, he's paid me some. But after Brussels she disappeared.'

'How d'you mean?'

'She did a runner with the stuff. She could have gone anywhere in Europe after Brussels. Trail's gone cold. If she knows where to sell that much hash, she'll make, let's see, twenty-odd grand, maybe more.'

'Shit.'

'Yeah! Mad, eh? Got to hand it out to her. Disappeared off the face of the earth, like a phantom.'

'Did she know you was in love with her?'

He looked at me straight. 'I told her in India.'

'Fuck man, you told her. You're fresh. That must've bin why she did a runner then.'

Andy rolled his paper up and hit me lightly round the head. 'Bastard.'

We both laughed. 'So you gonna try and find her then or what?'

'You bet.'

'Where you gonna look?'

'She told me she wanted to live in London, bright lights big city, you know the vibe. I'll start there.'

'London. You can get well lost in London.'

Andy did one of his sad faces.

'Won't Pads want her guts for garters if you find her?'

Andy nodded. 'I'm not sure I'll tell Pads.'

'Fuck that Pads, man, he's a tight bastard.'

'He's a businessman. He doesn't get sentimental. I can't knock him for that really.'

Right then I realized what it was about Andy I loved. He had his faults a course, we all do, but Andy forgave all mine, and all Bas's and Pads's and everyone's. He forgave everybody, he accepted everybody. All me life, Dad, Kev, all it was was hate and 'Get that fucker' and 'Twat that bastard' and 'They're to blame', not me, not us, and pretending I was hard so's I could fit in with it. But Andy . . . he understood about other worlds and love, even swastikas.

Andy ruffled me new-grown hair. 'You're sounding more like your old self every day, my man. It's good to have you back.'

'Good days and bad days, good days and bad.'

Course, Andy'd still ask me about the hotel and the dollars, hoping something would trigger me memory, but mostly he talked about the future. Praps he'd live abroad, he said, or knuckle down and have a go at being a professional musician instead of being half-arsed about it all. But mostly he talked about his girl and how he planned to find her. He said he'd kissed her in the airport before she got on the plane to do her run. Said he felt a whole new feeling flooding through him when he kissed her. Said it was like finding a key to a lock you didn't even know was there and opening the door to a secret world that had been inside your mind the whole time. Said his life was gonna change, that once Stitch'd been paid off he was leaving Cov for good. Said there'd always be a place for me with him. Said he meant it. I couldn't imagine him not being there to tell me what job we had on next and where we'd be going and what we'd all be doing. I couldn't imagine not being part of a crew, on a mission, doing the credit cards, running kilos across town, or over to Brum. But I knew it was over. That life. That time. There was no going back. Basil in prison. Me in the loony bin. Andy in love. And even though he meant that shit about having a place with him, he'd move on. It was how the world worked. I knew if I remembered the name of the hotel, Andy'd stop coming. Praps that's why it took me so long to dredge it up.

Course, I gradually remembered bits and pieces about the rooms and the layout of the place. I told Andy everything I could but Basil was the one he needed. It must've been hard for him having to rely on me for the details.

Then one night the hotel's name comes to me, no word of a lie. I'm wide awake, seriously, not sleeping, but I'm walking along this Spanish road, right, and it's Nerja and the sun's shining so bright I can barcly see. I can still see the hospital ward and all the beds, even the nurses' station, but there are little white clouds gliding across the sky above me and I can smell Spain in me nostrils. There's a person beside me. It's Andy, loping along, tall and good-looking, and his face is bright as floodlights. All the señoritas are winking at him as we walk and he's smiling one a them 'bloody women' smiles, pretending he's not enjoying the attention when really he is. Then up ahead I see the hotel, the front of it's rising up from the pavement high, high into the blue, higher than a skyscraper. I say, 'Look, man, there it is,' and as we come closer we scan the outside looking for the name. Then I spot it way up so we have to go over the other side of the road and crane our necks to read it. But the sign is so small and so high it's really frustrating cos we both want to know the name of it so bad and we can't make it out. Suddenly I notice all the señoritas have started screaming and crying, and all their pretty faces are screwed up in disgust, one or two of 'em are covering their eyes. I turn to Andy to ask what's going on but Andy's turned into a skeleton and his clothes have been blasted off his body and bits of skin and shit are hanging off his bones. Behind him is a rainbow of debris stretching up further than I can see. But his skeleton mouth chatters away like there's nothing wrong. He's saying, 'I'm in love, Jez, sure as day is day and night is night. I'm in love.' And I think, 'Maybe it's OK to get flayed cos there's always love,' as if love is like the afterlife. Then Andy points and says, 'Shit, would you look at that,' and I can see the name of the hotel suspended in the sky, lit up like a Christmas tree, *Puerta del Cielo*, so I write it down in case I forget.

Then BAM, I'm in me bed again and I know I have a wound or a cut but I can't work out where it is. It's only then I remember about the bullet, it's in me brain, and I don't know how I could've forgot it. I call the nurses. No one comes. So I scream and scream and soon they're all round me, but no one listens when I try to tell them about the bullet and the skeleton and that Andy's life's in danger. They won't listen. They hold me down. The fuckers.

17

MEHMET

A New Trade

The heat of late springtime now extends into the night and the tourists are in vests and shirtsleeves as they walk about the city. Romance is everywhere and the smell of a warming sea licks up from the port, reaching our nostrils like the memory of some favourite childhood dish that our mothers cooked us long ago. I am growing used to life by the water. I am a mountain man, but water is still a source of life and here it is also a gateway to other worlds. Ech, this city is a place of a million ins and outs, comings and goings, where huge liners empty their chattering loads into the port and planes whine across the dazzling skies. Coastal people are different from mountain people, I think. But the Pyrenees are close enough and I go to the mountains often, when my heart is low.

We have been working hard for months, Juan and I, saving and drinking. I am a good thief. I have a beady eye. In Albania I could spot the dancing leaf that told me of a change of weather, the nibbled shoot that signalled a roe deer was near. Here it is the same skill that leads me to the easy pickings, the unzipped rucksack pocket, the unfastened handbag, the wallet riding out the back of a fat man's trousers, the tourist plates on cars that promise doors that fall right open, the unattended swim bag full of camera and currency.

Tonight we work near the theatre district and Juan has popped the tinted window of a sleek black van off the Carrer Pujades. The charcoal glass attracted us and we can't resist checking for the treasure it is hiding. Juan tips the lock and lets me in first while he watches for *policia*. But once inside I am startled, for on the back seat there is what I first think is a voluptuous woman reclining. I jump back and scrabble off along the road, shouting, 'Run for it,' but Juan only stands and laughs.

'Hey, jumpy boy,' he mocks. 'What are you afraid of?'

He is relaxed, with one boot still inside the van. So I peer back inside and see the reclining woman is some kind of musical instrument.

It is cumbersome but we get it back to Ratto's back room with the rest of the night's haul, where I unzip the soft casing to reveal a beautiful wooden structure, elegant and shapely. It makes me think of Aisha. It smells of forests and tree resin and the varnish accents the gorgeous contrast in the wood grain even in the thin light of the single bulb.

'It's a cello,' says Juan. 'The van must have been a musician's, from the theatre.'

I bite my lip. 'It's like a woman.'

'Not like the women I know,' he teases. 'Maybe Albanian women are different, eh? Look, this girl has a hard heart.' And he delivers three hard raps on the soundboard and shouts through the curly cut-out carving into the hollow expanse inside. 'I'm coming in, pretty lady.'

'Don't!' I caution, irritated.

'Mehmet, it's a cello.'

I lower my eyes and leave the room.

Juan catches me as I step into the street. 'Where are you going, brother?'

I shrug.

'Come, I'll buy you a drink.'

We take a taxi to the Ramblas and drink cognac in a back street off the Plaça Reial.

'I have to leave this place, Juan,' I explain after he has tried in vain to cheer me.

'Why must you leave when we are becoming the best of friends?'

'Ah, it's hard to explain. In my head I want to stay with you and Ratto for ever. This is the happiest I have been for a very long time, in my whole life perhaps. But in my heart I know I have to keep a promise.'

Juan throws his arms up in frustration. 'What promise? What can be so important that you give your word to people you will never see again?' Then he says, 'Sorry,' with his eyes cast down, knowing this is hurtful and unfair.

'I promise them I will become a rich man and pay the debts of my past.'

'We all make promises like this when we are young, no? Promises that are impossible to keep, Mehmet. Even God cannot keep this promise you have made.'

'Ech, perhaps you're right. But you know I have to try. I owe a debt of honour to another *fis* and the women of my own *fis* rely on me, only me, to come to protect them.'

'Mehmet, from what you have told me it may already be too late. If your uncle has betrayed you then your mother is already –'

'Stop, I cannot think this. Jules will protect my mother. He made *me* a promise, and apart from you now I have no one else I trust.'

'But I think even Jules is no match for this Hoxha.'

We sit silently for a while and watch a small child bounce up to the fountain, his blond curls bobbing with each springy toddler step. He throws a penny in the water, turns and claps, gleeful, as his doting parents and several childless couples applaud him from their tables. I look at them and in each eye there is a light, a strand of under-standing that says this boy represents a future and from his loins more boys will spring. Why else do they give such importance to the sport of this dumpling thing?

'*Fis* do not exist in the real world, Mehmet,' Juan con-tinues, as if he hasn't watched this scene along with the rest. 'Here there is no honour and no *besa* and no *gjak* to pay for.' Juan is almost angry, as though I am a child he's told a thousand times to tie the door shut on the sheep fold and I have once again forgotten.

'How can you say that when everywhere in Spain I see the ties of the *fis* – here, right here, there are bonds of duty and loyalty that make even you do *this thing* rather than *that thing*. And your commitment to me, this is like *besa*. Believe me, without your *besa* I would be lost.'

'Then do me the honour of forgetting Albania. She is a ruined place and you can never go back. My God, it took all of your courage and your guile to get out, no?'

'You are wrong to ask this of me, Juan. But because I love you I am sad that I must do what will sadden *you*.'

Juan looks sullen and angles his face away from me to demonstrate his disappointment. 'You know, Mehmet, Ratto and I had to leave our parents. I miss them, but their hatred for Ratto's kind meant we could not stay. We will overcome their small minds by forgetting them, by making Catalunya our home, by disregarding their antique rules. I refuse the confines of my *fis*, as you call it . . . and so should you.'

'I am sorry about your parents . . . *and* like you I feel no guilt to live the way we do. But I have a love in my heart.'

'Love?'

'Yes, Juan, I confess. I am in love.'

Juan throws his arm across my shoulder, laughing. 'For the cello woman, yes?' And he knocks on the tabletop three times.

I smile. 'Yes, for the cello woman.'

'You are a romantic, hah! I knew it. I think I like you even more knowing this.' He slaps the table and calls for more cognac as if my revelation deserves some celebration. 'Why did you not tell me about love?'

I do not answer but I wonder why for love it is worth risking all, but for honour and duty it is not. Or maybe in Juan's country love *is* honour and duty by another name.

When we have said '¡Salud!' and slapped each other's backs, Juan says, 'So tell me. Where will you go? England?'

'Yes. To England, to make my fortune.'

'Hey, brother, I have a better idea. Do not go north. Go south . . . to Andalucia.'

'Why south?'

He makes himself more comfortable in his chair like he will tell a long story. 'Well, Englishmen, they love the hashish, even more than we. I knew a man, I know him still, who brings plenty hashish from Morocco to the south. He pays little for it there, but he tells me if I take it to Holland or Inglaterra then I would have the makings of a fortune.'

'How much money would this take?'

'I'll ask my friend but I would say . . . one hundred, one-fifty thousand pesetas.'

'Ech, I don't know this man or the south. I will take my chances in England without this hashish fortune.'

'*I* know the south, me, Juan.' He pats his chest with the palms of his hands. 'I am from the south. Besides, you are going to England for what? To beg on the streets, or clean the shithouses, or wheel dead bodies round at the morgue, or pull rats out of the drains? Brother, the best you can hope for in England is a life of drudgery, except fifteen degrees colder.'

'What are you talking about?'

'Everyone I know who has been to work in England has lived in squalor doing all the jobs the English hate, like picking vegetables for some fat pink farmer and living on *patatas fritas* soaked in pig fat. They will hate you and revile you there. You are no more than a gypsy to them.'

'But the money, the streets are full of money.'

'The only money is in the pockets of the rich. No, you must only *go* to England rich. If you go there poor you will become trapped in their miserable cold poverty for ever.'

I laugh. 'You are too dramatic, making myths and horror stories for me to believe.'

'And you would rather believe fairy stories, eh, my young romantic. Now look, over there, that is money walking down the street, ready for us to pluck.' And he points to a fresh young couple, English we both wager, he in khaki chinos, she in white shorts, their skin burnished with a hot blush from the day's relentless sun and both staggering to some absurd rhythm no one else can hear.

'They are milch-sheep, yes.' He grins.

'Drunk as skunks,' I say in English and we laugh.

We pay our bill and catch up with the couple as they turn off Las Ramblas into an altogether darker avenue.

But I cannot stop thinking of Aisha.

18

PADS

Slipping Up

Listen to this:
   Pads mon, I am in prison in Rome and I am writing to ask you for help. I may as well come out with it straight off. Me can't ask Andy now cos me know him have nothing to give and as you have been like a employer and a good good friend a Andy I and I know you will want to sort me out. Me need £800 fa lawyer and everything and from since you understand me predicament I is coming to you because you know that me can get off a this problem here if me tell some people some things directly, right here and right now. But of course I is a solid man, but me need help, y'understan' me? Lickle more, Basil.

   I can't do the accent of course, but you get the gist – the implicit threats. Imagine, Basil trying to finger me for cash, threatening *me* with Italian customs and whatnot. I ask you. I considered ignoring his letter but I couldn't resist writing back.

SHIVA HANDCRAFTS
282 FOLESHILL ROAD, COVENTRY

Dear Basil,
   I am sorry to hear about your situation but you will

appreciate my hands are tied. While I believe you have the potential to be a fine upstanding man you must understand me when I say 'crime doesn't pay'.

I realize my stance might anger you, or persuade you to try and blame the wrong people or – God forbid – me, for what was in the end your own choice to break the law, but I sincerely warn you not to make unfounded allegations. Anyone who accuses innocent people will suffer in the end. Sadly, I suspect that those who conspired in this crime with you will have covered their tracks by now.

I know it would be convenient to implicate someone like me simply to extract money – I travel regularly to India – but I am a legitimate businessman with a registered Indian import business, and I hope you will shy away from casting damaging aspersions.

I am sorry to hear Andy cannot be of more help. He is the one you should contact and I would like to point out that it was he who bought your ticket etc. and that you were in his employ, never in mine. Perhaps you could also ask your family for support at this difficult time.

Yours sincerely,

Mr T Padstock-Burroughs

PS: As a gesture of goodwill I enclose £20 for any personal items you might need during your confinement.

I thought the PS was a nice touch.

Basil had a nerve contacting me and although he had nothing 'on me' I knew he could do a good deal of harm if he decided to push things. He could at least arouse suspicions, enough to have me watched by Customs and Excise. So his threats made me take stock. An audit quickly confirmed I had a significant amount invested in the Indian businesses. Shiva Handcrafts, a genuine company I had set up to account for all my trips to Delhi and Kathmandu, yielded almost thirty per cent of my total overseas haul that year, and with no risk. But my rise to legitimate business success is another story.

Basil didn't have too much to worry about. Once his lawyers were paid off he'd probabaly be repatriated and get off with a couple of months in an Italian jail. I'd seen it time and again when runners got busted. It sounds implausible but the authorities in some European countries were so overrun with drug smugglers that their prison systems were buckling under the strain, so they were happy to send people like Basil packing with a slap on the wrist. To be honest, quite apart from Basil trying to blackmail me from an Italian prison, there were several other things on my mind; for example, the disappearance of Becca with more than £30,000-worth of *my* top quality Charras. Then of course there was mine and Andy's impending trip to Spain to retrieve the dollars. I was working on the Becca angle. I'd made enquiries, naturally. It appeared she'd disembarked in Brussels as planned, getting through customs there without a hitch. After that the trail went cold. Posing as her boyfriend, I contacted the consulates in France, Holland, Denmark and Germany. Nothing. I could only assume she'd headed back to England with the intention of keeping the dope for herself. Things between us had deteriorated steadily in Manali, although she had still done whatever I asked of her, if sullenly. She even spent a night in Basil's room smoothing things over on my instigation. I don't know precisely what transpired between them, but I do know that she convinced Basil she was more anxious than him about the 'coincidence' of them both being in India. She told me that much.

In Delhi I'd booked a room in one of the big colonial hotels. I liked to establish an atmosphere of calm before a run, to spend twenty-four hours in air-conditioned opulence, where the doormen and waiters, done up stiff in their Nehru collars and ceremonial turbans, were attentive but not intrusive. All this helped the couriers and the packers to feel relaxed, away from the street-level insanity that is India. Andy packed the bags. Becca would be carrying twelve kilos of hash, six kilos in each bag. The bags were Samsonites, soft cases with wheels so you could pull them along instead of lifting them. I went to reconfirm the flights and left Becca watching as Andy carefully cut the lining from inside each case to remove the base and expose the housing around the wheels. The packets of Charras had been sealed in twenty layers of cling film and packing tape and treated with the dog spray I'd developed. Each packet was then encased in cardboard and slotted into the false bottoms, after which Andy re-sewed the linings with fine stitches, using thread exactly the same colour as the material. Becca's job was to fill the cases with things she'd bought from the markets, light bulky fabrics and clothes. This would offset the fact that even though the bags looked empty they each weighed seven kilos with the hash inside.

That night I took Becca for dinner at Nirula's. I should have spotted it then, the difference in her, but I put her softness, sadness almost, down to fear. I mean, who wouldn't be petrified the night before carrying that much hashish across international borders?

Then Becca stole my dope. I felt strangely vindicated. I had discerned her nature and she had proved me right. This was Becca. That was what she'd do. It made me desire her even more, knowing she truly was devoid of fear and sentiment. It made me want to master her. I made calls, of course; the money was not unimportant. I got my boys to ask around in London and Manchester. Sometimes things filter through when a quantity of speciality dope comes on the market. But no one had heard anything. In time I phoned Val. She was reticent at first but she soon opened up. She said she hadn't heard from Becca in weeks, that even Becca's dad was going mad with worry. I believed her. Then I asked if we could meet face to face but Val was disinclined. We hadn't exactly hit it off in Spain. I managed to persuade her that Becca was in serious trouble and I had some information that might help. So the next day I met her in Manchester and, notwithstanding her unwillingness of the day before, Val duly arrived, wearing a typically tarty northern-girl get-up with violent pink high heels, a low-cut gypsy-style blouse and one of those awful tiered skirts that were fashionable at the time. Added to which Val had filled out further since Spain and came replete with hind of ham legs, wobbling flab and a painted, pudding face.

My plan was to offer Val money to let me know when Becca showed up but, as I listened to her dreary life story, I realized there was more mileage in stroking Val's ego, wooing her perhaps. She was desperate for attention and carped on for an hour about Becca, disloyalty and abandonment, only occasionally catching herself when she remembered who she was talking to and saying, 'Fuck, I don't know why I'm tellin' you this. You of all people.'

I watched the ripples and puckers in her cheeks as she spoke, noting that the mobility of her face was not only a consequence of the excess weight she carried but the peculiar tendency northern girls have to gurn at the end of each sentence. Val chain-smoked as she talked so that when I eventually steeled myself to move in on her I could smell the tar pits of her lungs.

'Listen,' I said at last. 'I know you were never keen on me, Val, but I have a confession to make.' I turned away, pretending I couldn't look in her eyes.

'What? Warris it?'

I paused for a moment. 'It was you, not Becca that I really liked . . . right from the start.'

I stole a glance. Val was gazing at me cod-mouthed. 'It

was never right between me and Rebecca,' I continued. 'She'd be the first to admit it.'

Her eyes had become suspicious piggy slits.

'Honestly,' I went on quickly. 'Becca and me . . .' I shook my head and squeezed out a whimper until Val's face finally relaxed into a pitying pout.

She reached out to place a dimpled hand on mine. 'I know . . . I mean, she told me it were crap and everything.'

'What?' I was suddenly eager to know how Becca had portrayed me to her chum.

'Y'know . . . like you're saying,' she said, encouraging, at once aware she might have pricked my vanity. 'Becca said, y'know, sex and everythin' was . . . really . . . y'know . . .' Her mouth contorted into a sympathetic grimace as she let the sentence hang. I could see her gums.

'Did she?'

'Yeah, but now I know you fancied me all along I understand you were both just, like, *incompatible*.' She said 'incompatible' with self-congratulatory surprise at recalling seldom-used vocabulary.

I clenched my fist. 'That's right, Val, we were *incompatible*. I tried to tell Becca that it was you and not her, but . . . well.'

'Fuck, did you really tell her? Did you really say you fancied *me*?'

I'd touched a sore point. Valerie, who had been grappling with inferiority all her life, was stung to think her beautiful, desirable friend would scupper an opportunity for romance.

'Oh yes, I spelled it out to her,' I went on. 'But she told me . . . No.' I stopped and bit my lip, as if I was holding back to protect her feelings.

'What? What did she tell yer?'

I took Val's hand and tried to emulate the pity she had offered me moments earlier. 'She said you had . . . *the clap*.'

I mouthed the last two words theatrically northern, like her, and gently squeezed her wrist. Val looked bewildered and I wondered if I'd overstepped the line, but I saw confusion quickly turn to rage. 'I'm sure Becca loves you to bits,' I went on quickly, while Val frowned and curled her lip, 'but people like her are vain, Val; they have to be top dog and they can't stand it if it looks like someone's going to usurp them.'

'Oh Pads, you're so right. She's always put me down, always. She doesn't believe I'll ever be anybody.'

'*I* believe in you, Val.'

'Do yer?' She was reassessing me.

'Oh yes, there's *even* more to you than meets the eye.'

'D'you really think so?'

'I *know*.'

At that point Val pushed her breasts into my shoulder and offered me her ashtray mouth with her eyes closed tight in expectation and, mustering a simulacrum of passion, I kissed her. When I eventually managed to break free she gasped breathlessly, 'What does usurp mean, Pads?'

I got us a room at one of the seedy hotels by the station and Valerie blubbered into bed with me with chubby, star-crossed enthusiasm. The details are irrelevant, but I prayed that one night would be enough to engender her loyalty. The next morning I left Val with instructions to call me the instant Becca arrived in town. Tearfully, she accepted some money 'for her pocket' and waved me off from the plat-form at Manchester Piccadilly. Through the carriage win-dow I promised unremitting lovemaking on my return. Relief overcame me as my train moved away. But despite my machinations Becca, as expected, was a clever vixen. She had calculated that I would nobble Val; watch her dad and her friends. She she was lying very low indeed.

Why didn't I go to Spain alone and look for the dollars? I knew exactly where the hotel was and as far as I was aware at the time I knew where Basil had stashed them. There was something else. It was a desire, no, not desire, a *need* to watch Andy's demise at close quarters, even though I hadn't completely worked out how I would precipitate it. Yet the further he slipped, the better I felt so that my need took on an unhealthy momentum. I'd felt the first seeds of that in Spain. Now I was struggling to keep my impulses in check.

It was excruciating waiting for Andy to wring the name of the hotel out of Jez; in fact my frustration nearly blew my cover, so to speak. One evening Andy came to see me after visiting Jez in hospital. He was bent over, carrying fear and failure on his shoulders like a deformity, so I said, 'You know, I think I could find that hotel myself if pushed.'

Andy was suddenly alert, not the world-weary soul of moments earlier, but looking at me askance, frowning. 'What do you mean?' he said. 'How could *you* find the hotel?'

I realized my mistake and felt my face redden. 'Basil . . . Basil described it to me.'

'When did he do that? Why would he tell *you*?'

Andy was right to be suspicious, of course. Basil would never have talked to me about Spain, or about any job he was doing for that matter, and Andy knew his man.

I needed to choose my words carefully. 'It was in India, we were talking about Nerja . . . anyway he knew that I knew he'd been to Spain with Jez . . . and I've been to Nerja a few times and I . . . we got talking . . . about the town. Well, he pretty well told me what street it was on . . . pretty well. And there can't be that many hotels on one street . . .'

I was over-explaining like a buffoon and I had to chill because Andy was focusing on me so precisely. It's the tiniest casting down of the eyes, that's the deadliest give-away to a lie. So I knew I had to avoid breaking eye contact with Andy at all costs. It was a good job I was practised at it.

'Ah man,' I sighed, suddenly concerned. 'Don't be angry with Basil for slipping up and talking about a job. He was a bit ratted one night in Manali, that's all. You know how he was over there.' I was nodding sadly, making my point.

Andy broke his stare and let his shoulders slump again.

'The good thing is,' I continued, not breaking my stride, 'I reckon I know which hotel they were in and ... *and* ... it's not as if Bas was indiscreet with someone you can't trust.' I risked holding Andy's shoulder and giving it a friendly shake.

'You're right,' he capitulated. 'It's just weird for Bas to ... Ah, forget it, you're right.'

There was something devilishly exciting about how close I was to exposure. It was an almost sexual sensation, knowing that at any moment Andy could discover that I was in Spain with Becca and Val. That I was trying to ruin him. It felt precipitate, and while it was certainly out of character for me to be taking such risks, I was exhilarated. Besides, what could he actually *do* if he found out? He could rail at me, write me off perhaps. Even if he attacked me I would simply endure it and I would still have won. It's hard to explain how predetermined my actions felt. Although how it would all work out still eluded me. I had all manner of fantasies; you know the thing, where you rehearse a scenario, again and again, playing both parts. Sometimes it turns out one way and sometimes another. In one scene I would secretly snatch the dollars before Andy could get to them, then watch his distraction when he realized he was destroyed. In another I would play a concerned father figure burning the dollars, in front of his face, to 'save him from himself'. And he'd be pleading with me not to do it while I held him off with one hand, saying, 'It's for your own good, Andy old chap.' In another he would admit his need of me, my counsel, begging my forgiveness for the humiliation he'd caused me ... Well, I can barely contain myself writing it. It still makes my blood run like vinegar. I just knew I had to watch it all, the failure . . . the pain. That's all.

Finally Jez remembered the name of the hotel. He wrote it down, apparently, before having some kind of seizure. Andy was in torment, blaming himself for Jez's mental health, or lack of it. Still, we arranged to go to Spain within days. Spud was enlisted to drive us to the airport, but when he arrived Andy was not in the car. He had sent Spud to collect me first. There was some 'last minute business to sort out'. So we waited around for a while then drove back to Spud's and beeped the horn.

Spud was one of those nerdy tokers with body odour and no girlfriend. He was easy to manipulate, being 'a pleaser' with very little confidence. He slid into the drug subculture at uni, like the rest of us, but later slid back out again and made a living writing software for a games company. While we waited, Spud spoke with a kind of forlorn resignation, like a family doctor telling an old friend his illness is terminal.

'This is the end, Pads. The end,' he sighed.

'Things change, Spud. Anyway, it's not over yet.'

'But the good old days?' He shook his head. 'It all feels so sad and I'm only twenty-one.'

He went on to say that Andy was 'on the edge' and was about to elaborate when a man I didn't recognize emerged from the entrance to the flats.

'Here we go,' sniffed Spud and opened the car door.

I had to double-take to recognize Andy. He was wearing a box-style jacket and polo shirt with perfectly white trainers sneaking a peek from underneath the turn-ups of stone-washed 501s. He was clean-shaven, shorn, the dreads that had taken so long to nurture gone. I was fascinated by the bony outline of his skull as he flumped into the seat in front of me, as if each divot and bulge was begging to be felt, to be measured by a phrenologist's hands. But his efforts meant only one thing: he was planning some escapade that demanded he look normal. He was going to play Babylon, as he called it, at its own game. Something about him looked final too, as if a part of his life was over and this was a new beginning.

'You're not taking any risks with the appearance then.' It was a statement.

'Time to get serious, Pads. I can't be too careful.'

Yes, Andy had a big plan for those dollars that didn't involve me. I fingered my own dreads thoughtfully. Everything pivoted on this trip. If he pulled it off, Andy would be able to pay the lawyers and get Basil out of prison, help Sharon kick the scag *and* pay his debt to Stitch. Then he could make a clean break and still be the hero. But I wasn't going to let him. It was all going to fuck up and I would be his undoing. I would break him, just as he had broken me. It took the whole journey to piece it all together from stories and memories and things he'd said but by the time we got to Nerja, I'd worked out Andy's plan. I don't want to blow my own trumpet, but by and large I turned out to be right.

Here was Andy's plan in a nutshell. He knew southern Spain pretty well *and* he had some good contacts in Morocco. We'd met a couple of Dutch chaps in Goa two Christmases before who regularly ran carloads of gear from the Atlas Mountains up into Holland and Germany. Andy had proposed this running route to me as a possible business plan but I remember saying I thought it sounded a bit *Cheech and Chong* so nothing ever came of it. I was reluctant to diversify at the time. We'd barely got our own partnership off the ground. I may have even blabbed about those Dutch guys to the wrong people and been inadvertently responsible for getting their house in Anjuna turned over by the cops. Yes, I did do that. Andy suspected it was me, but I denied it. The photo of Andy on my kitchen wall, on Anjuna beach, had been taken the next day.

Now Andy always had a lump of Double Zero in his tin. It was his dope of choice, so I knew he still had a live Moroccan connection. It turns out he stayed in touch with the Dutch guys without telling me. They knew some Moroccans who would be happy to take the counterfeit dollars in exchange for a quantity of soapbar so Andy wouldn't have to try and change any more of them into currency. Now some soapbar was passable, mildly good even, but the majority was low grade twigs and seeds with desperately few buds boiled up in a vat with a ton of fenugreek and black plastic bin liners that were then shaped into nine bars. These bars were then embossed with some 'seal' or other and shipped off to northern Europe, i.e. England, because we were the only suckers who'd smoke the shit. Here it could retail for as much as £500 a quarter-kilo.

It cost the Moroccans virtually nothing to produce, and as long as they were handing it over at source you could pay in buttons for it if you knew the right people. Not only that but fake dollars were almost as good as real dollars in parts of Africa, and Morocco is only a short hop from some of the poorest places on the planet. The dollars would get passed off as genuine currency – we're only talking fifty thousand piddling dollars minus what Jez and Bas had already changed – they probably wouldn't get noticed for years, if ever, in Sudan or Uganda or Ethiopia; they'd just get distributed throughout the continent before you could say 'Heart of Darkness' and the only risk to Andy would be getting the dope back to England. It made perfect sense to me that this was what he was planning. It was genius. In fact I worked out that he could make nearly twice as much from this gig than from the original deal with Mickey and the IRA boys. It was impressive.

The train of events began to run very quickly once Andy and I were in Spain but so much hinged on me staying in control of my excitement. We got to the hotel late – there'd been a fuck up with the car hire firm at the airport (they didn't have the specific car Andy wanted). Andy was insistent he got what he'd ordered and even when they offered to upgrade us he refused and walked along the company booths, looking pale and agitated, checking every hire firm for the make and model he wanted. In the end we waited for two hours for the right one to come in and get cleaned up (further corroborating my Moroccan theory). Then, at the hotel, we could only get a double room. Andy got stressed with the concierge and even when I said, 'Hey man, we can bunk up. I don't mind,' it was clear he wasn't happy about having to share a bed with me. Once in the room I made a half-hearted attempt to persuade him to retrieve the dollars that night but by now his behaviour was manifestly out of character. Perhaps my eagerness was beginning to arouse his suspicions at last. I got the impression he didn't want me there at all. I tried to keep a check on myself but I felt too tense to properly moderate my behaviour, I know that now. Things were slipping out of my control and I should have been more careful. I felt as if I was hanging over the edge of a cliff to reach a diamond on a ledge. I willed myself to be calm.

'I'm off for a walk then,' I announced casually as the light outside softened to sunset.

Andy barely acknowledged me.

'Do you want anything?'

'Uh . . . yeah, I'll have some *churros*,' he answered vaguely.

Damn, I'd have to go to the street vendors on the front when I had intended to hide and watch if he left the room to find the dollars. But I just said, 'OK.' As I closed the door I added, 'I might be a while though. I'm gonna stroll around.'

'Cool.'

In late August the Costa del Sol achieves the thick, sweating temperatures of the tropics. The evening air has a putrid sweetness, so instead of the freshness you expect when the sun goes down it feels as if you're wading through something dark and viscous. Nerja was 'letting it all hang out', and had changed from a springtime siren to summer strumpet, embarrassing herself by showing too much oily flesh. That day the skin of every tourist who wandered from the beaches to the bars and feeding stations reflected a carmine sunset that served to make their sunburn glow an even deeper red. The crush was irritating. Cobbled old town streets are not designed for scooters, buses and ubiquitous Mercedes. It felt as overpowering as rush hour, although I took some pleasure in it too. My malevolent purpose made me feel like a missile cutting through the mediocrity. People seemed to part the way for me.

You know, it was a pastime of mine to examine people's faces for signs of *intent*. Given a large enough crowd there will always be one or two planning nefarious deeds and I'd look for some mark or stain that singled them out. I'd say to myself, 'There, that man there, there's something in his eyes,' and I would invent a scenario where the man, perhaps dining alone, is scheming against his wife or his business partner. He wipes his mouth and stands to adjust the waistband of his trousers, then heads off to play out whatever drama he has planned, to exorcize his anger in a flurry of violence, something like that anyway. It was just a game I played. But I wondered if the crowd could discern that stain on me.

I bought the *churros* down by the Balcón de Europa and headed back to the hotel, but when I went up the room was empty. I was enraged. Andy had tricked me. He'd persuaded me to leave him unguarded so he could retrieve the dollars without me. I ran into the corridor, down to the window at the end and leaned out backwards, looking up towards the roof, then forwards, checking up and down the street. Then I ran to the stairs and craned my neck up and down the stairwell. How could I have been so stupid? I knew I should have waited and watched him from the upper landing. I hit the banister with unrestrained force so that I felt a bruise begin to swell the edge of my hand in spite of my free-running adrenalin. I had already determined that Basil must have hidden the dollars on the roof of the hotel; it was the most logical place. So I ran up the stairs, swearing through gritted teeth. On the fourth floor the stairs stopped and I was faced with a bland, tiled corridor extending to a dead end on my left and a balconied window to my right. After a few frustrating minutes, hanging over the edge of the balcony again, looking for a way up while forcing my mind to achieve some clarity, I tried each of the five doors on the landing. Bingo, one of the doors was open, behind it a service staircase leading up. Gingerly I climbed, aware that these tiptoe steps could be my last before a confrontation.

The metal door at the top of the narrow flight was already ajar. Adrenalin almost overcame me then, painful yet persuasive, like the chemical slap of amyl nitrate as it invades your nostrils. I gripped the edge of the door (for balance as much as anything) and pushed it into its hinges to prevent a creak or squeak. But it was well maintained and glided open silently. I was not surprised to step onto a tiled roof terrace. There were two sun loungers up there and, next to one, an open magazine with a Spanish title, face down. Several wires attached to metal poles on either side of the terrace were hung with rows of towels and hotel linen that dazzled white in the diminishing light. In the opposite corner, through the washing, was a large concrete structure I assumed was the water tank that fed the hotel. Crouching, I looked around, expecting to see Andy, but I was alone. Still erring on the side of caution, I made a dash for the tank, keeping my knees bent and look-ing all about me. The tank was six or so foot high and I had to pull myself up to lift the corrugated plastic that pro-tected it from the elements so I could look inside. The sur-face of the water was very dark and reflected what meagre daylight remained back at me. 'Plastic and tape,' Andy had said. Basil had wrapped the dollars, prepared them for submersion? The tank was lined with a black synthetic skin. I was certain this was where the dollars were hidden.

I stripped to my underpants and scrambled up and into the container, grazing my knee on the concrete. Despite the greenhouse humidity, the water was surprisingly cool and soon I was under, reaching to each corner, feeling along the edges for a package. It took several dives before I was convinced the dollars were not there. I was about to hoist myself back out of the tank, intending to steal one of the towels to dry off, when I heard voices. Whoever had used the sun loungers had returned to pack them away and remove the laundry from the lines. I waited nearly twenty minutes as the maids went about their work; even in Spanish I could tell their talk was mere gossip, the ped-estrian minutiae that seems to be the hallmark of female conversation. However, I prayed they would not notice my clothes in a heap behind the tank as I shivered in the water, cursing my lack of foresight. When they were gone I dried off as much as I could in the warm air, removing my underpants (the moisture would make a tell-tale water-mark on my trousers) before I got dressed, and headed for the door that led back downstairs. It was locked.

I am not insensible to the comic elements of this story, but at the time I kicked and punched the door and slapped my face forcefully, saying, 'Stupid, stupid,' before a needle of asthma panic made me crouch with one hand on the floor, breathing slowly. I had two choices. I could wait there until morning or I could try and get off the roof. I had to get off. So I lay down on my belly and inched backwards off the roof until I was hanging by one hand above one of the tiny balconies twelve foot below. I was worried I would fall badly, twist my ankle perhaps and be deflected away from the building to fall the eighty or so foot to the street. There was little margin for error. I let go, almost in a dream, and apart from a few scratches on my hands and a bruised shin to add to my now weeping knee, my stunt was successful. Still, I can feel acid rising in my throat as I remember the indignity.

Back in the room, Andy had eaten the *churros*; the greasy wrapper was discarded beside the bed. He lifted his head from his novel and looked me up and down, amused.

'Where've you been? You're wet, you look fucked, and your hands . . . ' he said, taking me in, in pieces.

I wasn't in the mood for explanations but he had to have one. 'It's nothing. I slipped on the rocks down by the beach and mashed my hands up.'

'Did you fall in?'

'Yeah I fell in. I meant to. Anyway, where were you?' I shouted, annoyed at his good humour.

I saw a muscle spasm at the hinge of Andy's jaw as he pointed to an open bottle of wine on the table. I had raised my voice. We didn't talk again that night.

I was supremely conscious of Andy's presence in the bed beside me as I tried to sleep. I am certain he felt the same. Side by side, we were like magnets repelling, attracting one another so there was a force field between us. Neither of us wanted to brush the other accidentally with a foot or a hand, but the bed was narrow and it seemed to take a huge effort to hold ourselves apart. I don't remember nodding off but I remember waking. It was early and a breeze was moving the long curtain at the window, allowing an occasional shaft of chalk-coloured light to fall gracefully across the room. I could hear the sea and smell a vague whiff of charred food. Andy was asleep beside me, the bed sheet pulled down to expose his torso. His face and arms were tan but his body was pale and some palpable muscularity seemed to encase each bone of his ribcage so that it gave the impression of ripples on wind-carved sand, and I could see the line that ran from his pelvis down either side of his abdomen towards his groin, defined and clearly visible, until the bunched up sheet prevented me from following it further. I caught myself then, and looked at his face, his long jawbone, the iron-filing specks of stubble emerging from his chin. I looked away and as I did I glimpsed my own reflection in the mirror. I was *sick*. I knew it then, sick and weak. The fingers of my left hand were gently touching my lips in childlike wonder, while a pathetic, saccharin expression played around my eyes. It had to stop. I must remove the object of my weakness from my life for ever. Andy stirred, disturbing the sheet as he turned onto his back, lifting one arm to support his head. Slowly he opened his eyes, rubbing them awake with his free hand, and as he did I smelled the half-must, half-musk that was released from the bedclothes and once more I was stupid with irreconcilable emotions. I thought I had turned every gramme of feeling I had for him into hate, but I had not.

We showered and I smoked a spliff, trying to calm myself. Andy was preoccupied and kept glancing at his watch until finally he said, 'Pack your stuff up, man. We're leaving.'

'We just got here,' I remonstrated.

'Just do it, Pads . . . or stay. It's up to you, but I'm leaving.'

'But the dollars . . .'

'They're not here.'

I closed my eyes and began, slowly. 'What do you mean? They're not here *full stop* or they're not where you thought they were?'

Andy rolled his shoulders, noncommittal, but didn't answer me.

'Listen, Andy, I thought we'd settled this. I'm running this now, eh?'

'NO . . . no. You've *been* running it and now we're gonna do this my way.'

My mind was lurching ahead. I was convinced he suspected me and doubly convinced he was already in possession of the dollars. He must have salvaged them while I was at the beach buying his bloody *churros*. He would have had just enough time to go up to the tank and swim about for them – shit, he was probably coming down the stairs as I was going up; he may have even seen me. Still, I was determined not to act as if I'd done anything wrong.

'So, you've got them,' I whispered, smiling with something approaching authenticity, I hoped.

'It's not important.'

'If the dollars aren't important then what the fuck are we here for, man?' I replied, unable to keep an even keel.

'We've got to be somewhere. Are you coming?' He was slinging his holdall across his back and I was tempted to rip it off him. I worried that my anger would show before I could conduct its power. It was as if skin alone could not hold in my fury and it would spill out as a rash – or boils? Why does emotion have to bring such combustion with it? But I managed to say, 'Yeah, yeah, keep your hair on, old chap,' or something ridiculous like that and followed him into the vivid morning using every muscle to contain myself.

Andy took the driver's seat of the hire car. He was the Andy I had met three years before but without the innocence, without the faith in human nature. Once on the main road he drove with a kind of glazed indifference, one hand at the top of the wheel, the other on his knee. After a few miles he turned off the main road – I missed the sign, he turned so abruptly – and soon we were on a winding coastal road I didn't know, part-canopied by ancient fir trees that made it feel cool even as midday approached.

'I thought we could have a last swim,' he stated.

'OK,' I said. 'But it sounds a bit final.'

He laughed flatly but kept his eyes on the road.

Presently he turned again onto a more open track that led to a sandy cliff-top parking space. A moped was propped under an ancient olive tree about twenty yards away and further down the track there was a solitary black campervan with shiny green sheeting in the window that made it look like a giant fly. But despite the vehicles I could see no signs of life on the sand below as we descended to the beach. I suspected there must be smaller, secret bays further along that could only be reached on foot.

'I don't know this cove,' I said as we picked our way down.

'Hidden gem,' Andy called behind him. 'They still exist, even on the Costa del Sol, if you know where to look.'

His attitude was more relaxed now and it was making me confused, but I followed him down the rough steps, foot-moulded rather than hand-hewn, carrying nothing more than our sarongs. Andy had locked everything else in the boot of the car. The cove was idyllic and despite all else I was desperate for a swim, although I didn't venture in the water until Andy was ten yards or so out, showing off his vigorous freestyle. I was afraid he would abandon me there. We swam for twenty minutes before Andy got out and stretched on his sarong. I lay beside him, on my back, and squinted as the sun polarized the salty droplets on my lashes, magnifying my own sleek eyebrows as I closed one eye then another. The cicadas were scraping in the brush behind us while the warmth lulled and embraced me. I watched as vaporous zephyrs slid, then evaporated, across the lapis sky and in the distance I caught the opulent drone of a speedboat and the whine of a scooter on the coast road far away. All this was suffused and muffled by the insistent foamy sussurus of warm wavelets soaking the sand before me. I fought the urge to sleep.

'What I don't understand,' Andy began abruptly so that I was wrenched from reverie with a jolt, 'is what I've done, you know, to piss you off.'

The words sizzled like spit on the seared air and, instantly, I gagged. The fear was so sudden and so strong. But I swallowed hard and shaded my eyes with my forearm, pulling an ignorant face.

'You what, man?' I said. It was a struggle to speak.

I shouldn't have asked a question. I didn't want revelations and counter revelations, or some cathartic confrontation on an isolated beach. I needed props, some physical thing I could do, some situation I could mould or shape or influence or at least somewhere to run. A place to hide. I think he knew that too, so he'd trapped me and I was as good as naked.

'I mean, when Basil phoned . . . just before we caught the plane on Tuesday . . .' Andy threw me a look, then just as quickly averted his gaze back to the blue gem sky '. . . I didn't want to believe what he told me. I told him, "No one is that fucking spiteful." I said, "You have to be mistaken."'

I was on my elbows now, still feigning perplexity, my head at a confounded angle. 'Man, Basil rang? What? From Italy? Is he OK?'

Andy wasn't going to be diverted but he was still supine and it occurred to me that I might attack him. I had no weapon, there wasn't even a rock near at hand and more importantly Andy could easily overpower me. We'd had enough play scuffles and rugby tackles for me to be assured of his superior strength.

'Please, would you not insult my intelligence for a minute longer, Tristan?' He sighed, exasperated. 'I know all about Becca, that she was here in June and, from what I can gather, most likely you were here too, stalking Jez and Bas. Then, hey presto, she's in India as one of your donkeys, uh uh, that's a fucking coincidence too far.'

'You're joking,' I gasped. 'Becca . . . in Spain . . . here? I swear, Andy, I don't know what you're talking about.'

We were both sitting up now, a vortex of tension between us, but Andy had screwed his eyes closed, maddened by my continuing denial. 'Aargh . . . I saw you,' he shouted, then looked at me directly. 'I watched your ridiculous antics on the roof last night.'

I opened my mouth in mock indignation and denial.

'You were diving in the fucking water tank, man,' he went on, 'hanging from the fucking roof.'

'How *could* you have seen me?'

But he didn't answer; he did what he always did when things got really intense, he laughed. I mean he really laughed, properly cracked up. 'Man, for some reason you want to hurt me really badly but you got your sorry arse in a fix last night, stuck up there,' and he slapped his thigh and shook his perfect head.

'How could *you* have seen me?' I said again.

Then he stopped laughing. 'So what? You get Becca to flirt with Bas and try to steal the dollars. Then you get Becca to sleep with me in India, make me think she's in love with me. Then you and she pretend she's not made it back, so you can get away without paying me for India while I've done your dirty work and still owe every mother-fucker. And still . . . *still* you're trying to steal the dollars. Even now, look at you, cogs turning, thinking what to say, can you get away with it? Fuck, Pads! Why? Why, man?'

Was that it? Was that all he had, conjecture? No proof, just Becca in Spain and me on the roof. I could have brazened it out. But his laughter, his derision and now my certain knowledge that he and Becca had slept together made the heat drain out of my emotion. They had secretly slept together and exchanged enough affection for him to believe she loved him. At once I remembered Becca's face when Andy had 'rescued' Bas in Paharganj; her salute whenever Andy told her what to do; the open-faced wonder they shared as they looked at the impossible Himalyan panorama; her anger, genuine anger, when she thought he was patronizing her on the mountain in Manali. I saw it all as if for the first time. She wasn't pretending infatuation to manipulate Andy and manouevre herself into a more powerful position. She was manipulating me.

My anger became as cold as a scalpel. It excised the fog in my brain, leaving pure intent, and I launched at him, caught him off guard, landing a fist on his lip with my first attempt. There was an instant of shock in his eye as his head jarred back but levelled up quickly, then he caught and held my fist as I swung a second time.

'Don't try it, Pads,' he snarled, blood spilling from the split and covering me with a fine pink spray as he said the P of my name.

I pulled away and scrambled to my feet. I was about six foot away from him and casting a shadow where he remained sitting, too casually for my liking.

'You know I'm ten times stronger than you, Tris. There really is no point fighting.' He was trying to undermine me but he couldn't look at me directly because the sun was bursting out from behind my head, blinding him. 'I just want to know why.'

'How could you have *seen* me?' I snapped.

'Come on, spill the fucking beans, Pads.'

'How *could you* have seen me?'

'Shit, this isn't about that summer . . . at your house . . .'

'How could you have seen me . . . on the roof?' I repeated again.

'Not about Jennifer, surely. I thought we were past that. It was a mistake, man. A stupid fucking mistake.'

'*Tell me* how you could have seen me.'

Andy was becoming unsettled, shaky even, and the sun was still inhibiting eye contact, which was good for me and shit for him.

'Look, Pads, if this about your mum, I promise I never meant to hurt you. You were my best friend, you know that.'

'Just – TELL ME.' I barked so hard it chafed my throat.

Andy swallowed and furrowed his brow, bewildered by our cross-purpose. 'I was on the roof across the road watching everything you did, the tank, hanging off the roof, dropping onto the balcony, everything,' he explained, thoughtful now, re-eliciting his betrayal at the farm, no doubt.

There are times when you become aware of a kind of mechanical quality to your brain. You can almost hear the clicks and whirs and ticks as facts fall into place and things align to create a clear passage for the shining ball-bearing of thought to roll along until it plops perfectly into the spherical hole prepared for it. Basil had hidden the dollars not on our hotel roof but on the roof of the building opposite, the roof he could most likely see from his own balcony when he was there in June. In that instant my respect for Basil increased while I experienced my own diminution even more keenly. Then the ball-bearing dropped down to the next level, this time setting off all manner of flashing lights and whistles. If Andy had been on the other roof retrieving the dollars, then I was right, the dollars must be in his bag, which was in the hire car parked on top of the cliff.

Andy tutted and shook his head as I came upon him a third time, but he hadn't accounted properly for my wrath and, as he tried to stand and defend himself, my fist caught him awkwardly on the temple (admittedly I had the advantage of height and the blinding sun), but *I knocked him out*. It felt almost miraculous. I stood above him for a few seconds, conflicting desires bisecting my heart, and I felt the heat of my emotion return. He was groaning as I bent over him but I rummaged in his trunks and found the car key in the little netting pocket at the waistband. He began to blink and focus on me so I struck him again, quite firmly, between the eyes. Then I struck him once more. And then again, to be safe. He had heroic, god-like features and as he lay there in the sand I couldn't help but touch the contours of his bruising face, running my fingers gently across his cheekbones and his chin. I wiped a line of blood from his mouth with my sarong, then sped across the scalding sand and raced back up the steps. I was weeping.

19

PADS

The Farm

I can picture Andy now, sitting on the faded sofa in Aylesford Street holding forth about, I don't know, anarchy probably. He's wearing that half-smile of his; just one corner of his mouth curled up, eyes alight. He's passionate and alive. Yes, if I concentrate and close my eyes I can see him sitting there, wearing his 'Heads Will Roll' T-shirt. And look, he's full to brimming with energy and enthusiasm, drawing everyone into his plans and ideas, lighting our fires. There are three or four of us sitting around, trying to emulate him. It happens with charismatic people: Spud, biting his bottom lip, nodding with faux-wisdom when someone puts their point across; Biff using that exuberant loose-wristed finger clack the black guys use, that Andy copied from them in his turn and we faithfully copied from Andy. The room's a mess, of course, there are scrunched up cans, an empty bottle of Bush or tequila perhaps, yes, tequila, and mugs of cold tea everywhere. The ashtrays are overflowing, full of roaches, foil, pipe detritus. We've been up all night, naturally. That's how it was.

I remember the party we threw at the end of the second-year exams; we were like godfathers on campus by then, so cool, everyone wanted to know us. Whizzing off his head, Andy held my face between his hands that night and roared at me, ecstatic, knowing we were it, I mean 'it', a top team, best friends. It was Pads and Andy, Andy and Pads. No one did anything without us knowing about it. Who'd have a party without inviting the dealers, eh? Then we dropped out and went to Glastonbury, feeling invincible and liberated. We spent a week afterwards camping in the woods, not wanting to abandon the festie vibe. We built fires, made a shelter, took too much acid, Andy played guitar. I was along for the ride, he was the 'outdoor expert' and I was so happy, in the wild, doing something that made him and me feel so . . . real. Then coming back to Cov, afternoons at the quarry in July, naked, hot-skinned before diving in the still, cool water, just able to discern the ghostly outlines of obsolete machinery beneath the surface, and me and Andy, pissing ourselves that a pike would think our penises were bait as we swam and fought and held one another under. I remember his manful grace, his physical perfection, the muscles in his buttocks, freckles on his shoulders, his leanness. Yes, his leanness. The insalubrious room, the fuck-ups with the insurance, the string of insipid girlfriends, our stupid disagreements . . . They were nothing, immaterial, things I could accept.

It was when the 'new' friendships began that I became uneasy: Jez, the twins, the rest of that disjointed crew. Perhaps I was jealous. If I was I couldn't help myself. I found the shift in emphasis disagreeable and he began to talk pointedly about his 'other friends' and 'women he was shagging', as if I was simple. Insinuating I was queer, that he needed to make hints about his separateness from me, and his red-bloodedness. It incensed me. Why must men *feel* incapable of loving one another? I only wanted to be with him, to mean something to him. Everything I felt was noble. He had loved me. He had. I didn't understand what had changed.

The next summer was different. It was the summer of 1983, a nondescript summer really. I don't particularly remember the weather or what was happening in the news. I don't remember what was Number One, or what album I was listening to most. I don't remember what my favourite shirt was or what the in jokes and phrases were. I can't even remember how long my dreads had grown. Actually, I remember almost nothing about that summer except what was in relation to him. I do remember that when the lease ended on our Victorian terrace I found us another without consulting him, a flat on Gloucester Street, two bedrooms, open plan kitchen and living room, opposite the park beside the parish church. I put down a deposit and signed the contract. When I told Andy he was livid. He said, 'You should have asked me, man.' He was ungrateful, after all my effort. I held my tongue of course.

I remember there was a two-week gap between contracts and Andy was at a loose end. His plans for Cadaqués with the 'current girlfriend' had fallen through and he said he was going to 'doss at Spud's' for the fortnight. So I worked on him, persuaded him to come to the farm instead.

'Come on, old chap, come on, man, it'll be great. Mother's in Devon, we'll have the whole place to ourselves, the snooker room, the swimming pool!'

I remember this as a significant moment. I remember the conversation where I coaxed and he countered, but eventually he gave in. 'OK, I'll come, for fuck's sake, I'll come,' or words to that effect, making it clear he was doing me a favour by acquiescing, I don't know. It's just ironic to think I made him come to the farm; he didn't want to and I made him. I often wonder what would have happened if I hadn't managed to persuade him. But I was overjoyed when he agreed. I would have him to myself for two whole weeks. I'd cook for him, look after him, all very relaxed and hands off, no pressure; an opportunity to salvage things, to recreate the friendship we'd had.

Despite it being Mother's place since Dad died, I still loved the farm. It wasn't a working farm any more; it hadn't been for some time. I suppose we called it 'the farm' out of habit as much as anything. Dad sold the land off years before to fund *her* frivolity. He told me that. Now there were only twenty acres, but it was pretty, undulating countryside with a wide stream and meadows, a small tract of woodland and some paddocks rented out to a local riding school.

The first week was bliss. Andy truly relaxed. It felt like when we first met, joking, laughing, talking about politics again. We smoked too much, took LSD and spent the night stumbling around the farm in the dark, then lying in the meadow looking at the stars, saying, 'Can you see what I can see?' and chuckling because we could both feel the pulse of the earth beneath us. One night Andy even pulled me to his breast, ruffling my hair, drunk and ebullient.

'God, you're a strange one, Pads.' He laughed, shaking his head.

'Am I?'

'Fuck yeah.'

'Is that bad?'

'Aah, we're all strange in our own ways, bro.'

I could barely think. My heart was bloated.

Then *she* came back. She, the bane of my existence, from whose cunt I'd slipped, gross, unthinkable. I was deformed when she bore me but she wouldn't watch them fix me. Dad said she couldn't even look at me until the wound had healed. I had the best that money could buy, Harley Street cleft-lip specialist. He only left a sliver of silver behind as evidence. You wouldn't know it was a hare-lip, but mother knew. She turned her face away whenever

I tried to kiss her. She despised me. I despised her. She ignored my disgust, preferring to refer to it publicly with embarrassing asides to red-faced visitors.

'Tristan hates me, of course,' she'd explain when I was still a child, touching a dinner guest's hand, feigning confidentiality, not bothering to mask the inappropriateness of her candour. 'He's our own little home-grown misogynist, isn't he, Hilary?'

My father would nod, then give me one of his secret winks. He could do no more. That was our triangle.

And there she was, come to ruin my time with the one person who meant anything to me. Of course, as soon as she arrived I told Andy we'd have to leave.

'Where to?' he asked.

'Anywhere but here with that bitch.'

'C'mon, Tris, she's OK. She's being really nice.'

I told Andy that ascribing such incidental pleasantries as 'OK' and 'nice' to my mother gave me to believe he was paying scant attention. I asked him how he or anyone could presume to know a woman more intimately or more fully than her own son.

'Everyone feels shit about their parents.'

'She's a witch,' I replied.

'Easy, mate.' Andy laughed. 'I may have to defend the lady's honour if you carry on like that. All I'm saying is we've got nowhere else to go right now. So let's just chill here. It's only a few days. We'll hardly see her.'

Andy had obviously fallen for the charms of the farm so he was trying to placate me, touching me soothingly as he spoke, making me want to please him. This time *I* gave in to *him*. It was bearable at first. Mother was busy visiting various friends, organizing the horse trials in the grounds of the big house. But soon she started hanging around us with her 'Andy this' and 'Andy that'.

'Oh Andy, would you mind awfully if I ask a teensy

favour? Tristan hates me asking him for anything, don't you, dahling?'

'It would be my pleasure, Mrs P.'

'Oh heavens, call me Jennifer, please. I've told you enough times.'

She got him shifting furniture from the drawing room to the outbuildings, or from the conservatory to the bedroom, or taking the Land Rover off to deliver something at the stables.

'Why do you say "yes" to her all the time?' I pressed him.

'I don't know, Pads. Why do you say "no"?'

I knew it would have been impolite for him to refuse her. But there was something else, something flirtatious, something dirty that flashed across his face when she blew him a thank you kiss. I told him not to fall for it.

So there it is.

It doesn't take much imagination. They fucked. Andy and my mother fucked in my father's bed. (Although she screamed in the ensuing hoo-ha that she'd burned the bed she'd shared with Dad. Burned it! Imagine!) So yes, I found them. I knew I would – deep down. It's hard to explain, and I've heard other people say this, but before calamity there is a premonition of doom. The phone rings in an ominous way, or a car pulls up outside and you don't recognize the sound of the engine, and you *know*. Maybe we're all tuned in to that stuff, or perhaps the air is charged with different ions when momentous events are afoot, and we are quite literally electrified. Whichever way it happens I felt it as soon as I walked in the house.

I had left Andy sunbathing (my mother was out riding) and had gone up to Eagle Point for a spliff. It was one of those hazy summer days with too much thin cloud, typically English, but I could see for a few miles, the odd steeple, fields stitched together by hedges with trees like dark green mushrooms blooming from the seams. I even nodded off briefly in the warmth. When I returned to the farm I went straight round to the pool. Andy's book was face down on his towel (he always bent the spines like that), so I went in through the french windows, hesitating while my eyes grew accustomed to the change in light, shouting his name. It was the silence that gave it away. I remember running my thumbnails over my fingertips and thinking how sensitive they were, all those nerve endings, right there, so we can appreciate the most delicate things. Then I saw her riding boots in the back porch. I suppose I didn't need to take the stairs so fast and burst into her room, panting . . . and ashamed. But it is disbelief, as well as knowledge, that compels us to bear witness, however painful.

Mother hid her face.

I waited for Andy at the bottom of the garden. Here a seat overlooked the pond that bordered the orchid meadow. All was tranquil, serene even, with the inchoate soundscape of summer: bees, cows lowing way off, the lap of birdlife on the water. The swans were back. They took up residence each year. Before me one swan, a juvenile male, was preening, his neck flexing as his beak made impossible figures of eight across his speckled breast, conditioning his feathers. The older female stood ungainly on dry land, the lateral swell of her flanks too solid above her stubby legs and comical feet. Duly primped, the male stopped and extended his regal neck to better regard me, it seemed, with one black-bead eye, before opening his wings wide, showing me his full span. He was magnificent, heraldic.

Andy came outside half an hour later with his holdall across his back and sat on his haunches beside me. I couldn't bring myself to look at him.

'I thought it was best I leave,' he said with something pathetic in his voice, something akin to remorse.

'Yeah.'

'Are you angry?'

'Only that you're still here.'

'Right. Cool. Understood.'

He reached out to touch me as he rose, but I flinched away.

Beginning on that day I bent my heart away from him until all the love was gone.

JEZ

Craven Choke Puppy

'Mi done got miself bust, mon. Stupid I.'
Basil's sitting in the chair next to me bed, large as life, come to check up on me, he says. He looks too big to fit in this ward, too big for the whole frigging hospital. I feel like I've been here for ever, listening to him spouting on the way he does when he's on a roll, yab yab yab. He never does tone down that patois.

'Beast pull mi up in Rome when I and I change plane, y'nah. Them haul mi out the queue and whisk me off a this lickle room where them search every pocket and hem and fold a mi clothes. Then them strip me down neked and slap on this rubber glove jivation and look pon me like I and I is a dog. Dem probe mi *hintimate* body places, bwoy . . . mi nah wan gwin to detail but bloodfire and tunderation, them rob me of me dignity. Them find the big drug in mi suitcase, twelve kilos a it, and me start shaking like a alcoholic in a mornin'.' Bas stops to kiss his teeth. 'So, dem lock mi up, mon. Mi hate bein' lock up.'

He's looking round the ward now. Dennis has gone. I was out of it when he was discharged but he left me a note by me bed. It said loads a stuff, but one bit got to me, it did. It said, 'You have been a comfort to me, young Jeremy, and I wanted, so much, to thank you. I hope that in the fullness of time you can learn to cope with your demons as I am learning to cope with mine.' I'd never had a toff say thank you to me, not ever.

'I can't believe you're out of nick so soon, Bas,' I says.

'It that Becca gal, mon, y'nah, the one from Spain. She call the lawyer and then wire the duns straight through and them repatriate me. No questions.'

'What are you talkin' about? Becca who?'

'Y'nah, har wid har friend dere, wid the meaty round arse, that come back a room in Spain.'

'You mean . . . those girls we pulled?'

'Yeah, mon! Becca! She come to India and everyting.'

I'm scratching me head now. 'How come?'

'Well now, it turn out Pads and she is thick as thieves fa true. But Andy fall fa her as if 'im divin' off cliff, y'nah. Andy nah believe me when me tell 'im she a *himpostor*. So mi say, "Dready, you is a blind fool, mon. That man Pads and that gal dere stripping you down of everyting let me tell you," tho mi wrong bout the gal in the end.'

'I can't believe what I'm hearin'.'

'Bwoy, y'know what I'm sayin'?'

'So where's Andy?' I can feel that bullet on the move. A little nudge of metal in me brain.

'Him gone, mon. Gone! Mi hear from Spud that Pads come back a Spain, but no one seen skin nah teeth a Andy. Spud say him hear rumour that Pads pack up him business. So mi decide to pay Pads a visit fi find out where is Andy and show him a reasoning bout hisself.'

'Well, what did he say?' I can feel tears start spurting out of me eyes. I'm embarrassed more than anything, having no control.

'Hey, ress yourself, mon. Look, seckle down now.' Bas is looking scared and making calm-down actions with his hands cos I'm bawling like a brat. He's wishing he hadn't brought Andy up. I can get right jittery when I'm stressed these days.

And I goes, 'Andy's dead. I knew it. He's dead.'

'Him not dead, star, 'im jos gone. Gone away. Run off to find that gal there. Him starry-eyed in love. Mi seen him with mi own eyes. All right?'

I'm chilling out a bit but Nurse Joanna's by the bed going, 'You'll have to leave if you're going to upset him,' and looking at Bas all flinty and wild.

So I goes, 'S'all right, nurse, he's me mate. He is.'

And she goes, 'Hmm,' and turns tail with a backward glance and one a them 'one more chance' looks on her face.

'Mm mm, that nurse feisty, even wid 'er screw face on,' says Bas, checking out Nurse Joanna's arse as she strides off. Then he turns to me again, all serious, and spells it out. He says he's roughed Pads up a bit; it was the least he deserved.

'Mi broke him nose a lickle an' give him a fat lip. I enjoy it.'

Basil said Pads looked tired, busted even before the licking, and when he'd pushed him around some, Pads had an asthma attack and comes all 'I can't breathe' so Bas had to fetch his Ventolin and rub his back while he got some air back in his lungs. Then Pads confessed to it all. Said he did bring that Becca to Spain to try and steal the dollars off us. Said he was angry with Andy for loads a things, borrowing money, other things we wouldn't understand. Then Pads said he knew it was all over for him in Cov and he was leaving . . . going home.

'Him mother emigrate and leave him some *farm*.'

'Pads's mother?'

'Yeah, mon. But him seem level about it, y'nah.'

'Hold on,' I says, scratching me head again. 'So where are those friggin' dollars?'

Then Bas laughs, this big old toothy laugh he has, and he goes, 'You won't believe this, mon,' and he shakes his head and laughs some more.

'What?'

'Well, Andy get the dollars from the hotel and 'im plan to tek them off to Morocco and tell Pads about hisself but them get in a fight on a beach.'

I'm about to get fired up but Bas goes, 'No, wait, you really won't believe this . . . Pads win the fight! Him knock Andy flat, box him head and lef' him fa dead, nah rakstone. And that not all. When Pads reach the hire car on the cliff top, bwoy, *everyting* been stolen out a it, bag, passport, money . . . dollars . . . everyting. So mi say, "Pads, you tellin' me that while you on the beach boxin' mi best friend some raasclot breaking and entering the car and them tek every lickle ting?" and him say, "That's *exactly* what I'm saying."'

I'm sitting up now, and that bullet's snaking its way in, so me heart's thumping and I feel sick as a pig, but I goes, 'Dollars, everything, stolen?' just so's I can get it straight in me head.

'Boot empty, mon. Them even steal him cigarette.'

Me and Bas sit quiet for a while, mulling it all over. I can't think, me head's throbbing so strong. But I knew it, see. We was being followed the whole time in Spain and it wasn't hoity-toity, wanky little Pads, oh no, it was them IRA fuckers. Yep, I knew it. Stitch and them IRA fuckers were in it together, biding their time. I knew the likes a Stitch from the old days. Why would he let Andy have a month, a whole month to pay him back? It didn't make sense to me at the time and now it was gelling. It was gelling all right.

'So what happened then, to Andy, I mean?'

'Mi seen Andy, mon. Him fine.'

'But what did he say?'

'Bout the dollars?'

I nod.

Bas stretches his neck back. 'Andy laugh, mon, I'm tellin' ya. After it happen him and Pads have to spend three night together in the same hotel waiting for new passports and then, *them* have to be *repatriated* . . . and it cost Pads hundreds a pounds cos them have no insurance. That mek Andy laugh, mon. Then me say, "If all your money gone and you on a beach in jos your swimsuit, what, star? You come back neked? You're dread!" and him say the hotel manager let them stay in a room and pay him back when they get home. She give them clothes fi wear from the lost and found.' Basil clacks his fingers and goes on. 'Pads him wear a seventies pinstripe bell-bottom jivation and a shirt with the big big collar and Andy wear T-shirt and dem Bay City Roller trousers, mi nah jest. Andy say it like fancy dress on the plane, in the airport. Mi wish I and I had seen it.'

Bas's cracking up, imagining Pads and Andy walking through customs, hating each other, but dressed up like a coupla clowns.

I touch Bas's arm. 'You know it was IRA, don't you, Bas?'

'Ress yourself, Jez, mon. It not IRA. If it anyone it that jancrow Pads still tryin' to set us all up nah. Not IRA.'

'So why hasn't Stitch Maginnis come lookin' for blood, eh? Why not?'

'Cos him paid off to blousebait.'

'Speak English, Basil, please.' I'm shaking me bonce trying to make head and tail of Bas's pattywah.

Basil shoots me a sharp look, then smiles and rolls his eyes. 'Becca steal all Pads's hash, then she sell it in London, then she pays fa lawyer fa I an' I, for me, Basil, y'understand? Then she give Andy all the money fa Stitch from Pads's dope money.'

'All of it?'

'Every lickle penny.'

Basil and me give each other one a them 'fuckinell' looks, cos we know that Becca must be pretty keen on Andy to do that, or feel right shit for what she done in the first place.

'So do you think Andy'll find her?'

'Oh yes. He will find her. Him have marriage on him mind, mi tellin' ya. But that Pads, mi don't trust him to steer clear a dem. In Jamaica we have a saying, y'nah, it goes *craven choke puppy*. It mean when you get so greedy you want a ting too much it kill you. Pads is like puppy, him cyaan let go a Andy till it kill him dead.'

'You think? You think he'll try and find them?'

Bas rubs his chin. 'Hm, *maybe*. Pads tell me some tings. Him tell me Andy parents no politican, nor diplomat, nah big shot anyting neither.'

'You what?'

'Nah mon, Andy never went to no posh school, not Eton nah Harrow. Him father beast, mon . . . *policeman*.'

'I don't believe you.'

'Dread, mi telling ya, mi check it out after, an' it true.'

'Why would Andy lie to us?'

'Him never lie to me. Him never say nothin' to me bout when him a pickney. It you who tell me . . .'

' . . . and Pads told me.'

Me and Bas take some time to let the new Andy take his shape in our heads, if you know what I mean. Andy who was brought up by a *pig*. Andy with a chip on his shoulder so big he had to mash it up and rub his parents' noses in it. The Marcher's hitting himself on the forehead with the flat of his hand now, over and over and barking some blue curse or other into thin air, and it sets me off cos I know this is it for me. I've known it since Andy left. It's me and madness, together for ever. Nothing feels real now.

Basil pulls his chair up closer and looks at me all soppy.

The white in his eyes is right creamy like old paper but the centre of 'em's brown and swimmy and sad.

'You're gonna be OK, my friend,' he says.

I can feel his voice in me brain, gentle as touch, too deep for reason.

'Bas, I think I'm done for,' I say.

'Nah man. Mi here. Mi here fa you, y'understan'?'

EPILOGUE

MEHMET

New Empires

The fire has burned low but the embers still radiate heat enough for comfort. This night has been a catharsis for me, tracing my route from farmer to entrepreneur, laying my heart bare again after all these years. My new friend has been filled with awe and sorrow. He has listened like a child and I think perhaps he might not feel rewarded by the ending.

I put one hand on my breast. 'Ech, my heart still beats. Besides, this story is enough. We are tired, no? I will call for my driver to take you to the hotel,' I say and I make to stand.

'You can't leave it like this, Mr Lucca. You've got to tell me the end or else I'll think you've brought me here to torture me.'

'This is the end, my friend. You look at the end right here,' I say and I spread my arms like the branches of a beech tree.

'But how did you make so much money? It can't have just been thieving. And what happened when you went back to Albania? You went to find Aisha?'

'Yes. Among other things.'

I offer him a Montecristo and he holds his hand up to say no, but lets me fill his glass again.

'Well,' he says. 'Did you find her?'

I take a big draw on my cigar and examine the glowing end, enjoying the suspense I am creating in my listener.

'I did,' I say at last. 'The two years I was away seeking my fortune were hard for my family. My absence was regarded as a repudiation of those left living and my mother died soon after I had left, some say of a broken heart, and yes, hearts can break, I know this. After Hoxha died I went back to Albania. I took my father's knife. It had exerted such a magic on me for so long and I needed to return it. So I buried it with him. It was good to put my hands in the dirt of his grave. This was necessary for *my* heart, yes. My uncle had taken charge of the whole *fis*, as Jules predicted. It was a mess and there was bitterness in everyone's blood. I could see for the first time how poor the people were, so I forgave my uncle. It was easy. Hoxha's fear meant Albania had no friends and no investment and this affect the mind of the Albanian man; it made him friendless, it made him invest nothing also. I do not mean money. I mean soul.'

'You are a noble man, Mr Lucca.'

I shake my head, dismissive. 'No, not noble, just tired of blood. And by then I was wealthy, of course. Wealth can be a salve, my friend, even to a man of integrity. So Jules marry my younger sister, praise be, and my older sister lives with them until she have a husband of her own. Ech, I think she will stay a spinster all her life but she is happy.'

'And Aisha?'

'Hah, you are a romantic like me and you are impatient, yes? Well, my friend, it pains me to say it but she would not marry me. There, I put you from your misery. She said she does not know me, that she only met me three times and all of them were full with tragedy and pain. I told her I had watched *her* all her life, knew the way she pushed the hair from her eyes, the way she smoothed her skirts and sang to the chickens, her dancing steps from the house to the grain store. I tried to convince her there was happiness in my heart and love enough for her and me and armfuls of babies –'

'What did she say?'

'She was unmoved. Why should it be different? Aisha was an idea I clung to for survival. She was my fantasy. I was not hers. She married a political man from Tirana. He was murdered in 1995 and she returned to the mountains. Jules is the lucky man, surrounded by the women I should have had to dote on me in *my* old age.'

'You're not tempted to go back and try again with her now she's widowed?'

'Hah, maybe I will, my friend, maybe I will.'

'And what about Ismail? It was him who tried to fit Jules up with Rafiq and Razlan's murders, he was the one, yeah?'

'Oh yes, he was the one.'

'And you didn't kill him when it was him who caused the whole thing, Gabriel's death – I mean, how did he have Rafiq's gun in the first place?'

'He killed them, I know it, perhaps to cover up for killing that poor thing, Yana. Such immoderate passion, perhaps because he has no discipline in his mind.'

'I can't believe you didn't find him and rip him limb from limb.'

'I did find him.'

'You did?'

'Yes.'

'And?'

'Look, my life has had a course that led me to this point, the place I am in now. It led me through tragedy and poverty and oppression. It led me to a little car parked on a cliff top. I had nothing, no hope, my dreams shattered. But in that car the *djinns* sent me a fortune. So when it came to it I did not kill Ismail, I let him live. I decided I would be the fortune in his life. I could have been the executioner. See, bad things can –'

'What car?' my new friend interrupts.

'Oh, in Andalucia, I have never told a soul about this car, except Juan, of course, as he was there. It changed my life, it is the pivot that all my fortune balanced on.'

'Go on.' My friend's face is alight with interest and it persuades me to continue.

'Juan was sleeping. We were both sleeping in the van.'

'Where?'

'On a cliff top near Malaga in Andalucia. I hear a car pull up so I pull the shade from the window just a little way and there are two men in swimming clothes with towels, gone down to the beach, leaving their little car all alone. It is a tourist car so I think, OK, some money, yes, a camera perhaps, a Walkman. So I wait a while for them to go down to the track. But for one minute I think I am so comfortable in my van, maybe I let these people keep their things. Maybe I sleep. But then my stomach gripe and I know I must get up. You see, so close. Fortune breathes one way and then another. Then I spy on them from the cliff, they are swimming and lying on the sand. That is when I break open their car, pop, like that. I am expert car breaker.'

'What did you find?'

I grin now and lean forward. 'You won't believe it.'

'Try me.'

'No, it is too impossible to believe, even for me, even now.'

'You've told me this much, you can't hold back now. Tell me what you found.'

'You'll never tell a soul?'

'Never, I swear.'

I look at my friend, right into his shining eyes, and pause for a few seconds but I am too keen to know how he will react.

'I find thousands and thousands of dollars,' I whisper.

You know, my new friend say, 'Hah,' like this. Then 'Hah hah' again. Then he laugh and laugh so long and so hard I think I will have to get some help for him and I am halted in the middle of my revelation. I don't even have a chance to tell him the dollars were not real. That me and Juan must take them to Morocco and barter for blocks of cannabis to sell to the English. The Moroccans take the fake dollars as if they were genuine. They did not care. They told us our dollars were worth at least half face value so we came back through Algeciras with so much black Moroccan in the van the chassis scraped half the rubber from the tyres.

But my new friend is still laughing hard, slapping at his thigh then rocking back against my leather chair like a man half mad. It brings a smile to my lips to see it.

But I say, 'Mr —, are you all right? Do you need some water?'

He wipes tears from his face and he says, 'Please, Mr Lucca, you must call me Andy.'

About the Author

© Tricia Belchere

Born in Essex, Mez Packer was a student at Warwick University in the 1980s and travelled in Europe and Asia. She experimented in alternative lifestyles in the 1990s, and travelled to India, Nepal and Thailand. She lives with her husband (a veteran of Coventry 2 Tone days) and her youngest daughter in Leamington Spa, Warwickshire.

Acknowledgements

I would like to acknowledge the usefulness of *The Accused Mountains: Journeys in Albania* by Robert Carver in my research. Thank you to Tonya Blowers for her suggestions and encouragement; Saskia Bakayoko and Mandy Elliott for reading and rereading; Orville Hall, Joëlle and Naomi for their love and support; Luke Brown, Emma Hargrave and Alan Mahar at Tindal Street for their editorial empathy; and Gil Scott-Heron for his kind permission to reproduce the lyric to 'The Revolution Will Not Be Televised'. Thank you also to Rick Gekoski, a friend and mentor.